William Henry Giles Kingston

The Cruise of the Frolic

A Sea Story

William Henry Giles Kingston

The Cruise of the Frolic
A Sea Story

ISBN/EAN: 9783743400511

Manufactured in Europe, USA, Canada, Australia, Japa

Cover: Foto ©Andreas Hilbeck / pixelio.de

Manufactured and distributed by brebook publishing software (www.brebook.com)

William Henry Giles Kingston

The Cruise of the Frolic

THE

CRUISE OF THE FROLIC.

A SEA STORY.

BY

WILLIAM H. G. KINGSTON,

AUTHOR OF "DICK ONSLOW AMONG THE REDSKINS," "ANTONY WAYMOUTH," ETC.

BOSTON:

J. E. TILTON AND COMPANY.

1866.

STEREOTYPED BY C. J. PETERS & SON,
No. 13 Washington Street.

PRESS OF GEO. C. RAND & AVERY.

PREFACE,

BY

BARNABY BRINE, ESQ., R.N.

THE "CRUISE OF THE 'FROLIC'" has already met with
so many marks of favor, that it is hoped it will be
welcomed not the less warmly in its new and more
attractive form. The yachting world especially received the narrative of my adventures in good part;
two or three, however, among whom was the O'Wiggins, insisted that I had caricatured them, and talked
of demanding satisfaction at the point of the sword,
or the muzzle of a pistol. I assured them then, as I
do now, that on the word of an officer and a gentleman, I had not the slightest intention of wounding the
feelings of any human being; and I entreated their
pardon, if in shooting at a venture I had hit an object
at which I had not taken aim.

I can only say, that I hope my readers may experience as much pleasure in perusing my adventures as

I had in writing them, and, I may add, again feel, in looking over the pages which recall so many of the amusing scenes and incidents of my yachting days — a pleasure which will, I feel sure, be shared by my companions in the adventures I have described.

No one with any yachting experience will venture to say that the tale is improbable, although it may be confessed that when an author takes pen in hand, he is apt to throw an air of romance over events which, if told in a matter-of-fact manner, would be received as veracious history; and such is the plea which I have to offer for the truth of the following narrative of my yachting experience many summers ago.

CONTENTS.

———•+❈+•———

CHAPTER I.

CHAPTER II.

CHAPTER III.

CHAPTER IV.

CHAPTER V.

vii

CHAPTER VI.

CHAPTER VII.

CHAPTER VIII.

CHAPTER IX.

CHAPTER X.

CHAPTER XI.

CHAPTER XVIII.

CHAPTER XIX.

CHAPTER XX.

CHAPTER XXI.

CHAPTER XXII.

CHAPTER XXIII.

CHAPTER XXIV.

CHAPTER XXV.

THE

CRUISE OF THE "FROLIC."

CHAPTER I.

WHAT yachtsman can ever forget the beautiful scene Cowes
Road presented on a regatta morning in the palmy days
of the club, when the broad pennant of its noble commodore flew at the mast-head of his gallant little ship, the
" Falcon," and numberless beautiful craft, of all rigs and
sizes, with the white ensign of St. George at their peaks,
and the red cross and crown in their snowy burgees aloft,
willingly followed the orders of their honored leader? Then,
from far and near, assembled yachts and pleasure-boats, of
all degrees, loaded with eager passengers to witness *the*
regatta; and no puffing, blowing, smoking, rattling steamers came to create discord on the ocean, and to interfere
with the time-honored monopoly of the wind in propelling
vessels across the watery plain. Small thanks to the man
whose impertinently-inquisitive brain could not let the lid
of his tea-kettle move up and down at its pleasure without
wanting to know the cause of the phenomenon ! Smaller

13

to him who insisted on boiling salt-water on the realms of
Old Neptune! Stern enemy to the romance and poetry of a
life on the ocean! Could you not be content to make carriages go along at the rate of forty miles an hour over the
hard land, without sending your noisy, impudent demagogues of machines to plough up the waves of the sea,
which have already quite enough to do when their lawful
agitator thinks fit to exert his influence? It was a work of
no slight difficulty and risk to cruise in and out among the
innumerable craft at anchor, and dodging about under sail
just when the yachts were preparing to start. I doubt
whether many of your "turn-a-head and back her" mariners, with their chimney-sweep faces, would possess seamanship enough to perform the feat without fouling each
other every instant. But I must not go on harping on the
smoke-jacks. Back, memory! back, to those glorious yachting days. Of the regatta I am treating. While afloat, all
was movement, gayety, and excitement; there was not less
animation on shore. The awning of the club-house shaded
crowds of gay visitors; and on the broad esplanade in front
of it were drawn up the carriages-and-four of the noble
house of Holmes, and those of Barrington and Simeon, with
blood-red hands emblazoned on their crests; while, in like
style, some might by chance come over from Appulder-
combe, and others of equal rank from the east and the west
end of the island; and thus, what with booths of ginger-
bread and bands of music, scarcely standing-room was to be
found on the quays during the day, while every hotel and
lodging was overflowing at night. And then the ball!
what lofty rank, what a galaxy of beauty was to be seen
there! And the fireworks! what a splutter, what a galaxy
of bright stars they afforded! Alas, alas! how have they
faded! how have they gone out! The pride of Cowes has

departed, its monopoly is no more, its regattas and its balls
are both equalled, if not surpassed, by its younger rivals!
" Tempora mutantur et uos mutamur in illis." I am now
about to speak of times when that change had already commenced, and the fleets of the Ryde, the Thames, the Western,
the Irish, and other clubs dotted the ocean. The first day
of a Cowes Regatta broke fair and lovely, then down came
the rain in torrents to disappoint the hopes of the pleasure-
seekers, like the clouds which at every turn beset our path
in life ; but again, as they do happily in our mortal course,
the clouds passed away, and the sun shone forth bright,
warm, and cheering ; a light air sprang up from the westward, and the whole scene on shore and afloat looked animated, joyous, and beautiful. While the rain-drops were
still hanging on the trees, a large party of ladies and gentlemen collected on the Yacht Club slip, by the side of which
were two gigs, their fine, manly crews, with their oars in
the air, ready to receive them. Three or four servants
followed, laden with cloaks and plaids, to guard against a
repetition of the shower ; and several white baskets, of no
mean proportions, showed that delicacies were provided
from the shore which might not be found afloat. Never
was a merrier set of people collected together. Cheerful
voices and shouts of laughter emanated from them on all
sides.

" Who's for the first boat ?" sung out Ned Hearty, the
owner of the " Frolic." Ned had tried shooting, hunting,
and every other amusement which the brain of man has
invented to kill time ; and he was now trying yachting,
which he seemed to enjoy amazingly, though practically he
knew very little about it ; but I never met a man, green
from the shore, so 'cute in taking in the details of marine
affairs. In a week he could box the compass, knew the

names of all the sails and most of the ropes of his craft, and had a slight notion of steering, though I'll wager he never touched a tiller in his life before. "I say, old fellow," he continued, turning to me — I had joined him the day before, and had taken up my quarters on board for a spell — "do you take charge of the first gig, and see some of the ladies safe on board. Send her back, though, for the two boats won't hold us all, and the Cardiffs and Lorimer have not come down yet."

"Very well: I can stow four ladies and three gentlemen," I answered, stepping into the boat, and offering my hand to Miss Seaton, who was considered the belle of the party by most of the men: at all events, she was the most sought after, for she was that lovable thing, an heiress. She took her seat, and looked up with her soft blue eyes to see who was next coming.

"We'll go in the first! we'll go in the first!" exclaimed the two Miss Rattlers, in one breath; and forthwith, without ceremony, they jumped into the boat, disdaining my proffered aid. Fanny Rattler, the eldest, was dark, with fine flashing eyes and a *petite* figure; but Susan was the girl for fun. She had not the slightest pretension to beauty, of which she was well aware; but she did not seem to care a pin about it: and such a tongue for going as she had in her head! and what funny things it said! — the wonder was it had not worn out long ago.

"Who'll come next?" I asked. "Come, Miss May Sandon, will you?" She nodded, and gave her delicate little hand into my rough paw. She was one of three sisters who were about to embark. They were all fair, and very pretty, with elegant figures, and hair with a slight touch of auburn, and yet they were not, wonderful as it may seem, alike in feature. This made them more attractive, and there was no mistaking one for the other. The three gentlemen who presented themselves were Harry Loring, a fine, good-looking fellow, a barrister by profession, but briefless, and the younger son of Sir John and Lady Loring. He was a devoted admirer of Miss Seaton. The next was Sir Francis Futtock, a post-captain, and a right honest old fellow. "Here, I must go, to act propriety among you youngsters," he said, as he stepped into the boat. The third, Will Bubble, the owner of a small yacht called the "Froth," laid up that year for want, as he confessed, of quicksilver to float her. Will, like many a man of less wisdom, had been, I suspect, indulging in railway speculations, and if he had not actually burnt his fingers, he had found his capital safely locked up in lines which don't pay a dividend. "Shove off!" was the word; and I, seizing the yoke lines, away we went towards the "Frolic."

"I say, Sir Francis, take care they behave properly, — don't discredit the craft," sung out her owner. "No flirtations, remember, till we get on board — all start fair."

"Hear that, young ladies," said Sir Francis, looking, however, at Miss Seaton, whereat a *soupçon* of rosy tint came into her fair cheek, and her bright eyes glanced at her own delicate feet, while Henry Loring tried to look nohow, and succeeded badly.

"I vote for a mutiny against such restrictions," cried Miss Susan Rattler. "I've no idea of such a thing. Come, Sir Francis, let you and me set the example."

The gallant officer, who had only seen the fair Susan two or three times before, stared a little, and laughingly reminded her that he, as a naval man, should be the last to disobey the orders of the commander-in-chief. "Though faith, madam," he added, "the temptation to do so is very great."

2

"There, you've begun already with a compliment, Sir Francis," answered Miss Susan, laughing; "I must think of something to say to you in return."

She had not time, however, before the whole party were put in terror of their lives by a large schooner-yacht, which, without rhyme or reason, stood towards the mouth of the harbor, merely for the sake of standing out again, and very nearly ran us down, as she went about just at the moment she should not. We did not particularly bless the master, who stood at the helm with white kid gloves on his hands, one of which touched the tiller, the other held a cambric handkerchief to his nose, the scent of which Bubble declared he could smell as we passed to leeward. Two minutes more took us alongside the "Frolic." She was a fine cutter of between ninety and a hundred tons; in every respect what a yacht should be, though not a racer; for Ned Hearty liked his ease and his fun too much to pull his vessel to pieces at the very time he most wanted to use her. She did not belong to the Cowes squadron; but Ryde owned her, and Ryde was proud of her, and the red burgee of the Royal Victoria Yacht Club flew at her mast-head. The water was perfectly smooth, so the ladies stepped on board without any difficulty. The gentlemen were busily engaged in arranging the cloaks and cushions for the ladies, while the other boats were coming off. In the next came, under charge of Captain Carstairs, who was yachting regularly with Hearty, Mrs. Sandon, and two more of her fair daughters. Mamma was a very amiable gentlewoman, and had been a brunette in her youth, not wanting in prettiness, probably.

Then came a Mrs. Skyscraper, a widow, pretty, youngish — that is to say, not much beyond thirty — and with a good jointure at her own disposal; and a very tall young lady,

Miss Mary Masthead by name, a regular jolly girl, though, who bid fair to rival the Rattlers. Then there was Master Henry Flareup perched in the bows, a precocious young gentleman, waiting for his commission, and addicted to smoking; not a bad boy in the main, however, and full of good nature. Hearty himself came off last with what might be considered the aristocracy of the party — Lady and Miss Cardiff, Lord Lorimer, and the Honorable Mrs. Topgallant; and with them was young Sandon, an Oxonian, and going into a cavalry regiment. Her ladyship was one of those persons who look well and act well, and against whom no one can say a word; while Clara Cardiff was a general favorite with all sensible men, and even the women liked her; she talked a great deal, but never said a silly thing, and, what is more, never uttered an unkind one. She was so incredulous, too, that she never believed a bit of scandal, and (consequently, or rather, for such would not in all cases be the *sequitur*) at all events she never repeated one. She was not exactly pretty, but she had a pair of eyes, regular sparklers, which committed a great deal of mischief, though she did not intend it; her figure was *petite* and perfect for her height, and she was full of life and animation. Mrs. Topgallant was proud of her high descent, and a despiser of all those who had wealth, the advantages arising from which they would not allow her to enjoy. It was whispered that her liege lord was hard up in the world — not a very rare circumstance now-a-days. I almost forgot Lord Lorimer. He was a young man — a very good fellow — slightly afraid of being caught, perhaps, and consequently very likely to be so. The Miss Sandons, in their quiet way, set their caps at him; Jane Seaton looked as if she wished he would pay her more attention; and Mrs. Skyscraper thought his title very pretty; but the Rattler girls knew

that he was a cut above them ; and Clara Cardiff treated
him with the same indifference that she did the rest of
the men. Such was the party assembled on board the
" Frolic."

I have not yet described the " Frolic," which, as it
turned out, was to be my home — and a very pleasant
home, too, for many a month on the ocean wave ; and yet
she was well worthy of a description. She had the first
requisite for a good sea-boat — great breadth of beam, with
sharp bows, and a straightish stem. Her bulwarks were
of a comfortable height, and she was painted black outside ;
her copper, of its native hue, was varnished so as to shine
like a looking-glass. Some people would have thought her
deck rather too much encumbered with the skylights ; but
I am fond of air ; provided there are ample means of batten-
ing them down in case of a heavy sea breaking on board,
they are to be commended. A thorough draught can thus
always be obtained by having the foremost and aftermost
skylights open at the same time ; in a warm climate, an
absolute necessity. Besides her main cabin, she had five
good-sized sleeping-cabins, a cabin for the master and chief
mate, store-rooms, and pantries ; a large fore cuddy for the
men ; and Soyer himself would not have despised the kitchen
range. I might expatiate on the rosewood fittings of her
cabin, on the purity of her decks, on the whiteness of her
canvas and ropes, on the bright polish of the brass belaying-
pins, stanchions, davits, and guns, and on the tiller with the
head of a sea-fowl exquisitely carved ; but, suffice it to say,
that, even to the most fastidious taste, she was perfect in all
her details. Before Hearty came down I had engaged a
crew for him, and as soon as he arrived on board, I mustered
them aft in naval fashion. They were, truly, a fine-looking
set of fellows, as they stood hat in hand, dressed in plain blue

frocks and trousers, the ordinary costume of yachtsmen, with the name of "Frolic" in gold letters on the black ribbon which went round their low-crowned hats. The name of the master was Snow. He was a thorough sea-dog, who had spent the best part of his life in smuggling, but not finding it answer of late, had grown virtuous, and given up the trade. He was clean and neat in his person; and as he appeared in his gold-laced cap, and yacht-buttons on his jacket, he looked every inch the officer. Odd enough, the name of one of the other men was Sleet, so Carstairs chose to dub the rest, Hail, Ice, Frost, Rain, Mist, Thaw, and so on; while one of the boys always went by the name of Drizzle. Hearty had brought down his own man, but was very soon obliged to send him on shore again; for John, though an excellent groom, proved a very bad sailor. Among other disqualifications, he was invariably sick, and could never learn to keep his legs. The first day we got under weigh, he caught hold of the swing table, and sent all the plates and dishes flying from it. After breakfast he hove overboard half a dozen silver forks and spoons when shaking the tablecloth; and as he went to windward, of course all the crumbs and egg-tops came flying over the deck. Indeed, it were endless to mention all the inexcusable atrocities poor John committed. On his retiring on sick leave, we shipped a sea-steward to serve in his stead, who, having been regularly brought up on board yachts, proved himself admirable in his department; but a more impudent rascal to all strangers whom he thought not likely to know his master, I never met.

Who can fail to look with pleasure at the mouth of the Medina on a fine summer's day, filled as the roadstead is with numerous fine yachts, as well fitted to contend with the waves and tempests in a voyage round the world as the

largest ship afloat! The scenery itself is beautiful — a
charming combination of wood and water. On one side,
to the east, Norris Castle, with its ivy-crowned turrets and
waving forest; on the other, the church-spire peeping amid
the trees; and the pretty collection of villas climbing the
heights, and extending along the shore from the Club-house
and Castle to Egypt Point, with the fine wild downs beyond.
On the opposite coast, the wooded and fertile shores of
Hampshire; the lordly tower of Eaglehurst, amid its verdant groves; and Calshot Castle on its sandy beach, at the
mouth of the Southampton Water; while far away to the
east are seen, rising from the ocean, the lofty masts and
spars of the ships-of-war at Spithead, and the buildings in
the higher parts of Ryde; altogether forming a picture perfect and unrivalled in its kind. Osborne — fit abode of Her
Majesty of England — has now sprung up, and added both
dignity and beauty to the scene.

CHAPTER II.

" WHAT shall we do? Which way shall we go?" was
the cry from all hands.

" Accompany the yachts to the eastward, and haul our
wind in time to be back before the flood makes," was Will
Bubble's suggestion, and it was approved of and acted on.

We watched the yachts starting, and a very pretty sight
it was; but I have not the slightest recollection of their
names, except that they are mostly those which have sailed
before at Ryde. It is the *tout ensemble* of a regatta which
makes up the interest; the white sails moving about, the
number of craft dressed out with gay colors, the bands of
music, the cheers as the winners pass the starting vessel,
the eagerness of the men in the boats pulling about with
orders, the firing of guns, the crowd on shore, the noise
and bustle; and yet no dust, nor heat, nor odors disagreeable as at horse-races, where abominations innumerable take
away half the pleasure of the spectacle. A gun was fired
for the yachts to take their stations and prepare; a quarter
of an hour flew by — another was heard loud booming
along the water, and up went the white folds of canvas like
magic — mainsail, gaff-topsail, foresail, and jib altogether.
A hand ran aloft to make fast the gaff-topsail-sheet the moment the throat was up, and while they were still swaying
away on the peak.

Every man exerts himself to the utmost — what muscular power and activity is displayed! There is not one on board who is not as eager for victory as the owner. What a crowd of canvas each tiny hull supports. What a head to the gaff-topsail, as long as that of the mainsail itself! And then the jib, well may it be called a balloon; it looks as if it could lift the vessel out of the water and carry her bodily along; it can only be set when she is going free; another is stopped along the bowsprit ready to hoist as she hauls close up to beat back. Huzza! away glide the beautiful beings — they look as if they had life in them; altogether, not two seconds' difference in setting their sails — a magnificent start! This beats the turf hollow: no slashing and cutting the flanks of the unfortunate horses, no training of the still more miserable jockeys; after all of which, you see a flash of yellow, or green, or blue jackets, and in a few minutes every thing is over, and you hear that some horse has won, and some thousands have slipped out of the hands of one set of fools into those of another set, who, if wiser, are perhaps not more respectable. Now, consider what science is required to plan a fast yacht, what knowledge to build her, to cut and fashion her canvas — to rig her. What skill and hardihood in master and crew to sail her. What fine manly qualities are drawn out by the life they lead. Again I say, Huzza for yachting!

Away glided the "Frolic" from her moorings, as the racing yachts, accompanied with a crowd of others, ran dead before the wind to the eastward through Cowes Roads. The whole Channel appeared covered with a wide spread of canvas, as we saw them stem on with their mainsails over on one side, and their immense square sails boomed out on the other. Everybody on board was pleased, some uttered loud exclamations of delight, even the Miss Sandons smiled. They never expressed their pleasure by any more extravagant method; in fact, they were not given to admiration, however willing to receive it.

I wish two persons to be noted more particularly than the rest — our hero and heroine, at least for the present; for what is a story, however true, without them? They were to be seen at the after-part of the vessel — the one, the fair Jane Seaton, sitting on a pile of cushions, and leaning against the side, while Harry Loring, the other, reclined on a wrap-rascal at her feet, employed in looking up into her bright blue eyes, as she unconsciously pulled to pieces a flower he had taken out of his button-hole and given her.

" Wouldn't it be delightful to take a cruise to the Antipodes?" he asked.

" Yes," she answered.

" Just as we are now," he added, " with such a heaven above me." He looked meaningly into her blue eyes.

Sweet Jane blushed, as well she might. What more in the same style he said I don't know, for as she bent her head down, and he put his face into her blue hood, not a word reached me. By the by, all the ladies wore blue silk hoods, formed after the model of the front of a bathing-machine, and they were considered admirable contrivances to help a quiet flirtation, as in the present instance, besides aiding in preserving the complexion.

Hearty was rather bothered, I fancied. He liked to be making love to somebody, he declared, and Jane Seaton appeared to be a girl so much to his taste, that, as he confessed, he felt rather spooney on her, and had almost made up his mind to try his luck. Foolish Jane! Here was ten thousand a year ready to throw himself at your feet instead of the penniless youth who had so easily placed

himself there.   How you would have kicked had you
known the truth !

"I say, Hearty, can't you find something for all these
young people to do to keep them out of mischief?" sung
out Sir Francis.   "Remember the proverb about idleness.
I tremble for the consequences."

"Fie, fie !" said Mrs. Skyscraper.

"Fie, fie ! echoed Mrs. Topgallant ; "I'm ashamed of
you."

"We'll try what can be done, Sir Francis," answered
Hearty.   "Can you, Bubble, devise something?"

"I have it," replied Will.   "Tablecloths, napkins, towels,
and all sorts of household linen came on board yesterday
at Portsmouth unhemmed, so I laid in a supply of needles
and thread this morning on purpose for the present emergency."

The rogue had put Sir Francis up to making the observation he had done.   In a few minutes a number of rolls of
various sorts of linen were brought on deck.   Some of the
damsels protested that they had no needles, and couldn't
work and wouldn't work, till Sir Francis slyly suggested
that it was a trial to see who would make the most notable
wife ; and without another objection being offered, all the
fair hands were employed in sewing away at a great rate,
the gentlemen, meantime, holding their parasols to shade
them from the sun.   Carstairs was the only exception.   He
slyly went forward, and, taking out pencil and paper, made
a capital sketch of the various groups, under which he
wrote, "All for Love," and headed, "Distressed Needle-
women ;" much to the scandal of those who saw it.

The ladies, old and young, soon got tired of doing any
thing, and the announcement that dinner would be ready as
soon as the company were, was received with evident signs

of satisfaction. Hearty was a sensible fellow, and determined to get rid of all bad London habits, so we dined early
on board; and then when we got back to port in the evening, we used generally to repair to the house of one or other
of the guests, and enjoy a meal called by some a glorious
tea, by others a yachting tea — in fact, it was something
like the supper of our ancestors, with tea and coffee. It
mattered, therefore, nothing to us whether we got back at
eight, nine, or ten; no one waited dinner for us; indeed,
Hearty never would undertake to get back in time. I
should advise all yachting people to follow the good example
thus set them.

By general acclamation it was determined that we should
dine on deck; and Sir Francis, Bubble, and some of the
more nautical gentlemen, set to work to rig tables, which
we accomplished in a very satisfactory manner, and never
was a better feast set before a more hungry party of ladies
and gentlemen. Champagne was the favorite beverage;
and certainly Hearty did not stint his friends in it, though
there was no lack of less refined liquors. Sir Francis, of
course, proposed the health of Ned Hearty; "and may
there soon be a Mrs. Hearty to steady the helm of the
'Frolic'!" were the last words of his speech.

Ned got up to return thanks. He looked at Jane Seaton,
but she had the front of her bathing-machine turned toward
Harry Loring, so did not see him. He made a long ora-
tion, and concluded by observing, —

"How can there be any difficulty in following the advice
my gallant friend, Sir Francis Futtock, has given me, when
I see myself surrounded by so many angelic creatures, any
of whom a prince might be proud to make his bride?"

Loud shouts of applause from the gentlemen — odd looks
and doubtful smiles from the chaperones — blushes deep

from the young ladies — each one of whom, who was not already in love, thought she should like to become Mrs. Hearty,
provided Lord Lorimer did not ask her to become Lady
Lorimer; while Henry Flareup was discovered squeezing
the hand of Miss Mary Masthead.

"Oh that I were a prince, then!" whispered Loring into
Miss Seaton's blue shade.

Thus passed on the day. If there was not much real
wit, there was a great deal of hearty laughter; and stores
of health and good spirits were laid in for the future.
Loring sang some capital songs, Carstairs spouted, and
Bubble floated about, throwing in a word whenever he saw
any one silent, or looking as if about to become dull; while
young Flareup, who was anxious to do his best, laughed
loudly, for want of any other talent to amuse the company.
As the vessels came to haul their wind in order to save the
tide back to Cowes, it was curious to observe how they
appeared to vanish. One could scarcely tell what had become of the immense crowd we had just before seen astern
of us. Scattered far and wide in every direction, there
seemed not to be one-quarter of the number which were
before to be seen. We got back soon after eight o'clock,
every one assuring Hearty that they had spent a most delightful day.

CHAPTER III.

A VOYAGE — THE MARINERS' RETURN.

"I SAY, old fellows, don't you find this rather slow?" exclaimed Hearty, as one morning Carstairs, Bubble, and I sat at breakfast with him ön board the "Frolic." "What say you to a cruise to the westward, over to the coast of France and the Channel Islands, just for ten days or a fortnight or so?"

"Agreed, agreed, agreed!" we all answered.

"Well, then, to-morrow or next day we sail," said Hearty. "But how can you, Carstairs, tear yourself away from your pretty widow? Bubble, you don't mean to say that you can leave sweet May Sandon without a sigh?"

"A little absence will try the widow; it will teach her to miss me, and she will value me more when I return," was Carstairs' answer. "But you, Bubble, what do you say?" for he did not answer.

Will was guilty of blushing, for I saw the rosy hue appearing even through his sunburnt countenance, though the others did not.

"That is the best thing we can do," he answered, with a loud laugh. "Hurrah for the broad seas, and a rover's free life!"

"I thought so — I thought there was nothing in it," said Hearty. "Happy dog! — you never fall in love; you never care for any one.'

"Ah, no: I laugh, sing, and am merry!" exclaimed Bubble. "It's all very well for you fellows with your five or ten thousand a year to fall in love; you have hope to live on, if nothing else — no insurmountable obstacles; but for poverty-stricken wretches, like me and a dozen more I could name, it can only bring misery: yet I don't complain of poverty — no cares, no responsibilities; if one has only one's self to look after, it matters little; but should one unhappily meet with some being who to one's eye is lovely, towards whom one's heart yearns unconsciously, and one longs to make her one's own, then one begins to feel what poverty really is — then the galling yoke presses on one's neck. Can you then be surprised that I, and such as I, throw care away, and become the light frivolous wretches we seem? Hearty, my dear fellow, don't you squander your money, or you will repent it!"

Bubble spoke with a feeling for which few would have given him credit. He directly afterwards, however, broke into his usual loud laugh, adding,—

"Don't say that I have been moralizing, or I may be suspected of incipient insanity."

"Will Bubble has made out a clear case that he cannot be in love, for no one accuses him of being overburdened with the gifts of fortune," I observed; for I saw that he was more in earnest than he would have wished to be supposed. "But do you, Hearty, wish to desert Miss Seaton, and leave the stage clear for Loring?"

"Oh, I never enter the lists with a man who can sing," answered Hearty. "Those imitators of Orpheus have the same winning way about them which their great master possessed. But, at the same time, I'll bet ten to one that the fair Jane never becomes Mrs. Loring. I had a little confab the other day with Madame la Mère, and faith, she's about as fierce a she-dragon as ever guarded an enchanted princess from the attempts of knights-errant to rescue her."

" I'll take your bet, and for once stake love against lucre ! " exclaimed Bubble, and the bet was booked.

But enough of this. We bade our friends farewell ; and, in spite of all their attempts to detain us, we laid in a stock of provisions to last us for a month, and with a fine breeze from the northward, actually found our way through the Needles just as the sun was tinging the topmost pinnacles of those weather-worn rocks.

As soon as we were through the passage, we kept away, and shaped a course for Havre de Grâce. The wind shifted round soon afterwards to the westward, and I shall not forget the pure refreshing saltness of the breeze which filled our nostrils, and added strength and vigor to our limbs. What a breakfast we ate afterwards ! There seemed no end to it. Our caterer had done well to lay in a store of comestibles. Our perfect happiness lasted till nearly noon, and then the wind increased and the sea got up in a not unusual manner. We went below to take luncheon, and we set to in first-rate style, as if there was no such thing as the centre of gravity to be disturbed. ' Carstairs began to look a little queer.

" ' Thus far into the bowels of the earth have we marched on without impediment,' Shakspeare, hum " — he began. He was going to give us the whole speech, but instead, he exclaimed, " O ye gods and little fishes ! " and bolted up on deck.

Hearty, the joyous and free, followed. They declared that they felt as if the cook had mixed ipecacuanha in the sausages they had eaten for breakfast. Bubble laughed, lighted a cigar, and sat on the companion-hatch with one leg resting on the deck, the other carelessly dangling down, with the independence of a king on his throne, pitying them.

Oh, how they envied him; how they almost hated him, as cigar after. cigar disappeared, and still there he sat without a sign of discomposure! At dark we made the Havre light, and an hour afterwards, the tide being high, we ran in and dropped our anchor in smooth water. Wonderful was the change which quietude worked on all hands!

"Supper, supper!" was the cry. Even Will and I did justice to it, though we had had a quiet little dinner by ourselves in the midst of our friends' agony, off pickled salmon and roast duck, with a gooseberry tart and a bottle of champagne.

Next morning we sailed with the wind back again to the north-east, and, notwithstanding the little inconveniences we had suffered on the passage across, we stood to the westward, and heroically determined to run through the Race of Alderney, to pay a visit to Jersey. There was a nice breeze, and I must say we were glad there was no more of it, as we ran through the passage between Alderney and the French coast. The water seemed possessed; it tumbled and leaped and twisted and danced in a most extraordinary and unnatural manner; and several seas toppled right down on our decks, and we could not help fancying that some huge fish had jumped on board. However, with a fair wind and a strong tide we were soon through it, nor was there danger of any sort; but from the specimen we had we could judge what it would be in a strongish gale. The wind had got round to the southward of west, and before we had managed to weather Cape Gronez the tide turned against us. Cape Gronez is the north-west point of Jersey, and bears a strong similarity to the nose of Louis Philippe, as his portrait used to be represented in "Punch." We had an opportunity of judging of it, for, for upwards of an hour did we beat between it and those enticing rocks called very properly the Paternosters, for if a ship once strikes on them, it is to be hoped that the crew, being Roman Catholics, will, if they have time, say their Paternosters before they go to the bottom.

At last it came on very thick, we ran back and anchored in a most romantic little cove called Bouley Bay, where we remained all night, hoping the wind would not shift to the northward, and send us on shore. I should advise all timid yachtsmen to keep clear of Jersey, for what with the rapid tides, and rocks innumerable, it is a very ticklish locality. The next morning we got under way at daybreak, and brought up off Elizabeth Castle, which guards the entrance of the harbor of St. Heliers. I have not time to describe Jersey. I can only recommend all who have not seen it, and wish to enjoy some very beautiful scenery, to go there. Two days more saw us crossing to Torbay, which we reached on the morning of the regatta. Had an artist been employed to carve the cliffs on which Torbay is situated, he could scarcely have made them more picturesque, or added tints more suitable, except perhaps that they are a little more red than one might wish. However, it is a very beautiful place, and admirably adapted for a regatta.

The bay before the town was crowded with yachts, and I counted no less than fourteen large schooners, among which I remember the "Brilliant," which, however, should be called a ship, "Gypsy Queen," "Dolphin," "Louisa," and a vast number of cutters, a large proportion of which were gayly dressed up with flags. The course is round the bay, so that the yachts are in sight the whole time — an advantage possessed by few other places. The "Heroine," "Cygnet," and "Cynthia," sailed, but the race was not a good one, as the "Heroine," driven to windward by her

3

antagonist, ran her bowsprit into one of the mark boats, and
another of them, the "Cynthia," making a mistake, did not
go round her at all.   Notwithstanding this, the sight was as
beautiful of its kind as I ever saw.   There was a ball at
night, to which we went, and we flattered ourselves that four
dancing bachelors were not unwelcome.   We met a number
of acquaintances.   Hearty lost his heart for the tenth time
since he left London.   The Gentle Giant, as the Miss Rattlers called Carstairs, looked out for a charmer, but could
find none to surpass Mrs. Skyscraper.   Bubble laughed with
all but sighed with none, though Hearty accused him of
flirtations innumerable ; and I never chronicle my own
deeds, however fond I may be of noting those of my friends.
However, if we did not break hearts, we passed a very
pleasant evening.   Hearty invited everybody he knew to
come on board the next morning, and we went as far as
Dartmouth, and a beautiful sail back we had by moonlight,
to the great delight of the romantic portion of the guests.
They were a very quiet set of ladies and gentlemen, and
more than one sigh was heaved when they had gone on
shore for our fast friends at Cowes.

We were present at the Plymouth Regatta, and were
going to several other places, when, one day after dinner,
Hearty thus gave utterance to his thoughts.   We were about
a quarter of the way across channel on our passage to the
French coast, with a stiffish breeze from the westward, and
a chopping sea :—

" It seems to me arrant folly that we four bachelors should
keep turning up the salt water all the summer, and boxing
about from place to place which we don't care to visit, when
there are a number of fair ladies at Cowes who are undoubtedly pining for our return."

" My own idea," exclaimed Carstairs.

"Your argument is unanswerable," said Bubble.

I nodded.

"All agreed — then we'll up stick for the Wight," said Hearty joyfully. "The wind's fair. We shall be there some time to-morrow. Hillo, Jack! beg the master to step below."

This was said to a lad who waited at table and assisted the steward.

Old Snow, the master, soon made his appearance. He had been a yachtsman for many years, and previously, if his yarns were to be believed, a smuggler of no mean renown. He was a short man, rather fat, for good living had not been thrown away on him, and very neat and clean in his person, as became the master of a yacht.

"We want to get back to Cowes, Snow," said Hearty.

"Yes, sir," answered the skipper, well accustomed to sudden changes in the plans of his yachting masters.

"How soon can we get there?" asked Hearty.

"If we keeps away at once, and this here wind holds, early to-morrow; but, if it falls light, not till the afternoon, maybe; and, if it chops round to the eastward, not till next morning," replied Snow.

"By all means keep away at once, and get there as fast as you can," said Hearty; and the master disappeared from the cabin.

Directly afterwards we heard him call the hands aft to ease off the main sheet, the square sail and gaff topsail were set, and, by the comparatively easy motion, we felt that we were running off before the wind. Not a little did it contribute to our comfort in concluding our dinner.

The next day, at noon, saw us safely anchored in Cowes Roads.

"There's Mr. Hearty and the Gentle Giant, I declare,"

exclaimed the melodious voice of Miss Susan Rattler, from out of a shrubbery, as my two friends were pacing along on the road towards Egypt, to call on Lady Cardiff.

"Oh, the dear men! you don't say so, Susan!" replied her sister.

Bubble and I were close under them, a little in advance, so they did not see us, though we could not avoid hearing what was said.

"Yes, it's them, I vow; we must attack them about the picnic forthwith," said Susan.

"Don't mention Jane Seaton, or poor Ned will be too much out of spirits to do any thing," observed her sister.

"Trust me to manage all descriptions of he-animals," replied Rattler minima. "Ah, how d'ye do?—how d'ye do? Welcome, rovers, welcome!" she exclaimed, waving her handkerchief as they approached.

"Lovely ladies, we once more live in your presence," began Hearty.

"'Oh that I were a glove upon that hand!'" shouted Carstairs.

"Oh, don't, you'll make us blush!" screamed Susan, from over the bushes. "But seriously, we're so glad you're come, because now we can have the picnic to Netley you promised us."

"I like frankness—when shall it be?" said Hearty.

"To-morrow, by all means,—never delay a good thing."

"'If 'twere done, 'twere well 'twere done quickly,'" observed the captain.

"That's what Shakspeare says about a beef-steak," cried Susan. "But I say then, it's settled—how nice!"

"What? that we are to have beef-steaks?" asked Hearty.

"They are very nice when one's hungry."

" No, I mean that we are to have a pic-nic to-morrow," said the fair Rattler.

" That depends whether those we invite are willing to join it," observed Hearty.

" ' I can summon spirits from the vasty deep; but will they come, cousin?' " exclaimed Carstairs.

"Oh, yes, in these parts, often," cried Rattler maxima; " the revenue officers constantly find them, I know."

" Capital — capital!" ejaculated Hearty. " You must bring that out again on board the ' Frolic.' You deserve a pic-nic for it; it's so original. You must consider this only as a rehearsal."

" How kind — then it's all settled!" exclaimed both young ladies in a breath. " There's Mary Masthead, I know, is dying to go, and so is Mrs. Topgallant, and I dare say, if Captain Carstairs presses Mrs. Skyscraper, she'll go, and the Sandons and Cardiffs, and all our set; I don't think any will refuse."

" Well, then, we've no time to lose," we exclaimed, and off we set to beat up for recruits.

We were not, however, without our disappointments. Lady Cardiff could not go, and without a correct chaperone she could not let her daughter be of the party — the thing was utterly impossible, dreadfully incorrect, and altogether unheard of. Mrs. Skyscraper was a great deal too young, and being a widow had herself to look after. If Mrs. Topgallant would go, she would see about it; so we tried next to find the lady in question, but she had gone to Carisbrooke Castle, and would not be back till late. Mrs. Sandon was next visited, but she had a cold; and if Lady Cardiff would not let her daughter go without a chaperone, neither could she. We by chance met Mrs. Seaton with the fair Jane, looking very beautiful, but mamma never went on the water

if she could help it. She could not come to the island
without doing so; but once safe there, she would not set
her foot in a boat till she had to go away again. Sooth to
say, that was not surprising; the good dame was unsuited
by her figure for locomotion. Every thing depended on
Mrs. Topgallant; never was she in so much request. The
gentlemen being able to come without chaperones, more
readily promised to be present. We fell in with Sir Francis
Futtock, Lord Lorimer, Harry Loring, and young Flareup,
and a young Oxonian, who had lately taken orders, and
created a great sensation among the more sensitive portion
of his audience by his exquisite preaching, and the unction
by which he privately recommended auricular confession
and penance.

The Rev. Frederick Fairfax was a pink-faced young man,
and had naturally a round, good-natured countenance, but
by dint of shaving his whiskers, elongating his face, and
wearing a white cravat without gills, and a stand-up collar
to his coat, he contrived to present a no bad imitation of a
Jesuit priest. The Miss Rattlers called him the Paragon
Puseyite, or the P. P., which they said would stand as well
for parish priest. How Hearty came to invite him I don't
know, for he detested the silly clique to whom the youth
had attached himself. We had just left the young gentleman when we met the two merry little Miss Masons. At
first they could not possibly go, because they had no chaperone; but when they heard that the Rev. Frederick was to
be of the party, all their scruples vanished. With such a
pastor they might go anywhere. They had only lately been
bitten, but had ever since diligently applied themselves to
the study of the " Tracts of the Times;" and though not a
word did they understand of those works (which was not
surprising by the by), they perceived that the Rev. Fred's

voice was very melodious, that he chanted to admiration, and looked so pious that they could not be wrong in following his advice. At last the hearts of all were made glad by the appearance of Mrs. Topgallant, who, without much persuasion, undertook to chaperone as many young ladies as were committed to her charge.

CHAPTER IV.

A PIC-NIC, AND ITS CONSEQUENCES.

THE morning came at last, fine as the palpitating hearts of expectant damsels could desire, and calm enough to please the most timid chaperone; so calm, indeed, that it was a question whether any craft with canvas alone to depend on could move from her moorings with a chance of going anywhere except to Hurst or the Nab; but, as few of our lady friends had any nautical knowledge, that in no way disconcerted them, and they would not have believed us had we assured them that there was too little wind for the excursion. By noon, however, a few cats'-paws appeared on the lake-like surface of the water, and soon after the deck of the "Frolic" once more began to rejoice in the presence of many of the former frolickers. They found it easy enough to come on board, but to collect all hands and get under way was a very different thing. The Miss Sandons and Jane Seaton, who came escorted by Loring, on finding no chaperone, thought they ought to go on shore again, as neither Mrs. Topgallant nor Mrs. Skyscraper had come; but Sir Francis kept them discussing the point till Carstairs had time to dive below, and presently returned with a Norman cap on his head, a shawl over his shoulders, and a boat-cloak as a petticoat.

"There," he exclaimed, crossing his arms before him, and putting his head on one side, sentimentally, "I'm as good a duenna as Mrs. Topgallant, or any other lady of

your acquaintance." All laughed and forgot to go. "Come,
my dear girls, sit down and behave yourselves; no flirting
with that naval officer, if you please," he continued, imitat-
ing the honorable dame. "You, Mr. Loring, and you,
Mr. Henry Flarcup, go forward and smoke your cigars. I
can't allow such nasty practices here."

Flarcup had, as usual, lighted his weed, and was sending
the smoke into the face of May Sandon. The roars of
laughter were not few as the real Mrs. Topgallant, with
Miss Mary Masthead, approached, and the Norman cap with
the good-natured face of the wearer was seen looking over
the side affectionately down upon them. The Rev. Fred
and the Miss Masons next arrived, and lastly Mrs. Skyscraper, Miss Cardiff, Lord Lorimer, and Hearty.

"Now, remember, Mr. Hearty, we must get back before
dark; it is on that condition alone that I have consented to
chaperone these young ladies," said Mrs. Topgallant, as we
were about to get under way.

"And I, also," exclaimed pretty Mrs. Skyscraper.

"Oh, we don't allow you to be a chaperone," said Carstairs; "you are far too young and too engaging," he whispered; and the Gentle Giant actually blushed as he said so;
luckily Miss Susan Rattler did not hear him.

"And mamma made me promise to be back at eight,"
cried Jane Seaton.

"And so did ours!" echoed the three Miss Sandons.

"You know we could not have come at all unless we
were certain of being at home in proper time!" exclaimed
the two Miss Masons; "could we, Mr. Fairfax?"

The pet bowed and smiled. He was meditating on the
Life of St. Euphemia, of Rhodes, and did not hear the
question.

"Remember, ladies, that time and tide wait for no man,"

answered Hearty. "Even such fair goddesses as honor
the 'Frolic' by their presence this day cannot govern the
winds and waves, however much they may every thing else.
Therefore all I can promise is, to do my best to follow the
wishes of your amiable mammas, and of yourselves."

"And of mine, if you please, Mr. Hearty," put in Mrs.
Topgallant.

"Certainly, my dear madam, I considered you among
the goddesses of whom I was speaking," answered Hearty,
with a flourish of his broad-brimmed beaver, which, with
the compliment, completely won the honorable lady's heart.

The anchor was at last weighed, and it being fortunately
slack tide, with a light air from the south-east, we were
able to fetch Calshot Castle.

Most of my readers probably know the Southampton
Water, and may picture us to themselves as we floated up
the stream with the round, solid, Stilton-cheese-like-looking
Castle of Calshot, at the end of a sandy spit, and the lordly
Tower of Eaglehurst, rising among the trees visible over it
on the one hand, and the mouth of the Hamble River on
the other, while, as far as the eye can reach on either hand,
are seen verdant groves, with the roofs and chimneys of
numerous villas peeping from among them. About three-
quarters of the way up, on the right hand, at a short distance
only from the water, stand the picturesque ruins of Netley
Abbey. The jolly monks of old — and I respect them for
it — always selected the most beautiful sites in the neighborhood for their habitations, and in fixing on that for Netley,
they did not depart from their rule. Several chambers remain ; and the walls which surround an inner court are entire, with fine arched windows, the tracery work complete,
looking into it. We brought up off it, and the boats were
instantly lowered to convey the passengers on shore. In

getting into one of them, Loring nearly went overboard, and a shriek of terror from Jane Seaton would have published her secret, had not everybody known it before. At last the hampers and the people reached the beach in safety; and now began the difficulties of the chaperone. She was like a shepherd with a wild flock of sheep and no dog; they would stray in every direction out of her sight. Some had brought sketch-books, and perched themselves about, far apart, to take views of the ruins; others preferred what they called exploring; and Jane and Loring vanished no one knew where. The Gentle Giant, who drew very well, was called on by the Miss Rattlers and several other ladies to fill up the pages of their books; and Hearty was running about talking to everybody and ordering every thing; while Bubble was exerting himself to do the same, and to take sketches into the bargain, though all his friends observed that there was a want of his usual vivacity. The Rattler girls quizzed him unmercifully, till they brought him back to the semblance, at all events, of his former self. The servants had been employed in laying the cloth under the shade of a tree which had sprung up in the courtyard, and thither Hearty's voice now summoned us. How can pen of mine do justice to the cold collation which was spread before our rejoicing eyes! I can only say that the party did it, and amply too.

" Are we all here?" exclaimed the master of the revels. " No, by Bacchus! two are wanting — Miss Seaton and Mr. Loring — where are they?"

" Good gracious! where can they be?" screamed the Honorable Mrs. Topgallant.

" What can have become of them?" cried Mrs. Skyscraper.

" They probably did not hear you call, and I dare say

they are not far off," suggested Miss Cardiff, always anxious to find a good excuse for her acquaintance.

" I should not wonder but what they have eloped," observed Miss Susan Rattler.

" What fun ! " said Miss Mary Masthead ; " we haven't had such a thing for a long time."

" How shocking ! " ejaculated the Miss Masons in a breath, and looked at the Rev. Frederick.

" I'll wager I find the truants," said Bubble, about to go ; but he was saved the trouble, for at that moment they appeared ; the fair Jane looking very confused — Harry Loring remarkably happy.

" We've all been talking about you two," blurted out Hearty. " No scandal though, so sit down and enable us to recover our appetites, for our anxiety nearly took them away. Now tell us, what have you been doing? "

Poor Jane did not know which way to look, nor what to say ; and it never occurred to Hearty that his question might possibly confuse her. Loring, however, came to the rescue.

" Admiring the architecture, exploring everywhere, and examining every thing, which no one else appears to have done, or the dinner-bell would not have been answered so speedily. And now, old fellow, I'll drink a glass of champagne with you."

This would not blind us, however. Every one saw what he had been about, and no small blame to him either. Of course, no one further hinted at the subject. After dinner we again wandered about the ruins, and the shades of evening surprised us while still there, to the great horror of Mrs. Topgallant, and not a little to that of the Miss Masons, who had been so earnestly listening to a discourse of the

Rev. Frederick on the importance of reviving monasteries, that they did not observe the sun set.

"Hillo, ladies and gentlemen! we ought to be on board again," sung out Hearty, from the top of a high wall to which he had climbed. "There is no time to be lost, if we would not displease our mammas."

A good deal of time, however, was lost in collecting the scattered sheep, and in carrying down the baskets to the boats, which the servants had neglected to do. When we did at length reach the spot at which we had landed, a bank of mud was alone to be seen, and one of the men brought us the pleasing intelligence that the nearest place at which we could possibly embark was about a mile down the river.

"We here have a convincing proof that time and tide wait for no one," cried Bubble; "or the latter would certainly have remained up for the convenience of so. many charming young ladies."

"Shocking!" exclaimed Mrs. Topgallant.

"What will our mammas say?" ejaculated all the fair damsels.

"That it's very improper," said the chaperone-general.

"It can't be helped now; so if we do not intend to spend the night on the beach, we had better keep moving," observed one of the gentlemen.

Henry Flareup expressed his opinion that the dismay their non-arrival would cause would be jolly fun, and the Miss Rattlers were in ecstasies of delight at the *contretemps*.

However, no one grumbled very much, and at last we reached the boats. A new difficulty then arose. They barely floated with the crews in them, but with passengers on board they would be aground. The men had to get out, and, as it was, the only approach to them was over wet mud of a soft nature, yet no persuasions would induce the ladies to be carried to them. Mrs. Topgallant would not hear of such a thing, and boldly led the van through the mud. The young ladies followed, nearly losing their shoes, and most effectually draggling (I believe it is a proper word) their gowns. Hearty counted them off to see, as he said, that none were missing; and then began the work of getting the boats afloat, one or two of the ladies, not accustomed to yachting, being dreadfully alarmed at seeing the men jump overboard, to lift them along. Huzza! off we went at last, and pulled towards the "Frolic."

"Let's get back as fast as we can, Snow," exclaimed Hearty, as soon as he stepped on deck.

"Beg pardon, sir, it won't be very fast, though," answered the master.

"Why, how is that?" asked Hearty; "an hour and a half will do it, won't it?"

"Bless your heart, no, sir," said old Snow, almost laughing at the idea. "It's just dead low water, so the flood will make up for the best part of the next six hours, and after that, if there doesn't come more wind than we has now, we shan't make no great way.

"But let us at all events get up our anchor and try to do something," urged Hearty, whose ideas of navigation were not especially distinct at the time.

"If we does, sir, we shall drive up to Southampton, or maybe, to Redbridge, for there ain't an hair in all the 'eavens," was the encouraging answer given by the master.

I never saw a more perfect calm. A candle was lighted on deck, and the flame went straight up as if in a room. If we had been in a tropical climate we should have looked out for a hurricane. Here nothing so exciting was to be apprehended. The conversation with the master was not overheard by any of the ladies, and Hearty thought it was as well to say nothing about it, but to leave them to suppose that we were on our way back to Cowes.

" It is much too dark to distinguish the shore, and as none of them ever think of looking at the sails, they will not discover that we are still at anchor," he observed ; and so it proved, as we shall presently see.

The after-cabin had been devoted to the use of the fairer portion of the guests, and when they got there and found the muddy condition of their dresses, there was a general cry for hot water to wash them. Luckily the cook's coppers could supply a good quantity, and two tubs were sent aft, in which, as was afterwards reported — for we were not allowed to be spectators of the process — the Honorable Mrs. Topgallant and her *protégées* were busily employed in rinsing their skirts, though it was not quite so easy a matter to dry them. Tea and coffee were next served up in the main cabin, and cakes and muffins and toast in profusion were produced, and as Carstairs quietly observed, " Never were washerwomen more happy."

There was only one thing wanting, we had not sufficient milk ; and that there might be no scarcity in future, it was proposed to send the steward on shore with Henry Flareup to swap him for a cow to be kept on board instead. He was fixed on as the victim, as it was considered that he had been making too much love to one of the Miss Sandons, conduct altogether unbecoming one of his tender years.

" We have passed a very pleasant evening, Mr. Hearty, I can assure you," said the chaperone ; " and as I suppose we shall soon be there, we had better get ready to go on shore."

" We shall have time for a dance first ; we have had the deck cleared, and the musicians are ready," replied Hearty ;

"may I have the honor of opening the ball with you, Mrs. Topgallant?"

"Oh, I don't know what to say to such a thing—I'm afraid it will be very incorrect; and at all events you must excuse me, Mr. Hearty, I shall have quite enough to do to look after my charges.

And as Mrs. Topgallant said this, she glanced round at the assembled young ladies.

"A dance, a dance, by all means!" exclaimed the Miss Rattlers; "what capital fun."

A dance was therefore agreed on, and.we went on deck, which we found illuminated with all the lanterns and spare lamps which could be found on board; and even candles without any shade were stuck on the taffrail, and the boom was topped up, so as to be completely out of the way. We owed the arrangements to Bubble, Carstairs, and the master, who had been busily employed while the rest were below at tea. An exclamation of delight burst from the lips of the young ladies; the musicians struck up a polka, and in another minute all hands were footing it away as gayly as in any ball-room, and with far more merriment and freedom.

> Ye gentlemen and ladies who stay at home at ease,
> Ah, little do ye think upon the fun there's on the seas!

How we did dance! No one tired. Even Mrs. Topgallant got up and took a turn with the Gentle Giant, and very nearly went overboard, by the by. We had no hot lamps, no suffocating perfumed atmosphere, to oppress us, as in a London ball-room. The clear sky was our ceiling, the cool water was around us. Every gentleman had danced with every lady, except that Loring had taken more than his share with Miss Seaton, before we thought of giving in.

"Well, I wonder we don't get there!" on a sudden exclaimed Mrs. Topgallant, as if something new had struck her.

There was a general laugh, set, I am sorry to say, by Sir Francis Futtock.

"Why, my dear madam, we have not begun to go yet."

"Not begun to go!" cried the Miss Masons. "What will be said of us?"

"Not begun to go!" groaned the Rev. Fred. "What will my flock do without me?"

"Why, I thought we had been moving all the time. We have passed a number of objects which I should have taken for ghosts, if I believed in such things," said Mrs. Topgallant.

"Those were vessels going up with the tide, my dear madam, to Southampton, where we should have gone also," observed Sir Francis.

Just then a tall dark object came out of the gloom, and glided by us at a little distance. It certainly had what one might suppose the appearance of a spirit wandering over the face of the waters.

"Cutter, ahoy! What cutter is that?" hailed a voice from the stranger.

"It's one of them revenue chaps," said Snow. "The 'Frolic' yacht; Edward Hearty, Esq., owner!" answered the old man; "and be hanged to you," he muttered.

"'I'll call thee king — father, royal Dane. Oh, answer me!'" continued Carstairs.

"He'll not answer you — so avast spouting, and let's have another turn at dancing!" exclaimed Hearty, interrupting the would-be actor, and dragging him to the side of Mrs. Skyscraper, who did not refuse his request to dance another quadrille.

4

Thus at it again we went, to the no small amusement of a
number of spectators, whose voices could be heard round us.
Their boats were just dimly visible, though, from the bright
lights on our deck, we could not see the human beings on
board them. At last the rippling sound against our bows
ceasing, gave notice that the tide had slackened, and that we
might venture on lifting anchor. A light air also sprang up
from the eastward, and slowly we began to move on our
right course. Some of the un-nauticals, however, forgot
that with an ebb tide and an easterly wind there was not
much chance of our reaching Cowes in a hurry. A thick
fog also began to rise from the calm water ; and after the
dancing, for fear of their catching cold, cloaks and ,coats,
plaids and shawls, were in great requisition among the
young ladies. Mrs. Topgallant insisted that they would all
be laid up, and that they must go below till they got into
Cowes harbor.

" She was excessively angry," she said, " with Mr. Hearty
for keeping them out in this way ; and as for Sir Francis
Futtock, a captain in Her Majesty's navy, she was, indeed,
surprised that such a thing could happen while he was on
board."

" But, my dear madam," urged Sir Francis, in his defence, " you know that accidents will happen in the best-
regulated families. Nobody asked my advice, and I could
not venture to volunteer it, or I might have foretold what
has happened. However, come down below, and I trust no
harm will ensue."

After some persuasion, the good lady was induced to go
below, and to rest herself on a sofa in one of the sleeping
cabins, the door of which Harry Flareup quietly locked, at
a hint from Hearty, who then told the young ladies that, as
Cerberus was chained, they might now do exactly what they

liked. I must do them the justice to say that they behaved
very well. There was abundance of laughter, however,
especially when Miss Susan Rattler appeared habited in a
large box-coat belonging to Captain Carstairs. It had certainly nothing yachtish about it. It was of a whity-brown
hue, with great horn buttons and vast pockets. It was
thoroughly roadish, it smelt of the road, its appearance was
of the road. It reminded one of the days of four-in-hand
coaches ; and many a tale it could doubtless tell of New-
market ; of races run, of bets booked. Not content with
wearing the coat, Susan was persuaded to try a cigar. She
puffed away manfully for some time.

" You look a very jemmy young gent, indeed you do,"
observed the Gentle Giant, looking up at her as he sat at
her feet. " What would your mamma say if she saw
you ? "

" What an odious custom you men have of smoking," cried
Hearty, pretending not to see who was the culprit.

" In the presence of ladies, too," exclaimed Loring, really
ignorant of the state of the case.

Poor Susan saw that she was laughed at, and, beginning
probably at the same time to feel a little sick from the fumes
of the tobacco, she was not sorry of an excuse for throwing
Carstairs' best Havana into the water.

As the fog settled over us rather heavily, not only were
the more delicate part of the company wrapped up in cloaks
and shawls, but we got up the blankets and counterpanes
from the cabins, and swaddled them up completely in them,
while the gentlemen threw themselves along at their feet,
partly in a fit of romantic gallantry, and partly, it is just
possible, to assist in keeping themselves warm. Carstairs
recited Shakspeare all night long, and Loring sang some
capital songs.

By this time we had got down to Calshot; and, as the tide was now setting down pretty strong, we appeared to be going along at a good rate.

"How soon shall we be in, captain?" asked one of the Miss Masons of the skipper, who was at the helm.

"That depends, miss, whether a breeze comes before we get down to Yarmouth or Hurst; because, if we keep on, we shan't be far off either one or the other, before the tide turns," was the unsatisfactory answer.

"Keep on, by all means, Snow," exclaimed Hearty, who had not heard all that was said; "I promised to do my best to get in, and we must keep at it."

So tideward we went; the little wind there had been dropping altogether. Presently we heard a hail.

"What cutter is that?"

"The 'Frolic.'"

"Please, sir, we were sent out to look for you, to bring Mrs. Topgallant and Miss Masons, and some other ladies, on shore."

There was a great deal of talk, but Hearty had determined that no one should leave the yacht. Mrs. Topgallant was below, and could not be disturbed; besides, the other young ladies could not be left without a chaperone. The Miss Masons wanted to go in company with their pastor, but it would not exactly do to be out in a boat alone with the Rev. Fred. As that gentleman was afraid of catching cold, he was at the time safe below, and knew nothing of what was taking place, so the boat was sent off without a freight. Hearty vowed that he would fire on any other boat which came near us to carry off any of his guests. Thus the night wore on.

It would be impossible to record all the witty things which were said, all the funny things which were done, and all the laughter which was laughed. All I can say is, that the ladies and gentlemen were about as unlike as possible to what they would have been in town during the season. Hour after hour passed rapidly away, and not a little surprised were they when the bright streaks of dawn appeared in the eastern sky, and Egypt Point was seen a long way off in the same direction, while the vessel was found to be turning round and round without any steerage way.

Now it was very wrong and very improper, and I don't mean for a moment to defend our conduct, though, by the by, the fault was all Hearty's ; but it was not till half-past eleven of the next day that the party set foot once more upon the shore. Never was there a merrier pic-nic ; and, what is more, in spite of wet feet and damp fogs, no one was a bit the worse for it.

Looking in at the post-office, I found a letter summoning me immediately to London.

Sending a note to Hearty, to tell him of my departure, I set off forthwith, and reached the modern Babylon that same night. How black and dull and dingy it looked ; how hot it felt ; how smoky it smelt ! I was never celebrated for being a good man of business ; but on the present occasion I worked with a will, and it was wonderful with what rapidity I got through the matter in hand, and once more turned my back on the mighty metropolis.

CHAPTER V.

TRUE LOVE RUNS ANY THING BUT SMOOTH — BEING A MEL-
ANCHOLY SUBJECT, I CUT IT SHORT.

THE day after my return I met Harry Loring. Alas,
how changed was the once joyous expression of his countenance!

"My dear fellow, what is the matter?" I asked.

"What, don't you know?" he exclaimed. "I thought all
the world did, and laughed at me. False, fickle, heartless
flirting!"

"What is all this about?" I asked. "I deeply regret,
'I feel" —

"Oh, of course you do," he replied, interrupting me petu-
lantly. "I'll tell you how it was. She had accepted me,
as you may have guessed, and I made sure that there would
be no difficulties, as she has plenty of money, though I have
little enough; but when there is sufficient on one side, what
more can be required? At last one day she said, 'I wish,
Mr. Loring, you would speak to mamma' (she had always
called me Harry before). 'Of course I will,' said I, thinking it was a hint to fix the day; but after I left her, my
mind misgave me. Well, my dear fellow, as I dare say you
know, that same having to speak to papa or mamma is the
most confoundedly disagreeable thing of all the disagreeables
in life, when one hasn't got a good rent-roll to show. At
least, after all the billing and cooing, and the romance and
sentiment of love, it is such a worldly, matter-of-fact, pounds-

shillings-and-pence affair, that it is enough to disgust a fellow. However, I nerved myself up for the encounter, and was ushered into the presence of the old dragon."

" You shouldn't speak of your intended mother-in-law in that way," I observed, interrupting him.

"My intended —; but you shall hear," he continued. " ' Well, sir, I understand that you have favored my daughter with an offer,' she began. I didn't like the tone of her voice nor the look of her green eye, — they meant mischief. ' I have had the happiness of being accepted by '— ' Stay, stay !' she exclaimed, interrupting me. ' My daughter would not think of accepting you without asking my leave ; and I, as a mother, must first know what fortune you can settle on her.' ' Every thing she has got or ever will have,' I replied, as fast as I could utter the words. ' My father and mother are excellent people, and they have kindly offered us a house, and ' — ' Is that it, Mr. Loring ? ' And you have nothing — absolutely nothing ? ' shrieked out the old woman. Oh, how I hated her ! ' Then, sir, I beg you will clearly understand, that from this moment all communication between you and my daughter ceases for ever. I could not have believed that any gentleman would have been guilty of such impertinence. What ! a man without a penny to think of marrying my daughter, with her beauty and her fortune ! There, sir, you have got my answer ; I hope you understand it. Go, sir ; go ! ' I did go, without uttering another word, though I gave her a look which ought to have confounded her ; and here you see me a miserable, heart-broken man. I have been in vain trying to get a glimpse of Jane, to ask her if it was by her will that I am thus discarded, and if so, to whistle her down the wind ; but I have dreadful suspicions that it was a plot between them to get rid of me, and if so, I have had a happy escape."

I have an idea that his last suspicion was right. Poor fellow, I pitied him. It struck me as a piece of arrant folly on the part of the mother, that a nice, gentlemanly, good-looking fellow should be sent to the right-about simply because he was poor, when the young lady had ample fortune for them both.

"Look here!" exclaimed Loring, bitterly; "is it not enough to make a man turn sick with grief and pain as he looks round and sees those he once knew as blooming, nice girls growing into crusty old maids, because their parents chose to insist on an establishment and settlement for them equal to what they themselves enjoy, instead of remembering the altered circumstances of the times? Not one man in ten has a fortune; and if the talents and energy of the rising generation are not to be considered as such, Hymen may blow out his torch and cut his stick, and the fair maidens of England will have to sing for ever and a day, 'Nobody coming to marry me, nobody coming to woo.' "

I laughed, though I felt the truth of what he said. "But are you certain that you are disinterested? Were you in no way biassed in your love by her supposed fortune?" I asked.

"On my word, I was not. I never thought of the tin," was the answer.

"Then," I replied, "I must say that you are a very ill-used gentleman."

CHAPTER VI.

HOW TO KILL TIME — THE O'WIGGINS — ENGLAND'S BUL-
WARKS — JACK MIZEN AND THE "FUN" — HER FAIR
CREW — NAVAL HEROES AND NAUTICAL HEROINES.

I HAD promised to yacht during the summer with Hearty ;
and as he paid me the compliment of saying that he could
not do without me, notwithstanding several other invitations
I had received, I felt myself in honor bound to rejoin the
" Frolic." I had no disinclination to so doing, though I own
at times we led rather a more rollicking life than altogether
suited my taste. Accordingly, I once more took up my
berth aboard the " Frolic." Hearty was growing somewhat
tired of the style of life he was leading. He wanted more
variety, more excitement. Indeed, floating about inside the
Isle of Wight with parties of ladies on board is all very well
in its way to kill time, but unless one of the fair creatures
happens to be the only girl he ever loved, or, at all events,
the only girl he loves just then, or the girl he loves best, he
very soon wearies of the amusement, if he is worth any
thing, and longs for the wide ocean, and a mixture of storms
with sunshine and smooth water. I found the party on
board the " Frolic " increased by the addition of two. The
most worthy of note was Tom Porpoise, a thorough seaman,
and as good a fellow as ever stepped. He had entered into
an arrangement with Hearty to act as captain of the yacht ;
for though Snow was a very good sailing-master, he was

nothing of a navigator, and Hearty was now contemplating a trip to really distant lands.

Porpoise was a lieutenant in the navy of some years' standing; he had seen a great deal of service, and was considered a good officer. He sang a good song, told a good story, and was always in good spirits and good humor. He had been in the Syrian war, in China, on the coast of Africa, and in South America; indeed, wherever there had been any fighting, or work of any sort to be done, there has dashing Tom Porpoise been found. He had a good appetite, and, as old Snow used to say, his victuals did him good. Porpoise was fat; there was no denying the fact, nor was he ashamed of it. His height was suited to the dimensions of a small craft, and then, having stated that his face was red, not from intemperance, but from sun and spray, I think that I have sufficiently described our most excellent chum.

The other addition of note was ycleped Gregory Groggs. How Hearty came to ask him on board I do not know. It could scarcely have been for his companionable qualities, nor for his general knowledge and information; for I had seldom met a more simple-minded creature — one who had seen less of the world, or knew less of its wicked ways. It was his first trip to sea, and he afforded us no little amusement by his surprise at every thing he beheld, and every thing which occurred. He had a tolerably strong inside; so, as we had fine weather, he fortunately for us and for himself, was seldom sea-sick. Our friend Groggs was a native of an inland county, from which he had never before stirred, when, having come into some little property, he was seized with a strong desire to see the world. He had been reading some book or other which had given him most extraordinary principles; and one of his ideas was, that people should marry others of a different nation, as the only way of securing peace throughout the world. He informed us that he should early put his principles into practice, and that, should he find some damsel to suit his taste in France, he should without fail wed her. We bantered him unmercifully on the subject; but, as is the case with many other people with one idea, that was not easily knocked out of his head.

Hearty, having fallen in with him on a visit to his part of the country, invited him, should he ever come to the seaside, to visit the "Frolic." By a wonderful chance, Groggs did find his way on board the yacht, as she one day had gone up to Southampton, and once on board, finding himself very comfortable, he exhibited no inclination to leave her. He therein showed his taste; and Hearty, though at first he would have dispensed with his company, at last got accustomed to him, and would have been almost sorry to part with him.

So much for Groggs.

We lay at anchor off Cowes. Several other vessels lay there also, mostly schooners — a rig which has lately much come into fashion.

"What shall we do next?" exclaimed Hearty, as we sat at table after dinner over our biscuits and wine.

"What shall we do next?" said Carstairs, repeating Hearty's question; "why, I vote we go on deck and smoke a cigar."

We had not time to execute the important proposal before the steward put his head into the cabin and announced a boat alongside.

"Who is it?" asked Hearty.

"Mr. O'Wiggins, of the 'Popple' schooner, sir," answered the steward. "She brought up while you were at dinner, sir."

"Oh, ask him down below," said our host, throwing himself back in his chair with a resigned look, which said, more than words, "What a bore!"

Before the steward could reach the deck, O'Wiggins was heard descending the companion-ladder. He was a tall, broadly-built man, with a strongly marked Hibernian countenance. Hearty did not think it necessary to rise to receive his guest, but O'Wiggins, no way disconcerted, threw himself into a vacant chair.

"Ah, Hearty, my boy! Faith, I'm glad to find any one I know in this dull place," he exclaimed, stretching out his legs, and glancing round at the rest of us, as he helped himself from a decanter towards which Hearty pointed.

"We are not likely to be here long, but we are undecided what next to do," returned Hearty.

"Och, then, I'll tell you what to do, my boy," said O'Wiggins. "Just look in at the regattas to the westward, and then run over to Cherbourg. I've just come across from there, and all the world of France is talking of the grand naval review they are to have of a fleet, in comparison to which that of perfidious Albion is as a collection of Newcastle colliers. There'll be rare fun of one sort or another, depend on it; and, for my part, I wouldn't miss it on any account. What say your friends to the idea? I haven't had the pleasure of meeting them before, I think?"

"I beg your pardon," said Hearty; "I forgot to introduce them." And he did so in due form; at which O'Wiggins seemed mightily pleased, and directly afterwards began addressing us familiarly by our patronymics, as if we were old friends. In fact, in a wonderfully short space of time he made himself perfectly at home. The proposal of the

Cherbourg expedition pleased us all; and it was finally agreed that we would go there. We could not help being amused with O'Wiggins, in spite of the cool impudence of his manner. He told some capital stories, in which he always played a prominent part; and though we might have found some difficulty in believing them, they were not on that account the less entertaining. Meantime coffee and cigars made their appearance. O'Wiggins showed a determination to smoke below, and Hearty could not insist on his going on deck: so we sat and sat on; Porpoise enjoying the fun, and Groggs listening with opening eyes to all the wonders related by our Irish visitor, for whom he had evidently conceived a vast amount of admiration. At a late hour O'Wiggins looked at his watch, and finding that his boat was alongside, he at length took his departure.

We were present at most of the regattas to the westward, but as they differed but little from their predecessors for many years past, I need not describe them. No place equals Plymouth for a regatta, either on account of the beauty of the surrounding scenery, or in affording a good view of the course from the shore. By the by, it was some little satisfaction to look at the two new forts run up on either side of the entrance to the harbor, as well as at the one with tremendously heavy metal between the citadel and Devonport, not to speak of the screw guardships, which may steam out and take up a position wherever required. I can never forget the superb appearance of that mammoth of two-deckers, the "Albion," with her ninety guns, and a tonnage greater than most three-deckers. It is said that she could not fight her lower-deck guns in a heavy sea; but one is so accustomed to hear the ignorant or unjust abuse and the falsehood levied at her talented builder, that one may be excused from crediting such an assertion. She is acknowledged to be fast; and,

from looking at her, I should say that she has all the quali-
fications of a fighting ship, and a great power of stowage.
What more can be required?* If she is not perfect, it is
what must be said of all human fabrics. If Sir William
Symonds had never done more than get rid of those sea-
coffins, the ten-gun brigs, and introduce a class of small craft
superior to any before known in the service, the navy would
have cause to be deeply indebted to him. He has enemies;
but in the service I have generally found officers willing and
anxious to acknowledge his merits.

There is no little satisfaction in cruising about Plymouth
Sound. I suspect that now our neighbors would not be
so ready to attempt to surprise the place and to burn its
arsenal, as they one fine night thought of doing some few
years back. People in general are so accustomed to believe
our sacred coasts impregnable, that they could not comprehend that such an enterprise was possible. Yet I can assure my readers that not only was it possible, practicable,
in contemplation, and that every preparation was made, but
that we were perfectly helpless, and that they would indu-
bitably have succeeded in doing all they intended. Neither
Plymouth nor Portsmouth were half fortified; and such
fortifications as existed were not half garrisoned, while we
could not have collected a fleet sufficient to have defended
either one or the other. Providentially the differences
were adjusted in time, and the French had not the excuse of inflicting that long-enduring vengeance which they
have a not unnatural desire to gratify. When they have
thrashed us, and not till then, shall we be cordial friends;
and, though electric wires and railroads keep up a constant
communication, may that day be long distant! We had

* Well we may say *Tempora mutantus.* A pygmy ram would send her
to the bottom in a few minutes.— EDITOR.

brought up just inside Drake's Island, which, as all who
know Plymouth are aware, is at the entrance of Hamoaze.
We were just getting under way, and were all on deck,
when a cutter-yacht passed us, standing out of the harbor.
Our glasses were levelled at her to see who she carried, for
bonnet-ribbons and shawls were fluttering in the breeze.

"What cutter is that?" asked Porpoise. "There's a remarkably pretty girl on board of her."

"That must be — yes, I'm certain of it — that must be
the 'Fun;' and, by Jove, there's jolly Jack Mizen himself
at the helm!" ejaculated Hearty, with for him unusual animation.

He waved his cap as the rest of us did, for Porpoise and
I knew Mizen. Mizen waved his in return, and shouted
out, —

"Come and take a cruise with us. We'll expect you on
board to lunch."

"Ay, ay!" shouted Hearty, for there was no time for a
longer answer before the yacht shot by us.

We had soon sail made on the "Frolic," and were standing after the "Fun" towards the westernmost and broadest
entrance to the Sound. It was a lovely day, without a
cloud in the sky, and a fine steady breeze; such a day as,
from its rarity, one knows how to value in England. Yachts
of all sizes and many rigs were cruising about in the Sound.
Largest of all was the "Brilliant," a three-masted square-
topsail schooner, of nearly 400 tons, belonging to Mr. Ack-
ers, the highly-esteemed Commodore of the Royal Victoria
Yacht Club; and as for the smallest, there were some with
the burgee of a club flying, of scarcely ten tons. We, meantime, were standing after the "Fun." Her owner, Jack
Mizen, had once been in the navy; but before he had risen
above the exalted rank of a midshipman he had come into

a moderate independence, and not being of an aspiring disposition, he had quitted the service, with the intention of
living on shore and enjoying himself.   He, after a few
years, however, got tired of doing nothing, so he bought a
yacht and went afloat, and, as he used to say, —

"Fool that I am! I have to pay for sailing about in a
small craft, not knowing where to go or what to do, when,
if I had stuck to the service, I might have got paid for
sailing in a large ship, and have been told where to go and
what to do.   Never leave a profession in a huff; you'll
repent it once, and that will be to the end of your days, if
you do."

Such was Jack Mizen.   He was a jolly, good-natured
fellow.   He sang a good song, told a good story, and everybody liked him.   He had seven ladies on board, two of
whom we judged to be chaperones; the other five were
young, and, if not pretty, were full of smiles and laughter.
The "Fun" was much smaller than the "Frolic," so we
easily kept way with her, and ran round the Eddystone and
hove-to, while the racing vessels came round also.   We
four bachelors then went on board the "Fun," and were
welcomed not only by her owner, but by the many bright
eyes she contained.   There were already four or five gentlemen on board, but they had not done much to make themselves agreeable, so nearly all the work had fallen on Mizen.
We gladly came to his assistance : poor Groggs, also, afforded them much amusement, but it was at his own ex-
pense — not the first person in a like position — unknown
to himself.   They were all talking about Cherbourg, and
had insisted on Mizen's taken them over there.   He, of
course, was delighted.   The main cabin was to be devoted
to them.   Fortunately, however, one chaperone and two
damsels could not go, so the rest might continue to rough

it for a few nights. We had a large luncheon and much
small talk. I mustn't describe the ladies, lest they should
be offended. If I was to say that one of the chaperones
was fat, and another tall, all the fat and tall elderly ladies
on the water that day would consider I intended to represent them. However, there can be no risk in saying that
the eldest dame was Mrs. Mizen, an aunt of the owner of
the " Fun," and chaperone-general to the party. The very
pretty girl was Laura Mizen, her daughter, and the other
married lady was Mrs. Rullock, wife of Commander Rullock, R. N., and who had also two unmarried daughters
under her wing. Of the other young ladies, one was Fanny
Farlie, a rival in beauty, certainly, of Laura Mizen — it
was difficult to say which was the prettiest — and another
was her cousin, Susan Simms, who read novels, played on
the piano, was devoted to the polka, and kept tame rabbits.
It was perceptible to us, before we had been long on board,
that Mizen affected Fanny, while Miss Mizen at once, with
some effect, set her cap at Hearty. She did not intend to
do so, but she could not help it. She was not thinking of
his fortune nor of his position, nor did she wish to become
mistress of the " Frolic." Of the gentlemen, one was in
the navy, Lieutenant Piper, an old messmate of Mizen's,
and Mr. Simon Simms, the brother of Susan, who had an
office in the dockyard, smoked cigars, and was very nautical in his propensities. There was a fat old gentleman and
a thin Major Clay, of a foot regiment ; but I have not
space to describe all the party. They will re-appear in their
proper places. We ate and drank, and were very merry,
and sailed about all day, most of us hoping to meet again
at Cherbourg.

5

CHAPTER VII.

A CROWD of yachts might have been seen one fine morning becalmed outside the Needles. We were among them. We had sailed from Cowes the previous evening, but had been unable to get further, from the light winds and calms which had prevailed. At last a breeze from the northward sprang up, and we went gayly along. It was a beautiful sight, and no one could fail to be in good spirits as we spoke the various vessels on board which we had acquaintances. The "Popple" was among them, but having started first, was ahead till we came up with her, much to her owner's disgust. O'Wiggins entertained the idea (very common not only to yachtsmen, but to masters of vessels and seaman in general, and a very happy one it is) that his vessel was the fastest, the most beautiful, and the best sea-boat going.

"Ah, Hearty, old fellow, how are you?" he hailed. "You've brought a nice breeze with you. We haven't had a breath of it till this minute; we shall now stand on in company." As he spoke, we observed his master trimming sails with the greatest care, for he saw that we were already shooting past him at a great rate. We laughed, for we knew that the "Popple" was a regular slow coach, as

ugly as she was slow. She had once, I believe, been a
cutter of the old build, with a high bow, and she was
then lengthened, and had a new stern stuck on to her, and
was rigged as a schooner. As a cutter she had been considered fast; but her new canvas was too much for her,
and she could not manage to wag with it. Her copper was
painted of a bright red, and she had altogether a very peculiar and unmistakable appearance. We saw O'Wiggins
walking his deck with very impatient gestures as we shot
past him. He could not make it out; something must be
the matter with the " Popple; " she was out of trim; it
was the master's fault, but what was wrong was more than
he could discover. His philosophy, if he had any, was
sorely tried as yacht after yacht passed him, and more than
all, when every one on board laughed at him. The fact
was, that poor O'Wiggins had done so many things to make
himself ridiculous, that every one considered him a fair
subject to exercise their merriment on. It was night before
we made the lights on the French coast. First the Barfleur
lights and Cape La Hogue to the south were seen, then
those of Pilee and Querqueville, and lastly the breakwater
and harbor lights, and we soon after ran in by the south
entrance, and anchored among the crowd of vessels of all
sizes already in the harbor. One by one the yachts came, and
last, though not least, the " Popple " appeared, and brought
up near us. O'Wiggins instantly came on board to explain
why the " Popple " had not got in first; but all we could
make out was, that she had not sailed as fast as she could
because she had not. We did not go on shore that night.
We had amusement enough, as we walked the deck with our
cigars in our mouths, in watching the lights on shore and
afloat, and the vessels as they came gliding noiselessly in,
like dark spirits, and took up their berths wherever they

could find room, and in listening to the hails from the ships-
of-war, and those from the yachts' boats, as they pulled
about trying to find their respective craft. We amused ourselves by marking the contrasts between the voices of the
two nations — the sharp shrill cry of the French, and the
deep bass of John Bull.

A good deal of sea tumbled into the bay during the
night, in consequence of the fresh northerly breeze, and
many an appetite was put *hors de combat* in consequence.
Poor Groggs, we heard him groaning as he lay in his berth,
"Oh, why was I tempted to cross the sea to come to this
outlandish place, for the sake of watching a few French
ships moving about, which, I dare say, after all don't differ
much from as many English ones?" He exclaimed, between the paroxysms of his agony, "Oh dear! oh dear!
it's the last time I'll come yachting, that it is!"· Poor
Gregory! — he was not the only one ill that night, I take
it; and I am sure Hearty pardoned his not very grateful
observations. We were early on deck, to inhale the fresh
breeze, after the somewhat close air of the cabin; then indeed a splendid sight met our view. In the first place,
floating in the bay were nine line-of-battle ships, in splendid
fighting order, their dark batteries frowning down upon us;
and, drawn up in another line, were a number of large war-
steamers, besides many other steamers, both British and
French; and lastly, and no unpleasing sight, there were
some seventy or eighty yachts; it was impossible to count
them — schooners, cutters, and yawls, besides some merchantmen and innumerable small craft of every description, all so mingled together that it appeared as if they
would never get free of each other again. To the south
was the town, with its masses of houses and churches,
and its mercantile docks in front. On the west, the

naval arsenal and docks, the pride of France and Frenchmen, and which so many had come to see. On the
other side were the shores of the harbor, stretching out to
Pilee Island, and not far from the town a scarped hill
looking down on it, with a fine view obtainable from the
top, while to the north, outside all, was the famous digue,
or breakwater, which the French assert eclipses that of
Plymouth, as the big sea-serpent does a common conger-eel.
It was begun by Louis XIV., and almost completed during
the reign of Louis Philippe ; during which period it was one
night nearly washed away, while some hundred unfortunate
workmen engaged on it were in the morning not to be
found ! but their place being supplied, the works were
continued.

The first day nothing of public importance took place.
Yachts came gliding in from all quarters, and steamers, if
with less grace, at all events with more noise, bustle, and
smoke, paddled up the harbor, with their cargoes of felicity-
hunting human beings, very sick and very full of regrets at
their folly at having left *terra firma* to cross the unstable
element. Among other English craft, the " Fun " came in
with Jack Mizen and a large party on board. We quickly
pulled alongside to welcome our friends. The ladies had
proved better sailors than most of the gentlemen ; and
though good Mrs. Mizen, the chaperone of the party, had
been a little put out, and still looked rather yellow about
the lower extremity of the face, the young ladies, who had
been cruising all the summer, and tumbling about in all
sorts of weather, had borne the passage remarkably well,
and were as frisky and full of laughter as their dear sex are
apt to be when they have every thing their own way.

We, of course, as in duty bound, undertook to escort
them on shore to show them the lions of the place. As the

President was not expected till the evening, there was
nothing particular to be done, so we had full time to walk
about and to lionize to our heart's content. Hearty took
especial charge of Laura Mizen, while the owner of the
" Fun " kept Fanny Farlie under his arm, and looked
unutterable things into her bonnet every now and then,
while Susan Simms fell to my share ; for Porpoise made it
a point of conscience, I believe, always to watch over the
welfare of the chaperone. It was one of his many good
points.

Remember, in forming a party of pleasure, never fail to
secure a man who likes to make himself agreeable to the
chaperone, or you will inevitably make some promising
youth miserable, and bore the old lady into the bargain.
Groggs was the only man not paired. It was a pity the
Miss Rullocks had not come ; no blame to them, but their
pa would not let them. Mizen had brought no other gentlemen, as he had to give up all the after-part of his craft to
his fair passengers, in order to make them comfortable.

The two gigs carried the party properly apportioned between each, and in fine style we dashed up under the eyes
of thousands of admiring spectators to the landing-place at
the entrance of the inner basin, now filled with a number
of yachts, which had got in there for shelter. The hotel
was, of course, full ; so the ladies resolved to live on board
the yacht while they remained.

Our first visit was to the dockyard, through which we
were conducted by a gendarme. We were particularly
struck by the large proportion of anchors, of which, as
Mizen observed, he supposed there was a considerable expenditure in the French fleet. The vast inner basins, yet
incomplete, look like huge pits, as if excavated to discover
some hidden city. There are lines of heavy batteries

seaward, which would doubtlessly much inconvenience an
approaching fleet; but as their shot would not reach a
blockading squadron, they could not prevent an enemy's
fleet from shutting up theirs inside the breakwater, while
it remained fine, supposing such a squadron ready to
convoy over a fleet of troop-ships to the opposite shore ; and
were it to come on to blow, they might be welcome to put
to sea as fast as they like, and a pleasant sail to them across
channel.

We went into a church where mass was being performed,
and had to pay a sou each for our seats ; the faithful who
do not like paying must kneel on the ground, which is kept
in the most holy state of filth, in order not to tempt them to
economize.

Our next visit was to the Museum.   Its attractions were
not great, with the exception of some large pictures of naval
combats, drawn by artists of merit, undoubted by the citizens
of Cherbourg, but who, nevertheless, had not read " James's
Naval History" to any good purpose ; for, by some extraordinary oversight, the English were invariably getting tremendously thrashed (without their knowing it), and the
French fleet were, with colors flying, proudly victorious.
Perhaps our histories differ ; for certain battles, which we
consider of importance, were not even in any way represented.   Trafalgar, St. Vincent, the Nile, were totally
ignored.   Porpoise said that, to show his gratitude for the
attention we received, he should present them with a correct
painting of the first-named battle.

" They'll alter the buntin', if you do, and hoist the French
over the English," observed Hearty.   " Though they may
suspect that they cannot deceive the present generation,
they hope to give their descendants an idea that they were
everywhere victorious.   They will boast of their glory,

even at the risk of being convicted of fibbing by their pos-
terity."

" They know pretty well that the easy credulity of their
countrymen will allow them to go any length, in direct
opposition to truth, without fear of contradiction," replied
Porpoise. " Why, the greater the scrape Nap. or any of
his generals got into, the more glowing and grandiloquent
was their despatch. Depend on it that humbug has vast
influence in the world, and the French knowing it — small
blame to them — they make use of it wherever it suits their
purpose."

After we had shown all the sights to be seen to our
fair companions, we were walking through the somewhat
crowded streets, on our return to the boats, when by some
chance we got separated from each other. We, however,
managed to find our way to the rendezvous, with the exception of Groggs, who was not forthcoming. As he was
guiltless of speaking a word of any other language than his
mother-tongue, we could not leave him to find his way by
himself on board, and accordingly Porpoise and I, handing
our charges into the boat, hurried off in search of him.
We agreed not to be absent more than a quarter of an hour,
and away we started, taking different routes among the
crowds of women with high butterfly muslin caps, and
bearded soldiers with worsted epaulettes, and sailors totally
unlike English, notwithstanding all the pains they had taken
to imitate them. We agreed that this dissimilarity arose
much from the different mould in which the men are cast,
and the utter impossibility of a French tailor cutting a seaman's jacket and trousers correctly. They all wore braces,
and though they tried to swagger a little in imitation of the
English seaman's roll, they had in appearance a very slight
similarity to their intended originals.

In despair of finding Groggs among such a collection of idlers, I was wending my way back, when I was attracted by a crowd in front of the shop of a marchand d'eau de Cologne, and above the din of shrill voices I heard one which, by its unmistakable accents, I recognized as that of our lost companion. At the same time, Porpoise appearing some way up the street, I beckoned him towards me, and together we worked our way through the grinning crowd. In the shop was a damsel with considerable pretensions to beauty, before whom, on his knees, appeared Groggs, fervently clasping her hand, while with no less fervor, and much more gesticulation, his hair was grasped by a little man, the father, we found, of the damsel, and whose dress and highly-curled locks at once betrayed the peruquier, or the hair-artist, as he would probably have styled himself.

"But I tell you, old gentleman, my intentions are most honorable towards the lady!" exclaimed Groggs, trying to save his head from being scalped entirely. "I tell you, sir, I have rarely seen so much beauty and excellence combined; and, if she is not displeased with my attentions, I don't see why you or any other man should interfere."

"Je suis son père, je vous dis, et je ne permets pas de libertés avec ma fille!" cried the irate Frenchman, giving another tug at his unlucky locks.

Groggs now caught sight of us, and appealed to us to save him. As we advanced, the young lady disengaged herself from his hand and ran behind the counter, the peruquier withdrew his clutches, and Groggs rushed forward to meet us. The Frenchman gazed at us with a fierce look of inquiry; but the uniform Porpoise wore on the occasion, and my yachting costume, gained us some respect, I suppose.

"What in the name of wonder is all this about?" I exclaimed, looking at Groggs; and then turning to the Frenchman I observed, in my best French and blandest tone, "that our arrival was fortunate, as I hoped instantly to appease his wrath, and put every thing on a pleasing footing."

Groggs then, in a few words, gave us his eventful history since he parted from us. He had been attracted by the words "Eau de Cologne" in the *affiche* over the door, and being anxious to show how well he could make a purchase by himself, he had entered. Instantly struck all of a heap (as he said) by the beauty and elegant costume of the lady, forgetting all about the eau de Cologne, he endeavored to address her. What was his delight to discover that she could speak some English! Forgetful of the quick passing of time, he staid on, till the father, hearing a stranger talking to his daughter in a tongue he could not understand, made his appearance. It was at the moment that Groggs, grown bold, had seized her hand to vow eternal constancy. The lady was not unmoved, though somewhat amused, and not offended. It was probably not the first time her hand had been so taken, she nothing loath ; of which fact her most respectable sire was doubtlessly cognizant. To pacify the irate barber, we interpreted the protestations of his honorable intentions which Groggs was pouring out. The daughter, Mademoiselle Eulalie Sophie de Marabout, ably seconded our endeavors, by assuring her papa that the gentleman had behaved in the most respectful manner, nor uttered a word to offend her modest ears. At length we succeeded not only in appeasing the wrath of the *artiste*, but in propitiating him to such a degree that, assuring us that he felt convinced we were most honorable gentlemen, he invited us all to a *soirée* in his rooms over the shop that

evening. Eulalie, with sweet smiles, seconded the invitation. Groggs was delighted ; and we, provided we could
manage it, consented to avail ourselves of the respectable
gentleman's kindness.

We now hurried off Groggs, for the ladies were all this
time waiting in the boats ; not before, however, he had
whispered to Eulalie that nothing should prevent him, at
all events, from renewing the acquaintance thus somewhat
inauspiciously begun. It was impossible to refrain from
telling the story when we got on board ; and had Groggs's
admiration for Eulalie been proof against all the raillery
and banter with which he was assailed, it would have been
powerful indeed. The ladies did not openly allude to his
adventure, but they said enough to show him that they
knew all about it, as he could not help discovering from an
occasional reference made to international matrimonial alli-
ances, and the advantages to be derived from them.

We returned on board just in time to get under way at
a signal from our respective commodores, when the yachts
of the various squadrons sailed in line outside the breakwater, under the command of the Earl of Wilton, who acted
as admiral of the fleet. We formed in two columns, and
performed a number of evolutions — we flattered ourselves,
in the most creditable manner — and then we re-entered the
harbor, and, running down the French line in gallant style,
took up our stations again according to signal. Our hearts
swelled with pride, and we felt very grand indeed, only
wishing that each of our little craft were seventy-four or
one hundred and twenty gun ships, and that the French fleet
were what they were. O'Wiggins's yacht was the only one
continually out of line, or somewhere where she ought not
to have been. This was owing partly to his imagining that
he knew more about the matter than the commodore or any
one else, and partly to the bad sailing of his craft.

Mizen invited us four bachelors to spend the evening on board the "Fun," and the attractions of our fair friends proved stronger than those held out by Mademoiselle Eulalie. There was an addition to our party in the person of O'Wiggins, who invited himself on board, and served as an assistant laughing-stock to poor Groggs. There was, consequently, a bond of union between the two — similar to that of two donkeys in a cart, both being lashed with the same whip. In the course of the evening O'Wiggins heard of Groggs's adventure, and, clapping him on his shoulder, assured him that he would take care it should not be his fault if he lost the lady.

We had all day been waiting in expectation of the arrival of the President, every craft being decked out with flags, and every gun loaded to do him honor. At the hour he was expected, enthusiasm was at its height; but as time drew on, it waxed colder and colder. People had come from far and wide to see a sight which was not to be seen; they had expended their time and money, and had a right to complain. Complain, therefore, they did, ashore and afloat; and had it at that time been put to the vote whether he should longer remain President, I fear he would instantly have been shorn of his honors.

At last the bright luminary of day sank behind the dock-yard, the commodores of the English craft fired the sunset gun, the flags were hauled down, and night came on. We had begun to fancy that the President's carriage must have broken down or been upset, or that he was not coming at all, when a gun was heard, and then another, followed by such a flashing and blazing and banging of artillery and muskets and crackers and rockets that we could have no doubt that the great man had indeed arrived.

Thus ended our first day at Cherbourg.

CHAPTER VIII.

By the time the world was up and had breakfasted, on
Friday, the harbor of Cherbourg presented a very gay appearance. The water was covered with hulls of vessels,
and on the decks of the vessels were crowds of gay people,
and above them a forest of tall masts, surmounted by flags
innumerable, showing all the hues of the rainbow, while in
every direction were dashing and splashing boats of every
description, men-of-war's boats and shore-boats ; and faster
moving than all, yachts' boats, which, like comets, seemed
to be flying about in eccentric orbits, without any particular
reason, and for no definite purpose. O'Wiggins made his
appearance on board the " Frolic," foaming with rage and
indignation at not having been invited to the grand banquet
to be given that day to the President.

" Neither have I, nor Mizen, nor any other of the
owners of yachts, except the commodores and a few noblemen."

" Faith, but that's no reason at all, at all, why I
shouldn't ! " exclaimed our Hibernian friend, drawing himself up ; " and, what's more, I intend to go, in spite of their
neglect."

77

We laughed, as usual, at his unexampled conceit; but fancying that he was joking, we thought no more about the matter. He soon took his departure, carrying off Groggs, who had conceived a high respect for him. O'Wiggins had promised to conduct him to the feet of the fair Eulalie, which was an additional temptation to the poor man. Never, perhaps, was there so much paying and receiving of visits as there was in the course of the day. The yachtsmen paid visits to each other, and then to the men-of-war; and to do the French officers justice, they treated us with the very greatest attention. I must say that all the French naval officers I have met are as gentlemanly a set of fellows as I know: they are highly scientific, and as brave as any men one could wish to meet.

It appeared as if all the inhabitants and visitors of Cherbourg were on the water also paying visits; and a report having got abroad that the owners of the English yachts were happy to show their vessels to all comers, we were all day long surrounded by visitors. The general joke was to send them all off to O'Wiggins's craft, the "Popple." Her cabins were, certainly, very gaudily and attractively furnished. It was hinted to the townspeople that he was a very important person, and that he would be highly offended if his vessel was not the first honored by their presence. O'Wiggins was at first highly flattered with the attention paid him, and had actually prepared luncheon for the first-comers; but he soon discovered that he had more guests than he could accommodate, and in a little time he was almost overwhelmed with visitors, who, for hours after, crowded his cabins, without a possibility of his getting free of them. Among others, while Groggs was on board, came the fair Eulalie and her respectable sire, habited in the costume of the National Guard, and looking very military and dignified. Groggs hurriedly advanced to receive the lovely maid ; her surprise equalled his delight ; when O'Wiggins stepped out from an inner cabin. There was a mutual start and a look of recognition, and Eulalie sank back, almost fainting, into the arms paternal, open to receive her, while, with a look which would have annihilated any man but O'Wiggins, she exclaimed the single word, " *Perfide !* " M. de Marabout, with paternal solicitude, endeavored to remove his daughter to the fresh air of the deck, but she recovered without that assistance, and exhibited signs unmistakable of a wish to abstract one or both of the eyes of the O'Wiggins from his head.

" What means all this, my dear sir ? " inquired Groggs, with a somewhat faltering voice, for suspicions most unpleasant were beginning to take possession of his imagination.

" Ask the lady," replied O'Wiggins, looking out for a mode to secure his retreat.

The lady saw that he was cowed, which, of course, gave her courage ; so, releasing herself from her father, she sprang towards him. The skylight hatchway was the only available outlet ; so he sprang on the table, and from thence was endeavoring to leap on deck, when she caught him by the leg. He struggled hard, for expose himself to her fury he dared not, and he did not like to summon his people to his assistance. At last he was obliged to do so ; when as the seamen, with shouts of laughter, were hauling him up, off came his shoe and a piece of his trousers ; and he was spirited away and stowed safely in the forepeak before the irate damsel could gain the deck, where she instantly hastened in the hopes of catching him. Of the distracted and astounded Groggs, Eulalie took no further notice, and having in vain sought for the object of her fierce anger, whom she supposed to have escaped in a boat to the shore, she and her father and friends took their departure, and Groggs saw his beloved no more. How O'Wiggins had thus mortally offended the damsel remains a secret; for, communicative as he was on most subjects, he took very good care on this matter not to enlighten any of us.

When O'Wiggins discovered that Eulalie was in reality gone, he retired to his cabin to compose himself, and to change his tattered garments for a magnificent uniform of some corps of fencibles, or militia, or yeomanry, of which he professed to be colonel; the said uniform being added to and improved according to his own taste and design, till it rivalled in magnificence that of a Hungarian field-marshal, or a city lieutenant's.

We had been giving the ladies a pull about the harbor, and were passing the "Popple," when her owner made his appearance on deck. The previous account, it must be understood, we received afterwards from Groggs, who recounted it with a simple pathos worthy of a despairing lover. On his head O'Wiggins wore a huge cocked-hat, surmounted by a magnificent plume of feathers, which, waving in the wind, had a truly martial and imposing appearance, while the glittering bullion which profusely covered his dress could not fail of attracting the notice of all beholders. With the air of a monarch he stepped into his gig, which was alongside, manned by a grinning crew, and seizing the yoke-lines he directed her head up the harbor. He was too much engrossed by his own new-fledged dignity to observe us, so we followed him at a respectful distance, to watch his movements. The boats of all descriptions made way for him as he advanced, and the men-of-war's boats saluted, every one taking him for a foreign prince, or an ambassador, or a field-marshal, at least. At length he reached the quay, and with a truly princely air he stepped on shore, taking off his plumed hat, and bowing to the admiring and wondering crowds who stood there to welcome him. A space was instantly cleared to allow full scope for the wave of his cocked-hat, and as he advanced the crowd made way, bowing to him as he progressed. In execrable French he signified his wish to know the way to the mayor's hotel, where the banquet was to be held ; and an officious official instantly thereon, perceiving the gestures of the great unknown, stepped forward, and profoundly bowing, advanced before him.

" Some dreadful mistake has doubtlessly occurred, and by an oversight which no one but I can remedy, no one has been deputed to conduct the prince to the banquet. For the honor of my country I'll tell a lie." So thought the patriotic official, as he observed, in an obsequious tone, " I have been deputed, mon prince, by monsieur the mayor, who deeply regrets that his multifarious duties prevent him from coming in person to conduct you to the banqueting-hall, where the great President of the great French republic will have the satisfaction of meeting you."

" I am highly pleased at the mayor's attention," answered O'Wiggins, with an additional flourish of his hat, and wondering all the time whom he could be taken for, that he might the better act his part. " A prince, at all events, I am, and that's something," he thought ; so he walked on, smiling and bowing as before.

Of all nations in the world, the French are certainly the greatest admirers of a uniform, and the most easily humbugged by any one who will flatter their vanity ; and certainly republicans are the greatest worshippers of titles. On walked the great O'Wiggins, admired equally by the vieux moustache of the Imperial Guard, by the peasant-girl, with her high balloon starched cap, by the dapper grisette, by real

6

soldiers of the line, by shopkeeping national guards, by citizen
gentlemen and ladies in plain clothes, and the queer-shaped
seamen and boatmen, of whom I have before spoken. His
step was firm and confident as he approached the hall, and,
as he got near, he saw with dismay that the guests arriving
in crowds before him were admitted by tickets. This we
also observed, and fully expected to have seen him turned
back, shorn of his honors, amid the shouts of the populace.
But the knowing doorkeeper, equally knowing as the officious
official, who now, with a glance of pride, announced him,
could not dream of insulting a prince by asking him for his
ticket, and only bowed the lower as he advanced, he bestow-
ing on them in return some of his most gracious nods. The
act was accomplished. He was safe in the banqueting-hall ;
but still there might be a turn in the tide of his affairs ;
some one who knew him might possibly ask how he had
managed to get there, and the mayor might request his absence. But O'Wiggins was too true a disciple of St. Impu-
dentia thus to lose the ground he had gained. Having
begun with blusters and bold confidence, he now called in
meek humility and modest bashfulness, with an abundant
supply of blarney. Stowing away his cocked-hat in a safe
corner, he retired among a crowd of betinselled officials,
and earnestly entered into conversation with them, expatiating largely on his satisfaction at the sight he had that
day witnessed, assuring his hearers that in Turkey, Russia,
or America, or any other of the many countries he had
visited, he had never seen any thing to equal the magnificence he had beheld in this important part of *la belle* France.
He endeavored also to bend down, so as to hide his diminished head among the crowd, and thus, as he had calculated, more wisely than a well-known wise man we have
heard of, he passed undetected.

Dinner being announced as served, he found himself, much against his will, forced upwards close to the English naval officers and yacht commodores ; but by a still further exertion of humility he contrived to take a seat a few persons off from those who knew him, and might put awkward questions. The French, however, could not fail to admire the admirable modesty of the foreign prince, and the liberals set it down to the score of his respect for republican institutions, while the royalists fancied that he was afraid of presuming on his rank before his republican host. From the information I could gain, and from his own account afterwards, his impudence carried him through the affair with flying colors, for no one detected him, though many wondered who he was ; and even some who were acquainted with him by sight, failed to recognize the O'Wiggins in the gayly-decked *militaire* before them.

Having seen him enter the hall, we returned on board the " Fun," to give an account of what had happened to our fair friends ; and of course we did not fail of making a good story of the affair, and surmising that O'Wiggins would be discovered and compelled to strip off his feathers. After dinner we prepared to go to the ball, to which the ladies wisely would not venture. Poor Groggs was very downcast at the events of the morning, and with the discovery that he could never hope to make the fair Eulalie Mrs. Groggs. As we were going on shore we met O'Wiggins pulling off in his gig with four highly-bedecked officers of National Guards, whom he had invited to visit the yacht. He had selected them for the gayness of their uniforms, which he fancied betokened their exalted rank. They had discovered that he was not a prince, but still were under the impression that he was at least a Mi Lord Anglais, imbued with liberal principles. He nodded condescendingly to us as he passed.

" I'm going to show my craft to these officers whom I brought from the banquet, and I'll be back soon at the ball," he exclaimed, with a look of triumph.

It is understood — for I cannot vouch for the truth of the statement — that he made the officers very drunk, and then, changing his gay uniform for his usual yacht dress-coat, he made his appearance at the ball, where he boasted of the polite manner in which the President had asked him to the banquet, quoting all the speeches which had been made, and many other particulars, so that no one doubted that he was there.

The ball-room was crowded to suffocation, and dancing was out of the question. I looked at the President with interest. The last time I had seen him was in a London ball-room, and at supper I had sat opposite to him and his cousin, the very image of their uncle. At that time, neither had more influence in the world than I or any other humble person. They were little lions, because they had the blood in their veins of the most extraordinary man our times has known ; but any Indian from the East, with a jewelled turban, created more interest. Now I beheld the same man the head of a nation — the observed of all observers — dispensing his courtesies with a truly regal air. One could not help feeling that there must be more of his uncle's spirit in the man than one was before inclined to suppose. A considerable number of ladies' dresses and men's coats were torn, and purses and handkerchiefs abstracted from pockets, and the ball terminated. I have not given a very lucid description of it ; but a crush in England is so very like a crush in France, that my readers who have endured one may easily picture the other.

Mrs. Mizen and her charges were anxious to sail to get back to Plymouth for Sunday, but we induced them to stop till the afternoon, by promising them to accompany them, that they might see the President visit the fleet, which it was understood he was to do on Saturday. The day was lovely, and every craft afloat, from the big " Valmy " to the smallest yacht, did her best to look gay, and to add to the brilliancy of the scene. The piers were crowded with people, and so were the decks of the vessels and boats and barges laden with passengers which were moving in every direction. It was amusing to watch the numerous parties on board the steamers at their meals : those forward indulging in bread and cheese and sausages, and vin ordinaire or beer ; the more aristocratic aft in chicken-pies, hams, champagne, and claret, in which beverages they drank prosperity to the republic and long life to the President, though they would as readily have toasted a king or an emperor. It was a day of excitement. The first thing in the morning there was a pulling-match, but who was the winner I am unable to say. Then the President paid a visit to the dockyard, and from that time every one was on the tiptoe of expectation to catch a glimpse of him as he pulled off to the ships-of-war he purposed visiting.

At length he appeared in a state-barge of blue and white and gold, and prow and stern raised and carved richly, which floated as proudly as that of any Lord Mayor of London, from Whittington downward ; for not altogether dissimilar was she in appearance. She pulled twenty-four oars, and a captain stood by the coxswain to con her. Under a canopy of purple cloth, the color reminding one of imperial dignity, sat the President of the republic, a tricolor flag waving in the bow from a lofty flagstaff, speaking, however, loudly of republicanism. As his galley shot out of the dockyard, there burst forth from the mouth of every cannon on board the ships and in every fort on shore, roars most tremendous, flashes of flame, and clouds of smoke. Never had I before heard such a wild, terrific uproar; crash followed crash, till it appeared that every soul afloat or on shore must be annihilated.

Thundering away went the guns, every ship firing every gun she had as fast as she could, and every fort doing the same. Bang — crash, crash, crash. The ladies stopped their ears, and looked as if they wished themselves well out of it. It appeared as if a fierce battle were raging, while the ships and the batteries and the shore were shrouded by a dense mass of smoke. On a sudden the firing ceased, the smoke blew away, revealing once more the masts and rigging of the ships-of-war, now crowded with men in the act of laying out on the yards. The crews cheered, and the bands of all the ships struck up martial music, which floated joyfully over the water, and one could not help fancying that something very important was taking place. In reality, it was only a *coup d'état* — Prince Napoleon was trying to supplant Prince de Joinville in the affections of the seamen of France. It is said that he made himself very popular, and gained golden opinions from all classes of men.

His first visit was to the "Friedland," the flag-ship of Admiral Deschenes, then to the "Valmy," and next to "Minerve," the gunnery-ship, on the same plan as our "Excellent." Here some practice took place, but I cannot say that the firing was any thing out of the way good. Having inspected his own ships, he paid a visit to Lord Wilton's beautiful schooner, the "Zarifa," and afterwards to the "Enchantress," Lord Cardigan's yacht, both perfect vessels of their kind. We yachtsmen had, indeed, reason to feel not a little proud of the display made by our peaceable crafts on the occasion.

We went on board several of the French ships, and were much struck with their beauty, cleanliness, and order, while every improvement which science has suggested has been introduced on board them. We were not particularly prepossessed in favor of the French seamen, either on shore or on board. There was a roughness in their manner which savored somewhat of national dislike, fostered for sinister purposes, to be pleasant; or, if it was put on in imitation of the manners of our own honest Jack Tars, all I can say is, that it was a very bad imitation indeed, and about as unlike the truth as when they attempt to represent the English national character on the stage.

From the French officers all who visited their ships received the very greatest attention and courtesy. We sailed that afternoon, as soon as the spectacle was over, in company with the " Fun." I cannot, therefore, describe the ball, with its overpowering heat and crush, which took place that evening, nor the sham-fight, when the boats of the squadron attacked the steamer " Descartes," nor the evolutions of the fleet, nor the awful expenditure of gunpowder from the ships, sufficient to make the economical hearts of the men of Manchester sink dismayed within their bosoms. O friends! think you this expenditure of gunpowder and noise breathes the spirit of peace? O merchants, manufacturers, and calculators well versed in addition and subtraction, is it not worth while to employ some portion of our own income, even a large portion maybe, to insure Old England against any freak our volatile neighbors may take into their heads? But I have done with public affairs. The " Frolic " and the " Fun " danced gayly together over the starlit ocean towards Plymouth, wind and tide favoring us. The voices of our fair friends, as they sang in concert some delicious airs, sounded across the water most sweetly to our ears. What a contrast to the loud roar of the cannon in the morning, and the glare and bustle of Cherbourg harbor, did that quiet evening present!

We arrived safely in Plymouth at an early hour next day. I am happy to say that, not long after, I received cards with silver ties from my friends Mr. and Mrs. Jack Mizen; but I am somewhat anticipating events. I think it right, however, to announce to the spinster world that Groggs, Porpoise, and Bubble are still bachelors.

CHAPTER IX.

PREPARATIONS FOR A LONG CRUISE—HEARTY CONFESSES TO
A SOFT IMPEACHMENT—THE O'WIGGINS AND HIS PASSEN-
GERS—HOW WE GOT RID OF THEM.

HEARTY had long projected a voyage up the Mediterranean, and invited Carstairs, and Bubble, and me to join him.
Groggs, as may be supposed, had become a bore, unbearable ;
and, as soon as we arrived at Plymouth, had been sent back
to cultivate his paternal acres and describe the wonders he
had seen during his nautical career. While Porpoise was
attending to the refitting of the yacht, Bubble and I were
busily engaged in laying in stores of comestibles, and drink-
ables, and burnables and smokables, of all sorts. Food for
the mind, as well as for the body, was not forgotten ; but
Hearty would not allow a pack of cards or dice on board.
It was a fancy of his, he said, that he did not much mind
being peculiar. "If a set of men with heads on their
shoulders and brains in their heads cannot amuse themselves,
unless by the aid of means invented for the use of idiots,
and fit only for the half-witted, I would rather dispense with
their society," he used to observe. We had, however, chess
and draughts, though he was no great admirer of either
game, especially of the. latter. "However," as he said,
"though those games kill time which I think it would be
wise of men if they tried to keep alive, as they, at all events,
won't let a fellow's mind go to sleep, we may as well have
them."

We exerted all our ingenuity and thought in laying in every thing which could possibly be required for a long voyage ; and seldom has a yacht, I suspect, been better found in this respect. Seldom, also, have five jolly bachelors been brought together more ready to enjoy themselves. Three is generally considered the best number to form a travelling party, and certainly on shore no party should exceed that number, unless there is some stronger bond of union than mere pleasure or convenience. Seldom when more men unite do they fail to separate before the end of the journey. For a yacht voyage, however, the case is different. In the first place, there is more discipline. The owner, if he is a man of judgment, assumes a certain amount of mild authority ; acts as captain over every one on board, and keeps order. Should a dispute arise, he instantly reconciles the disputants, and takes care himself never to dispute with any one.

Hearty was just the man for the occasion. "Now, my dear fellows," said he to all the party on giving us the invitation, "the first thing we have to do is to sign articles to preserve good fellowship, and to do our best to make each other happy. I don't want to top the officer over my guests ; but all I want you to promise me is, that if there arises any difference, you will allow me at once to be umpire. If I differ with any one, the rest must act the part of judge and jury." We, of course, were all too happy to agree to so reasonable a proposal, and so the matter was settled. With respect also to the numbers on board, in reality only Hearty and Carstairs were idlers ; Porpoise was officially master ; Bubble had originally fitted out the yacht, and acted as caterer ; while I had undertaken to keep my watch, and aid Will in his duties. We had with us guns and ammunition, and fishing-rods and nets, and camera-lucidas, and sketch-books; and musical instruments, flutes, a violin, a guitar, and accordeon. We had even some scientific apparatus; nor had we forgotten a good supply of writing materials. The truth was that Bubble and I had some claim to be authors. Will had written a good deal: indeed, his prolific pen had often supplied him with the means of paying his tailor's bill; while I had more than once appeared in print. We agreed, therefore, not to interfere with one another in our literary compositions. While he took one department, I was to take the other. At last we were all ready for sea. Mizen came out in the "Fun" to see us off, with Fanny Farlie, Miss Mizen, Mr. and Mrs. Rullock, and Susan Simms on board, as well as several of our friends, and we struck up, as the yachts at length parted, with our voices and all the musical instruments we could bring into action, "The Girls we leave behind us." Hearty heaved a sigh as he was looking through his glass at the fast-receding "Fun."

" What's the matter?" I asked.

" Yes, she is a sweet girl!"·he ejaculated, not answering me, however. I spoke again.

" Laura Mizen, to be sure," he replied. " Who else? She's unlike all the rest of our yachting set away at Ryde there. They are all young ladies, cast in the same mould, differing only in paint, outside show; one may be blue and the other red, another yellow, though I don't think you often find them of any primitive color; generally they are of secondary, or mixed colors, as the artists say. One again wishes to be thought fast, and another sentimental, another philanthropic or religious, and another literary. I don't know which of the pretenders I dislike the most. The fast young ladies are the most difficult to deal with. They do such impudent things, both to one and of one. If they knew how some of the fast men speak of them in return, it would make them wince not a little, I suspect, if they have not rattled away from all delicacy themselves. Oh, give me a right honest, good girl, who does not dream of being any thing but herself; who is a dutiful daughter, and is ready to be a loving, obedient wife of an honest man, and the affectionate mother of some fine hearty children, whom she may bring up with a knowledge of the object for which they were sent into the world."

"Well said, my dear fellow," I answered, warmly; for I seriously responded to his sentiments, though, it must be confessed, they were very different to the style which had been usual on board the "Frolic." "Why did you not ask her, though?" I continued.

"Because I was a fool," he answered. "Those Rattler girls, Masons and Sandons, and that Miss Mary Masthead, and others of her stamp, were running in my head, and I couldn't believe that Laura Mizen was in reality superior to them. I used to talk the same nonsense to her that I rattled into their willing ears; and it is only now that I have thought over the replies she made, and many things she lately said to me, and that I have discovered the vast difference there is between her and the rest."

"Well, 'bout ship, and propose," said I; "though sorry to lose the cruise, your happiness shall be the first consideration."

"Oh, no, no! that will never do," he answered. "I doubt if she will have me now. When we come back next summer I will find her out, and if she appears to receive me favorably, I will propose. Now she thinks me only a harum-scarum rattler. It would never do."

I could say nothing to this. I truly believed that though Hearty's fortune would weigh with most girls, it would but little with her; and I could only hope that in the mean time she would not bestow her affections on any one else.

Just as we got outside the breakwater we sighted a schooner, standing in for the Sound, which we had no difficulty in making out to be the " Popple." As soon as she discovered us, she bore down on us, signalizing away as rapidly as possible.

" What are they saying? " asked Hearty, as he saw the bunting run up to her mast-head.

" Heave-to, I want to speak to you," I answered, turning over the leaves of the signal-book.

" Shall we? " asked Porpoise.

" Oh, by all means," replied Hearty. " O'Wiggins may have something of importance to communicate."

" Down with the helm ; let fly the jib-sheet ; haul the fore-sail to windward," sung out Porpoise, and the cutter lay bobbing her head gracefully to the sea, while the schooner approached her.

Still they continued running up and down the bunting on board the " Popple." I had some difficulty in making out what they intended to say. " Ladies aboard — trust to gallantry," I continued to interpret, as I made out the words by reference to the book.

" What can they wish to say? " exclaimed Hearty.

" They wish to lay an embargo on us of some sort, and begin by complimenting us on our gallantry," observed Bubble.

" By the pricking of my thumbs, something evil this way comes," exclaimed Carstairs. " As I am a living gentleman, there are petticoats on board. Who has been acting the part of a perfidious wretch, and breaking tender vows? An avenging Nemesis is in his wake in the person of Mrs.

Skyscraper, or the Rattler girls, or Mary Masthead. Even
at this distance I can make them out."

So it was, as the schooner approached, the very dames
Carstairs had named were seen on board.

We had observed, as we went down the Sound, a large
schooner beating up from the westward. There had been
discussions as to what she was. Our glasses had now once
more been turned towards her, when we discovered her to
be the "Sea Eagle." Seeing our bunting going up and
down so rapidly, Sir Charles Drummore, her owner, curious
to know what we were talking about, stood towards us.

The "Popple" hove-to to windward of us, and a boat
being lowered, O'Wiggins pulled on board. "My dear
fellow, I'm so glad we've overtaken you," he began. "Your
friend, Mrs. Skyscraper, and those young ladies with
her, were so anxious to have another cruise on board the
'Frolic' before the summer is over, that I consented to
bring them down here, as I made sure that you would be
delighted to see them!" Never did Hearty's face assume a
more puzzled and vexed expression. "Heaven defend me
from them!" he exclaimed. "Tell them that we've got the
yellow fever — or the plague, or the cholera, or the measles,
or the hooping-cough, or any thing dreadful you can think
of; make every excuse — or no excuse; the thing is impossible, not to be thought of for a moment: they can't come.
We are bound foreign, say to the North Pole, or the West
Indies, or the coast of Africa, or the South Pacific, or to
the Antipodes. They don't want to go there, at all events,
I suppose."

"But if you don't take them, what am I to do with
them?" exclaimed O'Wiggins. "I'm bound down Channel, and if they don't worry me out of house and home,

they'll drive me overboard with the very clatter of their tongues."

A bright thought struck Hearty. Just then the "Sea Eagle" came up, and hove-to on our quarter.

"Much obliged to you for your kind intentions towards us, but, instead, just hand them over to Drummore," said he, rubbing his hands. "If any man can manage so delicate an affair, you can, O'Wiggins, without wishing to pay you an undue compliment."

Sir Charles Drummore was a baronet, one of our yachting acquaintances, and had lately purchased the "Sea Eagle." A worthy old fellow, though he had the character of being somewhat of a busybody. He certainly looked more in his place in his club than on board his yacht. "Well, I'll try it," answered the O'Wiggins, who was himself easily won by the very bait he offered so liberally to others. "Trust me, I'll do it if mortal man can. I'll weave a piteous tale of peerless damsels in distress, and all that sort of thing. Thank you for the hint; it will take, depend on it."

"Well, be quick about it," we exclaimed, "or Drummore will be topping his boom, and you will miss your chance." Thereon O'Wiggins tumbled into his boat, and pulled aboard the "Sea Eagle." What story he told — what arguments he used — we never heard; but very shortly we had the satisfaction of seeing the Misses Rattler and Mary Masthead, with their skittish chaperone, Mrs. Skyscraper, transferred to the deck of the "Sea Eagle."

We strongly suspected that the prim baronet had not the slightest conception as to who formed the component parts of the company with whom he was to be favored. He bowed rather stiffly as he received them and their bandboxes on deck; but he was in for it; his gallantry would not allow him to send them back to the "Popple," and he had, therefore, only to wish sincerely for a fair breeze, that he might land them as speedily as possible at Ryde. The O'Wiggins waved his cap with an extra amount of vehemence, and putting up his helm, and easing off his sheets, stood away for Falmouth. We, at the same time, shaped a course down Channel, mightily glad that we were free of all fast young ladies and flirting widows.

> "O'er the glad waters of the dark blue sea,
> Our thoughts as boundless, and our souls as free,
> Far as the breeze can bear, the billows foam,
> Survey our empire, and behold our home!"

spouted Carstairs, pointing to the wide Atlantic which rolled before us.

> "The sea, the sea, the open sea!—
> The wide, the blue, the ever free;
> Without a mark, without a bound,
> It runneth the earth's wide region round!
> I'm on the sea—
> I am where I would ever be:
> With the blue above, and the blue below,
> And silence wheresoe'er I go,"

chimed in Hearty, whose quotations and sketches were always from authors of more modern date.

"You'll sing different songs to those, gentlemen, if it comes on to blow a gale of wind while we are crossing the Bay," said Porpoise, laughing. "The sea always puts me in mind of a woman, very delightful when she's calm and smiling, but very much the contrary when a gale is blowing. I've knocked about all my life at sea, and have got pretty tired of storms, which I don't like a bit better than when I first went afloat."

"Never fear for us," answered Hearty. "I never was in

a storm in my life, and I want to see how the 'Frolic' will behave."

"As to that, I dare say she will behave well enough," said Porpoise. "There's no craft like a cutter for lying-to, or for beating off a lee shore; or working through a narrow channel, for that matter, though a man-of-war's man says it. We have the credit of preferring our own square-rigged vessels to all others, and not knowing how to handle a fore-and-after."

"Come what may, we'll trust to you to do the best which can be done under any chances which may occur," said Hearty. "And now here comes Ladle to summon us to dinner." To dinner we went, and a good one we ate, and many a good one after it. Many a joke was uttered, many a story told, and many a song was sung. In truth, the days slipped away more rapidly even than on shore.

"Well, after all, I can't say that there is much romance in a sea-life," exclaimed Carstairs, stretching out his legs, as he leaned back in an arm-chair on deck, and allowed the smoke of his fragrant Havana to rise curling over his upturned countenance, for there was very little wind at the time, and from what there was we were running away.

"I can't quite agree with you on that point: there is romance enough at sea, as well as everywhere else, if people only know how to look for it," observed Will Bubble, who had been scribbling away most assiduously all the morning in a large note-book which he kept carefully closed from vulgar eyes!

"Oh, I know, of course, 'Books in the running brooks, sermons in stones, and good in every thing,'" answered Carstairs, who was seldom at a loss for a quotation from Shakspeare. "But I mean, who ever meets a good, exciting, romantic adventure with pirate-smugglers, savages, or some

7

thing of that sort? Perhaps you, Bubble, have got something of that sort in your book there which you will give us, but then it will be only fiction: I want a stern reality. The world has grown too matter-of-fact to keep a fellow awake."

"I'll own to the soft impeachment," answered Bubble, laughing. "But my story's real; I've been merely putting some notes into form for our amusement, and I hope all hands will be duly grateful." We all thanked Bubble for his promise.

"I cannot agree with you, in any way, as to there being no romance in a sea-life," said I. "Only last year I took part in a very pretty little bit of romance, which would have made the fortune of any paper into which it had been allowed to find its way; but for the sake of the actors we kept the affair a profound secret, or you would certainly have heard of it."

"Let's have it all out now," exclaimed Hearty; "we won't peach: we'll be as tight as the 'Frolic' herself."

"I wouldn't trust you in the club," said I. "But, out here, I don't think it will go beyond the bulwarks, so you shall hear my story." While the rest of our party sat round, and drew, or netted, or smoked, I gave an account of the incident to which I alluded. As it is an important introduction to our subsequent adventures, it is, I feel, well worthy of a chapter to itself.

CHAPTER X.

AWAKENED one morning towards the close of the last
London season by the postman's rap, my friend Harcourt
found, on reading his letters, that he had become the owner
of the "Amethyst" cutter, and a member of the Royal
—— Yacht Club. Possessing an independent fortune, a
large circle of acquaintance, several stanch friends, and few
enemies, he ought to have been a happy man — but he was
not. The fact is, he did not know what to do with himself.
He had travelled not only over the Continent, but had
visited the three other quarters of the globe. He had gone
through several London seasons, and run the rounds of innumerable country-houses where there were marriageable
daughters, but had neither fallen in love, nor been drawn
into a proposal. In truth, he believed with his friends that
he was not a marrying man. He had become heartily sick
of dusty roads, passage-steamers, hot rooms, dissipation,
and manœuvring mammas, when I, who had of old been
his messmate, recommended him to try yachting for the
summer.

"What, go to sea for pleasure?" he exclaimed, in a tone
of contempt. "You surely cannot suggest such a folly. I
had enough of it when I was a poor young middy, and
obliged to buffet the rude winds and waves; but"——

"Well; think about it," were the last words I uttered as I left him.

He *did* think about it, and thought, too, perhaps, he might like it. He was not a novice, for he had for some years of his existence served his country in the exalted capacity of a midshipman; but on succeeding, by the death of an elder brother and an uncle, to some few thousands a year, he magnanimously determined, by the advice of his lady mother, not to stand in the way of the promotion of any of his brother officers, and retired from the career of glory he was following. I cannot say that the thoughts of leaving his profession gave him much regret, particularly as being too old to return to school, and too ignorant of Latin and Greek to think of the university, he was henceforth to be his own master. If now and then he acknowledged to himself that he might have been a happier man with a pursuit in life, I cannot say — I am not moralizing. So much for his past life.

After I left him he meditated on the subject I had suggested, he told me; and the next time we met, we talked it over, and as I was going down to Portsmouth, he gave me *carte blanche* to buy a vessel for him, there not being time to build one. This letter communicated the result of my search. Having made himself master of this and a few other bits of information, he turned round, as was his custom after reading his letters, to sleep off the weariness of body and mind with which he had lately been afflicted, but as he lay dozing on his luxurious couch, visions of the "Amethyst," flitted across his brain. A light, graceful craft, as she probably was, with a broad spread of white canvas, gliding like some lovely spirit over the blue ocean. "Who shall sail with me," he thought. "Brine, of course. Where shall we go? When shall we start? What adven-

tures shall we probably encounter? How shall I again
like to find myself on the surface of the fickle sea?" The
case, however, from the Then and the Now was widely
different. Then he was a midshipman in a cockpit, at the
beck and order of a dozen or twenty masters. Now he was
to enjoy a command independent of the admiralty and
their sealed orders, admirals, or senior captains. His own
will, and the winds and tides, the only powers he was to
obey.

"By Jove! there is something worth living for," he
exclaimed, as he jumped out of bed. " I'll forswear London forthwith. I'll hurry off from its scheming and heart-
lessness, its emptiness and frivolity. I'll go afloat at once.
Brine is right. He's a capital fellow. It was a bright
idea. I'll try first how I like channel cruising. I can always come on shore if it bores me. If I find it pleasant,
I'll buy a larger craft next year. I'll go up the Straits, perhaps out to visit my friend Brooke at Borneo, and round
the world."

He bathed, breakfasted, drove to his tailor's, looked in at
the Carlton and the Conservative, fulfilled a dinner engagement, and in the evening went to three parties, at all of
which places he astonished his acquaintances by the exuberance of his spirits.

" The fact is," he answered to their inquiries as by what
wonderful means the sudden change had been wrought,
" I've broken my trammels. I'm off. A few days hence
and London shall know me no more. To be plain, I'm
going to turn marine monster, don a monkey-jacket, cultivate a beard, wear a tarpaulin-hat, smoke cigars, and put
my hands in my pockets. We shall meet again at Cowes,
Torquay, Plymouth, or one of the other salt-water places.
Till then, au revoir."

As he was entering Lady L——'s door, who should he meet coming out but his old friend O'Malley, whom he had not seen for ages! He knew that his regiment had just come back from India, so he was not very much surprised. He took his arm and returned into the rooms with him. Now, O'Malley was an excellent fellow, agreeable, accomplished, and possessed of a fund of good spirits, which nothing could ruffle. He was, indeed, a good specimen of an Irish gentleman. He sang a good song, told a good story, and made friends wherever he went. Such was just the man under every circumstance for a *compagnon de voyage.* He hesitated not a moment in inviting him, and, to his infinite satisfaction, he at once accepted the offer.

A week after he had become the owner of the "Amethyst," O'Malley and he were seated in a Southampton railroad carriage, on their way to Cowes, where she was fitting out under my inspection. In the division opposite to them sat a little man whom they at once perceived to belong to the genus snob. He had a comical little face of his own, lighted by a pair of round eyes, with a meaningless expression, fat cheeks, a somewhat large open mouth, and a pug nose with large nostrils.

" Beg pardon, sir," he observed to O'Malley, on whose countenance he saw a smile playing, which encouraged him. " Hope I don't interrupt the perusal of your paper? Ah, no — concluded — topped off with births, deaths, marriages, and advertisements. See mine there soon. Don't mean an advertisement, nor my birth, ha, ha! too old a bird for that; nor death, you may suppose; I mean t'other — eh, you twig? coming the tender, wooing, and wedding — hope soon to fix the day : " — suddenly he turned round to Harcourt — " Reading the ' Daily ' ——? Ah, no, the ' Times,' I see. — Any news, sir? "

· They did look at him with astonishment, but, at the same time, were so amused that, of course, they humored the little man. Harcourt, therefore, unfroze, and smiling, offered him the paper.

"Oh dear! many thanks, didn't want it," he answered; "can't read in a railroad, afraid to interrupt you before you'd finished. Going down to the sea, I suppose? — So am I. Abroad, perhaps? — I'm not. Got a yacht? — national amusement. Sail about the Wight? — pretty scenery, smooth water, I'm told. Young lady, fond of boating — sure way to win her heart. Come it strong — squeeze her hand, can't get away. Eh, see I'm up to a trick or two."

In this absurdly vulgar style he ran on, while they stared, wondering who he could be. Finding that they said nothing, he began again.

"Fond of yachting, gentlemen?"

"I believe so," answered Harcourt.

"So am I. — Got a yacht?" he asked.

Harcourt nodded. .

"What's her name?"

Harcourt told him.

"Mine's the 'Dido.' Pretty name, isn't it? short and sweet. Dido was Queen of Sheba, you know — ran away with Ulysses, the Trojan hero, and then killed herself with an adder because he wouldn't marry her. Learned all that when I was at school. She's at Southampton, but I belong to the club. Only twenty-five tons — little, but good. Not a clipper I own — stanch and steady, that's my motto. Warwick Ribbons has always a welcome for his friends. That's me, at your service. Christened Warwick from the great Guy. Rough it now and then. You won't mind that. Eggs and bacon, and a plain chop, but weeds and liquor *ad*

lib. Brother yachtsmen, you know. Bond of union." They
winced a little. "Shall meet often, I hope, as my father
used to say each time he passed the bottle. David Ribbons
was his name. Good man. Merchant in the city. Cut
up well. Left me and brother Barnabas a mint of money.
Barnabas sticks to trade. I've cut it. Made a lucky spec.
in railroads, and am flaring up a bit. Here we are at the
end of our journey," he exclaimed, as the train stopped at
Southampton. "We shall meet again on board the ' Dido.'
Remember me. Warwick Ribbons, you know — good-by
good-by." And before they were aware of his friendly
intentions, he had grasped them both warmly by the hand.
"I must see after my goods — my trunks, I mean." So
saying, he set off to overtake the porter, who was wheeling
away his traps.

Harcourt never felt more inclined to give way to a hearty
fit of laughter, and O'Malley indulged himself to his heart's
content.

In an hour after this they were steaming down the Southampton Water on their way to Cowes. Just as they got
clear of the pier they again beheld their friend, Warwick
Ribbons, on the deck of a remarkably ugly little red-bottomed
cutter, which they had no doubt was the "Dido." He recognized them, apparently, for, holding on by the rigging,
he jumped on the gunwale, waving his hat vehemently to
draw their attention and that of the other passengers to himself and his craft, but of course they did not consider it
necessary to acknowledge his salute. This vexed him, for
he turned round and kicked a dirty-looking boy, which also
served to let everybody know that he was master of the
"Dido." The boy uttered a howl and ran forward, little
Ribbons followed him round and round the deck, repeating
the dose as long as they could see him.

I was the first person they met on landing at Cowes, and
Harcourt, having introduced O'Malley to me, we repaired
to the "Amethyst," lying off White's Yard. We pulled
round her twice, to examine her thoroughly before we went
on board. He was not disappointed in her, for though
smaller than he could have wished — she measured sixty
tons — she was a perfect model of symmetry and beauty.
She was also so well fitted within that she had accommoda-
dation equal to many vessels of nearly twice her size.

Three days more passed, and the "Amethyst" was stored,
provisioned, and reported ready for sea. Harcourt's spirits
rose to an elevation he had not experienced for years, as, on
one of the most beautiful mornings of that beautiful season,
his craft, with a light wind from the southward, glided out
of Cowes Harbor.

"What a wonderful effect has the pure fresh air, after the
smoke and heat of London!" exclaimed O'Malley. "Let
me once inhale the real salt breeze, and I shall commit a
thousand unthought-of vagaries, and so will you, let me tell
you; you'll be no more like yourself, the man about town,
than the 'Amethyst' to a coal-barge, or choose any other
simile you may prefer."

We had now got clear of the harbor, so I ordered the
vessel to be hove-to, that, consulting the winds and tides,
we might determine the best course to take.

"Where shall we go, then?" asked Harcourt. "The
flood has just done. See, that American ship has begun
to swing, so we have the whole ebb to get to the westward."

"We'll take a short trip to spread our wings and try their
strength," I answered. "What say you to a run through
the Needles down to Weymouth? We shall be back in time
for dinner to-morrow."

We all three had an engagement for the next day to dine with Harcourt's friends, the Granvilles, one of the few families of his acquaintance who had yet come down.

"As you like it; but hang these dinner engagements in the yachting season," exclaimed O'Malley. "I hope you put in a proviso that, should the winds drive us, we were at liberty to run over to Cherbourg, or down to Plymouth, or do as we pleased."

"No," he answered; "the fact is, I scarcely thought the vessel would be ready so soon, and we are bound to do our best to return."

"And I see no great hardship in being obliged to eat a good dinner in the company of such nice girls as the Miss Granvilles seem to be," I put in.

"Well, then, that's settled," Harcourt exclaimed. "We've no time to lose, however, though we have a soldier's wind. Up with the helm — let draw the foresail — keep her away, Griffiths." And the sails of the little craft filling, she glided gracefully through the water, shooting past Egypt Point, notwithstanding the light air, at the rate of some six knots an hour. Gradually as the sun rose the breeze freshened. Gracefully she heeled over to it. The water bubbled and hissed round her bows, and faster and faster she walked along.

"She's got it in her, sir, depend on't," said Griffiths, as he eyed the gaff-topsail with a knowing look. "There won't be many who can catch her, I'll answer. I was speaking yesterday to my brother-in-law, whose cousin was her master last summer, from the time she was launched, and he gave her a first-rate character — such a sea-boat, sir, as weatherly and dry as a duck. They were one whole day hove-to in the Chops of the Channel without shipping a drop of water, while a big ship, beating up past them, had her decks washed fore and aft."

Griffiths' satisfactory praise of the craft was cut short by the announcement of breakfast, and, with keen appetites, we descended to discuss as luxurious a meal as three bachelors ever sat down to. Tea, coffee, chocolate, hot rolls, eggs, pickled salmon, lamb chops, kaplines, and orange marmalade, were some of the ingredients. Then came some capital cigars, on which Harcourt and O'Malley had chosen a committee of connoisseurs at the Garrick to sit before they selected them.

" We bachelors lead a merry life, and few that are married lead better," sang O'Malley, as he lighted his first Havana.

" On my word you're right," chimed in Harcourt. " Now I should like any one to point me out three more happy fellows than we are and ought to be. What folly it would be for either of us to think of turning Benedict ! "

" Faith, an officer in a marching regiment, with only his pay to live on had better not bring his thoughts into practice, at all events," observed O'Malley. " Such has been the conclusion to which I have always arrived after having fallen in love with half the lovely girls I have met in my life ; and, as ill luck would have it, somehow or other if they have been heiresses, I could not help thinking that it might be their money which attracted me more than their pretty selves, and I have invariably run off without proposing. I once actually went down to marry a girl with a large fortune, whose friends said she was dying for me, but unfortunately she had a pretty little cousin staying with her, a perfect Hebe in form and face, and, on my life, I could not help making love to her instead of the right lady, who, of course, discarded me, as I deserved, on the spot."

As we opened Scratchell's Bay to the south of the Needles, O'Malley, who had never been there before, was delighted with the view.

"The pointed chalk rocks of the Needles running like a broken wall into the sea, the lofty white cliff presenting a daring front to the storms of the west, the protector, as it were, of the soft and fertile lands within; the smooth downs above, with their watchful lighthouse, the party-colored cliffs of Alum Bay, and Hurst Castle and its attendant towers, invading the waters at the end of the yellow sand-bank. Come, that description will do for the next tourist who wanders this way," he exclaimed. "Ah, now we are really at sea," he continued; "don't you discover the difference of the land wind and the cool, salt, exhilarating breeze which has just filled our sails, both by feel, taste, smell? At last I begin to get rid of the fogs of London which have hitherto been hanging about me."

As the sun rose the wind freshened, and we had a beautiful run to Weymouth. We brought up in the bay near a fine cutter, which we remarked particularly, as there were very few other yachts there at the time. Manning the gig, we pulled on shore to pass away the time till dinner, and as none of us had ever been there before, we took a turn to the end of the esplanade to view that once favorite residence of royalty.

As we were walking back we met a man in yachting costume, who, looking hard at O'Malley, came up and shook him warmly by the hand. I also knew his face, but could not recollect where I had seen him, and so it appeared had Harcourt. Slipping his arm through that of O'Malley, who introduced him as Mr. Miles Sandgate, he turned back with us. He seemed a jovial, hail-fellow-well-met sort of character, not refined, but very amusing; so, without further thought, as we were about to embark, Harcourt asked him on board to dine with us. He at once accepted the invitation, and as we passed the yacht we had admired, we found that she belonged to him. I remarked that she had no yacht burgee flying, and he did not speak of belonging to any club. He might, to be sure, have lately bought her, and not had time to be elected. But then, again, he had evidently been constantly at sea, and was, as far as I had an opportunity of judging, a very good seaman.

The dinner passed off very pleasantly. Harcourt's cook proved that he was a first-rate nautical *chef*. Our new acquaintance made himself highly amusing by his anecdotes of various people, and his adventures by sea and land in every part of the globe. There was, however, a recklessness in his manner, and at times a certain assumption and bravado, which I did not altogether like. After we had despatched our coffee, and a number of cigars, he took his leave, inviting us on board the " Rover," the name of his yacht; but we declined, on the plea of wishing to get under way again that evening. In fact, we had agreed to return at once to Cowes to be in time for our dinner at the Granvilles'.

" Oh, then you must breakfast with me to-morrow morning, for I am bound for the same place, and shall keep you company," he observed, with a laugh ; " though I have no doubt that the ' Amethyst' is a fast craft, yet I am so much larger that you must not be offended at my considering it probable that I shall be able to keep up with you."

On this Harcourt could not, in compliment to O'Malley, help asking him to remain longer with us, and he sending a message on board his vessel, both yachts got under way together. Perhaps he perceived a certain want of cordiality in Harcourt's manner towards him, as he was evidently a

keen observer of other men; for at all events he did his
utmost to ingratiate himself with him, and during the
second half of his stay on board he had entirely got rid of
the manner which annoyed him, appearing completely a man
of the world, well read, and conversant with good society.
At the same time he did not hint to what profession he had
belonged, nor what had taken him to the different places of
which he spoke. In fact, we could not help feeling that
there was a certain mystery about him which he did not
choose to disclose. At a late hour he hailed his own vessel,
and his boat took him on board her. The wind was so light,
that, till the tide turned to the eastward, we made but little
progress; but the moon was up, and the air soft and balmy,
and most unwillingly we turned in before we got through
the Needles.

As soon as our visitor had left us, O'Malley told us 'that
he had met him many years before in India, at the house of
a relation, he believed, of Sandgate's; that this relation
had nursed him most kindly through a severe illness with
which he had been attacked, and that he had, on his
recovery, travelled with Sandgate through the country.
He met him once or twice after that, and he then disappeared from India, nor had he seen him again, till he encountered him in London soon after his return. He believed
that he had been connected with the opium trade, and suspected that he had actually commanded an opium clipper in
his more youthful days, though he fancied he had engaged
in the pursuit for the sake of the excitement and danger it
afforded, as he appeared superior to the general run of men
employed in it.

The next morning, the tide having made against us, we
brought up off Yarmouth, when we went on board the
"Rover," to breakfast, and a very sumptuous entertain-

ment Mr. Sandgate gave us, with some cigars, which beat any thing I had ever tasted. The cabin we went into was handsomely fitted up ; but he did not go through the usual ceremony of showing us over the vessel. It was late in the afternoon when the two vessels anchored in Cowes Harbor.

Soon after we brought up we saw the " Dido " come into the harbor, and just as we were going on shore, Mr. Ribbons himself, in full nautical costume, pulled alongside. He insisted on coming on board, and taxed Harcourt's hospitality considerably before we could get rid of him. Hearing me mention the Granvilles, he very coolly asked us to introduce him. " Why, you see," he added, " there's an acquaintance of mine, I find, staying with them whom I should like to meet." We all, of course, positively declined the honor he intended us.

" Probably if you send a note to your friend he may do as you wish," I observed. " I am not on sufficiently intimate terms with the family."

" Oh ! why you see it's a lady — a young lady, you know — and I can't exactly ask her."

" I regret, but it is impossible, my dear sir," I answered. " You must excuse us, or we shall be late for dinner ; " and leaving him biting his thumbs with doubt and vexation, we pulled on shore.

The party at the Granvilles' was excessively pleasant. The Miss Granvilles were pretty, nice girls, and they had a friend staying with them, who struck me as being one of the most lovely creatures I had ever seen. She had dark hair and eyes, with an alabaster complexion, a figure slight and elegant, and features purely classical ; the expression of her countenance was intelligent and sweet in the extreme, but a shade of melancholy occasionally passed over it, which

she in vain endeavored to conceal. Harcourt at once became deeply interested in her, though he could learn little
more about her than that her name was Emily Manners,
and that she was staying with some friends at Ryde, the
Bosleys, he understood. Who they were he could not tell,
for he had never heard their names before. She sang very
delightfully; and some more people coming in, we even
accomplished a polka. During the evening, while he was
speaking to her, he overheard O'Malley, in his usually
amusing way, describing our rencontre with Mr. Warwick
Ribbons, and he was surprised, when she heard his name,
to see her start and look evidently annoyed, though she
afterwards could not help smiling as he continued drawing
his picture.

"And, do you know, Miss Granville," he added, "he
wanted us to bring him here, declaring that some mutual
and very dear friend of his and yours was staying with
you."

"Absurd! Who can the man be?" said Miss Granville.
"Miss Manners is the only friend staying with us, and I am
sure she cannot know such a person, if your description of
him is correct. Do you, Emily, dear?"

To my astonishment, Miss Manners blushed, and answered, "I am acquainted with a Mr. Ribbons; that is to
say, he is a friend of Mr. Bosley's; but I must disclaim
any intimacy with him, and I trust that he did not assume
otherwise."

O'Malley saw that he had made a mistake, and with good
tact took pains to show that he fully believed little Ribbons
had imposed on us, before he quietly dropped the subject,
and branched off into some other amusing story.

The Granvilles and their fair friend promised to take a
cruise in the "Amethyst" on the following day, but as the

weather proved not very favorable, Harcourt put off their visit till the day after. He thus also gained an excuse for passing a greater part of it in their society.

As we walked down to the esplanade in front of the club-house to look at the yacht, which they had expressed a wish to see, we encountered no less a person than Warwick Ribbons himself. He passed us several times without venturing to speak; but at last, mustering courage, he walked up to Miss Manners and addressed her —

"Good morning, Miss Emily. Happy to see you here. Couldn't tell where you'd run to, till old Bosley told me. Been looking for you in every place along the coast. Venture back to Ryde in the 'Dido'? Come, now, you never yet have been on board, and I got her on purpose " — he was, I verily believe, going to say "for you," but he lost confidence, and finished with a smirking giggle — "to take young ladies out, you know."

Harcourt felt inclined to throw the little abomination into the water.

"Thank you," said Miss Manners; "I prefer returning by the steamer."

"Oh, dear, now that is — but I'm going to see your guardian, Miss, and may I take a letter to him just to say you're well?" asked Mr. Ribbons; "he'll not be pleased if I don't."

"I prefer writing by the post," answered Emily, now really becoming annoyed at his pertinacity.

"You won't come and take a sail with me, then?" he continued; "you and your friends, I mean."

She shook her head and bowed.

"Well, then, if you won't, I'm off," he exclaimed, with a look of reproach, and, striking his forehead, he turned round and tumbled into his boat.

We watched him on board his vessel, and the first thing he did was to set to and beat his boy; he then dived down below and returned with a swimming belt, or rather jacket, on, which he immediately began to fill with air, till he looked like a balloon or a Chinese tumbler. The "Dido," then got under way; but her crew were apparently drunk, for she first very nearly ran right on to the quay, and then foul of a boat which was conveying a band of musicians across the river.

A most amusing scene ensued, Ribbons abused the musicians, who had nothing at all to do with it, and they retorted on him, trying to fend off the vessel with their trombones, trumpets, and cornopeans. At one time they seemed inclined to jump on board and take forcible possession of the "Dido," but they thought better of it, and when they got clear they put forth such a discordant blast of derision, finishing like a peal of laughter, that all the spectators on shore could not help joining them, and I wonder the little man ever had courage again to set his foot in Cowes.

We were still on the quay when Sandgate came on shore and passed us; as he did so, he nodded to us, and I observed him looking very hard at Miss Manners. He soon after, without much ceremony, joined us, and managed quietly to enter into conversation with all the ladies. After some time, however, I perceived that he devoted his attention almost exclusively to Emily. He was just the sort of fellow to attract many women, and I suspect that Harcourt felt a twinge of jealousy attacking him, and regretted that O'Malley had ever introduced him; at the same time I trusted that Emily would perceive that want, of innate refinement which I had discovered at once; but then, I thought, women have have not the same means of judging of men which men have of each other. He did not, however, speak of his vessel, nor offer to take out any of the party.

I shall pass over the next two or three days which we spent in the neighborhood, each day taking the Granvilles and their friends on the water ; and so agreeable did we find that way of passing our time that none of us felt any inclination to go further. It was, if I remember rightly, on the 24th of July that we went to Spithead to see those four magnificent ships, the "Queen," "Vengeance," St. Vincent," and "Howe," riding at anchor there. Though the morning was calm, a light breeze sprung up just as we got under way, and we arrived in time to see her Majesty and Prince Albert come out of Portsmouth Harbor in their yacht steamer, and cruise round the ships. We hove-to just to the southward of the "Howe," so as to have a good view of all the ships in line, and it was a beautiful and enlivening sight, as they all manned yards and saluted one after the other. From every ship, also, gay flags floated, in long lines from each masthead to the bowsprit and boom-ends, the bands played joyous tunes, and then arose those heart-stirring cheers such as British seamen alone can give. The ladies were delighted — indeed, who could not be so at the proud spectacle?

On our way back to Cowes we were to land Miss Manners, who, most unwillingly on her part, I believe, was obliged to return to her guardian. We accordingly hove-to off the pier, and all the party landed to conduct her to Mr. Bosley's house. After taking a turn to the end of the pier, as we were beginning our journey along its almost interminable length, we on a sudden found ourselves confronted by two most incongruous personages walking arm-in-arm — Warwick Ribbons and Miles Sandgate. The latter, the instant he saw us, withdrew his arm from that of his companion, and in his usual unembarrassed manner, advanced towards us, putting out his hand to O'Malley and me, and bowing to the ladies. He, as usual, placed himself at the side of Emily, who had Harcourt's arm, and certainly did his best to draw off her attention from him. Little Ribbons tried, also, to come up and speak to her, but either his courage or his impudence could not overcome the cold, low bow she gave him. By the by, she had bestowed one of a similar nature on Sandgate. After some time, however, he ranged up outside of Harcourt, for he had no shadow of excuse to speak to either Mrs. Granville or her daughters.

"Ah, Miss Emily," he exclaimed in a smirking way, "you said you would prefer returning here in a steamer to a yacht, and now you've come in one after all."

Emily did not know what to answer to his impudence, so Harcourt relieved her by answering —

"Miss Manners selected a larger vessel, and had, also, the society of her friends."

"In that case, I might have claimed the honor for my vessel, which is larger than either," observed Mr. Sandgate, with a tone in which I detected a sneer lurking under a pretended laugh.

"Ah, but then I'm an old friend," interposed the little man ; "ain't I, Miss Emily? — known you ever since you was a little girl, though you do now and then pretend not to remember it."

"Hang the fellow's impudence !" Harcourt was on the point of exclaiming, and perhaps might have said something of the sort, when his attention was called off by another actor in the drama. He was a corpulent, consequential-looking gentleman, with a vulgar expression of countenance, dressed in a broad-brimmed straw hat and shooting-coat,

with trousers of a huge plaid pattern, and he had an umbrella
under his arm though there was not a cloud in the sky. He
was, in fact, just the person I might have supposed as the
friend of little Ribbons, who, as soon as he espied him, with
great glee ran on to meet him. Poor Emily, at the same
time, pronounced the words, "My guardian, Mr. Bosley,"
in a tone which showed little pleasure at the *rencontre*, and
instantly withdrew her arm from Harcourt's. She was
evidently anxious to prevent a meeting between the parties,
for she turned round to the Miss Granvilles and begged
them not to come any further, and then holding out her
hand to Harcourt, thanked him for the pleasant excursions
he had afforded her. She was too late, however, for Mr.
Bosley advancing, bowed awkwardly to the Miss Granvilles, and then addressing Emily, said, —

"Ay, little missie, a long holiday you've been taking with
your friends ; but I shan't let you play truant again, I can
tell you. I've heard all about your doings from my friend
Warwick here — so come along, come along ;" and seizing
her arm, without more ceremony he walked her off, while
Mr. Ribbons smirked and chuckled at the thoughts of having
her now in his power, as he fancied. Miles Sandgate, at
the same time, bowing to the ladies, and nodding to us in a
familiar way which verged upon cool impudence, followed
their steps. We all felt excessively annoyed at the scene ;
but far more regretted that so charming a girl should
be in the power of such a coarse barbarian as Mr. Bosley
appeared.

On our passage back to Cowes, Miss Granville told me
all she knew of Miss Manners. She was the daughter of a
Colonel Manners, who had gone out on some mining specu-
lation or other, to one of the South American States, but it

was believed that the ship which was conveying him to England had foundered, with all hands, at sea.

He had left his daughter Emily under the charge of a Mr. Eastway, a merchant of high standing, and a very gentlemanly man. Mr. Eastway, who was the only person cognizant of Colonel Manners' plans, died suddenly, and Mr. Bosley, his partner, took charge of her and the little property invested in his house for her support. She had been at the same school with the Miss Granvilles, who there formed a friendship for her which had rather increased than abated after they grew up. This was the amount of the information I could extract from them. She never complained of her guardian to them ; but she was as well able as they were to observe his excessive vulgarity, though there was probably under it a kindliness of feeling which in some degree compensated for it. Harcourt certainly did his best to conceal the feelings with which he could not help acknowledging to himself she had inspired him, and was much pleased at hearing the Granvilles say that they intended writing to her to propose joining her at Ryde on the day of the regatta.

CHAPTER XI.

IN the mean time Harcourt made daily trips to Ryde, and promenaded the pier from one end to the other, and through every street of the town, in the hope of meeting Miss Manners, but in vain. He met Ribbons frequently, but of course he could not inquire after her from him, and consequently avoided him. Sandgate he encountered several times ; but he had conceived such an antipathy to the man, as well as a suspicion of his character, that, as O'Malley was not with us, he did not think it necessary to recognize him. Harcourt felt all the time that he was not treating O'Malley and me fairly in keeping about the island, and therefore promised to start on a long cruise directly after the regatta. The first day of the regatta was cold, and blowing fresh, so none of the ladies went. It was the schooner-match round the island, when the little "Bianca" carried off the cup from her huge competitors, though she came in last, so much time being allowed for the difference of tonnage. The next day of the regatta the weather was most propitious, and we had the pleasure of meeting Miss Manners on the end of the pier with Mr. Bosley, who saved Harcourt from inviting him, by telling us that "if we would give him a hundred pounds for every minute he was in that gimcrack-looking boat, he wouldn't come. Let him have a steady-going steamer, which didn't care for winds and tides." He made no objection to Emily's accompanying us ; though little

Ribbons coming up just as she was stepping into the boat, reproached her for not visiting the "Dido" instead.

The sight was beautiful in the extreme; for, independent of the racing-vessels, hundreds of other yachts were sailing about in every direction. The course also being round the Nab light, and a similar light-vessel moored at the mouth of the Southampton Water, the racing-yachts were the whole time in sight of Ryde. The Royal Victoria Yacht-Club-house was decorated with banners, and from a battery in front of it were fired the necessary signals and salutes, while several yachts anchored off the pier-head were also gayly decked with flags. In the afternoon the Queen came from Osborne on board the "Fairy," amid the animated scene, and made several wide circles; passing close to the pier, and as she glided by, each vessel saluted with their guns or lowered their flags. The whole day the "Dido" had most perseveringly endeavored to follow us, and several times we saw her nearly run foul of other vessels. At last, as she passed the "Fairy," Ribbons, in a fit of enthusiastic loyalty, I suppose, loaded his gun to the muzzle, and discharged it directly at the steamer, the lighted wadding almost falling on board, while the recoil of the gun upset the little man, who was looking with dismay at the effect of his achievement. He was not hurt, however, for he picked himself up, and managed to fire another wadding on board the "Amethyst." The last we saw of him that day, he was hard and fast on a mud-bank half-way between Ryde and Cowes. Sandgate's vessel was also cruising about, and passed us several times, though at a respectful distance; but I saw that his telescope was directed each time towards Miss Manners. On a sudden it struck me that Griffiths might possibly know something of the man, and I accord-

ingly asked him, in a mere casual way, if he had ever seen
him before he came on board us?

"Why, yes, sir, I have seen him more than once," he
answered. "Maybe he don't recollect me, though we've
gone through some wild scenes together."

"How is that?" I asked, with surprise.

"Why, you see, sir, I've done something in the free-trade
line myself, I own, and he's lent me a hand at it."

"What! you don't mean to say that Mr. Sandgate is a
smuggler?" I asked.

"Yes, I do, sir, though, and many's the rich crop he's
run in that ere craft of his."

"Impossible! why she's a yacht," I replied.

"No, sir, she's only a private vessel at the best, and if
she was a yacht, she's not the only one as ——. Howsomdever, I won't say any thing again yachts. It's the lookout
of the other members of the club that they don't smuggle,
and more's the shame of them who does."

"But I thought that smugglers were so bound together
that they would never speak against each other," I observed.

"So they are, sir; and though that Mr. Sandgate has no
reason to expect any favor from me, for reasons he well
knows, I wouldn't speak to anybody else of him as I do but
to you, or my master, because I don't think he's fit company
for such as you, sir, and that's the truth."

Thinking over what Griffiths had told me, I determined
in future to be on my guard against Sandgate. I, however,
did not repeat what I had heard to any one except Harcourt. In the afternoon we returned to Cowes, leaving Miss
Manners with the Granvilles.

Harcourt having promised to pay some friends a visit at
Torquay, the next morning we got under way, and, though

the winds were light, we got there on the following day. Taking all points into consideration, I think Torquay and its surrounding scenery is the most beautiful part of England. Our stay was short, for Harcourt was anxious to get back to Cowes, as he had found metal more attractive than even Devonshire could afford.

We reached Cowes late in the day, and after dinner went to the Granvilles', for we were now on sufficiently intimate terms to do so.. I missed Emily from their circle, and inquired if she was still staying with them.

"I am sorry to say that she left us suddenly yesterday evening," answered Miss Granville. "It was almost dark when a letter arrived from her guardian. It stated that he had gone over to Portsmouth on business connected with her affairs, and that when there he was taken dangerously ill; that something had transpired which he could alone communicate to her, and he entreated her to come to him without a moment's delay. The bearer of the letter was Mr. Miles Sandgate, who, it appeared, had met Mr. Bosley at Portsmouth, and volunteered to carry it, and to escort Miss Manners back. Emily immediately prepared for her departure, though she hesitated about accepting Mr. Sandgate's offer. We also sent down to the quay to learn if there was any steamer going to Portsmouth that evening, but the last for the day had already left. Mr. Sandgate on this requested Emily would allow his vessel to convey her, observing, in the most courteous way, that he saw the difficulties of the case, and would himself remain at Cowes till his vessel returned, saying, at the same time, that he thought he might be of service in escorting her to the hotel where Mr. Bosley was lying ill. Mamma herself would have gone with her, but she was unwell, and we girls should not much have mended the matter. Mr. Sandgate all the time stood by, acknowledging that he himself was perplexed, and would do any thing she wished; till at last I bethought me of sending our housekeeper, who was very ready to do her best to serve Emily, and to this plan, as Mr. Sandgate is a friend of yours as well as of Mr. Bosley's, Emily had no further hesitation in agreeing. We walked with her down to the quay, and saw her safely on board."

"And have you heard to-day from her?" I asked in a tone of anxiety I could not conceal.

"No," answered Miss Granville; "we thought she would have written."

"Good heavens! and has she trusted herself with that man?." exclaimed Harcourt.

Miss Granville stared.

"What do you mean?" she asked.

"That I have very serious suspicions of his character," answered Harcourt. "I wish that she had taken any other means of getting to Portsmouth: not that I for a moment suspect he would not safely convey her there, but I am unwilling that she should — that any lady, a friend of yours, should have even been on board that vessel."

"You surprise me!" exclaimed Miss Granville, now beginning to be really alarmed; and I volunteered to run over to Portsmouth at once, to inquire for Mr. Bosley, but she had not heard the name of the hotel where he was staying.

"That shall not stop me," replied Harcourt. "I will inquire at all of them till I learn."

She smiled at his eagerness, though, when he told her all he had heard of Sandgate, she saw that he had reason for his annoyance at what had occurred. We were engaged in paying our adieus, when the house-bell rang, and directly afterwards Mr. Warwick Ribbons was announced. Astonishment was depicted on the countenances of all present, at

the appearance of this most unexpected visitor, and all wondered what could have brought him there again.   He had,
by the by, already called in the morning to beg Miss Manners and her friends would take a sail in the "Dido," but
hearing that she was no longer there, had gone away.   He
gazed about the room, his round eyes blinking with the
bright light after having come out of darkness, and, with a
flourish of his hat, he bowed to the ladies.

"Beg pardon," he said, in a nervous tone; "but I've
come to ask where Miss Manners is."

"She has gone to see her guardian, Mr. Bosley, who
has been taken seriously ill at Portsmouth," answered Mrs.
Granville.

"No, she ain't, ma'am," he exclaimed, throwing his hat
down on the ground with vehemence; "Mr. Bosley isn't ill,
and isn't at Portsmouth, and Miss Manners isn't with him,
for I'm just come from Ryde, and there I saw him as well
as ever he was in his life, and he begged that I would come
and ask what has become of her.   Your servants this
morning told me that she wasn't here, so I made sure
that she'd gone back to Ryde, and started off to look after
her."

We were now seriously alarmed at what we had heard,
as were the rest of the party in a less degree.   Nothing
more could we elicit from Mr. Ribbons, though Miss
Granville convinced him that the account she gave of Miss
Manners's departure was true, and it appeared too certain
that she had been carried off for some reason or other by
Miles Sandgate.   I could have staked my existence that she
had been as much deceived by him as were her friends.
I need not attempt to describe what were Harcourt's feelings
on finding that his worst suspicions were more than realized.
She was in Sandgate's power, and his vessel was large

enough for him to carry her to any distant part of the world.
A bold and accomplished seaman as he was, he would not
hesitate, of course, to run across the Atlantic, and with the
start of upwards of twenty-four hours which he had, it would
be impossible to hope to overtake him, even if we could sail
at once ; but without a good supply of water and provisions,
it would be madness to attempt to follow him. This, however, as soon as by possibility we could, we determined to
do. Ribbons wanted to come also, but we recommended
him to employ his vessel in a different direction to ours ;
and while I was busy in collecting provisions and stores,
Harcourt made inquiries among all the boatmen and revenue
people to learn any thing about the " Rover," and what
course she had steered on leaving Cowes. The wind, it appeared, had been from the eastward, and as the tide was
ebbing, she must have gone to the westward, and could not
have got round by the Nab. At first he could learn nothing
about her ; but after some time he met a man who had
watched her getting under way, and, after she had stood
across as if turning up towards Portsmouth, had seen her,
or a vessel exactly like her, keep away and run past Cowes,
in the direction he supposed. One of the revenue-men, who
had been on duty in the guard-boat, had boarded her, and
her people said they were bound for Cherbourg. Harcourt
found, also, that her character was suspected, and that a
revenue-cutter was on the watch for her. This circumstance, he conjectured, if he could fall in with the cutter,
would give him the best chance of learning the course she
had steered. I believe that he ought to have called in the
aid of the law, but of that he did not think ; as soon as he
found that he could gain no further information about the
" Rover," he came to assist us in getting the " Amethyst "
ready for sea. We also shipped six additional hands, and

some cutlasses and pistols, for we felt certain that, should
we fall in with Sandgate at sea, he would resist an attempt
to rescue Emily from his power. By twelve o'clock at night
our preparations were completed, and we determined, in the
first place, to run across to Cherbourg, on the bare possibility of his having gone there, to complete his own supplies
for a long voyage. At the same time, we dispatched little
Ribbons in the "Dido," to look into every port along the
coast, and to wait for us at Penzance. Miss Granville, with
much judgment, undertook to send to every place to the
eastward, and to let Mr. Bosley know, that he might take
the proper measures to search for the daring scoundrel. I
need not say that Harcourt was in a perfect fever of excitement, and we were little less calm, particularly O'Malley,
whose indignation at Sandgate's conduct knew no bounds,
especially as he had acknowledged him as an acquaintance,
and introduced him to Harcourt.

Little Ribbons showed that there was something good
beneath the mass of absurdity, vanity, and vulgarity which
enveloped him, by the eagerness with which he undertook
the task we had assigned him; although he must have been
pretty well convinced that he had no chance of winning the
hand of the young lady, and we verily believed that, should
he fall in with Sandgate, he would attack him, even with
the fearful odds he would have against him. The weather
was clear, and the stars and moon shone bright from the
sky, as, with a fine fresh breeze from the eastward, and an
ebb tide, we got under way and ran through the Needles.
We then hauled up, and shaped a course for Cherbourg, for
we had no other clew by which to steer than the vague
report that the "Rover" had gone there. We thought also
that Sandgate would very probably have selected that place,
as being the nearest French port to the English coast, and

one into which he might at all times run, and from which he might as easily escape. For the sake of his victim he would probably go there, in the hopes that she might agree to the object, whatever it might be, which had induced him to venture on the atrocious exploit of carrying her off. We had understood that she was an almost portionless girl, so that her fortune could not have been the temptation : in fact, we were completely in the dark, and it was a subject too delicate and painful to discuss.

The wind held fair, and at daybreak we were running across the Channel at the rate of eight knots an hour. Just before sunrise, when the horizon is often the clearest, I went aloft to discover if any vessels coming from the direction we were steering for were in sight, to give me any information for the chase, but not a sail was visible any-where ahead of us, though several were seen off the island. For the next three or four hours not a cutter was seen, though many square-rigged vessels were standing down Channel. Almost worn out with mental and physical exertion, Harcourt threw himself into his berth, while I took charge of the deck, and promised to have him called should there be any vessel in sight either like the chase or from which we might gain any information about her. He had not been asleep an hour, when he heard a hail, and jumping on deck, just as O'Malley was coming to call him, he found that we were hove-to close to a revenue cutter, and that I had ordered a boat to be lowered ready to go on board her. He jumped in with me, and in another minute we were on the deck of the cutter. Her commander was excessively courteous, and ready to do every thing we might propose to overhaul the " Rover." From him I found that the information I had gained about Sandgate was correct; and he told us that, according to his orders, he had followed the

"Rover" at a distance, so as not to excite suspicion, and that he had seen her yesterday afternoon enter Cherbourg Harbor, where, supposing she would remain for some time, he had again stood off during the night.

"Then to a certainty she is still there!" exclaimed Harcourt, in a tone which somewhat surprised the officer.

The plan he instantly formed was to run in directly it was dusk, while the cutter remained in the offing, and to get alongside the "Rover" before Sandgate could have time to carry Miss Manners on shore. We thus should not lose much time, for the wind had fallen considerably, and we could scarcely expect to reach the mouth of the harbor before dark. The best formed plans are, however, liable to failure, particularly at sea; and as we got well in with the land, just put off Point Querqueville, it fell almost calm. There was still, however, a light air at times, which sent the cutter through the water, so that by degrees we drew in with the shore. We must have been for some time visible from the heights before it grew dark. The flood-tide was now sweeping us up to the eastward, and before we could get through the western passage we were carried past the break-water. The large fires lighted by the workmen engaged on that stupendous work dazzled our eyes so much, that we were almost prevented from seeing the entrance, and they totally disabled us from watching the western passage. At last, however, the wind freshened up, and we ran inside the breakwater. The moon had by this time risen, and we could see across that fine sheet of water, which, in extent and the shelter it affords to a fleet, rivals Plymouth Sound. Harcourt's impatience was excessive. We did not anchor; but as there was a light wind we kept cruising about among the men-of-war and large steamers lying there, in the hopes of finding the "Rover" brought up among them. In vain, however, did we search ; she was nowhere to be seen. At last we determined to go on shore, and endeavor to learn whether the " Rover " had been there at all. Pulling up between two fine stone piers, we landed at the end of the inner harbor, and repaired at once to the house of Monsieur. M——, who obligingly-assisted us in making the inquiries I desired. After some time we met a person who asserted that he had observed the " Rover " at anchor that very evening.

" Even with this light you can see her from the end of the pier," he observed ; " come, I will show you where she is."

We hurried to the spot, but the space where she had been was vacant. That she had not entered the inner harbor, Monsieur M—— was certain, as she could not have come without his knowledge. Baffled, but still determined to continue the pursuit, we returned on board ; and I was convinced that we had been seen from the shore before dark, and that Sandgate, suspecting we had come in quest of him, had slipped out by the western entrance while we were still outside the breakwater.

On making inquiries among other vessels anchored near where the " Rover " had lain, we found that, as we suspected, a vessel answering her description had got under way at the very time we supposed, and had stood off to the westward. After holding another consultation, we came to the conclusion that Sandgate would certainly avoid the open sea, and keep along the French coast, and we thought it probable would make for Jersey or Guernsey. At all events, thither we determined to run. Again we were under sail, and by the time we got clear of the harbor the wind had shifted round to the westward of north, and as the ebb had . then made, we suspected Sandgate would take advantage of the

9

.tide, and run through the Race of Alderney. We calculated, however, that by the time we could reach it, we should
have the full force of that rapid current in our favor, whereas
he would only have the commencement of it. No one on
board turned in, for the weather was too threatening, the
passage we were about to attempt too dangerous, and the
time too exciting, to allow us to think of sleep.

As we brought the bright light of Cape La Hogue a little
before the larboard beam, the wind increased considerably,
and we began to feel the short, broken sea of the Race.
Every moment it increased ; rapidly the water rose and fell
in white-topped pyramids, leaping high above our bulwarks,
and threatening to tumble on board and overwhelm us with
its weight.   The hatches were battened down and every
thing well secured on deck ; and well it was so, for sea after
sea came leaping over the side, now on the quarter, then
over the bows, and now again amidships.   It was impossible to say where it would strike the vessel, for not the best
steering could avoid it ; yet on we flew with the fast rising
breeze, rolling and pitching and tumbling, the water foaming and roaring, and literally drenching us with spray even
when we avoided the heavier seas.   The moon, too, which
shone forth on the wild tumult of waters, rather increased
the awfulness of the scene, by exhibiting to us the dangers
which surrounded us on every side ; yet so clear were the
lights, both of La Hogue on the left and the Casketts on
the right, that we had no difficulty in steering our course.
The dark outline of the small island of Sark at last appeared
in sight on the starboard beam, and in order to avoid the
wild shoal of the Dirouilles Rocks, towards which the early
flood sets, we hauled up more to the westward.

Still urged onward by the terrific force of the tide, we
continued plunging through the mad waters, till daybreak

showed us the Island of Jersey right ahead, and Guernsey on our weather beam. So strong was the current, however, that we had drifted considerably to the east, and in the gray light of the morning, not a cable's length from us, appeared the dark heads of the Dirouilles, while on the starboard hand the sea, in masses of foam, was breaking over the equally terrific rocks of the Paternosters. The wind had now got so far to the westward, and the tide set so strong against us, that finding we were drifting bodily to leeward, we ran close in shore, and dropped our anchor in a romantic little cove called Bouley Bay, on the north-east coast of Jersey. There was a narrow sandy beach, on which a few boats were drawn up, and a narrow ravine leading down to it, while on either side lofty cliffs towered high above our heads. On the side of the ravine was situated a small hotel, the master of which came off to us as soon as he saw us standing into the bay.

To the first question I put to him, as to whether he had seen any vessel off the coast that morning, he told us that at break of day he had been to the top of the cliffs, and had observed a cutter standing between the Paternosters and the land, and that he thought it probable she would be able to double Cape Grosnez before the tide made against her, in which case she would have little difficulty in getting round to St. Helier's, if she happened to be bound there.

" If she is, we shall catch her to a certainty," exclaimed O'Malley; and he forthwith volunteered to go across the island to try what he could do ; and I proposed accompanying him, as I thought I might be of assistance in getting hold of Sandgate. Of course Harcourt gladly assented to our offer, although he determined himself to remain in the vessel.

I have not described Harcourt's feelings all this time.—

his hopes and fears, his eager excitement, as he thought the
" Rover " was within his reach — his dread lest his Emily
should have suffered injury or alarm — they were too intense for utterance.

As soon as the " Amethyst " had made sail, O'Malley and
I started away across the little island as fast as our legs
could carry us.   We should have hired horses or a carriage,
but none were to be procured at the quiet little spot where
we landed, so we resolved to trust to our own feet, of which
we had by no means lost the use, as the way we made them
move over the ground gave full evidence.   As soon as we
reached St. Helier's, we hurried down to the pier, when, to our
infinite satisfaction, we beheld the " Rover " at anchor in the
outer roads.   We immediately hurried off to the authorities
to give information, and to procure assistance to rescue Miss
Manners.   On our way we suddenly came upon the villain
of whom we were in search, — Sandgate himself.   Something made him turn round, and he caught sight of us.
Without a moment's hesitation he darted off towards the
quay, where a boat was in waiting, and jumping into her,
pulled towards the cutter.   He had every reason to fear, we
learned ; for on his appearance in the morning he had been
narrowly watched by the revenue officers, who suspected
that some smuggling business had attracted him to the island.
Such in fact was the case, as he had gone there to settle with
his agents, and to procure certain stores before he commenced
the long voyage he contemplated, little thinking that we
should so soon have been able to track him thither.   Before
we had been able to engage a boat he had got on board, and
the " Rover " was under way for the westward.   I have an
idea that some of the boatmen were in league with him.   At
all events, they seemed to think that it was their business to
impede us as much as possible, and to do their best to help

the hunted fox to escape. Such a feeling is very general among that class. The more eagerness and impatience we exhibited, the more difficulties they threw in our way ; and it was not till the "Rover" was well clear of the harbor, and pursuit hopeless, that we could obtain a boat. We got one at last, and jumping into it, asked the men to pull away out of the harbor. Much to their vexation and to our satisfaction, we in a short time caught sight of our friend's cutter. She had just got off Elizabeth Castle, which stands on a rocky point, isolated at high water from the mainland. She hove-to, and in a few minutes we jumped on board, and gave Harcourt the information we had obtained on shore, and pointed out in the distance a sail which we had little doubt was the "Rover."

Harcourt then told us that after we had started overland, he had remained two hours at anchor, and then shipping an old pilot, in a Welsh wig, who only spoke Jersey French — the oddist *patois* he ever heard — he got under way for St. Helier's. The "Amethyst" beat along that rocky and lofty coast, inside the Paternosters, till she rounded Cape Grosnez — which, as she had had a fresh breeze, she had done without much difficulty. She was then kept away, passing the rugged and threatening rocks of the Corbière, rounding which with a flowing sheet, she was headed in among an archipelago of hidden dangers towards the town of St. Helier's. As they were passing the Corbière, Harcourt observed a cutter standing away to the westward, as if she had come out of St. Aubin's Bay. He pointed her out to Griffiths, but she was too far off to distinguish what she was, and he was unwilling to make chase till we had ascertained whether Sandgate had been there. He accordingly stood on, eager to receive our report.

Our first act was to tumble the pilot into the shore-boat,

and make chase after the cutter Harcourt had before observed. She had a very long start, but we trusted to the chances the winds and tides might afford us to come up with her — yet we could not but see that she had many more in her favor to aid her escape. There were, however, still some hours of daylight, and as long as we could keep her in sight, we need not despair. From the course she was steering, as much to the westward as she could lay up with the wind as it then stood, we felt certain that our worst suspicions would be realized, and that Sandgate fully intended to run across to America, or to some other distant land.

Never had the "Amethyst" before carried such a press of sail as she now staggered under; but little would it have availed us had the wind, which came in uncertain currents, not shifted round to the northward, while the "Rover" still had the breeze as before. It continued, however, increasing till we could no longer bear our gaff-topsail, and so much had we overhauled the chase, that, at sundown, we were within two miles of her. Now came the most critical time; as before the moon rose it would scarcely be possible to keep her in sight, and Sandgate would not fail to profit by the darkness if he could, to effect his escape — he, also, having the wind exactly as we had it, now sailed as fast as we did. So exciting had become the chase, even to those least interested in it, that every man kept the deck, and with so many well-practised eyes, Argus-like, fixed on her, any movement she made would scarcely escape us. The sky was clear, and the stars shone bright, but the wind whistled shrilly, and the foam flew over us, as the little craft, heeling over on her gunwale, plunged and tore through the foaming and tumbling waves. Thus passed hour after hour. If the "Rover" hauled up, so did we; if she kept away, the movement was instantly seen and followed by us, though all the time, as O'Malley observed, he could not, for the life of him, make out any thing but a dark shadow with a scarcely defined form stalking like an uneasy ghost before us ; as to know what she was about, it passed his comprehension how we discovered it. That she was, however, increasing her distance we became at length aware, by the difficulty we experienced in seeing her, and at last the shadowy form faded into air.

Every one on board uttered an exclamation of disappointment, and some swore deeply, if not loudly.

" Can no one make her out?" Harcourt asked.

The seamen peered through the darkness.

" There she is on the weather-bow," sung out one.

" I think I see her right ahead still," said another.

" No : I'm blowed if that ain't her on the lee-bow there," was the exclamation of a third.

One thing only was certain, she was not to be seen. We determined, however, to keep the same course we had been before steering, and as the moon would rise shortly, we trusted again to sight her. The intervening hour was one of great anxiety ; and when, at last, the crescent moon, rising from her watery bed, shed her light upon the ocean, we looked eagerly for the chase. Right ahead there appeared a sail, but what she was it was impossible to say ; she might be the " Rover," or she might be a perfect stranger. On still we steered due west, for, although we felt that our chance of overtaking Sandgate was slight indeed, yet our only hope remained in keeping a steady course. Thus we continued all night ; and the moment the first streaks of light appeared in the sky, Harcourt was at the mast-head eagerly looking out for the chase. Far as the eye could reach, not a sail was to be seen ; there was no sign of land, nothing was visible but the gray sky and the

leadcolored water. Still Harcourt remained at his post, for
he dared not acknowledge to himself that Emily was lost to
him for ever. In vain he strained his eyes, till the sun rose
and cast his beams along the ocean. A white object
glistened for a moment ahead ; it might have been the wing
of a sea-fowl, but as he watched, there it remained, and he
felt certain that it was the head of a cutter's mainsail.
Taking the bearings of the sail, he descended on deck, and,
as a last hope, steered towards it, sending a hand on the
cross-trees to watch her movements. The wind fortunately,
as it proved to us, was variable, and thus we again neared
the chase. As we rose her hull, Griffiths pronounced her to
be of the size of the "Rover," if not the "Rover" herself.

"Well, we'll do our best to overhaul her," I exclaimed ;
"set the gaff-topsail. The craft must bear it."

And, pressed to her utmost, the little "Amethyst" tore
through the foaming waves. Thus we went on the whole
day, till towards the evening the chase again ran us completely out of sight. The wind, also, was falling away,
and at sundown there was almost a complete calm. Still
the vessel had steerage-way, so we kept the same course as
before. At length I threw myself on a sofa in the cabin.
I know not how long I had slept, when I was awoke by
feeling the yacht once more springing livelily through the
water. I jumped on deck without awaking O'Malley, who
was on the opposite sofa. The morning was just breaking,
and, by the faint light of the early dawn, I perceived a large
dark object floating at some distance ahead of us.

"What is that?" I exclaimed to Griffiths, who had
charge of the deck.

"A dismasted ship, sir," was the answer. "I have
seen her for some time, and as she lay almost in our course,

I steered for her, as I thought as how you'd like to overhaul her, sir."

"You did well," I answered. "Rouse all hands, and see a boat clear for boarding her. But what is that away there just beyond the wreck? By heavens, it's the 'Rover,' and becalmed too. Grant the wind may not reach her!"

Awoke by hearing the people called, Harcourt and O'Malley were by my side. I pointed out the wreck and the cutter to them.

"Well," exclaimed O'Malley, "the big ship there may still float, but the breeze which has been sending us along, may at last reach the sails of the 'Rover;' so I propose we make sure of her first."

. To our joy, however, we found that the wind, instead of reaching her, was gradually falling away, and by the time we were up with the wreck, the sea was as calm as a sheet of glass. We were in hopes also that keeping, as we had done, the wreck between us and the "Rover," we might have escaped observation, and in the gray light of morning we might come upon her unawares. There were several people on board the ship, who cheered as they saw assistance at hand; and reason they had to be glad, for from the clear streams of water which gushed from her sides, they had evidently great labor to keep her afloat. No time was to be lost, the gig was soon in the water, and Harcourt, O'Malley, and I, with eight men fully armed, pulled towards the "Rover," while old Griffiths, the master, boarded the ship in the other boat. My friend's heart beat quick as we neared the cutter. She was the "Rover," there was no doubt, but whether Sandgate would attempt to defend his vessel was the question. A moment more would solve it. We dashed alongside; the men, stowed away in the bottom of the boat, sprang up, and before the crew of the "Rover" had time to defend themselves, we were on board. Except the man at the helm and the look-out forward, the watch on deck were all asleep, and those two, as it afterwards appeared, were glad to see us approach. The noise awoke Sandgate, who, springing on deck, found himself confronted by O'Malley and me, while half his crew were in the power of my people, and the fore-hatch was battened over the rest. A pistol he had seized in his hurry was in his hand; he pointed it at my breast, but it missed fire; on finding which, he dashed it down on the deck, and before we could seize him, retreated forward, where some of his crew rallied round him. With fear and hope alternately racking his bosom, Harcourt hurried below. He pronounced his own name; the old nurse opened the door of the main cabin—a fair girl was on her knees at prayer. She sprang up, and seeing him, forgetful of all else, fell weeping in his arms. I shall pass over all she told him, except that Sandgate had behaved most respectfully to her, informing her, however, that he should take her to the United States, where she must consent to marry him, and that, on their return to England, he would put her in possession of a large fortune, to which by some means he had discovered she was heiress, and which had induced him to run off with her. It was, I afterwards learned, his last stake, as the reduction of duties no longer enabled him to make a profit by smuggling; and as he had no other means of supporting his extravagant habits, he was a ruined man.

Sandgate's people seemed resolved to stand by him, but not to proceed to extremities, or to offer any opposition to our carrying off Miss Manners and her attendant. He evidently was doing all he could to induce them to support him; and I believe, had he possessed the power, he would, without the slightest compunction, have hove us all overboard, and carried off his prize in spite of us. As it was, he could do nothing but gnash his teeth and scowl at us with unutterable hatred. Handing the young lady and the old nurse into the boat, we pulled away from the "Rover." Of course, we should have wished to have secured Sandgate; but as we had come away without any legal authority to attempt so doing, we saw that it would be wiser to allow him to escape. We should probably have overpowered him and his lawless crew, but then the females might have been hurt in the scuffle, and we were too glad to recover them uninjured to think at the moment of the calls of justice.

What was our surprise, as Harcourt handed her on to the deck of the yacht, to see her rush forward into the arms of an old gentleman who stood by the companion-hatch.

"My own Emily!" he exclaimed, as he held her to his heart.

It was Colonel Manners.

"My father!" burst from her lips.

A young lady was reclining on the hatch near him; she rose as she saw Emily, and they threw themselves on each other's neck.

"My sister!" they both exclaimed, and tears of joy started to their eyes.

There were several other strangers on board, who, by Griffiths' exertions, had been removed from the wreck. Our boats were busily employed in removing the others, for there was no time to lose, as the ship was settling fast in the water. All the people being placed in safety, we proceeded to remove the articles of greatest value and smallest bulk on board the two vessels, which became then very much loaded, when, a breeze springing up, another sail hove in sight: she bore down towards us, and, in a short time, the little fat figure of Mr. Warwick Ribbons graced the deck of the "Amethyst." His delight at seeing Emily in safety was excessive, but, though he looked sentimental, he said nothing; and, when he heard that the colonel was alive, and that there was another sister in the case, his face elongated considerably. From motives of charity, I hurried him, with several of the passengers and part of the cargo, on board the "Dido," and the three vessels made sail together for Falmouth. Just as we were leaving the ship, a deep groan issued from her hold, and, her head inclining towards the water, she slowly glided down into the depths of the ocean. Landing all our passengers at Falmouth, except the colonel and his daughters, we had a quick run to Cowes. Colonel Manners established his claim to his property. O'Malley had made such good use of his time during the voyage, that he won the heart and hand of Julia Manners; while, as may be suspected, Emily owned, that if Harcourt loved her, their affection was reciprocal; and the same day saw them joined respectively together in holy matrimony.

Such was the result of my friend Harcourt's summer cruise, and I think you will all agree that the narrative is not altogether unworthy of the name of a romance. The last time I saw little Ribbons he was on board the "Dido," which lay high and dry on the mud off Ryde, and I afterwards heard that he married a Miss Bosley, who, I conclude, was a daughter of old Bosley's.

"And what became of the rascal Sandgate?" exclaimed Hearty; "by Neptune! I should like to come up with the fellow, and to lay my craft alongside his till I had blown her out of the water. Fancy a scoundrel in the nineteenth century venturing to run off with a young lady!" We laughed at his vehemence. Hearty always spoke under a generous impulse.

"Oh, it's not the first case of the sort I have heard of," said Carstairs; "more than one has occurred within the last few years in Ireland; but I agree with Hearty, that I should like to catch Mr. Sandgate, for the sake of giving him a good thrashing. Though I hadn't the pleasure of knowing Miss Manners, every man of honor should take a satisfaction in punishing such a scoundrel." Bubble and Porpoise responded heartily to the sentiment, and so strong a hold did the account take of the minds of all the party, that we talked ourselves into the idea that it would be our lot to fall in with Sandgate, and to inflict the punishment he had before escaped. Will Bubble had taken an active part in fitting out the yacht, and in selecting most of the crew; he consequently was on rather more intimate terms with them than the rest of us; not that it was the intimacy which breeds contempt, but he took a kindly interest in their welfare, and used to talk to them about their families, and the past incidents of their lives. Indeed, under a superficial coating of frivolity and egotism, I discovered that Bubble possessed a warm and generous heart, — fully alive to the calls of humanity. I do not mean to say that the coating was not objectionable; he would have been by far a superior character without it. Indeed, perhaps all I ought to say is, that he was capable of better things than those in which he too generally employed his time. He returned aft one day from a visit forward, and told us he had discovered that several of the men were first-rate yarn-spinners. "The master," said he, "seems a capital hand; but old Sleet beats all the others hollow. If it would not be subversive of all discipline, I wish you would come forward and hear them in the forecastle as one caps the other's tale with something more wonderful still."

"I don't think that would quite do," said Hearty; "if we

could catch them on deck spinning their yarns, it would be very well. But, at all events, I will invite Snow. into the cabin and consult him."

"According to Hearty's proposal, he invited Snow down. " Mr. Snow," said Hearty, " we hear that some of the people forward are not bad hands at spinning yarns, and, if you could manage it, we should be glad to hear them, but it would never do to send for them aft for the purpose."

" You are right, sir, they would become tongue-tied to a certainty," answered Snow ; "just let me alone, and I will manage to catch some of them in the humor. Several of them have been engaged, one time or another, in the free-trade, and have some curious things to tell about it."

" But I thought smuggling had been knocked on the head long ago," observed Hearty.

" Oh, no, sir ! of late years a very considerable blow has been struck against it ; but even now some people find inducements to follow it," answered the master. " I found it out to be a bad trade many years ago, and very few of those I know who still carry it on do more than live, and live very badly too ; some of them spending many a month out of the year in prison, and that is not where an honest man would wish to be."

However, I have undertaken to chronicle the adventures of the " Frolic," and of those who dwelt on board her, so that I must not devote too much of our time to the yarns, funs, witticisms, and anecdotes and good sayings with which we banished any thing like tedium during our voyage. No blue devils could stand for an instant such powerful exorcisms.

It was not, however, till some time after this that we benefited by Snow's inquiries among the crew.

CHAPTER XII.

THE "FROLIC" IN A GALE, IN WHICH THE FROLICKERS SEE
NO FUN — A SAIL IN SIGHT — HER FATE — AN UNEXPECTED
INCREASE TO THE CREW — BUBBLE SHOWS THAT HE CAN
THINK AND FEEL — INTELLIGENCE OBTAINED.

"WHAT sort of weather are we going to have, Snow?"
asked Hearty, as we came on deck after dinner one afternoon, when the cutter was somewhere about the middle of
the Bay of Biscay.

"Dirty, sir, dirty!" was the unenlivening answer, as the
old master looked with one eye to windward, which just then
was the south-west. In that direction thick clouds were
gathering rapidly together, and hurrying headlong towards
us, like, as Carstairs observed, "a band of fierce barbarians,
rushing like a torrent down upon the plain." The sea grew
darker and darker in hue, and then flakes of foam, white as
the driven snow, blew off from the hitherto smooth surface
of the ocean. The sea rose higher and higher, and the cutter, close hauled, began to pitch into them with an uneasy
motion, subversive of the entire internal economy of landsmen.

"The sooner we get the canvas off her the better, now,
sir," said Snow to Porpoise, who had come on deck after
calculating our exact position on the charts.

"As soon as you like," was the answer. "We shall have
to heave-to, I suspect; but that little matters, as we have
plenty of sea-room out here, and she may dance away for a
fortnight with the helm a-lee, and come to no harm."

The topmast was struck; the jib was taken in, and a storm-jib set; the foresail was handed, and the mainsail meantime was closely reefed. Relieved for a time, she breasted the seas more easily; but the wind had not yet reached its strength. Before nightfall down came the gale upon us with all its fury; the cutter heeled over to it as she dashed wildly through the waves.

"The sooner we get the mainsail altogether off her the better, sir," said Snow. This was accordingly done, and the trysail was set instead, and the helm lashed a-lee.

"There; we are as snug and comfortable as possible," exclaimed Porpoise, as the operation was completed. "Now all hands may turn in and go to sleep till the gale is over."

The landsmen looked rather blue.

"Very funny notion this of comfort!" exclaimed Carstairs, who had the worst seagoing inside of any of the party. "Oh, oh, oh! is it far from the shore?"

"Couldn't get there, sir, if any one was to offer ten thousand guineas," said Snow. "We are better as we are, sir, out here — by very far."

The cutter, which in Cowes Harbor people spoke of as a fine large craft, now looked and felt very like a mere cockle-shell, as she pitched and tumbled about amid the mighty waves of the Atlantic.

"Don't you feel very small, Carstairs?" exclaimed Hearty, as he sat convulsively grasping the sides of the sofa in the cabin.

"Yes, faith, I do," answered the gentle giant, who lay stretched out opposite to him. "Never felt so very little since I was a baby in long-clothes. I say, Porpoise, I thought you told me that the Bay of Biscay was always smooth at this time of the year."

"So it should be," replied our fat captain. "No rule without an exception though; but never mind, it will soon roll itself quiet; and then the cutter will do her best to make up for lost time."

The person evidently most at his ease was Will Bubble. Blow high or blow low, it seemed all the same to him; he sang and whistled away as happily as ever.

"Oh, oh, oh! you jolly dog, don't mock us in our misery!" exclaimed Carstairs with a groan.

"On no account," answered Will, with a demure look. "I'll betake myself to the deck, and smoke my weed in quiet."

On deck he went, and seated himself on the companion-hatch, where he held on by a becket secured for the purpose; but as to smoking a cigar, that was next to an impossibility, for the wind almost blew the leaves into a flame. I was glad to go on deck, also; for the skylights being battened down made the cabin somewhat close. The cutter rode like a wild fowl over the heavy seas, which, like dark walls crested with 'foam, came rolling up as if they would ingulf her. Just as one with threatening aspect approached her, she would lift her bows with a spring, and anon it would be found that she had sidled up to the top of it.

It was a wild scene — to a landsman it must have appeared particularly so. The dark, heavy clouds close overhead; the leaden seas, not jumping and leaping as in shallow waters, but rising and falling, with majestic deliberation, in mountain masses, forming deep valleys and lofty ridges, from the summits of which, high above our heads, the foam was blown off in sheets of snowy whiteness with a hissing sound, interrupted by the loud flop of the seas as they dashed together.

We were not the only floating thing within the compass

10

of vision. Far away I could see to windward, as the cutter
rose to the top of a sea, the canvas of a craft as we were
hove-to. She was a small schooner, and though we undoubtedly were as unsteady as she was, it seemed impossible, from the way she was tumbling about, that any thing
could hold together on board her.

I had rejoined the party in the cabin, when an exclamation from Bubble called us all on deck.

" The schooner has bore up, and is running down directly
for us ! " he exclaimed.

So it was ; and in hot haste she seemed indeed.

" Something is the matter on board that craft," said Porpoise, who had been looking at her through his glass. " Yes,
she has a signal of distress flying."

" The Lord have mercy on the hapless people on board,
then ! " said I. " Small is the help we or any one else can
afford them."

" If we don't look out, she'll be aboard us, sir," sung out
Snow. " To my mind, she's sprung a leak, and the people
aboard are afraid she'll go down."

" Stand by to make sail on the cutter ; and put the helm
up," cried Porpoise. " We must not let her play us that
trick, at all events."

On came the little schooner, directly down for us, stagger-
ing away under a close-reefed fore-topsail, the seas rolling
up astern, and threatening every instant to wash completely
over her. How could her crew expect that we could aid
them? still it was evidently their only hope of being saved
— remote as was the prospect. They might expect to be
able to heave-to again under our lee, and to send a boat
aboard us. The danger was that in their terror they might
run us down, when the destruction of both of us was certain. We stood all ready to keep the cutter away, dangerous

as was the operation — still it was the least perilous of two alternatives. We were, as may be supposed, attentively watching every movement of the schooner; so close had she come that we could see the hapless people on board stretching out their arms, as if imploring that aid which we had no power to afford them. On a sudden they threw up their hands; a huge sea came roaring up astern of them; they looked round at it — we could fancy that we almost saw their terror-stricken countenances, and heard their cry of despair. Down it came, thundering on her deck; the schooner made one plunge into the yawning gulf before her. Will she rise to the next sea?

"Where is she?" escaped us all. With a groan of horror we replied to our own question — " She's gone ! "

Down, down she went before our very eyes — her signal of distress fluttering amid the seething foam, the last of her we saw. Perhaps her sudden destruction was the means of our preservation. Some dark objects were still left floating amid the foam; they were human beings struggling for life; the sea tossed them madly about — now they were together, now they were separated wide asunder. Two were washed close to us; we could see the despairing countenance of one poor fellow; his staring eye-balls; his arms outstretched as he strove to reach us. In vain; his strength was unequal to the struggle; the sea again washed him away, and he sunk before our sight. His companion still strove on; a sea dashed towards us; down it came on our deck. "Hold on, hold on, my lads ! " sung out Porpoise.

It was well that all followed the warning, or had we not, most certainly we should have been washed overboard. The lively cutter, however, soon rose again to the top of the sea, shaking herself like a duck after a dive beneath the surface. As I looked around to ascertain that all hands were safe, I

saw a stranger clinging to the shrouds. I with others rushed
to haul him in, and it was with no little satisfaction that we
found that we had been the means of rescuing one of the
crew of the foundered schooner from a watery grave. The
poor fellow was so exhausted that he could neither speak
nor stand, so we carried him below, and stripping off his
wet clothes, put him between a couple of warm blankets.
By rubbing his body gently, and pouring down a few drops
of hot brandy and water, he was soon recovered. He
seemed very grateful for what had been done for him, and
his sorrow was intensely severe when he heard that no one
else of the schooner's crew had been saved.

"Ay, it's more than such a fellow as I deserve!" he
remarked.

I was much struck by his frank and intelligent manners,
when having got on a suit of dry clothes, he was asked by
Hearty into the cabin, to give an account of the catastrophe
which had just occurred.

"You see, gentlemen," said he, "the schooner was a
Levant trader. Her homeward-bound cargoes were chiefly
figs, currants, raisins, and such-like fruit. A better sea-
boat never swam. I shipped aboard her at Smyrna last
year, and had made two voyages in her before this here
event occurred. We were again homeward-bound, and had
made fine weather of it till we were somewhere abreast of
Cape Finisterre, when we fell in with some baddish weather,
in which our boats and caboose were washed away; and
besides this, we received other damage to hull and rigging.
We were too much knocked about to hope to cross the Bay
in safety, so we put into Corunna to refit. The schooner
leaked a little, though we thought nothing of it, and as we
could not get at the leak, as soon as we had got the craft
somewhat to rights, we again put to sea. We had been out

three days when this gale sprang up, and the master thought
it better to heave the vessel to, that she might ride it out.
The working of the craft very soon made the leak increase;
all hands went to the pumps, but the water gained on us,
and as a last chance the master determined to run down to
you, in the hopes that before the schooner went down, some
of us might be able to get aboard you. You saw what happened. Oh, gentlemen! may you never witness the scene
on board that vessel, as we all looked into each other's
faces, and felt that every hope was gone! It was sad to see
the poor master, as he stood there on the deck of the sinking
craft, thinking of his wife and seven or eight little ones at
home whom he was never to see again, and whom he knew
would have to struggle in poverty with the hard world! He
was a good, kind man; and to think of me being saved, —
a wild, careless chap, without any one to care for him, who
cares for nobody, and who has done many a wild, lawless
deed in his life, and who, maybe, will do many another! I
can't make it out; it passes my notion of things."

Will Bubble had been listening attentively to the latter
part of the young seaman's account of himself. He walked
up to him with an expression of feeling I did not expect to
see, seemingly forgetful that any one else was present, and
took his hand: " God in his mercy preserved you for better
things, that you might repent of your follies and vices, and
serve him in future. Oh, on your knees offer up your heart-
felt thanks to him for all he has done for you!"

Hearty and Carstairs opened their eyes with astonishment
as they heard Will speaking.

" Why, Bubble, what have?"——began Hearty.

" I have been thinking," was the answer; " I had time
while you fellows lay sick; and I bethought me how very
easily this little cockle-shell might go down and take up its

abode among the deposits of this Adamite age," — Will was somewhat of a geologist, — "and how very little we all were prepared to enter a pure state of existence."

"That's true, sir," said the seaman, not quite understanding, however, Bubble's remarks; "that's just what I thought before the schooner sank. I am grateful to God, sir; but, howsomdever, I feel that I am a very bad, good-for-nothing chap."

"Try to be better, my friend; you'll have help from above if you ask for it," said Bubble, resuming his seat.

"Why, where did you get all that from?" asked Carstairs, languidly; "I didn't expect to hear you preach, old fellow."

"I got it from my Bible," answered Bubble. "I'm very sure that's the only book of sailing directions likely to put a fellow on a right course, and to keep him there, so I hope in future to steer mine by it; but I don't wish to be preaching. It's not my vocation, and a harum-scarum, careless fellow as I am is not fitted for it; only all I ask of those present is to think — to think of their past lives; how they have employed their time — whether in the way for which they were sent into the world to employ it, in doing all the good to their fellow-creatures they can; or in selfish gratification; and to think of the future, that future without an end — to think if they are fitted for it — for its pure joys — its never-ending study of God's works; to think whether they have any claim to enter into realms of glory — of happiness."

Will sprang on deck as he ceased speaking. He had evidently worked himself up to utter these sentiments, so different to any we should have conceived him to have possessed. I never saw a party of gentlemen more astonished, if not disconcerted. Had not Tom Martin, the young seaman just

saved, been present, I do not know what might have been
said. Still the truth, the justice, the importance of what
Bubble had said, struck us all, though perhaps we thought
him just a little touched in the upper story, to venture on
thus giving expression to his feelings. While Tom Martin
had been giving an account of himself, I had been watching
his countenance, and it struck me that I had seen him somewhere before.

"You've been a yachtsman, I think," I observed; "I
have known your face, I am sure."

"Yes, sir," said he, frankly; "and, if I mistake not, I
know yours. I used to meet you at Cowes last year; but
the craft I belonged to I can't say was a yacht, though its
owner called her one. I'm sure you gentlemen won't take
advantage of any thing I say against me, and so I'll tell you
all about the matter. The craft I speak of was the 'Rover'
cutter, belonging to Mr. Miles Sandgate. I first shipped
aboard her about three years ago; he gave high pay, and
let us carry on aboard pretty much as we liked, when not
engaged in his business. An old chum of mine, a man
called Ned Holden, who was, I may say, born and bred a
smuggler, first got me to join; there wasn't a dodge to do
the revenue which Ned wasn't up to, and he thought no more
harm of smuggling than of eating his dinner. I didn't inquire how the 'Rover' was employed; she belonged to a
gentleman who paid well, and that's all I asked, though I
might have suspected something. She had just come from
foreign parts, and the people who had then been in her
talked of all sorts of curious things they had done. Smuggling was just nothing to what she'd been about. Mr. Sandgate seemed to have tried his hand at every thing. He had
been out in the China seas, running opium among the long
pigged-tailed gentlemen of that country. More than once he

had some hot fighting with the Government revenue-vessels, and several times he was engaged with the pirates, who swarm, they say, in those seas. I did not hear whether he made money out there, but after a time he got tired of the work, and shaped a course for England. On his way, after leaving the Cape of Good Hope, he fell in with a craft, which he attacked and took. She was laden with goods of all sorts fitted for the markets in Africa, and intended to be exchanged for slaves. Besides them she had the irons, and all the other fittings for a slaver. Such vessels sail without a protection from any government. After he had taken every thing he wanted, he hove the rest overboard, and then told the crew that he gave them their liberty, and that they might make the best of their way back to the parts from whence they came. With the goods he had thus obtained he stood for the slave-coast; he had acquaintance there, as every-where else; indeed it would be difficult to say in what part of the world he would not find himself at home. He was not long in fitting the 'Rover' inside into a regular slave-vessel, but outside she looked as honest and harmless as any yacht. He ran up the Gaboon, or one of those rivers on the slave-coast — I forget which exactly — where lived a certain Don Lopez Mendoza, the greatest slave-dealer in those parts; besides which, as I heard say, it would be difficult to find anywhere a bigger villain. Well, he and Mr. Sandgate were hand-in-glove, and one would have done any thing for each other. They were fairly matched, you may depend on it; however that might be, the Don took all the goods Mr. Sandgate brought him, and asked no questions, and filled his vessel in return with a lot of prime slaves and water, and farina enough to carry them across to Havana. As soon as he got them on board he was out of the river again, and, loosening his jib, away he went with some two

hundred human souls stowed under hatches, in a craft fit to
carry only thirty or forty in comfort. She had a quick run
across, and escaped all the ships-of-war looking after slavers.
Mr. Sandgate there sold the blacks for a good round sum,
and thought he had done a very clever thing. However, he
does not seem to be a man to keep money, though he is
ready enough to do many an odd thing to get it. He gave
his crew a handsome share of the profits ; he and they went
ashore at the Havana, and spent it as fast as they had
made it, just in the old buccaneering style I've heard tell of,
in all sorts of wild games and devilry, till I rather fancy the
Dons were glad to be rid of them. When their money was
nearly all gone, they went aboard again and made sail. I
don't mean to say but what I suppose Mr. Sandgate had
some left. He had also armed the cutter, and stored and
provisioned her completely for a voyage round the world.

" Once more he stood across for the African coast. He
had heard, it appears, that one of those store-ships I was
speaking of, which supply slavers with goods and provisions,
and irons and stores, was to be met with in a certain latitude. He fell in with her, and, without asking her leave or
saying a word, he ran her alongside, and, before her people
had time to stand to their arms, he had mastered every one
of them. He never ill-treated any one, but he just clapped
them in irons till he had rifled the vessel, and then, leaving
them a somewhat scant supply of provisions and water, he,
as before, told them that they were at liberty to make the
best of their way home again.

" Some men would, perhaps, have gone back to the coast,
taken in a cargo of slaves, and returned to the Havana or
the Brazils, but our gentleman was rather too cautious to
run any such risk. He knew that he had made enemies,
who would try to prove him a pirate, with or without law ;

so he just goes off the Gaboon, and sends in a note to his
friend Don Lopez, to say that he had got a rich cargo for
him, which he should have for so many dollars, two thousand or more below its value. The Don, in return, despatched two or three small craft with the sum agreed on
aboard, and all being found right and fair, the exchange,
was quickly made, and Mr. Sandgate once more shaped a
course for England. As you may suppose, every one was
sworn to secrecy aboard; but, bless you, the sort of chaps
he had got for a crew didn't much care for an oath; and
besides, as it was that they mightn't say any thing out of
the ship, they didn't mind talking about it to me and others
who afterwards joined her. He brought home a good round
sum of money; but he took it into his head to go up to
London, and what with gambling and such-like ways, he
soon managed to get rid of most of it. He had got tired,
it seems, of having his neck constantly in a noose, so he
took to the quieter occupation of smuggling. He didn't do
it in the common way like the people along the coast, but
in a first-rate style, like a gentleman. He had some rela-
tives or other, rich silk merchants in London, and he undertook to supply them with goods to any amount, free of duty.
There was nothing new in the plan, for it was an old dodge
of this house, by which they had made most of their money.
You would be surprised, gentlemen, to hear of the number
of people employed in the business, and who well knew it
was against the laws. First, there were the agents in
France to buy the goods, and to have them packed in small
bales fit for running; then they had to ship them; next
there were the cutters and other craft to bring them over,
and the people to assist at their landing; and the carters
with their light carts to bring them up to London; and the
clerks in the warehouse in London, many of whom knew

full well that not a penny of duty had ever been paid on the
goods; and the shop people too, who knew full well the
same thing, as they could not otherwise have got their
articles so cheap. It's a true saying, that one rascal makes
many; and so it was in this case."

Much to the same effect Tom told us about Sandgate;
but as with several of the points the readers are already
acquainted, I need not repeat them. Tom frankly acknowledged that he was on board the "Rover" when Sandgate
attempted to carry off Miss Manners; but he seemed to be
little aware of the enormity of the offence. He said that
he fancied the young lady had come of her own free will,
as Sandgate had made the crew believe a tale to that
effect.

"But what became of him after that?" I asked, eagerly.
"Did he return to the coast of Africa, and turn pirate
again?"

"No, sir," answered Martin. "He had several plans of
the sort though, I believe; but at last we stood for the
Rock of Gibraltar, and ran through the Straits into the
Mediterranean. We could not make out what Mr. Sandgate was about. We touched at two or three places on the
African coast, and he had some communication with the
Moors. To my mind, he scarcely knew himself what he
would be at. He spoke and acted very often like a person
out of his wits. Sometimes we would be steering for a
place, and our course would be suddenly altered, and we
would go back to the port from whence we came, However,
by degrees we got higher and higher up the Mediterranean.
We did not touch at Malta, but stood on till we got among
the Greek islands: there he seemed quite at home, and was
constantly having people aboard whom he treated as old
friends, Still we did nothing to make the vessel pay her

way, and that was very unlike Mr. Sandgate's custom.
After a time we ran on to Smyrna: we thought that we
were going to take in a cargo of figs and raisins, and to
return home. One day, however, a fine Greek polacca brig
stood into the harbor, and Mr. Sandgate, after examining
her narrowly, went on board her. On his return, calling us
together, he said that as he was going to sell the cutter, he
should no longer have any need of our services; and that
as he was very well pleased with the way we had more than
once stuck by him, he would therefore add five pounds to
the wages of each man. We all cheered him, and thought
him a very fine fellow; and so I believe he would have
been had he known what common honesty means. The
'Rover' was sold next day, and we all had to bundle on
shore and look out for fresh berths. When we were there
I heard some curious stories about that polacca brig; and
all I can say is, that if I had been aboard a merchantman
and sighted her, I shouldn't have been comfortable till we
got clear of her again. Whether Mr. Sandgate went away
in her or not I cannot say for certain; all I know is, that
the polacca brig left Smyrna in a few days. The crew of
the 'Rover' joined different vessels, and though I was very
often on shore, I saw no more of him. The rest of my story
you know, gentlemen. I shipped on board the schooner
which you lately saw go down."

"Very extraordinary story altogether," exclaimed Hearty,
as soon as Tom Martin had left the cabin, highly pleased
with his treatment. "If you had not been able to corrobo-
rate some of it, Brine, I certainly should not have felt inclined to believe it."

"I know the circumstance of one quite as extraordinary," said Porpoise. "Some day I will tell it you if you
wish it. I should not be surprised when we get up the

Straits if we hear more of Mr. Sandgate and his doings. He is evidently a gentleman not addicted to be idle, though, clever as he is, he will some day be getting his neck into a halter."

"I should think it was well fitted for one by this time," added Carstairs; "but I say, Porpoise, let us have your story at once; there's nothing like the present time for a good thing when it can be got, and we want something amusing to drive away all the bitter blue-devilish feelings which this confounded tumblefication of a sea has kicked up in our insides."

"You shall have it, with all my heart, and without delay," added Porpoise. "All I have first to say is, that as I was present during many of the scenes, and as descriptions of the others were given me, strange as the account may appear, it is as true as every thing we have just heard about that fellow Sandgate. I could almost have fancied that he and the hero of my story were one and the same person."

Our curiosity being not a little excited by this prelude, in spite of the rolling and pitching of the vessel, seldom has a more attentive audience been collected, as our jovial companion began his story.

CHAPTER XIII.

LIEUTENANT PORPOISE'S STORY — THE BLACK SLAVER — THE SPANISH MAIDEN — THE DESERTER'S DREAM — THE FLIGHT.

THE BRITISH CRUISER.

"KEEP a bright look-out, Collins, and let me be called if any thing like a sail appears in sight," said Captain Staunton, as he was quitting the quarter-deck of His Majesty's brig "Sylph," which he had the honor to command. She was then stationed on the coast of Africa. Some years have passed by, it must be remembered, since the time to which I now allude.

"Ay, ay, sir," answered the first lieutenant, who was the officer addressed. "With so many sharp eyes on board it shall be hard if we miss seeing him, should he venture to approach the coast, and if we see him, harder still if he escape us."

Captain Staunton descended to his cabin, and feverish and ill from long watching and the effects of the pestiferous climate, he threw himself into his cot, and endeavored to snatch a few hours' repose, to better prepare himself for the fresh exertions he expected to be called on to make. But sleep, which kindly so seldom neglects to visit the seaman's eyelids, when wooed even amid the raging tempest, refused for some time to come at his call.

"I would sacrifice many a year's pay to catch that fellow," he continued, as he soliloquized half aloud. "The monstrous villain! while he lives I feel that the stain yet remains on the cloth he once disgraced. We will yet show him that the honor of the service cannot be insulted with impunity, although·he dares our vengeance by venturing among us when he knows every vessel on the station is on the watch for him. And yet I once regarded that man as a friend; I loved him almost as a brother, for I thought his heart beat with the most noble sentiments. I thought him capable of the like deeds; but all the time he must have been a most accomplished hypocrite, though still he has one good quality, he is brave, or perhaps, it may be, he possesses rather physical insensibility to danger and utter recklessness of all consequences. He started fairly in life, and at one time gave good promise of rising in his profession. I knew him to be wild and irreligious; but I fancied his faults arose from thoughtlessness and high spirit, and I hoped that experience of their ill effects and a good example would cure them; but I now see that vice, from an ill-regulated education, was deeply rooted in him, and, alas! has that good example which might have saved him always been set him? I fear not. Ah! if those in command could foresee the dreadful results of their own acts, of their careless expressions, they would keep a better watch over themselves, and often shudder with horror at the crime and misery they have caused."

With a prayer to Heaven to enable him to avoid the faults of which he felt with pain that he had himself too often been guilty, the commander of the brig fell asleep.

The officer of the watch, meantime, continued his walk on the quarter-deck, his thoughts taking a turn very similar to those of his chief, for they had often together discussed the subject, and the same train of ideas were naturally suggested by the same circumstance, as he also had known the person of whom the captain was thinking.

The "Sylph" was at this time some miles off the African coast, which, although not seen from the deck, was faintly distinguishable from the mast-head; it appeared like a long blue line drawn on the ocean with a slight haze hanging over it, scarcely to be perceived by unpractised eyes. The part visible was about the mouth of the Pongos River, a well-known slave depot, the favorite resort of the Spanish South-American slavers.

The surface of the ocean was smooth, although occasionally ruffled by a light breeze, which, coming from seaward, served to cool the brows of the crew, and restore some vigor to their exhausted limbs; yet there was the usual swell, which seldom leaves the bosom of the Atlantic to perfect tranquillity. It came in from the west, slowly and silently, making the vessel roll from side to side like a drunken man. Though she was not, it must be understood, at anchor, she had not a stitch of canvas spread which would have contributed, had there been any wind, to steady her. All her sails were closely furled, but her studding-sail booms were at their yard-arms, their gear was rove, and the studding-sails themselves were on deck, ready to set in a moment. The boats, too, were clear to hoist out in an instant, and there was every sign on deck that the now apparently listless crew would, at first sound of the boatswain's whistle, spring into life and activity, and that the now bare tracery of spars and rigging would, the second after, be covered with a broad sheet of snowy canvas.

The "Sylph" had been about a year on the coast. When she left England, her officers and crew were a particularly fine, healthy set of men, and the whole of them could scarcely, in the course of their lives, have mustered a month's illness among them. Since they came to their present station, the second lieutenant and second master had died, as had two midshipmen and thirteen of the crew, and nearly all the remainder had, more or less, suffered, few retaining any traces of their former ruddy and healthy appearance.

They had, however, to be sure, before being well acclimated, or having learned the necessary precautions to take against illness, been exposed to a good deal of hard service in boats up the rivers, where were sown the seeds of the disease which afterwards proved so fatal among them. Fresh officers and men had been appointed to fill the places of those who had died, and the brig was now again the same model of discipline and beauty which she had before been. When Captain Staunton joined the brig, he is reported to have called the men aft, and to have made them a speech much to this effect: —

"Now, my men, that you may not have any long discussions as to the character of your new commander, I wish to let you clearly understand that I never overlook drunkenness, or any other crime whatever, either in my officers or men. I shall not say whether I like flogging or not, but while it is awarded by the articles of war, I shall inflict it. Remember, however, I would much rather reward than punish. The men who do their duty well and cheerfully, I will advance as far as I have the power. I wish this to be a happy ship, and it will be your own faults if you do not make it so. Now pipe down."

The men agreed, as they sat in knots together after they had knocked off work for the day, that they liked the cut of their new skipper's jib, and that his speech, though short, was good, and had no rigmarole in it.

He afterwards invited his officers to dine with him, and in the course of conversation impressed on their minds that he considered gross language and swearing not only ungentle-

11

manly, but wicked, and that he was certain the men did not
obey at all the more readily for having it applied to them;
that the men would follow the example they set them; that
their influence depended on their doing their duty, and that
if they did it the men would do theirs. "Drunkenness,"
he observed, "is by some considered a very venial offence,
but as the lives of all on board, as the discipline of the ship
depends on the judgment of those in command, however
much I shall regret the necessity, I shall break any officer
who is guilty of it." As Captain Staunton himself practised
what he preached, and set an example of all the high qualities which adorn his noble profession, the necessity he would
have deplored never occurred; punishment was very rare,
and the "Sylph" *was* a happy ship.

Having made this digression, we will return to the time
when the "Sylph" lay on the waste of waters, rolling her
polished sides in the shining ocean, while the drops of spray
which they threw off sparkled like diamonds in the rays of
the burning sun. Had it not been for the light breeze we
spoke of, the heat would have been intolerable on deck, for
there was not the usual shade from the sails to shelter the
seamen from the fury of the burning orb; but all were far
too eager for the appearance of a vessel they were looking
for to think of the inconvenience.

Three days before, an English homeward-bound merchantman had spoken them, and brought them the information that a large slaver was every moment expected in the
river; a very fast-sailing schooner, which had already once
before escaped them by the daring and good seamanship of
her commander, who was supposed to be an Englishman.
Thus much the crew knew, and they added their own com-
ments, believing him to be a character similar to the famed

Vanderdecken, or, at all events, in league with the prince
of terror, Davy Jones.

They had already been two days thus watching, after
having ascertained, by sending the boats up the river, that
the slaver was not there. Captain Staunton, knowing the
man with whom he had to deal, was aware that his only
chance of capturing him was by extreme caution. He had ·
therefore furled all the sails of the brig in the way we have
described, that she might not be discovered by the slaver till
the fellow had got close up to her, and he then hoped to be
able, without a long chase, to bring her to action. Each
night, as soon as it grew dusk, the "Sylph" made sail and
stood in shore, in order better to watch the coast, and before
daylight she was again at her former post. It has been asserted that the African cruisers have allowed the slavers to
get into port, and have not attempted to capture them till
they have got their slaves on board, in order either to gain
the head-money, or to make more sure of their condem-
nation; but if this was ever done, Captain Staunton was
not the person to do so; he knew, moreover, that the man
who commanded the slaver he was in search of would not
yield her up without a struggle, and, for the sake of saving
many lives which must otherwise inevitably be sacrificed, he
was anxious to bring her to action before she got her slaves
on board. The officer of the watch continued pacing the
deck with his spy-glass under his arm, every now and then
hailing the masthead to keep the look-outs on the alert, but
the same answer was each time given.

"Nothing in sight, sir."

Thus the day wore on. Towards the evening the breeze,
which had since the morning been sluggish, increased considerably; but as the current which is to be found in nearly
every part of the ocean set in an opposite direction to it,

the brig did not materially alter her position. A fresh hand had just relieved the look-out at the masthead at eight bells in the afternoon watch. His eyes, from not being fatigued, were sharper than his predecessor's, and he had scarcely glanced round the horizon, when he hailed the deck with words which roused everybody up —

"A sail in sight!"

"Where away?" asked the officer of the watch. The brig's head was now tending on shore.

"Right over the starboard quarter, sir," was the answer.

"Call the captain, Mr. Wildgrave," said the second lieutenant, who had charge of the deck, to the midshipman of the watch.

"Which way is she standing?" asked the officer.

"Directly down for us, sir," was the answer.

In five seconds the captain himself was on deck, and the remainder of the officers soon after appeared. The first lieutenant went aloft with his glass, and on his return pronounced the stranger to be a large square-rigged vessel, but whether a man-of-war, a slaver, or an honest trader, it was difficult to say, though he was inclined to suppose her belonging to either of the two former classes, from the broad spread of canvas she showed. On she came towards them, probably ignorant of their vicinity, as, stripped as they were, they would not be perceived by her till long after she was seen by them.

"What do you now make her out to be, Mr. Collins?" inquired the commander of the first lieutenant, who had again returned, after a second trip to the masthead.

"A large schooner, at all events, sir; and if I mistake not, she is the 'Espanto.'"

"Pipe all hands on deck, then, for we shall soon be discovered, and must make sail in chase."

The men were in a moment at their stations, and in silence waited the orders of their commander. Still the stranger came on, her sails slowly rising, as it were, from out of the ocean. She was now clearly seen from the deck of the " Sylph." Apparently there was a very bad look-out kept on board her, or else she was not the vessel they supposed, as otherwise the British cruiser must before this have been perceived by her.

Captain Staunton and his officers stood watching her with almost breathless anxiety, with their glasses constantly at their eyes, ready to observe the first indication of any alteration in her course. Nearer and nearer she approached, with studding-sails alow and aloft, on either side. Suddenly they were observed to be taken in, and the vessel's course was altered to the southward.

" Aloft there, and make sail! " shouted the commander, in a quick tone. The men, with alacrity, sprang up the rigging ; the sails were let fall, the tacks were sheeted home, and in a minute the " Sylph," under a spread of canvas, was standing on a bowline in chase of the stranger.

THE SPANISH MAIDEN.

We must now shift our scene to a different part of the world, and to a period much antecedent to that of which we have hitherto been speaking. The spot to which we allude is on the eastern coast of South America, in the northern part of that vast territory colonized by the inhabitants of Spain. There is a beautiful bay, or rather gulf, surrounded by lofty and picturesque cliffs, with deep ravines running up between them and several *haciendas*, or large farm-houses, on the surrounding ground, generally picturesquely situated, with a view of the sea in the distance. Several vessels lay at anchor, proudly pre-eminent among which was a frigate, from whose peak the ensign of Great Britain floated in the breeze.

Some way inland was a mansion of considerable size, though only one story, surrounded with deep verandas — the style of architecture general in the country. It stood at the head of a ravine, towards which the windows of its principal rooms opened, so that the inhabitants enjoyed a fine view of cliffs and rocks, and trees of every form and hue, between which a sparkling torrent found its way to the ocean, which was seen beyond the shipping in the harbor. In a room within the house, a beautiful girl was seated close to the window, but she looked not on the scene without. Her eyes were turned downwards, for at her feet knelt a youth ; his glance met hers ; and there was a wildness in his look, an expression of pain on his brow, which seemed to demand her pity. He was dressed in the British uniform, the single epaulet on his shoulder betokening that he held the rank of lieutenant ; but his complexion was swarthy in the extreme, and his tongue spoke with facility the language of Spain.

"Hear me, beloved one !" he exclaimed, passionately pressing her hand to his lips. "My ship sails hence in a few days, but I cannot tear myself from you. For your sake I will quit my profession, my country, and the thing men call honor, and will run the risk of death, if I am retaken, — all — all for your sake. Do you love me, dearest one ?"

The girl smiled faintly, and her eyes filled with tears. He again pressed her hand to his lips.

"Yes, yes ; I feel that I am blessed, indeed," he continued in the same tone. "But you must conceal me, beloved one. My life is in your hands. There will be a strict search made for me in every direction when I am missed.

You will hear vile tales invented to induce those who might be sheltering me to give me up, but believe them not. Will you promise to be my preserver, my guardian angel, my idol, and I will live but to show my gratitude?"

Where is the woman's heart which could resist such an appeal? The maiden's doubts and hesitations were gradually disappearing.

"But we have seen little of each other, señor. Your love for a poor girl like me cannot be so strong as for my sake to make you give up all men hold most dear. The sacrifice is surely not worth the price. I do not even know your name."

"Call me Juan, then," he answered. "But if my fiery, ardent love meets no return, I will quit you; though, perchance, to suffer death. On board yonder accursed ship I cannot live. I am hated there; and hate in return."

"Oh, no, señor! I will not expose you to such danger," answered the maiden. "I have heard sad stories of that ship. Even yesterday, it is said, one of the officers murdered another, and that the murderer has fled into the country."

The young man started and turned pale, but instantly recovering himself, he looked up affectionately into her countenance.

"But do you believe the tale?" he asked.

"I cannot but believe, señor," she answered; "one of our slaves saw the murdered man on the beach where he fell, and the dagger sticking in his bosom."

"But how can you suppose from that circumstance that an Englishman did the deed."

"Because the dagger was such as the young officers wear," answered the girl; "and they were seen walking together."

"Know you the name, then, of the supposed murderer?" he asked.

"I could not pronounce it if I did," she said.

"It matters not — but believe not the tale — at all events, you would not believe me guilty of such a deed?"

"Oh, heavens, certainly not!" she replied, casting a glance which told plainly the secret of her heart.

He saw that the victory was gained, and clasping her to his bosom, he urged her to form a plan for his conceal-ment.

"No one saw me approach the house," he observed, "so you will not be suspected; yet hasten, for should I now be observed, our difficulties would be increased."

Where woman's wit is sharpened by love, she finds no difficulties in serving him she loves. In a short time the stranger was concealed within the roof of the mansion, where she might, without exciting suspicion, constantly com-municate with him.

Juanetta, having thus obeyed the impulse of her heart, returned to her seat near the window to meditate on the act she had performed, and the responsible office she had undertaken.

"Yet who is the stranger to whom I have given my heart?" she thought; "he loves me, surely, or he would not tell me so; and I love him — he is so handsome, so eloquent — he narrates adventures so surprising — he has done such daring deeds. It is strange, too, that he should seek to leave the ship, and that another officer should have committed a murder — oh, horrible! what fierce, bad men those on board must be, except my Juan!"

Poor girl! she was young, loving, and ignorant of the wickedness in the world, or she would have suspected even him. Her meditations were interrupted by the appearance of her father, accompanied by the alcalde, and two officers in British uniforms. They were conversing earnestly as they passed the widow, and they thus did not observe her.

" There can be no doubt of it, señor," observed the alcalde to one of the English officers : " the murder must have been committed by him — his flight proves it."

" Where can he have concealed himself?" said the officer. " I would give a high reward to whoever discovers him, for such a crime must not go unpunished."

" He must still be wandering about near the coast, for without a horse — and I cannot learn that any person has supplied him with one — he cannot have escaped into the interior. The scouts also I sent out bring no intelligence of him."

On hearing these words Juanetta turned pale, for dreadful suspicions crossed her mind ; but she had vowed to protect the stranger, and she felt the necessity of appearing calm. She had scarcely time to compose herself before her father and his guests entered the apartment. Refreshments were ordered, and as she was obliged to busy herself in performing the duties of a hostess, her agitation was not observed. During the repast she listened eagerly to gain further information, but what she heard only served to increase her doubts and fears. At length her father, telling her that he would soon return, took his departure with his guests.

Unhappy Juanetta! she dared not believe what yet her reason told her was too true. Left alone, she burst into tears. They afforded some relief to her aching heart, and when calmness had again returned, she hastened to the place where she had concealed her dangerous guest. As she went, she resolved to tell him that she would see him no more, yet to assure him that her promise given, he was safe

while under her father's roof. She thought she would confess all that had passed to her father, and trusting to his generosity, entreat him to aid her in favoring the escape of the
suspected criminal.

Fortunate for her had she been firm in her resolve.
Alas! that passion should too often triumph over the dic-
tates of reason! yet who can fathom the deep well of a
woman's heart? Surely not she herself, while it remains
free from the rubbish, the wickedness, the knowledge of
the world, those things which choke it up and foul its pure
waters. Juan lay sleeping on the hard floor, yet so lightly,
that he started the moment she slowly raised the trap-door
which opened into the chamber, and grasping a pistol on
which his hand had rested, he sprang to his feet. When he
saw who was his visitor, his glance became less fierce, but
still he did not quit his hold of his weapon. He was about
to speak, but she, placing her finger to her mouth, signified
to him to be silent till she had carefully closed the place of
ingress.

" I have come, señor, to bid you prepare for instant
flight." She spoke in a low tone, and her voice faltered.
" You cannot remain here in safety, for I have heard dreadful stories, and I feel sure you will be sought for here.
They cannot be true; I know they cannot; but yet I wish
they had not been spoken."

" Should all the world desert me, my Juanetta will still
believe me true," exclaimed the young man as he approached
her and knelt at her feet. " Do not credit those tales, dearest; they are told by my foes and tyrants to destroy me; but
my vengeance will yet alight on their heads. Yet what
care I what they they say or do while you, sweet angel, are
my protector? "

He took the maiden's hand, and she did not withdraw it.

He pressed her hand to his lips, and his imploring glance met her eyes, already suffused with tears. She smiled, for she could not believe him false ; that youth with his gallant air and bold look ; crime cannot be an inhabitant of a figure so noble, she thought.

An arch-traitor was within the garrison, and the deceiver was victorious over the simple maiden. She dared not remain long in his company, lest her absence might betray her guest. · To one person alone did she confide her secret, a black slave who had attended her from a child, and loved her faithfully. Her word was his law, and Mauro promised that no harm should befall the stranger. His own conceptions of right and wrong were not very clear, nor did he make very minute inquiries as to the truth of the story his mistress told him. He believed that the Englishman had been ill-treated, and had avenged himself, and he was acute enough to discover that his young mistress loved the handsome stranger. He therefore considered it his duty to please her to the utmost of his power.

THE DESERTER'S DREAM.

Left again alone, Juan's weary limbs sank once more beneath the power of sleep ; but though the frame was still, the mind refused to be at rest. He dreamed that he was again a boy, young, innocent, and happy ; but yet all the time a consciousness of the bitter truth mocked the vain illusion, like some dark phantom hovering over him ; he felt and knew that the dream was false, still it seemed vivid and clear like the reality.

He thought that he lay at the feet of his fond and gentle mother, while his proud father smiled at his youthful gambols. It was in a princely hall, decked with all the luxury wealth can supply; other children were there, but he was the eldest and best beloved, the inheritor of almost boundless riches — of title and power. He had early learned his own importance; foolish nurses had not been slow to give him the baneful lesson; and while his parents believed him to be all their hearts could wish, the noxious seeds were already taking root. Years rolled on; he had gained knowledge at school, and beneath the care of his tutor, but, as regards self-government or religious feelings, he was still less educated than the poorest peasant on his father's broad domains. At last the truth had burst on his father's mind. His son was passionate, headstrong, self-willed, and, worse, deceitful. Every means of reclaiming him had been tried in vain, and he had determined to send him to sea under a strict captain, who promised to curb, if not to break, his spirit, if severity could influence him.

Young Hernan stood before his father, while his mother sat overpowered with grief. The carriage was waiting which was to convey him to Portsmouth. He was unmoved, for filial affection had been swallowed up by selfishness, and he fancied that he was about to lead a life of freedom and independence. He had yet to learn what a man-of-war was like. His mother pressed him to her heart, and his father strove to bless him as he turned to quit the room, for he was still his son.

The carriage rolled off, and in a few hours he was on board the ship which was to be his home and school for three long years. He learned many a lesson, it is true, but the great one came too late for him to profit by it. The first three years of his naval career passed by, and many a wild act had he committed, such as had often brought him under the censure of his superiors. That he was unreformed his father felt too surely convinced, and he was accordingly again sent to sea.

He was no longer a boy, and the irregularities of that age had grown into the vices of manhood. Yet among his equals he had friends, and, knowing their value, he took care to cultivate them. The most intimate was Edward Staunton, his superior in age by two years — one whose generous spirit, believing that he had discovered noble qualities in his companion, longed to win him back to virtue. Together they paced the deck in the midnight watch, and spoke of their future prospects, till even Hernan believed that he had resolved to amend. There are calm and often happy moments in a sailor's life, when all the dangers of their floating home, except the watch on deck, are wrapped in sleep ; and then many a youth pours into his attentive shipmate's ears the tale of his love, his hopes and fears, and pictures the beauty of the girl he has left behind — the lady of his heart, with whom he fondly fancies he shall some day wed. Such a tale did Staunton tell ; and Hernan listened carelessly at first, but afterwards with interest, as the ardent lover, delighting in the picture he was conjuring up, described the surpassing beauty of his mistress.

" Then you must introduce me to your lovely Blanche, and let me judge whether she is as fair as you paint her," said Hernan to his companion ; and Staunton, guileless himself, promised to gratify his wish.

" I shall not allow you to break your word, remember," added Hernan.

" Never fear," answered Staunton, laughing. " But see what a sudden change has come over the sky while we have been speaking ! We shall have a reef in the topsails before many minutes are out."

It was true. When they began their watch the sky was studded with a million stars, the dark sea was calm, and a gentle breeze filled the sails of the noble frigate. Now wild clouds were coursing each other across the arch of heaven, the light foam flew over the ocean, and the ship heeled over to the rising blast.

Scarcely had he spoken, when the voice of the officer of the watch roused his sleeping men with the order to furl the topgallant-sails quickly, followed by that to take a reef in the topsails. Hernan's duty had led him aloft. He was careless in keeping a firm hold. The ship gave a sudden lurch, and he found himself struggling in the wild waters. He could swim, but the fall had numbed his limbs, and the ship flew past him. Despair was seizing him, when he heard the cry which arose from the deck of "a man overboard!" echoed by a hundred voices. He was sinking beneath the waves, when he felt a friendly hand grasping his arm, and once more he rose to the surface of the water, and the voice of Edward Staunton cheered him to fresh exertions. He saw, too, the bright light of the life-buoy, which floated at a short distance only from them. It was a fearful thing, though, to be left thus alone on that stormy sea, for the dim outline of the frigate was scarcely visible, and she might be unable to fetch again, while the light continued burning, the spot where they were. For his sake, Staunton had thus risked his life. With great exertions Staunton dragged him to the life-buoy, and hanging on to it, they anxiously watched the approach of the frigate.

"The boat has been swamped, and we shall be left to perish miserably here," exclaimed Hernan. "Curses on my fate!"

"No," cried Staunton; "hark, I hear the shouts of the people in the boat pulling towards us. The frigate must have gone far to leeward before she could be hove-to to lower one.

Again the shouts were heard, and a dark object emerged from the obscurity which surrounded them. In a few minutes they were on board, and scarcely was the boat hoisted in than down came the tempest with tenfold fury, and vain would then have been any attempt to save him had he still been struggling in the waves. He was profuse in his professions of gratitude to Staunton, and he thought himself sincere.

The frigate returned home, her crew were paid off, and Staunton and his friend received their promotion.

"And now, Staunton, you must keep to your word, and introduce me to your beautiful friend, Miss Blanche D'Aubigné," said Hernan, after they had been some time on shore, and had met by chance in London.

"Gladly," answered Edward; " I have told her all about you, and she will be most glad to see you."

So they went together to the village where the fair girl resided; it was at no great distance from the country-seat of Sir Hernan Daggerfeldt, the father of Edward's friend. Staunton had won his promotion by his own exertions; and another step, his commander's rank, was to be gained before he could hope to make Blanche his bride. Such was the decree of her father, who had given an unwilling consent to their union, and he felt that he had no right to murmur at the decision. A short stay on shore was all he could hope to enjoy, before he must again go afloat for two or three more weary years; but she was still very young, and he confided in her truth and love.

This Hernan knew; he was surprised and delighted when first introduced to Miss D'Aubigné, for her beauty far surpassed his expectations. He thought her far more lovely than any one he had ever met, when, with artless simplicity, she received him as the friend of her betrothed. Edward went to sea, and Hernan took up his abode at his father's seat. Every week his visits to the village of Darlington grew more frequent, and Blanche unsuspectingly received him with pleasure, while her father, who knew his prospects, welcomed him cordially.

Hernan knew that Blanche looked on him as a friend of her intended husband, and he at first thought not of inquiring into his own feelings regarding her. Soon, however, a fierce passion sprang up in addition to the simple admiration he at first had felt. Indeed, he scarcely attempted to conceal it; but she was too pure-minded and unsuspecting to perceive the existence of the feelings she had inspired.

Thus matters went on till even she could no longer deceive herself as to Hernan's real feelings. Horrified at the discovery, she refused to see him more, and Hernan saw that he must make a bold stroke or lose her forever. He called falsehood and treachery to his aid. He went to her father; he spoke of his own ardent love, of his future wealth, of the position he could offer; then he continued to express his regret that Edward, his friend, was unworthy of her, that he had expressed his anxiety to break off the connection, but was unwilling to wound her feelings by doing so abruptly, and therefore intended to write, when he had reached his station, to free her from her engagement. Mr. D'Aubigné listened, and believed what he wished to be true; but Blanche was long incredulous, and refused to credit the tale of her intended's disloyalty. At last, however, the cruel letter came; it was enclosed in one to Hernan. It spoke of the impolicy of early engagements, of the misery of married poverty, of the difficulty of governing the affections, and of the danger of wedding when love has begun to decay.

Hernan watched the effect of the letter, and congratulated himself on its success; still Blanche disbelieved her senses, but dared not utter her suspicions. Hernan knew, too, that it was so, yet he trusted in the versatility of his talents to bring his schemes to a successful issue.

Her father's influence was exerted in his favor, and Blanche was told that she must discard her former lover from her heart. She had loved too truly, however, to obey the command, and she determined not to wed another till she had heard from his own lips that he was indeed changed.

Hernan Daggerfeldt knelt at the feet of Blanche D'Aubigné. He had seized her hand, and was pressing it with rapture to his lips, while she in vain endeavored to withdraw it.

" Rise, sir, rise," she said ; " you wrong me — you wrong him who is away — your friend, the preserver of your life. While he lives, I am his, and his alone ! "

" I do not wrong him," he answered. " His nature is fickle, and if he no longer loves you, will not woman's pride teach you to forget him ? "

" I know not that he no longer loves me," she replied.

" Did not his letter convince you ? " he asked.

" That letter ! No, sir," she replied, rising proudly from her seat, and a smile of unwonted bitterness curling her lip. " That letter was a forgery."

" On my sacred word, on my soul, it was not ! " he cried, vehemently. " It is you who wrong me and my devoted love. Be mine, and let me enjoy the only heaven I seek. If I speak not the truth, may the Powers above strike me this moment dead at your feet ! "

12

Blanche shuddered at his words. At that instant a dark form seemed to rise up between them, and to gaze with threatening aspect at Hernan, while it shielded Blanche from him. Soon it assumed the form of Edward Staunton, and beckoning Hernan to follow, slowly receded from the room. Even the deceiver trembled, and daring not to disobey, followed the phantom.

It led him through dark chambers, beneath roaring waterfalls, along dizzy heights, whence the sea-birds could scarce be seen in the depths below, on the wild shore, where the fierce waves dashed with terrific fury, while the tempest raged, and the lightnings flashed around his head, and then with a derisive shriek which sounded high above the furious turmoil, disappeared amid the boiling ocean.

"Such, traitor, shall be thy fate!" were the words it spoke.

Again Hernan dreamed that Blanche had promised to be his, — a prize bought at the cost of further perjury. Edward for long had been unheard of; he was still a rover in far-off climes. Mr. D'Aubigné was satisfied and rejoiced at the thoughts of finding a wealthy husband for his daughter. Hernan was with his intended bride when a messenger arrived, breathless with haste, to summon him to the death-bed of his parent.

He hurried thither to listen to a tale the old man falteringly whispered into his ear; it was enough to freeze up the current in his veins. A stigma was on his birth, and instant precautions were necessary, or the fatal secret would be discovered which would consign him to poverty and disgrace.

"You are my child," said the proud baronet, "yet for long my wife had borne me none; at length one came into the world and died. You took its place, and my wife

believed you to be her own offspring. The change was ill-
managed, and the deceit is discovered by one who is my
enemy, and will be yours. I fancied that no one knew it,
till some years ago he came and convinced me that he was
aware of the truth. He then told me that should you be
worthy to succeed to my rank and fortune, the secret should
die with him; but if not, my first lawful child, whom he
insisted on educating under his own inspection, should be
declared to have his rights. Though the terms seemed hard,
I was obliged to yield to his demands, and have ever since
been his slave. By his orders you were sent to sea, and will
be compelled shortly again to go; and by his orders I have
made you acquainted with the dreadful tale I have now told
you. I know him well, and you too must become his slave.
He will probably insist on your again going to sea, and you
must obey him, or rue the consequences."

Scarcely stopping to close his father's eyes, who died
shortly after this disclosure, Hernan hurried off to endeavor
to propitiate the arbitrator of his destiny. The old man was
inflexible. He insisted on his forthwith returning to sea,
and refused to sanction his marriage with Blanche. Hernan
had good cause to suspect that his character was seen
through; he dared not disobey. His appointment to the
—— frigate soon arrived, and framing an excuse to Blanche,
he prepared for his departure. Blanche received the account
without any regret, for though she was prepared to obey her
father, she did not love Hernan, as he well. knew. Her
heart was still with one whom she had been told was false
to her. The frigate on board which Hernan Daggerfeldt
was the junior lieutenant sailed for the coast of South America. Hernan felt that he was no favorite with his brother-
officers; his fierce temper and overbearing manner was one
cause, while his constant scoffs at religion and honor was

another.   When off Rio, they fell in with a frigate carrying
despatches to England.   It was a dead calm, and a boat
from her was sent on board them to learn intelligence from
home.   Two officers were in the boat; one was Staunton.
Hernan in vain endeavored to avoid him.   Staunton had a
thousand questions to ask, which Hernan might be able to
answer respecting his beloved Blanche.   Was she well?
Had she received his letters? — none of hers had reached
him.   Hernan made the most plausible answers he could
invent.   They spoke in the presence of two of his brother-
officers, and one of them, an old friend of Staunton's, knew
the truth.   Accordingly, drawing him aside, he told him at
once that he believed Hernan had been speaking falsehoods.
Staunton's indignation knew no bounds, and he taxed Hernan with his duplicity and falsehood, though the sanctity of
the quarter-deck prevented him from proceeding to extremities.   Hernan defended himself from the accusation, though
he felt that he was discovered, and he determined to revenge
himself on the man who had unmasked him to Staunton.
He, however, bided his time; but he suspected that by some
means or other more of his secrets might be known to his
shipmate.

The frigate had been for some time on the coast of
America, when, receiving some damage in a heavy gale,
she put into the harbor of —— to refit.   She lay there
for some time, and the officers were constantly, when duty
allowed, on shore.   It was a dark night, when Hernan,
accompanied by young Selwyn, the friend of Staunton,
was returning, after an excursion into the country, on
board.   They had left their horses at the town, and were
walking along the beach on foot; young Selwyn thoughtlessly alluded to Staunton and Blanche D'Aubigné, and
while he spoke the spirit of a demon entered into Hernan

Daggerfeldt's heart. A sharp cry awoke the stillness of night — a deed had been done no power on earth could recall. He fled he knew not whither; vipers seemed twining round his heart; burning coals were raining on his head, and while heavy weights were clogging his limbs, a thousand fierce bloodhounds urged him to fly. He awoke, the perspiration standing in large drops on his brow, while he gasped for breath; yet there he still lay in the loft where Juanetta had concealed him. Was all that had occurred an empty dream, or was it the re-acting of a dreadful reality?

THE FLIGHT.

The following morning Juan, or rather Hernan Daggerfeldt, was awoke by the entrance of Señor Ribiera's black slave, with a basket of provisions.

"Why does not your mistress come to me herself?" inquired Hernan, who dreaded being abandoned by the only human being in whom he could trust.

"Donna Juanetta is with her father, and till he goes out she cannot come to see you," answered the slave. "He is a stern man, and were he to discover that you are here without his leave, and that his daughter loved you, he would kill you without ceremony. Ah, señor! you do not know what these Spanish gentlemen are capable of."

"Well, you must take care that he does not discover I am here till that cursed ship in the harbor has sailed away; and now listen to me — what is your name, though?"

"Mauro, at your service, señor," said the slave.

"There, Mauro — there is a piece of gold. You shall have a larger piece by and by. It will go towards buying your freedom."

"My freedom!" muttered the African. "What does that mean?—Ah, yes, I know. It would be of no value to me now. Had it come when I was yet young, and could have returned to those I loved across the ocean, I should have prized it. Now they are all dead, and those I love best are in this house. My mistress told me to do your bidding. What is it you require of me, señor?"

"First, I wish you to procure me a suit of Spanish clothes, fit for a gentleman to appear in, and then you must take this uniform, coat, and hat, and as soon as it is dark, carry them down to the sea-shore, and place them as if the waves had thrown them there. They will certainly be discovered, and it will appear that I have been drowned, and then no further search will be made after me."

"A very good idea, señor," said Mauro, rubbing his hands with pleasure, for he was delighted to be employed in a scheme by which those in authority, whom he looked upon as oppressors, might be deceived. Such is the feeling of slaves in general.

While her father took his siesta, Juanetta visited her prisoner, and Hernan employed the time in endeavoring to convince her of his love for her, and his innocence of the crime of which he was suspected. In both he succeeded too well.

In the evening Mauro returned with the suit of clothes he had purchased; and Hernan having exchanged them for his own, pierced the latter with his sword, and deliberately drawing blood from his arm, soaked them in it.

Mauro, who well understood what he was to do, wrapped them up in a bundle, and as soon as it was dark carried them off.

We will pass over several days, during which Daggerfeldt

remained concealed without any one in the house suspecting
that he was in the garret.

At last one morning Mauro came in rubbing his hands
with delight. "You are free, señor, you are free!" he
exclaimed; "the big ship with the many guns is even now
sailing out of the harbor, and all you have got to do now
is to come down to beg Señor Ribiera's pardon for living
so long in his house without his leave, and to marry his
daughter."

"Curses go with her!" ejaculated Hernan, fiercely. "I
will still wreak my vengeance on some of those who sail on
board her. But tell me, Mauro, did your lady say I might
venture into her father's presence?"

"Not exactly, señor, and perhaps it might be as well to
prepare the old gentleman for your appearance, as he yet
believes, like the rest of the world, that you are food for the
sharks."

"Then, my good Mauro, go and urge her to come here
to concert the best way to release me. I pant once more to
stretch my limbs on the open shore, and to breathe the pure
air of heaven."

Some time elapsed after the slave had gone to fulfil his
mission before Juanetta appeared. She then came with a
sad countenance and tears in her eyes.

"Oh, señor!" she said, "the ship has sailed, and I hoped
that the news would have made us both happy; but, alas!
when I told my father what I had done, and how I had
preserved your life from those tyrants, he stormed and raved,
and declared that I had behaved very wickedly, and that he
would deliver you up to the authorities. Fortunately I did
not tell him that you were still here; but, as Mauro had
cautioned me, I led him to suppose that you had made your
escape up the country."

"That was a happy idea of yours, my Juanetta," said Daggerfeldt. "Your father must in some way be gained to our wishes. You are his only child, and he is enormously rich, you say — plenty of gold stored up in bars in his house. Stay, I must think over the subject. Sit down by me, and I will unfold my plans."

He was silent for some time, and then he continued, while Juanetta, who was incapable of fathoming the depths of his deceit, listened to him without suspicion.

"Now, Juanetta, dear, you must not be startled by the plan I am going to propose. From what you tell me, your father is prejudiced against me, and will not willingly give his consent to our marriage, so we must marry first, and ask his forgiveness afterwards. He will·then, I have no doubt, pardon us, and give us as much gold as we may require. Now, as I have no money, and no priest will marry us without, we must contrive to borrow some of his. We can return it afterwards, you know. I propose, therefore, that you show me some night where he keeps his gold, and then I will take a little of it, as much as we may require, and then we will fly together to the nearest place where we can find a priest to unite us. Shall we not do so, dearest? The plan may seem to you dangerous and wrong, but let no fears alarm you. We will afterwards explain our motives, and the old man will forgive you."

Poor Juanetta, had she known this world and the wickedness in it, would have flown with horror from the betrayer ; but she was ignorant of its evil ways — she listened and hesitated. No arguments which sophistry could invent were left untried. The deceiver was victorious.

That night the keys of the old man's money-chests were stolen from beneath his pillow. The following morning he found them where he had placed them, and, unsuspecting, did not think of counting his hoarded gold.

His daughter dared not again speak to him of the stranger she had preserved. He believed that he had long ago escaped into the interior, and forbore to make further inquiries about him. Daggerfeldt was no longer an inhabitant of his house.

A foreign merchant, of considerable wealth at command, had arrived, it was said, from the interior, and had taken up his abode in the town. He had become the purchaser of a large schooner, which was taking in a cargo of goods for the African coast. Don Manuel Ribiera, on hearing this, invited the stranger to his house, for he himself was a dealer in slaves, and wished to make some arrangements respecting the return cargo.

On the unexpected appearance of the stranger, Donna Juanetta started ; but her presence of mind quickly returned, for she felt the importance of discretion. Her father observed her momentary confusion, and apologized to his guest, attributing it to her being unaccustomed to receive strangers.

Soon afterwards, some business called Señor Ribiera from the room, and Juanetta was left alone with their guest.

" Oh, Juan, how could you venture here? " she exclaimed to the pretended merchant, who was no other than Daggerfeldt. " My father will discover you, and your ruin and mine must follow."

" No fear, dearest. He is blinded by the prospect of profit," answered Hernan. " He has, too, scarcely seen me before, and then only in uniform. It was also necessary to run some risks to gain our ends. I have made all the necessary arrangements, and this night you are to be mine.

The cost, however, has been considerable, and we must borrow a little more from your father's money-chests to pay the priest who is to unite us."

Daggerfeldt had scarcely arranged his plans with his credulous dupe when Señor Ribiera returned. As may be supposed, he was induced to arrange a plan to dispose of his slaves on his return on terms highly advantageous to the old slave-dealer; and after being entertained magnificently, he was conducted to his sleeping apartment. Instead of retiring to rest, Daggerfelt employed himself in loading his pistols and listening attentively for the arrival of some one apparently, but not a sound disturbed the silence of the night. At last, losing patience, he opened his door, and was met by Juanetta. The poor girl was pale and trembling.

"Here are the keys," she said; "but, oh, señor, I do not like this work — surely it is very wicked!"

"Pretty fool," he answered, abruptly, "it is too late to recede now. There is nothing to alarm you. Wait in this room till I return." Saying this, he was about to leave her, when footsteps were heard approaching the house. He listened attentively.

"It is right," he observed; "those are some people I have engaged to assist us in our flight."

Just then some men sprang into the room through the open window. Poor Juanetta uttered a cry of terror, but it was instantly silenced by Daggerfeldt, who ordered two of the men to take charge of her while the rest followed him to the chamber of Don Ribiera. The unhappy girl listened, horror-struck and bewildered. There was a cry and a groan, and soon afterwards Daggerfeldt returned, accompanied by the men carrying several heavy chests between them.

"Onward," said the traitor, " and you, my fair lady, must accompany us. The ship is waiting to bear us to far-off lands, where you may become my bride."

The next morning, the new slave schooner was seen in the offing, and when people went to the house of Don Ribiera, he was found dead in his bed, his money-chests were gone, and his daughter had fled, while his slaves were only just awaking from a heavy sleep, for which none of them could account. Mauro, too, had disappeared, and all the watch-dogs were dead.

CHAPTER XIV.

THE CHASE.

WE left her Britannic Majesty's brig " Sylph" in chase of a strange sail on the coast of Africa. The wind was from the westward, and she was standing on a bowline to the southward, with the coast clearly seen broad on the lee-beam. Captain Staunton ordered every expedient he could think of to be tried to increase the speed of his vessel, for the stranger was evidently a very fast sailer, though it was at first difficult to say whether or not she was increasing her distance from them. At all events, the British crew soon saw that it would be hopeless to expect to come up with the stranger before dark, for the sun was just sinking below the horizon, and the thick mists were already rising over the wooded shore, and yet they appeared to be no nearer to her than they were when they first made sail in chase. It was a magnificent sailing breeze, just sufficient for both vessels to carry their topgallant-sails and royals without fear of springing their spars, and the sea was per-fectly smooth, merely rippled over by the playful wind. In-deed, as the two vessels glided proudly along over the calm waters, they appeared rather to be engaged in some friendly race than anxious to lead each other to destruction. All the officers of the " Sylph" were on deck with their glasses constantly at their eyes, as the last rays of the sun tinged

188

the royals of the chase, and so clearly was every spar and rope defined through that pure atmosphere, that it was difficult to believe that she was not within range of their guns. Captain Staunton and his first lieutenant walked together on the weather side of the deck.

" Do you think she is the ' Espanto,' Mr. Collins? " asked the captain.

" I have no doubt about it, sir," answered the officer addressed. " I watched her narrowly when we chased her off Loanda the last time she was on the coast, and I pulled round her several times when she lay in the harbor of St. Jago da Cuba, just a year and a half ago."

" She has had a long run of iniquity," said the captain ; " two years our cruisers have been on the look-out for her, and have never yet been able to overhaul her."

" That Daggerfeldt must be a desperate villain, if report speaks true," observed the lieutenant ; " I think, sir, you seemed to say you once knew him."

" I did, to my cost," answered Captain Staunton ; " that man's life has been a tissue of treachery and deceit from his earliest days. He once disgraced our noble service. He murdered a shipmate and ran from his ship on the coast of America. It was reported for some time that he was dead, by his clothes having been found torn and bloody on the shore, and his family, fortunately for them, believed the story. It was, however, afterwards discovered that he had been sheltered by a Spanish girl, and, in gratitude for his preservation, he carried her off, robbed her father of all his wealth, and either frightened him to death or smothered him. The unhappy girl has, it is said, ever since sailed with him, and it is to be hoped she is not aware of the enormity of his guilt. Pirate and slaver, he has committed every atrocity human nature is capable of."

" A very perfect scoundrel, in truth, sir," answered Mr. Collins. " It was said, too, I remember, that he was going to marry a very beautiful girl in England. What an escape for her ! "

" No, he was not going to marry her ! " exclaimed the captain, with unusual vehemence. " Her father, perhaps, wished it, but she would never have consented. Collins, you are my friend, and I will tell you the truth. That lady, Blanche D'Aubigné, was engaged to me, and never would have broken her faith to me while she believed me alive. By a series of forgeries, Daggerfeldt endeavored to persuade her that I was false to her, though she would 'not believe him. On my return home she is to become my wife. We were to have married directly I got my promotion, but I was so immediately sent out here that I was able to spend but one day in her society. I wished to have secured her a pension in case this delightful climate should knock me on the head, but she would not hear of it. Poor girl, I have left her what little fortune I possess, Collins ; I could not do less. Those who live on shore at ease can't say we enjoy too much of the pleasures of home, or don't earn the Queen's biscuit. Bless her Majesty ! "

" I don't know that, sir. There are, I hear, though I never fell in with any of them, a set of lying traitors at home, who say we are no better than pirates, and want to do away with the navy altogether. If they were to succeed in their roguish projects, there would be an end of Old England altogether, say I."

" They never will succeed, Collins, depend upon that. There is still too much sense left in the country ; but if her Majesty's government were to employ her cruisers in any other part of the world than on this pestiferous coast, the cause of humanity would benefit by the change. For

every prize we capture, ten escape, and our being here
scarcely raises the price of slaves in the Cuban and Brazilian markets five dollars a head ; while the Spaniards and
Portuguese, notwithstanding their treaties, do all they can
to favor the traffic. Do we gain on the chase, do you think,
Collins?"

"Not a foot, I fear, sir," answered the lieutenant.
"That brig is a fast craft, and though I don't believe, as
some of the people do, that the skipper has signed a con-
tract with Davy Jones, she is rightly called by them the
'Black Slaver.'"

"If the breeze freshens, we may overhaul her, but if not,
she may double on us in the dark, and again get away,"
observed the captain. "Take care a bright look-out is
kept for'ard."

"Ay, ay, sir," answered the lieutenant, repeating the
order and adjusting his night-glass ; "she hasn't altered her
course, at all events."

By this time daylight had totally disappeared, although a
pale crescent moon in the clear sky afforded light sufficient
for objects to be distinguished at some distance. Few of
the officers turned in, but the watch below were ordered to
their hammocks to recruit their strength for the services
they might be required to perform on the morrow, as Captain Staunton had determined, should the wind fail, to attack
the chase in his boats. When the enemy is well armed and
determined, this a very dangerous operation, and in the
present instance there could be no doubt that he who commanded the "Black Slaver" would not yield without a desperate resistance. Look-outs were stationed at the mast-
heads as well as forward, and every eye was employed in
endeavoring to keep her in sight — no easy task with the
increasing darkness — for a light mist was gradually filling

the atmosphere, and the moon itself was sinking into the ocean. The breeze, however, appeared to be increasing; the brig felt its force, and heeled gracefully over to it as the water bubbled and frothed against her bows.

"What are the odds we don't catch her after all?" said young Wildgrave to his messmate; "I hate these long chases, when one never comes up with the enemy."

"So do I," answered his companion. "But to tell you the truth, I have a presentiment that we shall come up with her this time, and bring her to action too. She has escaped us twice before, and the third time will, I think, be fatal to her. By-the-by, where is she though?"

"Fore-yard, there!" sang out the first lieutenant, "can you see the chase?"

"I did a moment ago, sir;—no, sir, I can see her no-where."

A similar answer was returned from the other look-outs. She was nowhere visible.

THE SLAVER.

The "Black Slaver" well deserved her name. Her hull was black, without the usual relief of a colored ribbon; her masts and spars were of the same ebon hue, her cargo was black, and surely her decks were dark as the darkest night. She was a very large vessel, certainly upwards of three hundred tons, and also heavily armed with a long brass gun amidships, and ten long nines in battery, besides small brass swivel-guns mounted on her quarter, to aid in defending her against an attack in boats.

Her crew was composed of every nation under the sun, for crime makes all men brothers, but brothers who, Cain-like, were ready any moment to imbrue their hands in each other's blood; and their costume was as varied as their

language — a mixture of that of many nations. A mongrel
Spanish, however, was the language in which all orders
were issued, as being that spoken by the greater number of
the people. She was a very beautiful and powerful vessel,
and all the arrangements on board betokened strict attention
to nautical discipline. For more than two years she had
run her evil career with undeserved success, and her captain
and owner was reputed to be a wealthy man, already in possession of several estates in Cuba. Slaving was his most
profitable and safe occupation, mixed up with a little piracy,
as occasion offered, without fear of detection. Several
slavers had unaccountably disappeared, which had certainly
not been taken by English cruisers, and others had returned
to the coast complaining that they had been robbed of their
slaves by a large armed schooner, which had put on board a
few bales of colored cottons, with an order to them to go
back and take in a fresh cargo of human beings. The
" Espanto " was more than suspected of being the culprit ;
but she was always so disguised that it was difficult to bring
the accusation home to her, while they themselves being ille-
gally employed, could obtain no redress in a court of law.

She had for some time been cruising, as usual, in the
hopes of picking up a cargo without taking the trouble of
looking into the coast for it, when, weary of waiting, and
being short of water and provisions, the captain determined
to run the risk of procuring one by the usual method.

From the ruse practised by the " Sylph," she was not seen
by his look-outs till he was nearly close up to her. He was
in no way alarmed, however, for he recognized the British
man-of-war, and knowing the respective rate of sailing of
the two vessels, felt certain, if the wind held, to be able to
walk away from her. To make certain what she was, he
had stood on some time after he had first seen her, a circum-

13

stance which had, as we mentioned, somewhat surprised
Captain Staunton and his officers. Having ascertained that
the sail inside of him was the "Sylph," he hauled his wind,
and making all sail, before an hour of the first watch had
passed, aided by the darkness, he had completely run her
out of sight. When he stood in he had been making for
the Pongos River ; but being prevented from getting in there,
he determined to run for the Coanza River, some forty miles
further to the south, before day-break, and as the mouth is
narrow, and entirely concealed by trees, he had many
chances in his favor of remaining concealed there while the
British man-of-war passed by. A slave-agent, also, of his
resided in the neighborhood, who would be able to supply
him at the shortest notice, and at moderate prices, with a
cargo of his fellow-beings. At this rendezvous he knew
there would be a look-out for him, and that there were pilots
ready to assist him in entering the river.

"Square the yards and keep her away, Antonio," he sung
out to his first mate, a ferocious-looking mulatto, who was
conning the vessel. "We are just abreast of —— Point,
and Diogo, if he has his eyes open, ought to see us."

The helm was kept up, the yards were squared, and the
vessel stood stem on towards the shore.

Before long the dark line of a tree-fringed coast was visible, when she was again brought to the wind ; her lower
sails were furled, and she was hove-to under her topsails.

"We must make a signal, or the lazy blacks will never
find us out, señor captain," observed Antonio to his chief.

"Yes, we must run the risk : we shall not be in before
daylight if we do not, and the enemy will scarcely distinguish from what direction the report of the gun comes. Be
smart about it though."

A gun from the lee quarter was accordingly discharged,

the dull echoes from which were heard rebounding along the shore, and directly afterwards a blue-light was fired, the bright flame giving a spectre-like appearance to the slaver and her evil-doing crew. They might well have been taken for one of those phantom barks said to cruise about the ocean either to warn mariners of coming danger or to lure them to destruction.

Soon afterwards a small light was seen to burst out, as it seemed, from the dark line, and to glide slowly over the water towards them. Gradually it increased, and as it approached nearer, it was seen to proceed from a fire burning in the bow of a large canoe pulled by a dozen black fellows. When it came alongside, two of them scrambled on board, and recognizing the captain, welcomed him to the coast. Their language was a curious mixture of Spanish, Portuguese, English, and African.

" Ah, señor captain, berry glad you et Espanto, come esta nocha, viento es favoravel, for run up de river Diogo — me vos on the look-out you, sabe."

Having thus delivered himself, the chief pilot went aft to the helm with much the same air as one of his European brethren, habited in Flushing coat and tarpaulin hat, although the only garment he boasted was a blue shirt, secured at the waist by a piece of spun-yarn, and a red handkerchief bound round his head.

" Up with the helm, then square away the yards ! " sung out the captain, and the vessel, under the direction of the negro, was standing dead on to the apparently unbroken line of dark shore.

It required great confidence in the honesty and knowledge of the pilot for the crew not to believe that he was running the schooner on shore, for such a thing had been more than once before done.

"Remember," whispered Antonio, as he passed him, "if the vessel touches, my pistol sends a ball through your head."

"No tien duvida, señor, contremestre," answered Quacko, quite unmoved by the threat, as being one to which he was well accustomed.

"Viento favoravel, rio fundo. Have de anchor pronto to let go."

The bowsprit of the schooner was now almost among the mangrove bushes.

"Stivordo!" sung out the pilot.

A yellow line of sand was seen over her quarter. This seemed to spring up from the sea on either side, like dark, shapeless phantoms, eager to destroy the slaver's crew, the spirits of those their cruelty had sent from this world. Taller and taller they grew, for so calmly did the vessel glide on, that she appeared not to move, yet the broad open sea was completely shut out from the view of those on board; a narrow dark line, in which the reflection of a star was here and there visible, was the only water seen as still, on the schooner moved.

"Bombordo!" sung out the pilot.

The helm was put to port, and the schooner glided into another passage, her yards, as they were squared away or braced up to meet the alterations in her course, almost brushing the branches of the lofty trees. For some minutes more she ran on, till the stream grew suddenly wider, and a little bay, formed by a bend of the shore, appeared on the starboard hand, into which she glided. The anchor was let go, the topsails were furled, and so entirely was she concealed by the overhanging boughs, that a boat might have passed down the centre of the stream without seeing her.

At dawn the next morning a busy scene was going on on

board and round the slaver. Her crew, aided by a number of negroes, were employed in setting up her rigging and fitting slave-decks, while several canoes were assisting her boats in bringing water and provisions alongside. Thus they were employed without cessation for two days. There was no play, it was all hard, earnest work. It is a pity they were not laboring in a good cause instead of a bad one.

In the mean time the King of ——, as he was called, in reality the principal slave-dealer and greatest rogue in the district, was collecting the negroes who had been kidnapped by him or his allies, from whom he had bought them in the neighboring provinces — some as they were quietly fishing in their canoes on the coast, others as they were seated beneath the shade of the palm-tree in their native forest, or were coming from the far interior with a load of oil or ivory, to sell to the nearest trader — untutored savages, who perhaps had never before seen the face of a white man, or the blue dancing ocean. It is no wonder that they paint the Devil white, and believe the sea is the passage to his realms. Eight hundred human beings were thus collected to be conveyed in that fell bark to the Far West, there to wear out their lives in hopeless slavery.

The greater part of the fourth day was spent in receiving half the number on board, and stowing them below. This operation was performed by men whose especial trade it is. The unhappy wretches are compelled to sit down with their legs bent under them, so closely packed that they cover but little more space than the length of their feet, between decks, little more than a yard high ; and thus they remain, bolted down to the decks, the whole voyage, a few only being allowed to come up at a time to be aired, while the smallest quantity of water possible is afforded them to quench their burning thirst.

THE CAPTURE.

The work for the day was nearly concluded, and the captain of the slaver was walking by himself beneath the awning spread over the after-part of the deck, when he observed a canoe suddenly dart out of the main stream into the bay where the schooner lay concealed. It was soon alongside, when a black jumped on board.

"Señor capitan, you must be pronto," he said. "Big man-of-war come, big canoe, mucho hombres, come up river."

"Ah, have they found me out?" muttered the captain to himself. "I'll give them a warm reception if they do come. Very well, Queebo," he said aloud, "now pull back and watch them narrowly. Take care they don't see you, and come and report their movements to me."

At a signal all the crew were summoned on board, the awning was handed, boarding-nettings were triced up, the guns were double-shotted and run out, and a thick screen of boughs was carried across the part of the bay so as still further to conceal the schooner from the eye of any stranger. Two guns were also sent on shore and planted in battery, so as to command the entrance of the bay. Every other precaution was likewise taken to avoid discovery; all fires were extinguished, and the blacks were ordered to remove from the neighborhood.

By the time these arrangements had been made, the scout returned to give notice that two boats had entered the river, and were exploring one of the numerous passages of the stream. The captain on this ordered the scout to remain on board, lest he might betray their whereabouts to the enemy. He had no wish to destroy the boats, as so doing would not benefit him; concealment, not fighting, was his object. When night, however, came on, he sent out the scout to gain further intelligence. Scarcely had the man gone, when he returned, and noiselessly stepped on deck.

"Hist, señor, hist!" he whispered. "They are close at hand, little dreaming we are near them."

"Whereabouts?" inquired the captain.

"On the other side of the long island which divides the middle from the southern stream," was the substance of the reply.

"We'll attack them then, and either kill or make them all prisoners. They may be useful as hostages," muttered the captain, and calling Antonio to him, he ordered him to man two boats with the most trustworthy of their people, and carefully to muffle the oars. This done, both boats left the schooner, under his command, in the direction indicated by the scout.

They pulled across the channel to a thickly-wooded island indicated by the scout. The negro landed, and in a few minutes came back.

"Dere dey are, señor," he whispered; "you may kill all fast asleep; berry good time now; no make noise."

On hearing this, the slavers, all of whom were armed to the teeth, advanced cautiously across the island, by a path with which Queebo seemed well acquainted. The black pointed between the trees, and there was seen the head of a man, fast asleep in the stern-sheets of a boat. Just then a light rustling noise was heard, and a figure was seen advancing close up to where the slavers were crouching down, ready for the command of their officer to fire.

He advanced slowly, looking out for the very path apparently by which they had gained the spot. He reached within almost an arm's length of the captain. The impulse was irresistible; and before the stranger was aware any one was near him, he was felled to the ground, and a handkerchief was passed over his mouth, so that he could not utter a cry for help. Two other men, who were doing duty as sentinels on shore, were in like manner surprised and gagged, without uttering a sound to alarm the rest. The slavers then advanced close up to the nearest boat, and pouring a volley from their deadly trabucos into her, killed or wounded nearly all her crew. A larger boat was moored at some little distance farther on, and her people being aroused by the firing, they at once shoved off into the stream, which the survivors of the other also succeeded in doing. They then opened a fire on the slavers, but sheltered as they were among the trees, it was ineffectual.

The contest was kept up for some time; but reduced in strength as the crews of the boats were, they were at last obliged to retreat, while the slavers returned with their prisoners to the schooner. As the slavers' boats were left on the other side of the island, which extended for more than a mile towards the sea, they were unable to follow their retreating enemy had they been so inclined; but in fact they did not relish the thought of coming in actual contact with British seamen, as they had good reason in believing the enemy to be, although weakened and dispirited by defeat.

When the prisoners, who had not uttered a word, were handed up on deck, the captain ordered lights to be brought, for he had no longer any fear of being discovered. One evidently, by his uniform, was an officer; the other two were seamen. The captain paced the deck in the interval before lights were brought, grinding his teeth and clinching his fists with rage, as he muttered to himself,—

"He shall die — he wears that hated uniform: it reminds me of what I once was. Oh, this hell within me! blood must quench its fire."

A seaman now brought aft a lantern ; its glare fell as well on the features of the prisoner as on that of the slave captain. Both started.

" Staunton ! " ejaculated the latter.

" Daggerfeldt ! " exclaimed the prisoner.

" You know me, then? " said the captain of the slaver, bitterly ; " it will avail you little, though. I had wished it had been another man ; but no matter — you must take your chance."

The slaver's crew were now thronging aft.

" Well, meos amigos," he continued, in a fierce tone, " what is to be done with these spies? You are the judges, and must decide the case."

" Enforca-los — hang them, hang them — at least the officer. The other two may possibly enter, and they may be of service : we want good seamen to work the vessel, and these English generally are so."

" You hear what your fate is to be," said Daggerfeldt, turning to Captain Staunton. " You had better prepare for it. You may have some at home to regret your loss. If you have any messages, I will take care to transmit them. It is the only favor I can do you."

While he spoke, a bitter sneer curled his lip, and his voice assumed a taunting tone, which he could not repress.

The gallant officer, proud in his consciousness of virtue, confronted the villain boldly.

" I would receive no favor, even my life, from one whose very name is a disgrace to humanity. Even if the message I were to send was conveyed correctly, it would be polluted by the bearer. It would be little satisfaction for my friends to know that I was murdered in an African creek by the hands of a rascally slaver."

While Staunton was uttering these words, which he did

in very bitterness of spirit, for, knowing the character of
the wretch with whom he had to deal, he had not the remotest hope of saving either his own life or that of his
people, the rage of Daggerfeldt was rising till it surpassed
his control.

" Silence ! " he thundered, " or I will brain you on the
spot ! "

But Staunton stood unmoved.

" Madman, would you thus repay me for the life I saved ? "
he asked, calmly.

" A curse on you for having saved it," answered the
pirate, fiercely, returning his sword, which he had half
drawn from its scabbard. " My hand, however, shall not
do the deed. Here, Antonio Diogo, here are the spies who
wish to interfere in our trade, and would send us all to
prison, or to the gallows, if they could catch us."

" The end of a rope and a dance on nothing for the
officer, say I," answered the mulatto mate. " See what his
followers will do ; speak to them in their own lingo, captain,
and ask them whether they choose to walk overboard or
join us."

While he was speaking, some of the crew brought aft the
two British seamen, with their hands lashed behind them.
Others, headed by Antonio, immediately seized Captain
Staunton, and led him to the gangway, one of the men
running aloft to reeve a rope through the studding-sail-sheet-
block on the main-yard. Staunton well knew what the
preparations meant, but he trembled not ; his whole anxiety
was for the boats' crews he had led in the expedition which
had ended so unfortunately, and for the two poor fellows
whose lives, he feared, were about also to be sacrificed by
the miscreants.

The British seamen watched what was going forward,

and by the convulsive workings of their features, and the exertions they were making to free their arms, were evidently longing to strike a blow to rescue him. Daggerfeldt was better able to confront them than he had been to face Staunton.

"You are seamen belonging to a man-of-war outside this river, and you came here to interfere with our affairs?"

"You've hit it to an affigraphy, my bo'," answered one of the men, glad, at all events, to get the use of his tongue. "We belongs to her Majesty's brig ' Sylph,' and we came into this here cursed hole to take you or any other slaver we could fall in with ; and now you knows what I am, I'll just tell you what you are — a runaway scoundrel of a piccarooning villain, whom no honest man would consort with, or even speak to, for that matter, except to give him a bit of his mind ; and if you're not drowned, or blown up sky high, you'll be hung, as you deserve, as sure as you're as big a rascal as ever breathed. Now, put that in your pipe, my bo', and smoke it."

While he was thus running on, to the evident satisfaction of his shipmate, who, indifferent to their danger, seemed mightily to enjoy the joke, Daggerfeldt in vain endeavored to stop him.

"Silence ! " he shouted, " or you go overboard this moment ! "

"You must bawl louder than that, my bo', if you wants to frighten Jack Hopkins, let me tell you," answered the undaunted seaman. "What is it you want of us? Come, out with it ; some villany, I'll warrant."

The captain of the slaver ground his teeth with fury, but he dared not kill the man who was bearding him, for he could not explain to his crew the nature of the offence,

a very venial one in their eyes, and he wanted some good
seamen.

" I overlook your insolence," he answered, restraining his
passion. " My crew are your judges. You have been convicted of endeavoring to capture us, and they give you your
choice of joining us, or of going overboard ; the dark stream
alongside swarms with alligators. That fate is too good for
your captain : he is to be hung."

" Why, what a cursed idiot you must be to suppose we'd
ship with such a pretty set of scoundrels as you and your
men are," answered Jack Hopkins, with a laugh. " I speak
for myself and for Bob Short, too. It's all right, Bob; I
suppose?" he said, turning to his companion. " There's no
use shilly-shallying with these blackguards."

" Ay, ay ; I'm ready for what you are," replied Bob
Short, who had gained his name from the succinctness of
his observations apparently, rather than from his stature,
for he was six feet high, while the name by which Jack
Hopkins was generally known on board was Peter Palaver,
from his inveterate habits of loquacity.

" Well, then, look ye here, Mr. Daggerfeldt, I knowed
you many years ago for an ill-begotten spawn of you knows
what, and I knows you now for the biggest scoundrel un-
hung, so you must just take the compliments I've got to give
you. Now for the matter of dying, I'd rather die with a
brave, noble fellow like our skipper than live in company
with a man who has murdered his messmate, has seduced
the girl who sheltered him from justice, and would now
hang the man who saved his life. Your favors ! I'll have
none on 'em."

The fierce pirate and slaver stood abashed before the
wild outbreak of the bold sailor, but quickly recovering
himself, livid and trembling with rage, he shouted out to
his crew,—

"Heave these fools of Englishmen overboard; they know more of our secrets than they ought, and will not join us. Send this talkiug fellow first."

"If it comes to that, I can find my tongue too, let me tell you," exclaimed Bob Short; "you're a murderous, rascally, thieving" —

"Heave them both together," shouted Daggerfeldt.

"Stay," said Antonio, who was refined in his cruelty; "let them have the pleasure of seeing their captain hang first, since they are so fond of him. He well knows what their fate will be, and perhaps he would rather they went overboard than joined us."

"Do as you like, but let it be done quickly," answered Daggerfeldt. "I'm sick of this work, and we must be preparing to get out of the river, or their friends will be sending in here to look for us."

Hopkins and Short did not understand a word of this conversation, and finding themselves brought close up to where their captain stood engaged in his devotions, and preparing like a brave man for inevitable death, they believed that they were to share his fate.

"Well, I'm blowed if that ain't more than I expected of the beggars," whispered Jack Hopkins to his companion; "they're going to do the thing that's right after all, and launch us in our last cruise in the same way as the captain."

"Jack, can you pray?" asked Bob Short.

"Why, for the matter of that I was never much of a hand at it," answered Jack; "but when I was a youngster I was taught to thank God for all his mercies, and I do so still. Why do you ask?"

"I was thinking as how as the skipper is taking a spell at it, whether we might ask him just to put in a word for us. He knows more about it, and a captain of a man-of-war

must have a greater chance of being attended to than one
of us, you see, Jack."

Poor Bob could never thus have exerted himself had he
not felt that he should only have a few words more to speak
in this life. Jack looked at him in surprise.

"I'll ask him, Bob, I'll ask him; but you know as how
the parson says, in the country we are going to all men
are equal, and so I suppose we ought to pray for ourselves."

"But we are still in this world, Jack," argued the other;
"Captain Staunton is still our captain, and we are before
the mast."

He spoke loud, and Captain Staunton had apparently
overheard the conversation, for he smiled and looked towards
them. He had been offering up a prayer to the throne on
high for mercy for the failings of the two honest fellows,
whose ignorance it was now too late to enlighten. Antonio
was a pious Catholic, and, villain as he was, he was unwilling not to give the chance of a quiet passage into the other
world to his victims.

"What are you about there?" shouted Daggerfeldt; "is
this work never to end?"

"The men are praying, señor, before they slip their cables
for eternity," answered Antonio.

"Is there an eternity?" muttered the pirate, and shuddered.

On Captain Staunton's turning his head, on which the
light from the lantern fell strongly, Antonio believed it was
the signal that he was prepared,—"Hoist away!" he
shouted, in Spanish; but at that instant a light female form
rushed forth from the cabin, and seizing the whip, held
it forcibly down with one hand while she disengaged the
noose from the captain's neck.

"Oh, Juan! have you not murders enough on your head

already that you must commit another in cold blood?" she exclaimed, turning to Daggerfeldt, "and that other on one who saved your life at the risk of his own. I knew him — before all my misery began, and recognized him at once. If you persist, I leave you; you know me well, I fear not to die; Antonio, you dare not disobey me. Unreeve that rope, and leave me to settle with our captain regarding these men."

The slaver's crew stood sulky and with frowning aspect around her, yet they in no way interrupted her proceedings, while Daggerfeldt stood a silent spectator in the after-part of the vessel.

"Unreeve that rope! again I say," she exclaimed, stamping on the deck with her foot. The order was obeyed without the captain's interference. "Your lives are safe for the present," she said, addressing the Englishmen. "I know that man's humor, and he dares not now contradict me. I am the only thing who yet clings to him, the only one he thinks who loves him, the only being in whom he can place his trust; that explains my power." She spoke hurriedly and low, so that Staunton alone could hear her, and there was scorn in her tone. "Cast those men loose," she continued, turning to the crew, while with her own hands she undid the cords which lashed Staunton's arms, and as she did so she whispered, "Keep together, and edge towards the arms-chest. There are those on board who will aid me if any attempt is made to injure you."

Saying this she approached the captain of the slaver; she touched his arm: "Juan," she said, in a softened tone, totally different from that in which she had hitherto spoken; "I am wayward, and have my fancies. I felt certain that your death would immediately follow that of those men. I was asleep in my cabin, and dreamed that you were struggling in the waves, and they, seizing hold of you, were about to drag you down with them."

Daggerfeldt looked down at her as she stood in a supplicating attitude before him. " You are fanciful, Juanetta; but you love me, girl."

" Have I not proved it?" she answered in a tone of sadness ; "you will save the lives of these men?"

" I tell you I will. We will carry them in chains to Cuba, and there sell them as slaves."

" You must let them go free here," she answered.

" Impossible, Juanetta ; do you wish to betray me?" he asked, fiercely. " Go to your cabin. The men shall not be hurt, and they will be better off than the blacks on board."

She was silent, and then retired to her cabin, speaking on her way a word to a negro who stood near the entrance. " Mauro," she said, " watch those men, and if you observe any signs of treachery, let me know."

The black signified that he comprehended her wishes, and would obey them.

THE ESCAPE.

Captain Staunton and his companions were not allowed to remain long at liberty ; for as soon as the lady had retired, at a sign from Daggerfeldt, the slaver's crew again attempted to lash their arms behind them, not, however, without some resistance on the part of Hopkins and Short. The most zealous in this work was the negro Mauro, who contrived, as he was passing a rope round Captain Staunton's arm, to whisper in his ear, " Make no resistance, señor, it is useless. You have friends near you. Tell your followers to keep quiet. They can do themselves no good."

Staunton accordingly told his men to follow his example, when they quietly submitted to their fate. Before this, he had contemplated the possibility of their being able to succeed in getting arms from the arms-chest, and either selling their lives dearly, or jumping overboard and attempting to reach the shore. In most slavers the lower deck is devoted entirely to the slaves and the provisions, the men sleeping under a topgallant-forecastle, or sometimes on the open deck, and the captain and mates under the poop deck. There was, therefore, no spare place in which to confine the prisoners, and they were accordingly told to take up their quarters under an awning stretched between two guns in the waist. This was better accommodation than they could have expected, for not only were they sheltered partially from the dew, but were screened from the observation of the crew, and were not subject to the suffocating heat of the between-decks.

A night may, however, be more agreeably spent than on a hard plank, up an African river, with a prospect of being sent to feed the alligators in the morning, and the certainty of a long separation from one's friends and country, not to speak of the nine hundred and ninety-nine chances out of a thousand of one's losing one's health, if not one's life, by the insatiable yellow-fever.

The reflections of Captain Staunton were most bitter. He thought not of himself, but of her he had loved so long and faithfully ; she would believe him dead, and he knew how poignant would be her grief. He felt sure that she would not be faithless to his memory, but months, even years, might pass before he might escape, or have the means of informing her of his existence. While these ideas were passing through his mind, it was impossible to sleep. There were, too, the midnight noises of the African clime : the croaking of frogs, the chirrup of birds, the howl of wild beasts, the cries, if not of fish, of innumerable amphibious

14

animals of flesh and fowl, and, more than all, the groans
and moans of the unhappy beings confined in their noisome
sepulchre below; all combined to make a concert sounding
as might the distant echoes of Pandemonium. At length,
however, towards the morning, nature gave way, and he
forgot himself and his unfortunates in slumber. It had not
lasted many minutes when he was aroused by a hand placed
on his shoulder, while a soft hush was whispered in his ear.
At the same time he felt that there was a knife employed
in cutting the ropes which bound his arms. Something
told him that the person performing this office was a friend,
so he did not attempt to speak, but quietly waited to learn
what he was next expected to do. Again the voice whispered in his ear, —

"Arouse your companions, if possible, but beware that
they do not speak aloud; caution them in their ear as I did
you — their heads are near where yours lies."

The voice which spoke, from its silvery tones, Staunton
felt certain was that of a female, as was the hand which
loosened his bonds. Without hesitation, therefore, he did
as he was desired, and putting his mouth down to Hopkins's
ear, he ordered him on his life not to utter a word. Jack was
awake in a moment, and alive to the state of affairs. They
had more difficulty in arousing Bob Short, who uttered several very treacherous groans and grunts before he was quite
awake, though he fortunately did not speak. Had Captain
Staunton been aware that a sentry was actually posted outside the screen, he would have trembled for their safety.
Fortunately the man was fast asleep, reclining against the
bulwarks — a fact ascertained by Jack Hopkins, who poked
his head from under the screen to ascertain how the coast
lay. Not a sound was heard to give notice that any of the
crew were stirring on deck. Staunton, feeling that his best

course was to trust implicitly to his unseen guide, waited till he received directions how to proceed. He soon felt himself pulled gently by the arm towards the nearest port, which was sufficiently raised to enable him to pass through it. On putting his head out, he perceived through the obscurity a canoe with a single person in it, hanging on alongside the schooner. His guide dropped noiselessly into it, and took her place in the stern; Staunton cautiously followed, and seating himself in the afterthwart, found a paddle put into his hands; Jack and Bob required no one to tell them what to do, but quickly also took their places in the boat. As soon as they were seated, the man who was first in the canoe shoved her off gently from the side of the schooner; and while the guide directed their course, began to paddle off rapidly towards the centre of the stream. So dexterously did he apply his oar, that not a splash was heard, though the canoe darted quickly along through the ink-like current without leaving even a ripple in her wake. Not a word was uttered by any of the party; every one seemed to be aware of the importance of silence, and even Peter Palaver forebore to cut a joke, which he felt very much inclined to do, as he found himself increasing his distance from the black slaver.

THE PURSUIT.

The canoe held her silent course down the dark and mirror-like stream towards the sea. Not a breath of wind moved the leaves of the lofty palm-trees which towered above their heads, casting their tall shadows on the calm waters below, while here and there a star was seen piercing as it were through the thick canopy of branches; the air was hot and oppressive, and a noxious exhalation rose from the muddy banks, whence the tide had run off. Now and then a lazy alligator would run his long snout above the surface of the stream, like some water demon, and again glide noiselessly back into his slimy couch.

"Tell your people to take to their paddles and ply them well," said the guide, in a louder tone than had hitherto been used.

Staunton was now certain that it was Juanetta's voice — that of the lady who had preserved his life.

"We are still some distance from the sea, in reaching which is our only chance of safety; for if we are overtaken — and the moment our flight is discovered, we shall be pursued — our death is certain."

The instant Bob and Jack had leave to use their paddles they plied them most vigorously, and the canoe, which had hitherto glided, now sprang, as it were, through the water, throwing up sparkling bubbles on either side of her sharp bows.

"Pull on, my brave men," she exclaimed to herself, more than to the seamen, "every thing depends on our speed. The tide is still making out, and if we can clear the mouth of the river before the flood sets in all will be well."

She spoke in Spanish, a language Staunton understood well. Her eye was meantime turning in every direction as her hand skilfully guided the boat.

"There are scouts about who might attempt to stop us if they suspected we were fugitives. I have, however, the pass-word, and can without difficulty mislead them if we encounter any. Your own people, too, may be in the river looking out for the schooner."

"I think not," answered Staunton. "We had lost one of our boats, and as I am believed dead, my successor (poor fellow, how he will be disappointed!) will, if he acts wisely, not attempt to capture the 'Espanto' except with the 'Sylph' herself."

"The greater necessity, then, for our getting out to sea. It is already dawn. Observe the red glare bursting through the mist in the eastern sky, just through the vista of palm-trees up that long reach. We shall soon have no longer the friendly darkness to conceal us."

As she was speaking a large canoe was seen gliding calmly up the stream, close in with the bank. The people in her hailed in the negro language, and the man who was first in the canoe promptly answered in the same.

"Ask them if they have seen the English man-of-war," said Juanetta.

The negroes answered that she was still riding at anchor off the mouth of the river.

"We shall thus be safe if we can reach the open sea," she observed ; " but we have still some miles to row before we can get clear of the treacherous woods which surround us ; and perhaps when our flight is discovered, our pursuers may take one of the other channels, and we may find our egress stopped at the very mouth of the stream. This suspense is dreadful."

"We may yet strike a blow for you, and for our own liberty, señora," answered Staunton. "It was fortunate the obscurity prevented the people in the canoe from discovering us."

"That matters little. No one would venture to stop me but that man, that demon rather in human disguise, Daggerfeldt, as you call him," she replied, bitterly, pronouncing the name as one to which she was unaccustomed. "Ah, señor ; love — ardent, blind, mad love — can be turned to the most deadly hatred. Criminal, lost as I have been, I feel that there is a step further into iniquity, and that step I have refused to take. The scales have fallen from my eyes, and I have seen the enormity of my wickedness, and have discov-

ered the foulness of my wrongs. From his own lips the
dreadful information came. In the same breath he acknowledged that he had murdered my father and deceived me.
As he slept he told the dreadful tale ; the sight of you conjured up the past to his memory; other murders he talked
of, and treachery of all sorts attempted. He mocked, too,
at me, and at my credulity. I learned also that he still contemplated your destruction as well as mine. I who had preserved his life, who had sacrificed my happiness here and
hereafter for his sake, was to be cast off for another lady
fairer and younger, so it seemed to me, but I could not understand all his words, for sometimes he spoke in his native
language, sometimes in Spanish. Enough was heard to decide me. I had long contemplated quitting him. I knew
that it was wrong remaining, but had not strength before to
tear asunder my bonds, till the feeling that I might rescue
you, and make some slight reparation to heaven for my
wickedness, gave me strength to undertake the enterprise.
There, señor, you know the reason of your liberation ;
my trusty Mauro, who has ever been faithful, provided the
means."

She spoke in a hurried tone, and her sentences were
broken, as if she hesitated to speak of her disgrace and
misery, but yet was urged on by an irresistible impulse.
Even while she was speaking her eye was on the alert, and
her hand continued skilfully to guide the canoe. The stars
had gradually disappeared, sinking as it were into a bed of
thick leaden-colored mist, which overspread the narrow
arch overhead, while in the east a red glow appeared which
melted away as the pale daylight slowly filled the air. It
was day, but there was no joyousness in animated nature,
or elasticity in the atmosphere, as at that time in other
regions. A sombre hue tinted the trees, the water, and the

sky; even the chattering of innumerable parrots, and the cries of those caricatures of men, many thousands of obscene monkeys, appeared rather to mock at than to welcome the return of the world to life.

The canoe flew rapidly on. Suddenly Juanetta lifted her paddle from the water; her ears were keenly employed.

"Hark!" she said, "cease rowing; there is the sound of oars in the water. Ah! it is as I thought. There is a boat endeavoring to cut us off by taking another channel; she is still astern of us though, but we must not slack our exertions."

Captain Staunton redoubled his efforts, as did his men on his telling them they were pursued. After the story he had heard, he was now doubly anxious to rescue the unfortunate girl from the power of the miscreant Daggerfeldt. They now entered a broader reach of the river below the fork, where the channel which Juanetta supposed their pursuers had taken united with the one they were following. They had got some way down it when Staunton observed a large boat emerging from behind the woody screen. Juanetta judged from his eye that he had caught sight of the boat. -

"Is it as I thought?" she asked, calmly.

Staunton told her that he could distinguish a boat, evidently pursuing them, but whether she belonged to his ship or to the slaver, he could not judge.

"We must not stay to examine; if we were mistaken we should be lost," she observed; "but we have the means of defending ourselves — see, I had fire-arms placed in the bottom of the canoe, and here are powder-horns under the seat. Mauro has carefully loaded them, and if they attempt to stop us we must use them."

On they pulled, straining every nerve to the utmost, but the canoe was heavily laden, and the boat gained on them. Staunton trusted that their pursuers might be his own people, but his hope vanished when one of them rose ; there was a wreath of smoke, a sharp report, and a bullet flew over their heads and splintered the branch of a tree which grew at the end of a point they were just then doubling.

"Aim lower next time, my bo', if you wish to wing us," shouted Jack Hopkins, who saw no use in longer keeping silence.

"Ah!" exclaimed Juanetta, "the blue sea — we may yet escape."

As she spoke, another shot better aimed took effect on the quarter of the canoe, but did no further injury. It showed, however, that there were good marksmen in the boat intent on mischief, and that they were perilously near already. For some time they were again shut out from their pursuers, but as the latter doubled the last point, they had, too evidently, gained on them.

"If any one again rises to fire, you must take also to your arms, señor," said Juanetta, a shudder passing through her frame ; "and if it is he, kill him — kill him without remorse. He has shown none. That rifle at your feet was his — it was always true to its aim."

She had scarcely ceased speaking, when a figure stood up in the boat. It seemed to have the likeness of Daggerfeldt. Staunton seized the rifle to fire — he was too late. Ere he had drawn the trigger, a flash was seen, and Juanetta, with a wild shriek, fell forward into the canoe. Staunton fired ; the man who had sent the fatal shot stood unharmed, but the oar of one fell from his grasp, and got entangled with those of the others. This would have enabled the canoe to recover her lost ground, had not Mauro, on seeing his beloved mistress fall, thrown up his paddle, exclaiming that he wished to die with her.

"She may yet be saved if you exert yourself," cried Staunton, in Spanish; "row — for your life row; I will attend to your mistress."

Urged by the officer's commanding tone, the negro again resumed his paddle. Staunton, still guiding the canoe, raised Juanetta, and placed her back in the stern-sheets — she scarcely breathed. The ball had apparently entered her neck, though no blood was to be seen. He suspected the worst, but dared not utter his fears lest Mauro should again give way to his grief. Several other shots were fired at them from the boat, which was rapidly gaining on them. They were close on the bar, in another moment they would be in clear water.

The slaver crew shouted fiercely; again a volley was fired, the balls from which went through and through the sides of the slight canoe, without wounding any one, but making holes for the water to rush in. One more volley would sink them, when a loud cheerful shout rung in their ears, and two boats with the British ensign trailing from the stern were seen pulling rapidly towards them.

Jack Hopkins and Bob Short answered the hail; the pirates, too, saw the boats, they ceased rowing, and then pulling round, retraced their course up the river. The canoe, with the rapid current, flew over the bar, and had barely time to get alongside the barge of the "Sylph," when she was full up to the thwarts. We need not say that his crew welcomed Captain Staunton's return in safety with shouts of joy, after they had believed him dead.

With the strong current then setting out of the river it was found hopeless to follow the slaver's boat. They were soon alongside the brig.

Poor Juanetta was carried carefully to the captain's cabin, watched earnestly by Mauro. The surgeon examined.her wound.

"Her hours are numbered," he said. "No art of mine can save her."

THE ACTION.

Calm and treacherously beautiful as was the morning on which Captain Staunton regained his ship, scarcely had she got under way to stand in closer to the mouth of the river, in order to watch more narrowly for the schooner, should she attempt to run out, than a dark cloud was seen rising over the land. It appeared on a sudden, and extended rapidly, till it spread over the whole eastern sky.

"I fear that it will not do with the weather we have in prospect to send the boats up the river again to retrieve our defeat, Mr. Collins," said Captain Staunton, pointing to the threatening sky.

"I think not, sir, with you," answered the lieutenant; "in fact, if I may advise, the sooner we shorten sail the better, or we may have it down upon us before we are prepared."

"You are right, Mr. Collins; shorten sail as soon as you please," said the captain.

"All hands shorten sail," was sung along the decks.

"Aloft there" — "Lay out" — "Be smart about it" — "In with every thing" — "Let fly" — "Haul down" — "Brail up" — "Be smart, it will be down upon us thick and strong, in a moment" — "Up with the helm" — "Look out there aloft" — "Be smart, my lads."

Such were the different orders issued, and exclamations uttered in succession by the officers.

A moment before, the sea was smooth as glass, and the brig had scarcely steerage-way. Now the loud roaring of the angry blast was heard, and the flapping of the yet un-folded canvas against the masts; the ocean was a sheet of white foam, and the sky a canopy of inky hue. Away the brig flew before it, leaving the land astern, her sails were closely furled, and she remained unharmed, not a spar was sprung, not a rope carried away, not a sail injured. Thus she flew on under bare poles till the squall subsided as quickly as it had arisen, and sail was again made to re-cover the ground they had lost.

Land was still visible, blue and indistinct, but many fears were naturally entertained lest the slaver, which had already given them so much trouble, should have got out of the river with her living cargo, and by keeping either way along shore, have escaped them. For some minutes the wind en-tirely failed, and curses loud and deep were uttered at their ill luck, when, as if to rebuke them for their discontent, the fine fresh sea-breeze set in, and, with a flowing sheet, car-ried them gayly along.

Every eye was employed in looking out for the slaver, for they could not suppose she would have lost the opportu-nity of getting out during their absence. They were not kept long in suspense.

" A sail on the starboard bow," cried the look-out from the mast-head.

" What is she like?" asked the first lieutenant.

" A schooner, sir. The slaver, sir, as we chased afore," answered the seaman, his anxiety that she should be so making him fancy he could not be mistaken.

" The fellow must have sharp eyes indeed to know her at this distance," muttered the lieutenant to himself with a smile; " however, I suppose he's right. We must not, though, be chasing the wrong craft while the enemy is es-caping. Which way is she standing?" he asked.

"To the southward, sir, with every stitch of canvas she can carry," was the answer.

The officer made the proper official report to the captain.

"We must be after her at all events," said Captain Staunton. "Haul up, Mr. Collins, in chase. Send Mr. Stevenson away in the barge to watch the mouth of the river."

The brig was forthwith brought to the wind, the barge in a very short space of time was launched and manned with a stout crew well armed and provisioned, and she shoved off to perform her duty, while the "Sylph" followed the strange sail. The man-of-war had evidently an advantage over the stranger, for while the sea-breeze in the offing blew fresh and steady, in shore it was light and variable.

On perceiving this, Captain Staunton kept his brig still nearer to the wind, and ran down, close-hauled, along the coast, thus keeping the strength of the wind, and coming up hand over hand with the stranger, who lay at times almost becalmed under the land. The breeze, however, before they came abreast of her reached her also, and away she flew like a startled hare just aroused from sleep.

"Fire a gun to bring her to," exclaimed the captain; "she shall have no reason to mistake our intentions."

The British ensign was run up, and a gun was discharged, but to no effect. Two others followed, which only caused her to make more sail; and by her luffing closer up to the wind, she apparently hoped to weather on them, and cross their bows. She was a large schooner, and by the way sail was made on her, probably strongly-handed, so that there could be little doubt that she was the vessel for which they were in search.

"Send a shot into the fellow," exclaimed the captain; "that will prove we are in earnest, and make him show his colors."

The shot clearly hit the schooner, although the range was somewhat long, but it did slight damage. It had the effect though of making him show his ensign, and the stripes and stars of the United States streamed out to the breeze.

"Those are not the fellow's colors, I'll swear," said Mr. Collins, as he looked through his glass. "Another shot will teach him we are not to be humbugged."

"Give it him, Collins, and see if you can knock away any of his spars," said the captain. "We must follow that fellow round the world till we bring him to action, and take or sink him. He'll not heave-to for us, depend upon that."

"Not if Daggerfeldt is the captain," answered the first lieutenant.

"I think she is his schooner; but he is so continually altering her appearance that it is difficult to be quite certain."

"Though I was some hours on board of her, as I reached her in the dark, and left her before it was light, I cannot be certain," observed Captain Staunton, as he took a turn on the quarter-deck with his officer. "By the by, there is that poor girl's black attendant; he will know the vessel at all events. Tell him to come up and give us his opinion."

The lieutenant went into the captain's cabin, and soon after returned, observing, —

"He will not quit his mistress, sir; and the surgeon tells me he has sat by her side without stirring, watching every movement of her lips as a mother does her only child. As no one on board can speak his language but you, sir, we cannot make him understand why he is wanted on deck."

"Oh, I forgot that: I will speak to him myself," answered the captain. "Keep firing at the chase till she heaves-to, and then see that she does not play us any trick. Daggerfeldt is up to every thing."

Captain Staunton descended to his cabin. Juanetta lay on the sofa, a sheet thrown over her limbs, her countenance of a corpse-like hue, but by the slight movements of her lips she still breathed. The black hung over her, applying a handkerchief to her brow to wipe away the cold damps gathering there. Her features, though slightly sunk, as seen in the subdued light of the cabin, seemed like those of some beautiful statue rather than of a living being. The surgeon stood at the head of the couch, endeavoring to stop the hemorrhage from the wound.

"I dare not probe for the ball," he whispered, as if the dying girl could understand him; "it would only add to her torture, and I cannot prolong her life."

"And this is thy handiwork, Daggerfeldt — another victim of thy unholy passions," muttered the captain, as he gazed at her for a moment. "Poor girl, we will avenge thee!"

. He had considerable difficulty in persuading Mauro to quit his mistress; but at length the faithful black allowed himself to be led on deck. He looked round, at first bewildered, as if unconscious where he was; but when his eye fell on the schooner, it brightened up, as if meeting an object with which it was familiar, and a fierce expression took possession of his countenance.

"*Es ella, es ella, señor!*" he exclaimed, vehemently. "It is she, it is she — fire, fire — kill him, kill him, he has slain my mistress!"

A gun was just then discharged, the shot struck the quarter of the schooner, and the white splinters were seen flying from it. On seeing this he shouted with savage joy, clapped his hands, and spat in the direction of the slaver, exhibiting every other sign he could think of, of hatred and rage. Having thus given way to his feelings, the recollection of his mistress returned, and with a groan of anguish he rushed down below.

The two vessels had been gradually drawing closer to each other, in consequence of the schooner luffing up to endeavor to cross the bows of the brig, and if she could, to get to windward of her, the only chance she had of escaping. The eyes of the officers were fixed on her to watch her movements.

" She's about — all right !" shouted the captain. " Give her a broadside while she is in stays, and knock away some of her spars. Fire high, my lads, so as not to hurt her hull."

The brig discharged her whole larboard battery, and the fore-topmast of the schooner was seen tumbling below.

" By Jingo, we've dished him !" exclaimed Jack Hopkins, to his chum, Bob Short ; " and I'm blowed, Bob, if it wasn't my shot did that ere for him. I never lost sight of it till it struck."

" Maybe," answered Bob ; " hard to prove, though."

The schooner had sufficient way on her to bring her round before the topmast fell, and she was now brought into a position partially to rake the brig, though at the distance the two vessels were from each other, the aim was very uncertain.

That Daggerfeldt had determined to fight his vessel was now evident, for the flag of the United States being hauled down, that of Spain was run up in its stead, and at the same moment a broadside was let fly from the schooner. The shot came whizzing over and about the brig, but one only struck her, carrying away the side of a port, a splinter from which slightly wounded Bob Short in the leg.

"Ough!" exclaimed Bob, quietly binding his handkerchief round the limb without quitting his post, "they're uncivil blackguards."

"Never mind, Bob," said Jack Hopkins, "we'll soon have an opportunity of giving them something in return. See, by Jingo, we've shot away his forestay! we'll have his foremast down in a jiffy. Huzza, my boys, let's try what we can do!"

Whether Jack's gun was well aimed it is difficult to say, but at all events the shot from the brig told with considerable effect on the rigging of the schooner. The brig did not altogether escape from the fire of the enemy, who worked his guns rapidly; but whenever a brace was shot away it was quickly again rove, so that she was always kept well under command. The loss of her fore-topmast made the escape of the schooner hopeless, unless she could equally cripple her pursuer; but that she had not contrived to do, and accordingly, as the two vessels drew closer together, the fire from each took more effect. Daggerfeldt, to do him justice, did all a seaman could do, and in a very short space of time the wreck of his topmast was cleared away, and he was preparing to get up a new one in its place. The sea was perfectly smooth, and the wind gradually fell till there was scarcely enough to blow away the smoke from the guns of the combatants, which in thick curling wreaths surrounded them, till at intervals only could the adjacent land and the ocean be seen.

Although Daggerfeldt could scarcely have hoped to succeed either in escaping or coming off the victor, he still refused to haul down his colors, even when the "Sylph," shooting past ahead of him, poured in her whole broadside, sweeping his decks, and killing and wounding several of his people. Dreadful were the shrieks which arose from the poor affrighted wretches confined below, although none of them were injured. The "Sylph" then wore round, and, passing under her stern, gave her another broadside, and then luffing up, ran her alongside — the grappling-irons were hove on board, and she was secured in a deadly embrace. The miserable blacks, believing that every moment was to be their last, again uttered loud cries of horror ; but the slaver's crew, some of whom fought with halters round their necks, still refused to yield, and, with cutlass in hand, seemed prepared to defend their vessel to the last, as the British seamen, led on by their captain, leaped upon the decks. Staunton endeavored to single out Daggerfeldt, but he could nowhere distinguish him ; and after a severe struggle, in which several of the Spaniards were killed, he fought his way aft, and hauled down the colors.

At that instant a female form, with a white robe thrown around her, was seen standing on the deck of the brig ; the crew of the slaver also saw her, and, believing her to be a spirit of another world, fancied she had come to warn them of their fate. The energies of many were paralyzed, and some threw down their arms and begged for quarter. A loud, piercing shriek was heard.

"I am avenged, I am avenged!" she cried, and sank upon the deck.

It was Juanetta. Mauro, who had followed her from the cabin, threw himself by her side, and wrung his hands in despair. They raised up her head, and the surgeon felt her pulse. She had ceased to breathe.

No further resistance was offered by the crew of the slaver. Eight hundred human beings — men, women, and children

15

—were found stowed below, wedged so closely together, that none could move without disturbing his neighbor. Some had actually died from sheer fright at the noise of the cannonading.

Instant search was made for Daggerfeldt; he was nowhere to be found, and the crew either could not or would not give any information respecting him. The prize was carried safely to Sierra Leone, where she was condemned; the slaves were liberated, and became colonists; and Captain Staunton, and his officers and crew, got a handsome share of prize-money.

The " Sylph " was in the following month recalled home, and a few weeks afterward the papers announced the marriage of Captain Staunton, R.N., to Miss Blanche D'Aubigné.

CHAPTER XV.

CORUNNA — OPORTO — PULL UP THE DOURO — NOTICE OF
THE SIEGE OF OPORTO — LINE-OF-BATTLE SHIP.

PORPOISE's story lasted out the gale. We were not sorry
to see the conclusion of the latter, though it left old ocean
in a very uncomfortable state for some time. A downright
heavy gale is undoubtedly a very fine thing to witness — at
least the effects are — and every man would wish to see one
once in his life ; but having experienced what it can do, and
how it makes the ocean look and human beings feel, a wise
man will be satisfied, at all events if he is to fall in with it
in a small cutter in the Bay of Biscay when that once is
over. I've had to go through a good many in the course of
my nautical career ; and though I've often heard sung with
much gusto —

> " One night it blew a hurricane,
> The sea was mountains rolling,
> When Barney Buntline turned his quid,
> And cried to Billy Bowline:
>
> "' Here's a south-wester coming, Billy;
> Don't you hear it roar now?
> Lord help 'em, how I pities those
> Unhappy folks ashore now!
>
> "' While you and I upon the deck
> Are comfortably lying,
> My eyes! what tiles and chimney-tops
> About their heads are flying!' "

I mustn't quote more of the old song; for my own part I like a steady breeze and a smooth sea, when plates and dishes will stay quietly on the table, and a person may walk the deck without any undue exertion of the muscles of the leg.

The gale had driven us somewhat into the bay, and finding it would cause us little delay to look into Corunna, we determined to go there. The entrance to the harbor is very easy — a fine tall lighthouse on the south clearly making it. We brought up off the town, which is situated along the circular shore of a bay something like Weymouth. After paying our respects to the consul, we mounted a troop of steeds offered us for hire, and galloped off to inspect the chief scenes of the engagement between the English and the French, when the former retreated under Sir John Moore. On our return we visited his tomb, situated on the ramparts on the sea side of the town; the tomb is surrounded with cannon, with their muzzles downward — a fit monument to the hero who sleeps beneath. Carstairs did not fail to repeat with due effect —

> " Not a sound was heard; not a funeral note."

They are truly magnificent lines, rarely equalled. Some, however, of a like character appeared lately on Havelock, which are very much to my taste.

But where am I driving to with my poetry and criticism? We got on board the same night, and made sail by daybreak the next morning. We looked into the deep and picturesque Gulf of Vigo, and thought the town a very nasty one, in spite of its imposing castle on the top of a hill. Had we come from the south we might have formed a different opinion of the place. We hove-to off Oporto, and should have gone in, but though exempt from harbor-dues, we found that the pilotage would be heavy, and that we might have some difficulty in getting out again over the bar which has formed across the mouth of the Douro. The city stands on a granite hill on the north side of the river, and about three miles from the sea. Fortunately for us, while we were hove-to there, the steamer from England came in sight, and we were able to obtain a passage on shore in the boats which brought off the mail bags. Hearty, Bubble, and I formed the party; Carstairs and Porpoise remained to take care of the ship. Away we pulled with the glee of schoolboys on a holiday excursion; the boat was large, but of the roughest description — with the stem and stern alike — probably not changed since the earliest days of the Portuguese monarchy; she was double-banked, pulling twelve oars at least. The men mostly wore red caps, with a colored sash round their waists, and had shoeless feet; some had huge wooden slippers, almost big enough to go to sea in. Many of them were fine-looking fellows, but they were very unlike English sailors, and oh! how they did jabber. To those who understood them their observations might have been very sensible, but to our ears their voices sounded like the chattering of a huge family of monkeys in their native woods. The view before us consisted of the blue shining sea, a large whitewashed and yellow-washed village to the north, called St. João da Foz, with a lighthouse on a hill at one end of it, a line of black rocks and white breakers before us, and to the south a yellow beach with cliffs and pine-trees beyond, and a convent, and a few of the higher standing houses and churches of Oporto in the distance. When we got near the white foam-topped rollers, all the jabbering ceased, our crew bent to their oars like men worthy of descendants of Albuquerque's gallant crew; and the boat now backed for an instant, now dashing on, we were in smooth water close under the walls of a no very formidable-looking fortress. A little farther on we landed at a stone slip, at the before-mentioned village, among fishwomen, and porters, and boatmen, and soldiers, and custom-house guards, and boys, all talking away most vociferously. As we had no luggage to carry, we were allowed to look about us. What we should have done I scarcely know, had not Bubble, who never failed to find acquaintance in every place, recognized an English gentleman who had come down to the river to embark for the city. Bubble's friend was invaluable to us; he first invited us to go up the river in his boat, and pointed out numerous spots of interest on the way. The boat was a curious affair; it had a flat bottom and sides, and narrowed to a rising point forward. The greater part was covered with a wooden awning painted green, and supported by wooden stanchions; and the seats run fore and aft round the sides; it had yellow curtains to keep out the sun or rain; the crew, three in number, stood up with their faces to the bow, pressing against the oars; two stood on a deck forward, and one, who occasionally brought his oar in a line with the keel, rowed aft. Dressed in red caps with red sashes, and mostly in white or blue-striped garments, they had a picturesque appearance.

Although the civil war which overthrew despotism, and planted the present line on the throne, had occurred so long before, our new friend spoke of it with as much interest as if it had but lately been concluded. Such an occurrence, indeed, was the great event in the lives of a generation.

On the south side of the entrance of the river is a long sandbank; on the north side is the castle of Foz, or the mouth. This castle was built by the Pedroites, and it was literally the key on which depended the success of the enterprise. Had it been taken, the communication with the sea and Oporto would have been cut off, and the Liberals would have been starved out. For the greater portion of the time occupied by the struggle, Dom Pedro's followers held little more than the city of Oporto and a line of country on the north bank of the Douro scarcely a mile wide, leading from the city to the sea. They held the lighthouse at the north point of the village ; but a few hundred yards beyond was a mound on which the Miguelites erected a strong battery. Not a spot along the whole line but what was the scene of some desperate encounter ; and most certainly the Portuguese Constitutionalists of all ranks, from the highest to the lowest, fought as bravely as men could fight in the noblest of causes. Heaven favored the right, and in spite of apparently overwhelming hosts opposed to them, of disease and gaunt famine, they won their cause, and the mother of the present enlightened King of Portugal ascended the throne.

But I am writing the cruise of the " Frolic," and not a history of Portugal. Still I must dot down a few of our friend's anecdotes. While the north side of the river was held by the Constitutionalists, the south was in the hands of the Miguelites, and the two parties used to amuse themselves by firing at each other across the stream, so that it was dangerous to pass along the lower road by daylight.

On one occasion, the Miguelites, wishing to attack the castle, brought a number of casks to the end of the spit of sand at the entrance of the river, and erected a battery on it, but they forgot to fill the casks with sand or earth ; when morning broke there was a formidable battery directly under the walls of the castle. Some unfortunate troops were placed in it to work the guns ; all went very well till the guns of the castle began to play on it, and then a few shots sent the entire fabric to the four winds of heaven, and either killed the soldiers placed in it, or drove them flying hurry-skurry across the sand, where many more were picked off by the rifles of the Constitutionalists.

What could be more unpleasant than having on a hot day to run along a heavy shingly beach, with a number of sharp-shooters taking deliberate aim at one's corpus? Happy would he be who could find a deep hole into which to roll himself out of harm's way.

The banks of the Douro are picturesque from the very entrance. On either side are broken cliffs; on the south covered with pine-groves, on the north with yellow, white, and pink houses and churches, and orange-groves. On the south we passed the remains of the old convent of St. Antonio, where once the jovial monks feasted and sang and prayed, well supplied with the spoils of the sea. Here pious fisher-men used to stop and ask a blessing on their labors, on their way down the river, and on their return they failed not to offer the choice of their spoil to the worthy friars. The gardens of the convent were profusely ornamented with statues of curious device, and flowers, and vases, and orange-trees, and grottoes, and temples; all now swept away by the scythe of war — the convent walls now forming part of a manufactory. The monks have disappeared from Portugal, and few people regret them less than the Portuguese. At best they were drones; and, if we are to credit one-quarter of the tales told of them, they continued to do no little amount of evil in their generation. On the same side of the river, but much higher up, where the Douro forces its way be-tween two lofty cliffs, on the summit of the southern one, stands the once very celebrated convent of the Sierra. From beneath its walls the Duke of Wellington led his army across the river into Oporto, and drove Marshal Soult out of the city. This convent, and its surrounding garden, was the only spot held by the Pedroites, and most heroically held it was, against the whole army of the usurper Miguel, led by his best generals. Day after day, and night after night, were his legions led to the attack, and as often were they repulsed by the half-starved defenders of its earth-formed ramparts. We may speak with pride of the siege of Kars and of Lucknow, and of many another event in the late war; but I hold that they do not eclipse the gallant defence of the Portuguese Constitutionalists of the Sierra convent. Below the convent the two banks of the river are now joined by a handsome iron suspension-bridge, which superseded one long existing formed of boats. The city stands below this point, rising on the converse steep sides of a granite hill, and with its numerous church-steeples, its tinted-walled houses, its bright red roofs interspersed with the polished green of orange-trees in its gardens, is a very picturesque city. Along its quays are arranged vessels of various sizes, chiefly Portuguese or Brazilians, those of other nations anchoring on the other side, in the stream, to be away from the temptations of the wine-shops. On the south side is a bay with gently sloping shores; and here are found the long, low, narrow lodges in which are stowed the casks of Port wine, which has perhaps made Portugal and the Portuguese more generally known to Englishmen of all classes than would have been done by the historical associations connected with that beautiful country.

As Bubble's friend was on his way to visit his wine-pipes, he took us first to Villa Nova, the place I have been speaking of. One lodge he showed us contained three thousand pipes, ranged in long lines, two and three pipes one above another, which, at fifty pounds a pipe, represents a capital of one hundred and fifty thousand pounds. Some of the English houses are said to have two or three times that quantity; but of course the young wine is not of the value I have mentioned. The Port wine is grown on the banks of the Douro, in a district commencing about fifty miles above the city. It is made in the autumn, and remains in large vats on the farms till the spring, when it is put into casks, and brought down in flat-bottomed boats to the lodges at Villa Nova. Here it is racked and lotted to get rid of impurities, and has brandy put to it to keep it. Our friend assured us that Port wine will not keep for any length of time without brandy; the experiment has been tried over and over again. The only way to make it keep for a short time is to rack it constantly; but then it becomes spiritless, vapid, and colorless. To one conclusion we came, that Port wine in the lodge at Villa Nova and Port wine out of decanter at an English dinner-table are very different things; for Port wine racked and lotted for the English market, and kept some years in a temperate cellar, is undoubtedly vastly superior to the juice of the grape before it is so prepared.

Having satisfied our curiosity, with our friend as guide, we crossed the river to Oporto. We landed at a gateway in the brown old wall of the city, which runs along the river and up the hill to the east and west, surmounted by high, pointed battlements of a very Moorish appearance, though the Moors did not plant their conquering standard so far north as Oporto. Passing along a very narrow, cool, dirty, and somewhat odoriferous street, we entered a wide, well-paved one, called the Rua Nova. In the middle of it congregate the merchants every afternoon, at the exchange hour, to transact their public business. At the end of the street is a fine stone building, called the Factory House, a sort of club belonging to the English, who become members by election. High above the end of the street, on a hill covered with houses, rises the old cathedral of Oporto. We found our way to it along some narrow, twisting streets, with oriental-looking shops on either side — tinmen and goldsmiths and shoemakers and stationers — a line of each sort together. The cathedral, as well as all the churches we saw at Oporto, were rather curious than elegant.

For the greater part of our walk we were continually ascending along tolerably well-paved and clean streets, with stone houses and wide, projecting balconies, some with stone, others with iron balustrades. We passed through a street called the Street of Flowers; the chief shops in it were those of jewellers, who showed us some very beautiful fili-gree work in gold — brooches and ear-rings and rings. We next found ourselves in a square at the bottom of two hills, with wide streets running up each of them, and a church at their higher ends. One has a curious arabesque tower, of great height, which we saw a long way out at sea, called the Torre dos Clerigos. Going up still higher we reached a large parade ground, with barracks at one end, and near them a granite-fronted church, called the Lappa, where, in an urn, is preserved the heart of the heroic Dom Pedro — the grandfather of the present King of Portugal. Oporto is full of gardens, which make the city spread over a wide extent of ground. We were agreeably surprised with its bright, clean, cheerful look. Built on a succession of granite hills, which afford admirable materials for the construction of its edifices, it has a substantial comfortable look. It is also tolerably well drained, and wayfarers are not much offended with either bad sights or smells. The variety of the cos-tume of the inhabitants gives it a lively look; for although gentlemen and ladies have taken to French fashions, the townspeople still generally wear the graceful black mantilla, or colored or white handkerchief over their heads, while the peasantry appear with broad-brimmed hats and cloth jack-ets, gay-colored petticoats, and a profusion of gold ear-rings

and chains.   There are beggars, but they are not very im-
portunate, and the smallest copper coin seemed to satisfy
them.   Our friend told us that he has seen a Portuguese
gentleman, wanting a copper, take his snuff-box and present
it to a beggar, who would take a pinch with the air of a
noble, and shower a thousand blessings on the head of the
donor in return.   "The truth is, that the Portuguese as a
nation are the kindest people I have ever met," observed our
friend.   "They think charitably and act charitably, and do
not despise each other; they are kindly affectionate one to
another.   A good government and a reformed church would
make them a very happy people."

Our walk through the city was a hurried one, as we wished
to be on board again before dark.   We passed near a large
palace, with some ugly visages garnishing the front.   Here
Dom Pedro lived, and here Marshal Soult's dinner had been
prepared, when the Duke of Wellington entered the city and
ate it up.   We found a boat ready to carry us down the
river, which we reached by a steep, winding road.   Our
friend kindly insisted on accompanying us.

At Foz a catria was prepared by our friend's directions to
put us on board the yacht.   Oh, how refreshing to our olfactory senses, after the hot air of the streets, was the fresh
sea-breeze as we reached the mouth of the river, and once
more floated on the blue Atlantic!   The sun descended beneath the far western wave in a blaze of glory, such as I
have seldom seen equalled in any latitude; the glow lit up
the Lappa church, the Clerigos tower, and the Sierra convent in the distance, suffusing a rich glow over the whole
landscape.   All sail was set, but we made little way through
the water; a calm succeeded, and then the hot night-wind
came off the land in fitful gusts, smelling of parched earth
and dry leaves.   Having stood off the land sufficiently to

clear every danger, we kept our course. The night was somewhat dark, and we had all turned in, leaving the mate in charge of the watch.

I know not what it was made me restless and inclined to turn out, and breathe the fresher air on deck; probably I was heated with the long and exciting excursion of the day. As I put my head up the companion-hatch, sailor-fashion, I turned my eyes towards every point of the compass. Did they deceive me? "Hallo, Sleet, what's that?" I exclaimed. "Port the helm; hard aport, or we shall be run into." What was the look-out about? Where were Sleet's eyes? All, I suspect, were asleep. There, directly ahead of us, like some huge phantom of a disordered dream, came gliding on a line-of-battle ship, her tall masts and wide-spreading canvas towering up into the sky — a dark pyramid high above our heads; our destruction seemed inevitable. With a hail which horror made sound more like a shriek of despair, I summoned all hands on deck. Happily, the man at the helm of the yacht obeyed my orders at the moment, and the agile little craft slipped out of the way as the huge monster glided by, her side almost touching our taffrail, and her lower studding-sail booms just passing over our peak — so it seemed; our topmast, I know, had a narrow squeak for it.

"What ship's that?" shouted Porpoise, springing on deck.

"Her Britannic Majesty's ship 'Megatherium,'" so the name sounded.

"Then let a better look-out be kept aboard her Britannic Majesty's ship 'Megatherium' in future, or the Duke of Blow-you-up will have to report to the Lords Commissioners of the Admiralty," replied Porpoise, through the speaking-trumpet. "I hauled in the duke just to frighten them a

bit," he added; "they wouldn't care for the plain mister.
The chances are that some of the look-outs had their eyes
shut, and the officer of the watch had gone to freshen his
nip a bit. No one dreams of danger on a fine night like
this, and if a few small fishing-boats had been run down, no
one would have heard any thing about it; there would be
just a cry and a shriek from the drowning people, and all
would be over. There's more danger of being run down on
a calm night like this than in a gale of wind, when everybody has his eyes open."

"What cutter is that?" hailed some on board the ship,
through a speaking-trumpet, before Porpoise had done
speaking.

"Bow-wow-wow! I leave you to guess," he answered.

By this time the vessels were so far apart that a hail
could scarcely be distinguished, and so we separated. I
only hope those who deserved a reprimand got it, and that
any of my brother-officers, or other sea-going men who read
these pages, will take the hint, and have as bright a look-
out kept in fine weather as in foul.

CHAPTER XVI.

CINTRA — THE TAGUS — LISBON — CADIZ — GIBRALTAR —
SANDGATE AGAIN — OLD FRIENDS — NEWS OF MY HEROINE.

Two days after our narrow escape, as the rising sun shed
his bright rays over the world of waters, we again made
the land a little to the northward of the Rock of Lisbon.
We could see with our glasses the vast convent and palace
of Mafra, built by that debauched devotee, Don John V.
He had .a notion, not uncommon at the present day, that,
by rearing edifices of brick and mortar, he might thus
create for himself a few stepping-stones towards heaven.
The building shows a front of seven hundred feet at least
towards the sea, with a lofty portico in the centre, and is
capable of quartering all the troops in the kingdom. When
monks dwelt there they must have had ample space for
exercise.

Soon afterwards we came under the rocky heights of
Cintra. They surround a perfect oasis, rising from the arid
plains about Lisbon. Every one knows Cintra on account
of its Convention, not over creditable to its executors ; its
convent cut out of the rock, and lined with cork to keep the
old monks warm ; and its palace, built by the talented and
eccentric Beckford, now a mass of ruins. We just got a
glimpse through a break in the rocks of its cork, orange,
and citron groves, surrounded with sweet-scented shrubs.

Passing the Bay of Cascaes, a fresh breeze carried us by
the white circular Bugio Fort, standing on a rock at the

mouth of the Tagus, and with a fair tide we ascended
the river.

In our company were a number of craft of all sorts,
carrying flags of all nations. Iron-moulded and weather-
stained Indiamen, and Brazilian ships surrounded by boats
full of people, who had come out to welcome relations and
friends after a long absence ; men-of-war, with their polished
sides and snowy, wide-spreading canvas ; heavily laden and
heavy-looking English merchant-brigs, more esteemed for
capacity than for speed, like London aldermen ; tub-shaped,
yellow-sided Dutchmen, laden with cargoes more formidable in appearance than in reality. Instead of being
bomb-shells or round shot, proving, on nearer inspection,
to be Dutch cheeses, to be dreaded only by those of weak
digestion.

Contrasted with the heavy-looking foreign vessels were
the Portuguese rascas, employed chiefly in the coasting
trade, with their graceful, high-pointed, lateen sails, sharp
bows, and rounded decks, and the native schooners or
hiates, with hulls not destitute of beauty, but rigged with
masts raking at different angles, and gaffs peaked at unequal heights. There were also numberless sloops, and
schooners, and boats of various sorts, the most curious
being the Lisbon fishing-boat, shaped like a bean-pod, curv-
ing up at stem and stern, with a short rounded deck at
either end, and a single high lateen sail. A pilot whom
we received on board off the Bugio Fort took us close to
the white tower of Belem, and its Gothic church at the
western end of Lisbon, and brought us to an anchor among
a crowd of other vessels off Blackhorse Square. Lisbon
rising on several hills from the waters of the wide-flowing
Tagus — here many miles across — is noted as a very picturesque city ; its white buildings glittering in the sun,

crowned by the dark frowning castle, and surrounded by suburbs intermixed with gardens filled with richly-tinted orange-trees and flowers of many hues.

Gold and Silver Streets are handsome streets ; and there are some fine palaces, and the Opera House is a respectable edifice, and has, moreover, a very good opera ; but, though improved of late years, we were told, in cleanliness, it is still a very dirty city, and the lower orders have a marked inferiority to those we saw at Oporto. They are a darker, smaller race, with much Moorish blood in their veins, without any mixture of the nobler Gothic stream from which the inhabitants of the north have sprung. They are the fellows who have gained for the Portuguese the character of being assassins and robbers, which certainly those in the north do not deserve. However, a strong government, liberal institutions, and a street police have pretty well put a stop to such proceedings even there.

The best account I have ever read of Lisbon and its people, as they were before the French Revolution changed affairs not a little in most of the countries of Europe, is to be found in Beckford's " Visit to the Convents of Alcobaça and Batalha," and in his " Tour to Italy and Portugal." There is a rich, racy humor in his descriptions, which has seldom been surpassed. At one of the convents a dance is proposed for the entertainment of the illustrious strangers, and while a few act as musicians, the greater number of the oleaginous, obese monks tuck up their frocks, and begin sliding and whirling and gliding about with as much gusto as a number of school-girls at play. But we must be off to sea again.

We lionized Lisbon, and paid a visit to Cintra, but as no adventure occurred worthy of note to any of our party, I will not enter into details.

16

Once more the "Frolic" breasted the waves of the Atlantic, her course being for fair Cadiz. On the third day after leaving the Tagus, we dropped our anchor off that bright, smiling city. Its flat-roofed houses give it somewhat of an eastern look, but it is far cleaner than any eastern city. The houses are built after the Moorish fashion, and very like the residences excavated at Pompeii. The coloring of the outside is more in accordance with the taste of the luxurious Romans in the days of their degeneracy, than with that of the ancient Greeks, which made them satisfied with softer hues; while the interior, on the other hand, is as cool and simple as the purest taste can make it. No sooner had we furled sails than all hands were eager to go on shore, to have a glimpse at the often talked of mantilla-wearing, fair, flirting, fascinating Gaditanas. The gig was lowered, and on shore we went.

We were not disappointed in the appearance of Cadiz. The streets are narrow, that the sun of that torrid clime may not penetrate into them, and those only who have lived in a southern latitude can appreciate the luxury of having a cool, shady road in which to walk. Verandas in front of every window reach nearly half-way overhead; they are closely barred, and sometimes glazed, so that no impertinent eye can penetrate their recesses. These verandas are full of flowers, and overhung with ivy or other luxuriant creepers.

The fronts of the houses are ornamented with various colors, as red, blue, yellow, green, and other tints; while the separation between each house and each floor is marked by lines of red, thus giving the whole street a singularly bright and cheerful appearance.

The gateway is the pride of a Cadiz house. Many we passed were very handsome. It was pleasant to look

through them into the interior, where the column-sur-
rounded patios with cool, sparkling fountains in their centres,
and shrubs and flowers of every hue, were indeed most
refreshing to the senses. Every house is a square, with one
or more patios in the centre, their only roof the bright blue
sky. Into this court of columns all the rooms of the house
open. Shade and coolness are the great things sought for
in that clime.

· We wandered up and down the narrow streets till we
began to wish that some one would take compassion on us
and ask us in ; but nobody did, and our only satisfaction
was the belief that we created a mighty sensation in the
bosoms of numberless lovely damsels whose bright eyes we
saw flashing at us through the thickly-barred jalouses.

" Ah, my good fellows, but you did not see their small
noses, thick lips, and swarthy skins," observed that unsen-
timental fellow, Bubble, thus cruelly depriving us of the
only consolation we enjoyed. The fact was that at that
early hour of the day no one goes abroad who can stay at
home, except, as the Spaniards say, dogs and Englishmen,
putting the canine tribe before the biped. Fatigue drove
us into a café, where we took some refreshment, and in the
evening we were somewhat repaid by watching the crowds
of bewitching damsels and gay cavaliers, who sauntered
forth to enjoy the cool air, and each other's conversation.

Cadiz is joined to the mainland by a narrow strip of sand,
deprived of which it would be an island. Opposite to it,
across the bay, is Port St. Mary's, the port of Xeres, where
the sherry wine is embarked.

The next day we visited that place to taste some of its
celebrated wines. We were much captivated with some
deliciously dry Mansanilla, inferior as it is in flavor, however, to the still more valuable Amontillado.

But interesting as was our visit to Cadiz to ourselves, attractive as were its far-famed dames, and delicious as were its wines, my readers will undoubtedly rather hear some of the more stirring events of our cruise.

Away, away, once more we went, bounding over the blue ocean. We were, however, destined not to find ourselves so soon inside the Mediterranean as we expected. A dead calm came on, and for many hours we lay sweltering under a sun not much less fierce than that of the tropics.

It was very tantalizing to remain thus almost in sight of the entrance of that classic sea we all wished to behold, and yet not be able to get there. Once within the influence of that strange current which from age to age has unweariedly flowed into that mighty basin, and yet never has filled it, we should have advanced with sufficient rapidity. Another whole day tried our patience, and Hearty had begun to declare that, after all, he thought the Mediterranean could not be worth visiting, when, on the morning of the third day, a breeze sprung up, and the cutter began to slip through the water towards the Straits.

The chief strength of the current is in the centre, far out of reach of shot and shell from the shore on either side. I mention this because many people have a notion that the fortress of Gibraltar defends the entrance to the Straits. The fact is, that the narrowest part is seven and a quarter miles wide ; but that narrowest part we passed through at a distance of fifteen miles from Gibraltar, before we reached it. We did not, indeed, see the Rock before we had passed the Narrows.

The distance from the Rock to Ceuta, opposite to it on the African coast, is twelve miles.

Gibraltar is formed by a tongue of land three miles long and one broad, with a sandbank joining it to the main, and terminating with a high promontory. No one ever expected to make it defend the Straits, even before steamers were introduced. The heaviest guns are turned towards Spain; at the same time the sea-side is made inaccessible by scarping. Below the Rock is a belt of level land, on which the modern town is built. The Rock has the form of a lofty ridge with three elevations on it, one at each end, and one in the centre. That in the centre is the highest, and has the flag-staff planted on it. When we landed, we went through the wonderful galleries excavated in the Rock. These excavations have been going on since the time of the Moors, who, I believe, made by far the largest number of them.

They were wonderful fellows, those Moors. I have always felt a vast respect for them when I have beheld their remains in the south of Spain. The reason of their success is, that they were always in earnest in whatever they undertook. However, I don't want to talk here about the Moors. Gibraltar is a very curious place, and well worth a visit; with its excavated galleries, its heavy guns, its outward fortifications, its zig-zag roads, its towers and batteries, its narrow streets, its crowded houses, its ragged rocks, and its troops of monkeys, the only specimens of the family of simia, which reside, I believe, in a wild state in Europe. Gibraltar, in reality, from its geological formation, belongs rather to Africa than to Europe, it being evidently cut off from the African mountains, and having no connection with those of Europe.

It is a question for naturalists to solve how the monkeys came there — I don't pretend to do so. We brought up in Gibraltar Bay, where the yacht lay very comfortably, and so do now our men-of-war. Should, however, a war break out with Spain, they would find the place too hot to hold

them, as the bay is completely commanded by the Spanish
coast, where batteries could speedily be erected, nor could
the Rock afford the ships any protection.

Now I have talked enough about Gibraltar; I'll however
just describe it, like a big tadpole caught by the tail as it
was darting away towards Africa. We spent some pleasant
days there, and were very hospitably treated by some military friends in the garrison. Malta, the Isles of Greece,
and the Levant, was our destination. I did not fail to make
inquiries respecting Sandgate; and, curious enough, I fell
in with a merchant who had in his youth fought in the
Greek War of Independence. He told me that a youth of
that name, and who in every way answered Sandgate's
description, had come out from England and joined the
patriot forces. He was a brave, dashing fellow, but most
troublesome from his unwillingness to submit to any of the
necessary restraints of discipline, and utterly unprincipled.
He had, however, plenty of talent, and managed to ingratiate himself with some of the Greek chiefs, though the more
respectable, as did the English Philhellenes, stood aloof from
him.

" The truth is," said my friend, " many of those Greek
chiefs had been notorious pirates themselves, and I have no
doubt Sandgate learned his trade from them."

" I suspect very strongly that the man you describe and
Sandgate are one and the same person," I remarked. " It
is curious that I should so soon have gained a clew to
him."

The next day I again met my friend. " I have some
further account of Sandgate to give you," said he, taking
me by the button; " he'll give some little trouble before his
career is closed, I suspect. My Smyrna correspondent is
here, and he tells me that he knew of Sandgate's being

there, and of his selling his yacht. He served with me in the war, and knew him also : consequently, when he made his appearance he kept his eye upon him. He traced him on board a vessel, in which he went to one of the Greek islands. From thence he crossed to a smaller island owned by a chief who had once been a notorious pirate, and was strongly suspected of still following the same trade in a more quiet way. There he lost sight of him ; but several piracies had been committed during the spring by a craft which it was suspected had been fitted out in the island in question."

" We certainly have in a most unexpected way discovered a clew to Mr. Sandgate's whereabouts and course of life," I remarked. " It would almost read like a romance were it to be put into print."

" Oh, we have had many heroes of that description from time to time in the Mediterranean," replied my friend. " There was that fellow Delano, who was hung at Malta a few years back, he was an Englishman — or a Yankee, I believe rather. How many piracies he had committed I do not know before he was found out, but at last he tried to scuttle a brig, which did not go down as he thought she had, so happily his intended victims escaped and informed against him. He was captured by a man-of-war's boat's crew, and he and his followers were carried in chains to Malta. Then there was a very daring fellow, a Greek, Zappa by name, who commanded a brig, and on one occasion attacked an Austrian man-of-war which he believed had treasure on board, and took her. Then there has been no end of Greek pirates of high or low degree. Gentlemanly cut-throats, princes and counts with fleets under their command, down to the disreputable owners of small boats which lie in wait behind headlands to rob unwary merchantmen who cannot defend themselves. Oh! the Mediterranean has reason to be proud of the achievements of its mariners from the times of the pious Æneas down to the present day."

From all I heard of Sandgate, indeed, I felt more and more thankful that Miss Manners had so fortunately escaped from his power.

Nothing worthy of note occurred to us during our very pleasant stay at Gibraltar. The day before we had arranged to leave the place, who should we fall in with but Jack Piper, a lieutenant in the navy, and a friend and old messmate of Tom Mizen's. "Why, I thought we had left you at Plymouth!" I exclaimed as I wrung his hand.

"So you did," he answered; "but I had been ordered to come out here and to join my ship. You know old Rullock, Mizen's uncle. He had just before commissioned the 'Zebra' brig, for this station, and as she was the first vessel to sail, I got a passage in her. We had a fast run, and they only put me on shore here yesterday while she has gone to Malta. We had Mrs. and Miss Mizen on board, and Mrs. Mizen's niece, Miss Susan Simms" (Jack, I knew, rather affected Miss Susan, and he looked very conscious as he mentioned her name). "Very nice girl," he continued; "so kind of her, too, to come out just at an hour's notice to take care of her cousin, Miss Rullock, you know. You haven't heard, perhaps, that they are rather alarmed about Miss Laura. Caught a cold, somewhat ugly symptoms. Think her consumptive, so it was judged best to bring her out to spend a winter at Malta, and as her uncle was coming, the opportunity was a good one."

"Ah! this news will be matter of interest to Hearty," thought I. "We shall now see whether his feelings for Miss Mizen had any root, or whether he was affected by a mere passing fancy."

"Poor girl! I am sorry to hear of her illness," said I aloud. "Malta is as good a place as she could come to, and I hope the change will do her good. We shall see her there, I dare say. Have you any commands for the ladies?"

"Say I hope that my ship will be there before long," answered Piper, absolutely blushing through the well-bronzed hue of his cheek.

He had been appointed as first lieutenant of the "Thunder," sloop-of-war. She was expected at the Rock every day. Jack Piper was not very dissimilar in appearance and manner to Porpoise, and he was the same sort of good-natured, frank, open-hearted fellow — just the man to do a gallant, noble action, and not to say a word about it, simply because it would not occur to him that it was any thing out of the way. There are plenty of such men in the service, and England may be proud of them.

On quitting Piper I went on board the yacht, where we had agreed to assemble in the evening, to be ready for a start by daybreak. Should Hearty not have heard of the "Zebra's" touching at the Rock, I resolved to say nothing about the matter. If he really was in love with Miss Mizen, I might chance to spoil him as a companion, and if he did not care about her, there was no harm done.

CHAPTER XVII.

A SUSPICIOUS SAIL — AN EXPECTED VISIT FROM AN UNINVITED STRANGER — WE PREPARE TO RECEIVE HIM.

THE Rock of Gibraltar was fading from our sight in the far distance, as the sun in a blaze of glory went down into his ocean bed between the pillars of Hercules. The yacht lay in a dead calm, her canvas idly flapping for want of more useful employment, while every spar and rope was reflected in the mirror-like surface of the watery expanse ; yet she was not immovable, for the current which runs in at the mouth of the Mediterranean was sending her on at the rate of some knots an hour, over the ground pretty well in her direct course. We sat on deck and smoked our cigars, and spun many a yarn, and told many an adventure of bygone days. It was with difficulty that we could persuade ourselves to turn in, so enjoyable was the cool sea atmosphere after the burnt-up, baked, oveny air of the old Rock.

The next morning, when we came on deck, although there had not been an air in all the heavens, as Snow informed us, we had sunk Gibraltar completely beneath the sea. That day passed much like the previous one. Now and then a light breeze from the westward filled the cutter's sails, and made her step through the water at a speed which must have astonished some of the ancient fish, which looked up at her from out of their caverned homes beneath the waves. As the day wore on we made out, away to the westward, the mastheads of a brig. As we gradually rose them it appeared that she was a polacca-rigged brig, probably a Greek laden with corn, bound out of the Straits, perhaps to supply the insatiable maw of old England with food. We had just made this discovery when we were summoned to dinner. To people who have nothing to do, any small thing affords subject of interest. I remember a story of two noblemen, shut up at a country inn on a rainy day, betting large sums on the speed of two small flies running over a pane of glass, and of others equally wise, staking larger amounts than many a naval and military officer receives in his life-time, on two spots of rain, the bet being a drawn one by the drops uniting. When we returned on deck after dinner no change had taken place. The canvas of the cutter gave every now and then an idle flap, while the sails of the Greek brig seemed very much in the same humor. We, however, were so far better off than the stranger, because the current was sweeping us, slowly indeed, but still in the direction we wanted to go, while it was carrying her away from it.· Still we appeared by some mysterious influence to near each other. It was not, however, for some time that we discovered that her crew were towing her ahead, and that she had also long sweeps out, which probably sent her through the water two or three knots an hour.

"I thought those Greek seamen were idle dogs, who would not think of taking so much trouble as these fellows appear to do, even to save their lives."

"Oh, there's little enough to be said in their favor," replied Porpoise. "These fellows want to get through the Straits, as they fancy they shall find a fair wind outside, so they take a little trouble now in the hopes of perfect idleness by and by." Odd as it may seem, I could not help fancying that there was something strange about that brig, yet what it was of course I could not tell.

"Well, I shall always think favorably of the industry of Greeks, after watching those fellows," said Carstairs.

The strange brig kept creeping up closer and closer to us; still, except an occasional glance which we took of her, as being the only object in sight, she appeared in no way to excite the interest of my messmates. I, however, as I remarked, clearly remember to have had a strange feeling of doubt and mistrust as I looked at her. It is impossible to account for similar sensations, experienced frequently by people on various occasions; had she been a rakish-looking, low, black schooner, with a wide spread of canvas, met with in the latitude of the West Indies, I might very naturally have guessed her to be a pirate or slaver; but the brig in sight was a harmless, honest-looking trader, and still I could not help frequently during the day looking at her, very much as I should have done had she been of the character of the craft I had described.

"Bubble!" exclaimed Hearty, "you know that you have promised us a tale of your own composition, and you have very frequently been missed from the deck and found pen in hand in the cabin, covering sundry sheets of paper, and when we have been wrapped in slumber you have been supposed to have sat up continuing your work. Come, man, have compassion on our curiosity, and give us the result of your lucubrations."

"Oh, no! spare my blushes," answered Will, with a comic sentimental look: "I don't aim at the world-wide celebrity of an author: I am content to please a select circle of friends like yourselves. Who would read a story published under the signature of Will Bubble? No! I say, let me float on adown the quiet stream of insignificance. The post of safety is a humble station — hum!"

" Over-modesty, over-modesty, Will," answered Hearty. " Pluck up courage, man ; you will do well if you try."

The best of the joke was, that the rogue, as I well know, had for many a year past been dabbling in literature, and often had I enjoyed a quiet laugh when reading an article from his pen.

" Well, perhaps some day I'll try," said he, demurely.

" Hillo ! what can the fellow be wanting?" exclaimed Porpoise, interrupting our talking (I won't call it conversation).

We all turned our eyes in the direction in which he was looking. The brig had lowered a boat, which with rapid strokes was pulling towards us.

" She seems to have a good many hands in her," he added, holding his glass to his eye. " I don't quite like the look of her."

" Nor do I either, I confess," said I. " There are some craft in this sea not altogether honest, we must remember, though they are generally met with higher up towards the Levant."

" What ought we to do, then?" asked Hearty.

" Just serve out the cutlasses and pistols, and cast the guns loose," said Porpoise. " Tell the people to keep an eye on the strangers, and if more than two or three attempt to come on board, to tumble them into their boat again. There's not the slightest danger if we put on a bold front, but if we are caught napping, I would not be answerable for the consequences.

CHAPTER XVIII.

THE STRANGER COMES ON BOARD — THE GREEK CHIEF — A WHITE SQUALL — WHAT HAS BECOME OF THE BRIG ? — THE SUSPICIOUS STRANGER AGAIN — PREPARATIONS FOR A FIGHT.

THE advice Porpoise gave seemed so rational that although it might have gone somewhat against the grain with so thorough a John Bull as Hearty to put himself in a posture of defence before he was attacked, Snow was summoned aft to superintend the distribution of the contents of the arm-chest. The men buckled on their cutlasses with looks of no small glee, snapping the locks of their pistols to try them before loading, as they eyed the advancing boat.

"There's no fear, gentlemen, but what they'd give an account of twice the number of chaps as are aboard that craft, if they ever come to close quarters," said Snow, approvingly casting his eye over the crew.

I could not help thinking the same, for a finer set of broad-shouldered, wide-chested fellows I never saw, as they stood around us with their necks bare, and the sleeves of their blue shirts tucked up above the elbows, handling their weapons with the fond look which a child bestows on a newly-given toy.

"Go forward again, my men, and keep on the opposite side to which the boat comes," said Porpoise.

"Just stand about as if you did not suspect there was any thing wrong; very likely there may not be, you know, and

254

perhaps the Greek has lost his reckoning, and is sending aboard us only to ask his whereabouts."

" A craft like that wouldn't send away a boat with twelve men in her, or more, to ask such a question," observed Snow to old Sleet ; " I know better nor that."

" You may well say so," answered the old man. " I've heard of such rum tricks being played, that I always like to be prepared for squalls."

I must say that after the strange misgivings I had experienced in the early part of the day, when the polacca-brig first hove in sight, I was well satisfied to see the yacht put in a perfect state of defence. It was more than possible that the stranger might after all be an honest trader, and that her crew might be not a little surprised to find an English yacht with so formidable an appearance. Still again, I have always seen the wisdom of not despising an antagonist, and of being as prepared as circumstances will allow for any emergency.

The boat, a heavy launch, was meantime advancing towards us. I examined her narrowly with my glass ; she had what looked very like a gun mounted in the bows, though a' capote, or piece of dark canvas, was thrown over it. She pulled twelve oars, beside which three or four other people sat in the stern-sheets. I observed Porpoise, who had been, as may be supposed, attentively watching the boat, go up to the foremost gun, and draw the shot.

" Carpenter," said he, to Chips, " bring me up a shovel of old nails and bits of iron."

The articles in question were soon brought to him, and he proceeded forthwith to load the gun with them up to the muzzle.

" Sleet," said he, " you have charge of this gun ; if our friends there show fight, and I give the word, slap this

mouthful right in among them ; it will soon bring them to
reason, I guess."

" Ay, ay, sir," answered the old man, slapping the breech
of his gun with a quiet smile, " I'll make her speak, depend on't."

Thus prepared, we awaited the arrival of the suspicious-
looking strangers. Had there been any wind, we might
easily have prevented their coming on board by running out
of their way, but as it was we could not help ourselves without fighting. In a few minutes more they pulled alongside,
rather awkwardly ; however, we did not order them to keep
off, as it was agreed it would not be wise to show any suspicion of them. They were all dressed in the Greek costume ; one of the men who sat in the stern-sheets, a full-
bearded fellow, with a capote thrown over his shoulders and
a fez on his head, stood up in the boat, and in broken English asked to come on board.

" Oh ! let him," said Hearty, who began to fancy we had
been over-cautious. " There can't possibly be any harm."

The side was accordingly manned, and our friend with
the capote, followed by two less ill-looking fellows, stepped
unceremoniously on board.

" I speak to de captain," said the stranger, in a blunt
tone.

" I am the captain, at your service," answered Porpoise,
standing before him, and preventing his farther advance on
deck.

" Oh ! I come to know where you come from," said the
Greek stranger, casting his eyes furtively round the deck,
as if to discover the state of defence in which we might be.

The look of our sturdy fellows, with their cutlasses by
their sides, might possibly have surprised him, and at all

events he must have seen that there was little chance of surprising us.

"We come from England," answered Porpoise, bluntly.
"A civil question requires a civil answer, but I don't know
by what right you ask it."

"Where you bound for?" continued the Greek, not notic-
ing the last remark it seemed.

"Malta, Alexandria, Smyrna, and a few other places up
the Levant," said Porpoise.

"Ah! will you take letter for me? You do me great
favor," said the Greek, putting his hand in his bosom.

While the Greek was speaking, I had been eyeing him
narrowly from the after-part of the vessel, where I had
placed myself. Most of my readers have heard of the famed
Vanderdecken, the terrible Flying Dutchman, who in his
phantom ship goes cruising about to the southward of the
Cape of Good Hope, sailing right into the eye of the heaviest gale. When he falls in with a vessel, he comes aboard,
and requests a packet he presents may be taken on shore.
Just such another as Vanderdecken did our present visitor
appear, except that the Dutchman is habited in a somewhat
different costume to the Greek, in broad-brimmed hat, big-
buttoned waistcoat, and wide breeches. By the way Porpoise looked at him, I had a notion some such idea was
passing through his mind. Perhaps he suspected that the
gentleman had a pistol instead of a letter inside the folds of
his vest. The boat's crew meantime sat scowling at us,
and surveying the vessel with a no friendly look; I guessed,
indeed, that nothing would have given them greater pleasure
than to have been able to jump on board, and to cut all our
throats.

"We shall be happy to take your letter or any commands
17

on shore," answered Porpoise, putting his hand in his pocket in imitation of the Greek.

The stranger furtively eyed the movement of his hand, as much as to say, " Why, have you got a pistol there likewise ? "

However, withdrawing his own hand from his bosom, he exclaimed, " Ah ! I have by some omission left my letter on board."

The man spoke with as downright an English pronunciation as I ever heard in my life. Pretty well for a Greek, thought I, stepping forward to examine his features more narrowly. I had had my suspicions from the time he stepped on board; so, it appeared, had Tom Newton. There could be very little doubt about the matter; the man who stood before us in the guise of a Greek, was no other than the *ci-devant* pirate — slaver — smuggler, the outlaw Miles Sandgate. I thought his keen eye glanced at my countenance for a moment, as if he recognized me ; but so completely did he maintain his self-possession, that he did not exhibit the slightest sign of fear or hesitation. He bit his lips though, as if he found that he had betrayed himself by speaking English too fluently, and he instantly fell back into his former mode of expression. Porpoise had either not remarked his slip of the tongue, or thought it best not to comment on it.

" I go send letter aboard," he continued, stepping back a pace as if to be ready to spring into his boat. His crew in the mean time had begun to vociferate something I could not understand. He replied to them in the same language, and I have no doubt it was to tell them that their enterprise was fruitless, and that it was not quite so easy to catch the crew of an English yacht napping as they might have supposed. He still hesitated to take his departure. Some plan

or other was passing through his fertile, ever-active brain.
Perhaps he did not suspect that I had recognized him.
However, whatever might have been his intentions, he was
summoned hurriedly into the boat by his crew. He turned
hastily round and cast his eye to the northward, so did I and
Porpoise. There, rising out of the water as it were, was a
small white cloud, which, as we looked, every instant increased in size.

"You'd better shorten sail, or you'll repent it," exclaimed
the seeming Greek, as he leaped into his boat.

The crew pulled lustily away in the direction of their own
vessel. Nothing comes on so rapidly and gives so little time
for preparation as does a white squall in the Mediterranean.
Porpoise, taking the advice offered, gave the necessary orders.
All hands rushed to the halliards and downhauls, but before
a rope could be let go the squall was upon us. A drift of
white foam came rushing towards the cutter, driven on by
some irresistible power, which at the same time curled up
the whole hitherto calm and shining sea into rolling, breaking waves. Our eyes were almost blinded with the salt
mist which dashed over us. Terrific was the blow we received. The cutter having no steerage way offered a dead
resistance to it. Over she went as does a stately tree, its
stem cut through by the woodman's deadly axe and saw.

"Hold on! hold on for your lives!" sung out Porpoise.

There was good reason. I thought she would never rise
again. The water rose up her decks. We began to look at
boats and spars as the only hope of safety. Then shrouds
and stays and bolts gave way, and the stout mast cracked
off at the deck with a loud crash; and the little craft rising
on an even keel floated in safety, but presented a forlorn
wreck compared to the gay and gallant trim in which she
had lately appeared. Not a moment was to be lost in ascer-

taining whether the cutter had received any vital damage, and in endeavoring to put her to rights. Everybody was busily engaged in the work. Hearty and our landsmen friends took the matter very coolly.

" Just sing out where you want us to lend a hand, and we are four men," cried Hearty, pulling and hauling away with a will, while we were getting in the wreck of our mast and spars.

The drag of the rigging astern brought the vessel up into the wind's eye, and then she lay pitching and bobbing away into the short seas, sending the spray flying over us like a regular shower-bath, and surrounding us with a mist impervious to the sight. It was heavy work, and as part of the bulwarks had been knocked away there was no little danger of being washed overboard. Where, however, all labor with a will, the hardest task is soon performed ; and no fellows could have worked harder than did our crew of yachtsmen. Before, however, the craft was in any way put to rights, the squall and its effects on the sea had completely passed away, but night coming down had shrouded us in total darkness. No one had thought of the Greek brig or her boat, and now not a glimpse of either was to be perceived.

What had become of her ? Had the boat with the rascal Sandgate been swamped ? Had the brig been caught by the squall and gone down ? Such had been the fate of many a craft in the Mediterranean. When we had got the yacht somewhat to rights we made inquiries among the men, but no one had observed her. Old Sleet, it was said, had watched the boat pulling away for her even during the hurly-burly of the squall. I therefore called him up to examine him more particularly.

" When we was on our beam-ends, and I thought we was

over for good, still I couldn't help keeping my eye on the boat," said the old man ; " I can't say as how I liked the look of that ere curious chap the Greek captain who came ·aboard us, and as for his crew, a bigger set of cut-throats I never saw. Well, thinks I to myself, if the boat goes to the bottom, and all her people goes in her, there's no great harm done : but if she floats and gains the brig, they may just come back when we are not prepared for them, and try to knock us all on the head ; but, says I to myself, there's no use talking about it, for the gentlemen won't believe such a thing possible, and I shall only get laughed at for my pains."

· I was very much inclined to agree with the old man, that if our Greek friend had escaped drowning, and could discover our whereabout, he would be apt to try his hand at playing us some scurvy trick ; but I said nothing to this effect. I, however, resolved to speak to Porpoise, so that we might be prepared to resist any attack he might attempt to make on us. Porpoise was rather inclined to laugh at my fears.

" My belief is that the fellow went to the bottom," he replied. " Serve him right, too, if he is the rascal you suppose him ; or if he got aboard his ship he saw enough of us to know that we should prove rather a tough morsel, should he attempt to swallow us."

A council of war having been called, it was resolved that we should try to get back to Gibraltar as fast as we could. To effect this, however, it would be necessary to rig jury-·masts, and this could not very well be done till daylight. We proposed turning the cutter into a schooner or lugger, and happily, as we had saved most of our spars and canvas, we expected to have no great difficulty in getting sufficient sail on her to navigate with ease the poor little closely-shorn craft.

I have often had in my naval career to pass through nights of toil and anxiety, and this gave every promise of being one of that character. In a few hours we had gathered in all our ruffled feathers, or, in other words, our masts and spars and sails and rigging; and having stowed them along the decks as best we could, there we lay floating helplessly like a log on the water. Not having discarded my suspicions of the polacca-brig, notwithstanding my fatigue I felt no inclination to go to sleep. I now was left in charge of the deck while Porpoise and the rest of my messmates turned in, all standing. I walked the deck for some time, ever and anon turning my gaze upward to the dark blue vault of heaven glittering with a thousand stars, each but a centre of some mighty system, each more complex and marvellous, probably, than our own. I thought of the all-potent Being who made them as well as all the wondrous specimens of animal life which dwell on this globe we call our own, and my heart swelled with gratitude to Him who had preserved me and my shipmates from the danger to which we had been exposed. My spirit, as I thought, seemed to take its flight through the calm atmosphere, and to wander far far away among those distant spheres. How long it was away I know not. I was not conscious of the existence of my body on the surface of the globe. A splash aroused me from my reveries. It was caused by a fish leaping out of its liquid home to avoid some monster of the deep wishing to make a supper off it. It called me back to earth and things earthly. My first impulse was to cast my eye round the horizon. It was rather a circumscribed one at that hour of darkness. Once I made the full circuit and could see nothing. I took a few more turns on deck, and again I swept my eye round the watery circle more slowly than before. As I reached the south-eastern point of the heavens

I was certain I saw a dark object. I rubbed my eyes. The sails of a vessel appeared before me, rising up like a thin dark pencil-line against the sky. I wetted my fingers and held up my hand. The cold struck it on that side. Whatever she might be she was well to windward of us. I took the night-glass, which hung on brackets just inside the companion-hatch. She was still too far off to enable me to make out what she was. I had not, however, forgotten my suspicions of the polacca. The stranger was evidently approaching us. If she was the Greek, her crew would scarcely resist the temptation of attempting to plunder us. Still I felt that my suspicions were almost absurd, and I did not like to arouse my friends without some better grounds for my fears. I, however, felt it would be wise not to run the risk of being taken altogether unprepared. I therefore went up alongside old Snow — so we called him, though he was young enough to be old Sleet's son. I was not long in waking him up to the proper pitch of caution by narrating a variety of stories about pirates and slavers and savages, and such like gentry, with a due admixture of instances where people from carelessness were caught napping and lost their lives.

"Now," said I, "let us get these spars cleared away enough to work the guns. The watch on deck will do it without rousing the rest. We'll have a supply up of round shot and ammunition. The people have not restored their pistols and cutlasses to the arm-chest. Send a couple of hands to collect them all ready, and then if yonder stranger proves to be the polacca, and wishes to taste our quality, we'll let her have her will, and show her what we are made of."

I spoke thus confidently that there might be no risk of taking any of the pluck out of the people. I cannot say, however, that I at all liked the notion of a brush with the well-manned and probably well-armed polacca-brig in our present dismantled condition, however little I might have feared her at close quarters had we been all to rights. I watched the approach of the stranger, therefore, with no little anxiety. She was evidently bearing right down upon us, though, as there was but little wind, her progress was slow. The hours of the night wore on. I was leaning against the wreck of the mast which lay fore and aft along the deck, and at length I fell asleep. I do not know how long I had slept when I heard Porpoise's voice close to me.

"Hillo, Brine! what in the name of wonder is that away there to windward?" he exclaimed.

"The polacca-brig, there's no doubt about it," I answered, as I beheld a vessel like a dark phantom stealing up towards us. I then explained to him the preparations I had made in case the brig should really be of the piratical character we suspected, and at the same time inclined to attack us. This relieved his mind not a little. My belief, however, was that the Greek might not have seen us. She might, of course, have calculated our whereabouts. Perhaps even now she might not see us. Perhaps, also, as Porpoise suggested, if the boat was swamped in the squall, the rest of the crew would probably cruise about to look for their companions. He agreed with me, therefore, that we need not yet rouse up Hearty and our other two friends. By the by, in consequence of all the delays we must endure, I was doubly glad that we had not told Hearty of Miss Mizen's expedition to Malta. It would have made him undergo them with much less than his usual philosophy, I suspect.

"I doubt if even now the brig sees us," said I as I watched her through the night-glass. So low down in the water as we were, she was very likely to miss us.

"See, she is passing us," exclaimed Porpoise, after we had watched her for some time. "It is just as well she should miss us, for in our present state we could not exactly do ourselves justice."

"Perhaps after all our friends may be very well disposed, and in no way inclined to do us any harm," said I, not that I could in reality divest myself of the idea that the polacca was commanded by Sandgate, and that he would have delighted to do us all the mischief in his power. With daylight, however, I don't think I should fear him, even now, I thought to myself.

It still wanted nearly an hour to sunrise, and daylight in that clime does not come very long before the glorious luminary of day rushes up from his ocean bed. We hoped by that time that the brig would have pretty well run us out of sight. Still neither Porpoise nor I felt inclined to go below again. We intended, indeed, to rouse out all hands to get up the jury-masts the moment we had light to work by. We, however, were not so clear of danger as we fancied. The brig had got about a mile to leeward of us, when we saw her brace up her yards, and, close hauled, she stood back so as soon to fetch us. There was no longer any time to spare.

"Rouse up all hands fore and aft," sung out Porpoise, with a stentorian voice.

In a minute every one was on deck busily employed in casting loose the guns, in priming pistols, and buckling on cutlasses.

"If the fellow will but come to close quarters, we have no reason to fear him," exclaimed our gallant skipper, surveying his crew with no little pride.

"I only wish we may have a brush with him," added Hearty; "it would tell well in the Club; only I wish we had our mast standing." I cannot say that I participated altogether in the satisfaction of my friends. The brig, if she did attack us, I knew, we must find an ugly customer, and the pirates could only venture to do so with the full intention of sending every one of us, with the yacht into the bargain, to the bottom, on the principle that dead men tell no tales.

The Greek was not long in showing us his intentions. No sooner had he got us within range of his guns, than brailing up his courses and lowering his topsails, he opened his fire upon our almost helpless craft. Happily for us his gunnery was very bad, and he evidently had a fancy for long bowls, and a wholesome dread of coming to close quarters with us. Our people went cheerily to their guns, not a bit afraid of our big enemy.

" Only just do ye come on, ye confounded scoundrels, and we'll just give ye a taste of what we are made of," sung out Tom Hall, a broad-shouldered fellow, standing six feet high or more in his stockings, as he shook his cutlass in an attitude of defiance at the enemy ; and no one was better able to give an account of them than he would have been when the day's work was over.

Will Bubble threw off his coat, fastened a silk handkerchief round his waist and another round his head, and worked away at his little gun in fine style. Carstairs did the same in a more deliberate manner, whistling the fag end of a hunting song. If we had possessed guns four times the size of ours, I verily believe, crippled as were, we should very soon have sent our antagonists to the bottom, instead of running the risk of going there ourselves. Finding his shot fall short or wide of us, he ran on a little way, and then tacking, stood closer up to us.

CHAPTER XIX.

THE ENGAGEMENT — OUR DESPERATE CONDITION — A FRIEND
IN SIGHT — OUR ENEMY FLIES — MALTA.

BY this time the first faint streaks of early dawn had
appeared in the sky; but in that latitude the sun does not
take long to get above the horizon, and daylight was on us
almost as soon as the brig had again got us within range of
her guns. Two or three shots struck our hull, and at the
same time the enemy opened a fire of musketry on us; but
the pirates did not prove themselves better marksmen with
their small arms than they had hitherto done with their
heavier guns.

"Oh, I wish the rascals would but attempt to run us
aboard!" exclaimed Hearty. "To think of their impudence
in daring to knock holes in the side of my yacht!"

"There spoke a true Briton," observed Bubble as he once
more ran out his gun. "He does not think any thing of
being shot at; but the idea of having his property injured,
or his home invaded, rouses all his anger. Here goes
though; I'll see if we can't pay them off in their own coin,
with some change in our favor."

Will was a capital marksman, and as cool as a cucumber,
which was more than most of our men were, though not one
was wanting in pluck. He pulled the trigger, and as I
watched to see the effects of his fire, I saw two men fall on
the pirate's deck, while some white splinters flying from the
mainmast showed us that the shot had, as well, done some
damage to the vessel herself.

267

"Hurra! bravo, Bubble!" I shouted, and the crew echoed my cry, which, rising in full chorus, must have reached the ears of our enemy, and showed them that we were not likely to prove as easy a prey as they might have fancied. "Another such a shot as that, and I believe they will up helm and be off," I exclaimed.

"I'll do my best," answered Bubble, fanning himself with his broad-brimmed hat, for the weather was very hot, and he had been making, for him, somewhat unusual exertions.

Will now trained his gun with great care: a great deal depended on a fortunate shot. "If we could but bring down one of his masts, or make a hole through his sides, we should win the day even now," he exclaimed, kneeling down to aim with more deliberation; "a ten-pound note to the man who wounds a mast, or sends a shot between wind and water." As he afterwards acknowledged, the ten pounds was truly a widow's mite with him, for he hadn't another such sum in his locker to back it.

"I'll make it twenty," cried Hearty, who really seemed to enjoy the excitement of the adventure; "come, let us see who will win it."

"I have," cried Bubble, jumping up and clapping his hands like a schoolboy, as he watched with intense eagerness his shot strike the hull of the brig just at the water-line, sending the white splinters flying in every direction.

"Fairly won, Bubble, fairly won!" we all exclaimed; "if they don't plug that hole pretty quickly, they will soon find their jackets wetter than they like."

In return for the mischief we had done him, the pirate let fly his whole broadside at us. He was every instant drawing nearer and nearer, either to give his guns more effect, or to attempt carrying us by boarding. He probably fancied that we were by this time weakened by loss of men, as he very likely was not aware of the little effect produced by his own guns. Dismasted as we were, and low in the water, we presented, indeed, a somewhat difficult mark to hit. The pirate's approach gave us another advantage, as we were now able to bring our own musketry into play, which somewhat made up for the lightness of our guns. We had a great advantage also in the rapid way we were able to load our guns, which were of brass, while our opponents' were probably of iron. Our muskets, too, were kept constantly at work; Ruggles, the steward, and Pepper, the boy, being set to load them as fast as they were discharged, while Carstairs had a first-rate rifle, with which he picked off every fellow whose red cap appeared above the bulwarks with as much *sang froid* as he would have knocked over a partridge on the 1st of September.

As our yachtsmen had had no practice with their guns, they were not particularly good shots, so that none of them surpassed Bubble in the accuracy of their aim, greatly to his delight. The enemy's shot now began to fall rather thicker around us, while two or three of our people were hit with their musket-balls. None of them were hurt sufficiently to make them leave the deck; we could not, however, expect that this state of impunity would long continue. I every now and then turned an eye on Bubble to watch his energetic proceedings, though I had enough to do to load and fire away with my own musket. On a sudden, as he jumped up to watch the effect of his shot, I saw him stagger back and fall on the deck; I sprang forward to raise him up, " Oh, it's nothing, nothing," he exclaimed, turning, however, at the same time very pale; " only the wind of a shot or a little more; but it's a new sensation; took me by surprise; just set me on my legs again, and I shall be all to rights soon."

This, however, was more than I could do, poor fellow. He had been hit, and badly too, I was afraid; I sent Ruggles down for a glass of brandy and water. "Just bring up a flask, and a jug of water also," said I, "others may want it." Bubble was much revived by the draught, and binding a handkerchief over his side, which was really wounded, though not so badly as I feared, with the greatest pluck he again went to his gun.

During this interval the enemy had ceased firing, having shot some way ahead of us, but he now again tacked, and, looking well up to windward, stood towards us on a line which would enable him to run us aboard, if he pleased, or to strike us so directly amidships, that there was every probability of his sinking us. This last proceeding was the one most to be feared, and I felt sure that he would not scruple so to do. I could not tell if my frriends saw the terrific danger we were in; I thought not, for they went on peppering away with their fire-arms, and laughing and cheering, as if the whole affair was a very good joke. I confess that my heart sank within me as I contemplated the fate which awaited us. "How soon will those gay and gallant spirits be quenched in death," I thought. "How completely will our remorseless enemies triumph. They have all this time been merely playing with us as a cat does with a mouse." Five minutes more would, I calculated, consummate the catastrophe. A minute had, however, scarcely passed, when I saw the brig square away her yards; and putting up her helm, off she went before the wind. Her courses were let fall; topgallant-sails were set, studding-sails and royals soon followed. Every stitch of canvas she could carry was got on her, while not the slightest further attention did she pay to us. I rubbed my eyes, for I could scarcely believe my senses. We, however, continued firing away as long as there was the chance of a shot reaching her, and then our men set up such a jovial, hearty cheer, which if it could have reached the ears of the pirates, would have convinced them that we had still an abundance of fight left in us.

What had caused the enemy so suddenly to haul off was now the wonder. At all events, I trust that we were thankful for our unexpected deliverance. When I pointed out to my companions the danger we had been in, they at once saw it themselves. Porpoise had seen it, indeed, all along, but had concealed his apprehension as I had done mine.

"The rascal found we were too tough a morsel to swallow, so thought he had better let us alone at once," said Hearty.

"I cannot think that," I observed; "he had some other reason, depend on it." I was right; the mystery was soon solved. All hands at once set to work to fit and rig the jury-masts, when we were called from our occupation by a cheer from Bubble, whose wound made it clearly dangerous for him to exert himself in any way.

"A sail, a sail!" he exclaimed; "a big ship, too, I suspect."

I looked in the direction in which he pointed away to windward, where the topsails of a ship appeared rising above the horizon; from their squareness I judged her to be a man-of-war. The rising sun just tinged the weather-side of her canvas, as she bore down on us with a streak of light which made her stand out in bold relief against the deep blue sky. The pirate crew had, of course, seen her from aloft long before we could have done so. She was welcome in every way, as she would probably enable us to get into port. The only provoking part of the business was,

that the pirate would in all probability get away with impunity. Had she but come on the scene an hour earlier,
she would, probably, have been down upon us before either
we or the pirate could have seen her, and would most assuredly have nabbed our amigo.

"Never mind," said Porpoise, "the fellow can scarcely
get out of the Straits, even if he wishes it, and if I ever fall
in with him within the boundaries of the Mediterranean, I
have no fear of not knowing him again ; we shall hear more
of him by and by, depend on it."

Our fighting had given us an appetite, so we went to
breakfast with no little satisfaction, though we had not
much time to spare for it. Bubble would not acknowledge
that his wound was of consequence, though he let me look
to it, as I did to the hurts of the other poor fellows who
were hit. From the appearance they presented, I was truly
glad that there was a good prospect of their having surgical
aid without delay. They did not know, as I did, that their
wounds would be far more painful in a few hours than they
were at that time, so they made very light of them. As
the stranger drew nearer, we made her out to be a sloop-of-
war, and the ensign flying from her peak showed her to be
British ; she had been standing so as to pass a little way to
the westward of us. When, however, she made us out,
which she did not do till she was quite close to us, she
altered her course and was soon hove-to, a few cables' length
to leeward. A boat was lowered, and, with an officer in the
stern-sheets, came pulling towards us.

"What in the name of wonder is the matter?" exclaimed
the officer, standing up and surveying us with no little
surprise.

"Why, Sprat, the matter is that we have been dismasted
in a white squall, which would have sent many a craft to

the bottom," answered Porpoise, who in the officer recognized an old shipmate; "we since then have been made a target of by a rascally pirate, whose mast heads have scarcely yet sunk beneath the horizon."

"If that is the case, we must see if we cannot catch her," answered Lieutenant Sprat, who was second lieutenant of the corvette.

"What, sir! leave us rolling helplessly about here like an empty tub?" exclaimed Hearty, in a dolorous tone. "But never mind, if you think you can catch her, I dare say we can take care of ourselves."

"I'll report the state of things to Captain Arden, and learn what he wishes," quoth Lieutenant Sprat, as he pulled back to his ship.

In another minute the corvette's jolly-boat was seen leaving her side, while she, putting up her helm, stood away in the direction the pirate had taken. The jolly-boat soon came alongside, with a midshipman and six men.

"Captain Arden has sent me with the carpenter's mate and some of his crew to help you in," quoth Master Middie, addressing Porpoise; "we'll soon get a new mast into you, and carry you safely to old Gib, or wherever you want to go."

Porpoise looked at him, and evidently felt very much inclined to laugh. He was one of the shortest lads in a midshipman's uniform I ever saw; but he was broad-shouldered, and had a countenance which showed clearly that he very well knew what he was about.

"Thank you," answered Porpoise; "we shall be much beholden to you I doubt not, though we should have been glad if your captain had sent us a doctor as well, May I ask your name, young gentleman?"

"Mite, sir; Anthony Mite," answered the midshipman, a little taken aback at Porpoise's manner.

18

The old lieutenant did not quite like his patronizing airs.

"I thought so," observed our worthy skipper; "your father was a shipmate of mine, youngster, and you are very like him."

"In knowing my father you knew a brave man, I hope, sir, you will allow," replied Master Mite, with much spirit.

"But I did not know that you were in the service. A better or braver fellow never stepped," answered Porpoise, warmly, putting out his hand. "I've no doubt you are worthy of him, youngster. We'll have a yarn about him by and by. However, just now, we must try to get the craft in sailing trim again."

Small as the young midshipman was in stature, he soon made it evident that he was of the true stuff which forms a hero. He was here, there, and everywhere, pulling and hauling, directing and encouraging. So rapid were his movements, that his body seemed ubiquitous, while the tone of his voice showed that he was well accustomed to command and to be obeyed. We had no reason to complain of either the officer or laborers Captain Arden had sent us. Meantime I had been keeping my eye on the proceedings of the corvette. She at first stood away steadily to the northward and eastward, in the direction the brig had taken, and it seemed evident that she had her in sight; then she altered her course to the westward, but finally disappeared below the horizon, steering nearly due north.

"If the man-of-war has still the brig in sight, the latter must be making for some Spanish port, where the pirates hope to lie concealed till the search for them is over," I thought to myself. "However, Sandgate, if he really is the commander, is up to all sorts of dodges, and will very likely, somehow or other, manage to make his escape."

As may be supposed, we watched very anxiously for the

re-appearance of the corvette, but the sun went down, and we saw nothing of her. However, we had by this time got up apologies for three masts, and, moreover, managed to make sail on them.

It was a great satisfaction to feel the poor little barkie once more slipping through the water, though at a much slower pace than usual.

As I feared, both Bubble and the men who had been wounded began, towards midnight, to complain somewhat . of their hurts. While we were all sitting round the table in the cabin at supper, before turning in, Hearty, as Porpoise had done, expressed his regret that Captain Arden had not sent us a surgeon.

" Oh, we didn't know that any one was hurt," observed Mr. Mite. " But never mind, I understand something of doctoring. I can bleed in first-rate style, I can tell you. Don't you think I had better try my hand?"

" Thank you, they have been bled enough already, I suspect," answered Hearty. " I'm afraid no one on board can do much good to them. I only pray the wind may hold, and that we may soon get into Gibraltar."

But Master Mite was not so easily turned aside from his purpose of trying his hand as a surgeon. He begged hard that he might, at all events, be allowed to examine the men's wounds.

We of course assured our young friend that we did not doubt his surgical talents ; but still declined allowing him to operate on any of the yacht's crew. We were not sorry, however, to let him take the middle watch, which he volunteered to do, for both Porpoise and I and old Snow were regularly worn out. The wind held fair, and there was not much of it. The night passed away quietly, and when morning broke we saw the corvette standing after us. She had been, as I expected, unsuccessful in her chase of the Greek brig. She had made all sail after a craft which she took for her, but on coming up with the chase, discovered her to be an honest trader laden with corn. She now took us in tow, and in the afternoon we reached the Rock.

Hearty very soon heard that the "Zebra" had gone on to Malta, with Miss Mizen on board, and from the way he received the information, I suspected that his feelings towards her were of a warmer character than I at first supposed. He was very anxious to be away again, and urged on Porpoise to do his utmost to expedite the refitting of the yacht. Fortunately, we were able to procure a spar intended for the mast of a man-of-war schooner, and which was not refused to the application of an M.P. In a week the little craft was all to rights again, and once more on her way to that little military hot-house — the far-famed island of Malta.

CHAPTER XX.

MALTA lay basking on the bright blue ocean, looking very white and very hot under the scorching rays of a burning sun, as, early in the afternoon, we stood towards the entrance of the harbor of Valetta. Passing St. Elmo Castle on our right, and Fort Ricasoli on our left, whose numberless guns looked frowning down upon us, as if ready, at a moment's notice, to annihilate any enemy daring to enter with an exhibition of hostile intent, we ran up that magnificent inlet called the Grand Harbor.

Malta Harbor has been so often described, that my readers will not thank me for another elaborate drawing. Only, let them picture to themselves a gulf from three to four hundred yards across, with several deep inlets full of shipping, and on every conspicuous point, on all sides, white batteries of hewn stone, of various heights, some flush with the water, others rising in tiers one above another, with huge black guns grinning out of them, the whole crowned with flat-roofed barracks, and palaces and churches and steeples and towers, with a blue sky overhead, and blue water below, covered with oriental-looking boats, and lateen-rigged craft, with high-pointed triangular sails of snowy whiteness, and boatmen in gayly-colored scarfs and caps, and men-of-war, and merchant-vessels — and a very tolerable idea will be formed of the place.

Valetta itself, the capital, stands on a hog's back, a nar-

row but high neck of land, dividing the Grand Harbor from
the quarantine harbor, called, also, Marsa Muceit.   The
chief streets run in parallel lines along the said hog's back,
and they are intersected by others, which run up and down
its steep sides.   In some parts they are so steep that flights of
steps take the place of the carriage-way.   The best known
of these steps are the Nix Mangiari Stairs, so called from
the troops of little beggars who infest them, and assure all
passers-by that they have had nothing to eat for six days.
" *Oh, signori, me no fader no moder; me nix mangiari seis
journi !* "   An assertion which their fat cheeks and obese
little figures most undeniably contradict. · Few people will
forget those steep steps who have had to toil to the top
of them on a sweltering day, not one, but three or four
times, perchance ; nor will those noisy, lazy, dirty beggars
— those sights most foul — those odors most sickening —
fade from his memory.

We ran up the harbor and dropped our anchor not far
from the chief landing-place, abreast of Nix Mangiari Steps.
There were several men-of-war in the harbor.   Among them
was our old friend the " Trident."

" If Piper sees us, we shall soon have him on board to
tell us all the news," observed Porpoise.   " I don't think
Master Mite will forget us, either, if he can-manage to come.
Our good things, in the way of eating and drinking, made
no slight impression on his mind, whatever he may have
thought of us as individuals.   If he has an opportunity,
that little fellow will distinguish himself."

While stowing sails, the rest of the party having gone
below to prepare for a visit to the shore, my eye, as it
ranged round the harbor, fell on the sails of a Greek brig,
which was just then standing out of the galley port.   I
looked at her attentively, and then pointed her out to Snow,

who was so earnest in seeing that his mainsail was stowed
in the smoothest of skins, that he had not observed her.

"What do you think of her?" said I.

"Why, sir, if she isn't that rascally craft which attacked
us, she is as like her as one marlinspike is to another!" he
exclaimed, slapping his hand on his thigh. "I'll be hanged
but what I believe it is her, and no mistake about it."

"I think so, too. Call Mr. Porpoise," said I.

Porpoise jumped on deck with his coat off, and a hair-
brush in each hand, to look at her.

"I couldn't swear to her; but she is the same build and
look of craft as our piratical friend," he answered. "Hang
it! I wish that we had come in an hour or two sooner; we
might have just nabbed her. As it is, I fear, before we can
have time to get the power from the proper authorities to
stop her, she will be far away, and laughing at us. At all
events, there is not a moment to be lost."

By this time all hands were on deck, looking at the Greek
brig; but all were not agreed as to her being the pirate.
However, the gig was lowered, and we pulled on shore, to
hurry up as fast as we could to the governor's palace, to
make our report, and to get him to stop the brig before she
got out of the harbor.

Landing among empty casks and bales on the sandy
shore, we hurried up Nix Mangiari Stairs, greatly to the
detriment of Porpoise's conversational powers, and then on
to the residence of the governor, once the palace of the
Grand Master of the far-famed Knights of Malta; a huge
square structure, imposing for its size, rather than for the
beauty of its architecture. The governor was within, and
without delay we were ushered through a magnificent suite
of rooms into his presence. He received us politely, but
raised his eyebrows at the account of our adventure with

the pirate, and seemed to insinuate that yachting gentlemen might be apt to be mistaken, and that we had perhaps after all only found a mare's-nest.

"But, hang it, sir," exclaimed Hearty, "the villain fired into us as fast as he could; and that gentleman, Mr. Bubble, and several of my people, were hit. There was no fancy in that, I imagine."

"Ah, I see; that alters the case," said the governor. "We will send and stop the brig; but understand, that you will have to prove that she is the vessel which fired into you; and, if she is not, you must be answerable for the consequences."

"By all manner of means," sung out Hearty. "I suppose the consequences won't be very dreadful."

"Hang the consequences," he exclaimed, as soon afterwards we were left to ourselves, to await the report from the telegraph-station. "I cannot bear to hear these official gentlemen babbling of consequences when rogues are to be punished, and honest men protected. A thing must be either right or wrong. If it's right, do it—if it's wrong, let it alone. I hate the red-tape system which binds our rulers from beginning to end. We must break through it, and that pretty quickly, or Old England will come to an end."

We were all ready enough to argue with Hearty in this matter, though the said breaking through an old deep-rooted system is more easy to propose than to carry into effect.

After we had waited some time, word was brought to the palace that, as I expected would be the case, the suspicious brig had got out of the harbor; and was out of the range of the guns on the batteries before the message had reached them. A gun was fired to bring her to, but of course she paid no attention to the signal. Once more we were ushered into the presence of the governor. He was very civil and very kind, be it understood.

" Your best course is to go to the admiral, and tell him your story, and perhaps he will send a man-of-war after her."

" Thank you, sir," said Hearty, rising. " We will do as you advise ; though I fear, before a man-of-war can get under way, our piratical friend will be safe from pursuit."

" It matters little. He is very certain to be caught before long ; and we will have him hung at his own yard-arm, like some of his predecessors," observed the governor, politely bowing us out.

" Humph ! " muttered Hearty, as we descended the superb steps of the palatial abode. " It matters not, I suppose, how many throats may be cut, and how many rich cargoes sent to the bottom, in the mean time. Hang official routine, I say again. We must get these things altered in Parliament." *

The admiral was living on shore, and to his residence we repaired as fast as our legs would carry us, with the thermometer at 90.

" I wish that we had taken the law into our own hands, and made chase after the fellow in the yacht," exclaimed poor Porpoise, wiping the perspiration from his forehead. " A few hours' fighting would have been better than this hot work."

" All very well if we could prove that she was the vessel which attacked us ; but if it should have turned out that we were mistaken, we should have been in the place of the

* Let no one suppose that this incident is intended to reflect on any particular governor of Malta. It is, unhappily, only too characteristic of many of our governors, ambassadors, and consuls, and other authorities in various parts of the world, both at home and abroad. Certainly, old Tom, well known to fame, would not have so acted.

pirates, and have been accused of murder, robbery, rapine, and all sorts of atrocities," remarked Bubble. "No, no; depend on it, things are better as they are. Retribution will overtake the fellows one of these days."

The admiral's abode was reached at last; but the admiral was not at home, though his secretary was. The admiral had gone into the country, and would not return till the cool of the evening. The secretary received us very politely, though he seemed rather inclined to laugh at our suspicions.

A pirate sail into Malta Harbor, — beard the lion in his den! The idea was too absurd. It was scarcely possible that any pirates could exist in the Mediterranean. A few had appeared, from time to time, it was true; but several had been hung, and the example had proved a warning to other evil-doers. He would, however, as soon as the admiral returned, mention the circumstance to him, and if he thought fit he would undoubtedly send a vessel in chase of the suspected polacca.

Such was the substance of the worthy secretary's remarks to us. We could not go in search of the admiral, as it was uncertain where he was to be found, so, very little satisfied with our morning's work, we left the house.

"What shall we do next?" exclaimed Hearty. "There seems to be no chance of our catching Master Sandgate."

"Oh, by all means, let us go on board and get cool," answered Porpoise.

"Certainly," said Bubble, "I want to look out some zephyr clothing. One can bear nothing thicker than a cobweb this sultry weather."

So on board we went, and lay each man in his cabin with all the sky-lights off, and wind-sails down, an awning over the deck, and a pulkah invented by Bubble, kept working, which sent a stream of air through every portion of our abode, so that we were far more comfortable than we could have been anywhere else. When yachting I always make a point of going everywhere in the yacht, and living on board her, scarcely ever entering an hotel. We thus spent two or three hours — some reading, others smoking or talking, Bubble every now and then giving vent to his feelings in snatches of song. I am not certain that we did not all drop asleep. We were aroused from our quietness by the sound of footsteps on deck, and by the descent of the steward into the cabin.

"Please, sir, that young gentleman that came aboard from the sloop-of-war, after we lost our masts, wants to know if he may come below to see you," said he to Hearty.

"By all means," cried Hearty, springing up; "glad to see him."

Master Mite had followed the steward, and heard the last observation.

"Thank you, sir," quoth he, helping himself to a seat. "Glad to see you, too. Scarcely thought you would be here so soon. Just in time for a grand ball. You'll like it. We can take you there. I'm a great favorite with the signora. Told me to bring all my friends — the more the better — very hearty people for Smaitches. That's what we call the Maltese here, you know. I saw your craft come in, and wanted to come on board before, but couldn't. A midshipman is not always his own master, you know. At last I got leave from our jolly old first, Tom Piper. He told me to say that he would come as soon as he could. I know that he wants to press you to come to the ball, also."

Thus did the young midshipman run on. Hearty told him that he should be very happy to go to his friend's house under his chaperonage, and that so should we all, which mightily pleased Master Mite.

"That's right," he exclaimed. "It will be jolly good fun, I can tell you. There are some very nice English people, too, great friends of mine. Such a splendiferous girl, too — a Miss Mizen — came out with her uncle, old Rullock, in the 'Zebra.' I dance with her whenever I can. If you could but see her I'm sure you'd say my taste was very good. Some people think that she is cut out by another fine girl, a Miss Jane Seton; but I don't. Jane's all very well in her way, very fine to look at, and all that sort of thing; but to say the truth, she's rather addicted to snubbing midshipmen, and that we don't approve of. As for her mother, she wouldn't touch one of us with a boarding-pike. She's a terrible old harridan, and that's not in Jane's favor. Oh, no, give me Laura Mizen for my money, and all our mess say the same. She's the toast of the mess just now, I can tell you."

While the youngster was running on thus I watched Hearty's countenance. He fairly blushed, and looked more pleased and astonished and puzzled than I had ever seen him before in my life. He evidently did not like to stop the boy, though he winced at hearing Miss Mizen spoken of as the toast of the mess. He was astonished, and clearly delighted at hearing that she was so near him, for, as may be remembered, I had not told him that she and her mother had come out to Malta, nor did he hear of the circumstance during our stay at Gibraltar. Dinner was soon brought on the table, and Tom Mite did not fail to do ample justice to it.

"Well, you yachtsmen do live like princes," quoth the

young gentleman, as he quaffed his cool claret. "When I come into my fortune, I'll get a yacht, and cut the service. Then, if Miss Mizen, or some other fine young girl like her, will have me, she shall become the rover's bride. Oh, wouldn't it be jolly! Here's to her health in the mean time!"

I could stand the joke no longer, and burst into a fit of laughter.

"What's the matter?" asked Tommy, guessing he might have been saying something he had better not have said.

"Only that Captain Rullock and his sister and niece are great friends of ours, and that they will be highly flattered at the high estimation in which they are held by your mess," I answered.

Mite, who had plenty of tact, very adroitly replied, "Well, gentlemen, I hope that you will come to the ball, and meet your friends."

His invitation was backed by Lieutenant Piper, who soon afterwards came on board, and it was arranged that we should call alongside the "Trident" for them just before sunset.

CHAPTER XXI.

A BALL — WHAT OCCURRED AT IT — THE GREEK COUNT —
MRS. SKYSCRAPER.

WE were conducted by our friends to a handsome palace
in one of the principal streets of Valetta. The ball-room
was full of naval and military officers in uniform, and ladies
in dresses of every hue and gossamer texture. Many were
fair and blooming, but the dark skins and flashing eyes of a
southern clime predominated.

Hearty and I walked in together. He cast a glance
eagerly round the room. Laura Mizen against the field, as
Carstairs would say, thought I. How will she receive him,
however, is the question? We men are too often apt to
forget that point. He was not long in finding her; he
walked up hastily, and put out his hand. She looked up, a
gleam of pleased surprise lighted up her eyes, and a slight
blush suffused her cheek, and then she put out her hand with
the same frankness he had offered his. All right, I thought;
that is just as people should meet; they will understand
each other very soon. Miss Mizen had entirely overlooked
me when meeting Hearty, which, however complimentary
to him, might, under some circumstances, have hurt my
feelings.

After allowing them to talk a little, I went forward and
was cordially received as his friend. I was surprised that
Carstairs and Bubble had not found their way to that end
of the room. On returning towards the door, after ex-

286

changing a few words with some old naval acquaintance,
I caught sight of him bending over a lady who was leaning
back in an arm-chair flirting with her fan. Her face was
thus hidden from me, but on getting nearer I beheld no less
a personage than Mrs. Skyscraper ; at a little distance was
Bubble, carrying on an animated conversation with Miss
Jane Seton, greatly to the chagrin, as it appeared, of a
magnificently dressed Albanian who stood near them. The
stranger's face was turned away from me, so that I could
not see the expression of his countenance ; but the convulsive clutch which he ever and anon made at the handle of
his jewel-hilted dagger showed the irritation of his feelings ;
and so strongly did this movement impress me with his evil
intentions, that I kept my eye fixed on his weapon to hold
him back should he attempt to do any mischief. Just at
that moment Mite came up to me.

" This is fun, isn't it? " quoth my young friend. " Now
to my mind there's a fine woman, the one Mr. Carstairs is
talking to ; but by Jupiter Ammon she's cut out by that girl
there Mr. Bubble has ranged up alongside. She's superb,
isn't she? What a Juno-like head! Still, do you know
that I don't think I should quite like to offend her. She
looks as if she could twitch a fellow by the ear pretty sharply.
Look there now, there's another girl, she's much more to
my mind, though she has nothing of the stunner about her.
The primrose style is what I like, or the violet, if that's
more to your taste — quiet and neat. Now, that's what I
should call that little fair girl there. I say, I must just try
and have a dance with her ; I ought to, for the skipper
made me toe and heel it with a little Smaitch girl, who was
wonderfully heavy to haul about ; and as she didn't understand a word I said, and as I couldn't make out a word she
said, there was no great fun in it."

Thus the youngster ran on somewhat flippantly, perhaps, drawing off my attention from Bubble and the Greek. I was, however, conscious that the latter had turned his head and looked at me. Directly afterwards he walked off to another part of the room. As I was neither lazy nor too old to dance, nor blind to the charms of beauty, I was soon after this engaged in moving about to the sound of music among the laughing throng. Among others, the fair Jane honored me with her hand. I found her any thing but a lively companion; somewhat absent, and far from haughty as before. Had the avenging Nemesis of an unrequited passion punished her for her treatment of my friend Loring? It looked very like it; she answered my most brilliant sallies of wit by monosyllables, and smiled faintly, putting her bouquet to her nose — but I am certain the sweets therein conveyed no sensation to her olfactory nerves. What was the matter with her I could in no way make out. I was leading her to a seat, somewhat weary with my vain endeavors to arouse her, when we encountered Sir Lloyd Snowdon, one of the officers of the garrison, and evidently an admirer of hers.

" It's all arranged, Miss Seton; we have fixed to have the pic-nic to-morrow. Mrs. Seton has promised and so has Mrs. Mizen, and Mrs. Rowley, and Mrs. Gray, and her daughters, and that charming personage Mrs. Skyscraper only waits to be asked." I recollected the pic-nic we had had to Netley, when my friend Loring had apparently made such way into the good graces of the fair Jane, but she made no sign to betray any recollection of the event. I was acquainted with Sir Lloyd, and he knew Hearty well, so he invited all our party to join the pic-nic on the morrow. Old Rullock of the " Zebra " of course was asked, and so was Captain Arden of the " Trident," and requested to bring some of their officers, rather an unusual stretch of military politeness at Malta, where midshipmen, and even lieutenants, are held often in but slight estimation. We were to visit the old capital of Citta Vecchia and the catacombs, and the grotto of St. Paul's, and then to go on to a sheltered bay on the sea-shore, where the operation of dining was to be performed. The whole plan was soon arranged, and everybody was pleased. I was talking to Mrs. Skyscraper when Sir Lloyd Snowdon came up to us.

" By the by," said he to the widow, " I quite forgot to ask your friend the Greek Count; can you, my dear madam, tell me where he is to be found? I would remedy my neglect."

" Indeed, I cannot," answered the lady with a toss of her head ; " I saw Count Gerovolio, but I have not watched his proceedings."

" Oh, Mrs. Skyscraper — Mrs. Skyscraper ! " thought I, " what were your eyes about when they wandered just now so often towards Miss Seton and that finely dressed Albanian?" I had missed the fair Jane after supper, and heard her mother inquiring for her. I had wandered out on a narrow terrace which ran under the windows of a long corridor, to enjoy the fresh air and the moonlight. As I passed under one of the windows, I saw two figures standing in the recess. One I saw was Count Gerovolio, the other I felt sure was Miss Seton. I would not have willingly been an eavesdropper, but I could scarcely help hearing what was said. I was arrested, also, by finding that the speakers were conversing in English.

" Beautiful girl," exclaimed the Count, in a tone of deep devotion, " you have enslaved me completely. I sought you but for my amusement, and you have thrown your golden

19

chains around me, so that I could not break from them if I would."

" Oh! who are you?" exclaimed Miss Seton, in an agitated tone. " You did not tell me you could speak English. Surely you are not an Englishman."

" Whatever I am, I am a Greek at heart and by adoption," answered the stranger, with a slight hesitation in his voice. " I was first led to the shores of that classic land to fight for the cause of her long-oppressed children. My sword raised me to my present position. Let that suffice you. And now, lovely girl, do not longer hold me in torturing suspense. You know how deeply, how earnestly, I love you. Your mother, you tell me, will not consent to our union. Fly with me at once. My beautiful vessel waits off the coast to receive us on board, and to convey us to a land of freedom and romance ; and where, emancipated from the trammels of the cold, calculating world, we may enjoy that bliss reserved for so few on earth."

Miss Seton's answer I could not hear. I could scarcely believe that she could be influenced by such palpable sophistry. Still I knew that there are moments when even the wisest among the daughters of Eve, thrown off their guard by the wiles of the Evil One, are ready to listen to his most barefaced falsehood ; if they trust to their own strength — their own wisdom — and seek not protection from the only source whence it can come. " Oh, you consummate scoundrel ! " I muttered to myself, as I retreated to the doorway, whence I had come out. I had no longer a doubt as to the identity of the pretended Greek. I resolved to put the matter to the test. Entering the house, I walked briskly along the gallery, towards the window where I had seen the two speakers. Miss Seton was there — more like a statue than a living being — leaning against the wall, with her hands pressed to her forehead ; but the pretended Greek was gone.

" Miss Seton," said I, going up to her, " tell me what has become of Mr. Sandgate."

" I know not of whom you speak," she answered. " I know no one of that name."

" The man in the Greek dress," I replied, calmly, for I felt that much depended on my tone and manner.

" What! do you know him?" she asked in a faltering voice.

" I do," said I ; " and, Miss Seton, I would save you from him. He is worthless. He lives with a halter around his neck, and he will some day find it hauled taut."

She stood perfectly silent for some time. I allowed her to remain so that she might regain her composure. She did this in a wonderfully short space of time. I suspected that her feelings were not very acute.

" You know my secret. I throw myself on your generosity, and I am sure that you will not betray me, Mr. Brine."

" Indeed, you may trust me, Miss Seton," I replied ; " I shall rejoice at being the means of saving you from a very great danger. Let me entreat you, therefore, not to see that man again on any account. Keep close to your mother, and let nothing separate you from her. Another time I will tell you his history, and you will see that you have reason to be guarded."

" Oh, tell me now, tell me now!" she exclaimed. " I will follow your advice ; but I would hear all about him, and then shut him out of my thoughts forever."

I saw that she was right, so I told her briefly all I knew about Sandgate. She shuddered several times at the narrative. She was not particularly romantic, and fully alive to the advantages of a good position, thanks to her mother's instruction. Though she had seen no great objection to be- coming a Greek countess, she had reason to be thankful at having escaped falling into the power of a villain of the stamp of Sandgate. "Now let me lead you to Mrs. Seton," I replied, offering my arm. She took it. Hers trembled as it pressed mine.

"Why, Jane, my dear, you look very ill; what is the matter?" exclaimed the old lady, starting up with a look of real alarm in her countenance. I believe she loved her daughter, and fancied she showed it by helping her to make what she called a good match.

"Oh, nothing, nothing — the heat, I believe," she answered, turning still paler. "I think that I had better leave the room."

Her mother thought so likewise. I found their carriage. They lived not far off; so, following on foot, I watched them till they were safely within their own doors. On returning to the ball-room I heard Mrs. Skyscraper making anxious inquiries as to what had become of Count Gerovolio.

"Never mind, we shall see him to-morrow at the pic-nic. He promised to be there," she observed. I saw from the look Carstairs gave that the Count had better behave himself should he venture to make his appearance, which I did not think very likely.

CHAPTER XXII.

My friends were not a little astonished when I told them, on getting on board the yacht, that Sandgate was in the island. The question was, how to catch him. We had no moral doubt whatever that he had come on board our vessel with the intention of plundering us, and that he had afterwards endeavored to send us to the bottom by attacking us in the polacca-brig; still no one could swear to the fact. We were not certain that the brig which left the harbor that morning was the one which had engaged us — we could not prove that he belonged to her; scarcely, indeed, could we expect to induce the authorities to believe that the Greek Count and Sandgate the smuggler were one and the same person.

" Take my advice," observed Carstairs ; " don't let us fash ourselves on the subject, but give the rogue a long rope, and he will soon hang himself."

We all agreed to the wisdom of this remark, and resolving to wait the course of events, turned in and went to sleep.

A large and merry party set off to the scene of the picnic, some in calèches, and others in carriages of higher pretensions, and vehicles of all sorts, and others on horseback. I will not stop to describe the scenery. Stone walls, and here and there an orange grove, form its chief characteristics. It is wonderful that there is any cultivation, considering that the greater portion of the soil has been brought from other lands. That which is produced on the island is formed from the crumbling away of the surface of the rock of which it is composed.

Our party met by agreement near the gatés. Hearty, greatly to his satisfaction, managed to undertake the escort of Mrs. Mizen and her daughter ; the widow fell to the lot of Carstairs, and I took charge of Mrs. and Miss Seton.

" Oh ! but where is Count Gerovolio?" exclaimed Mrs. Skyscraper, as we were driving off. " I fully expected to have him of our party. Has anybody seen him? Miss Seton, do you know what has become of him ? "

Poor Jane for a moment looked dreadfully disconcerted at hearing the name of the impostor ; but she soon recovered her self-possession, and I did my best to rattle on, so as to draw off the attention of her mother and Mr. Mite, who had been admitted as a fourth in the carriage. Mrs. Skyscraper looked about in vain for the Count ; I thought that he would scarcely have the boldness to make his appearance. Our drive, as far as we four ill-matched beings were concerned, was any thing but a pleasant one. Old Mrs. Seton was annoyed at not having Sir Lloyd Snowdon, or any other eligible gentleman, to act the suitor to her daughter.

Poor Jane could not drive away her own bitter thoughts. Mite would infinitely rather have been in the company of one of his jolly little Maltese acquaintances, and I felt oppressed at being the keeper of a young lady's secret. At last we arrived at the spot where our lionizing was to commence — the old capital of the island, Citta Vecchia, and had to descend from our conveyances.

The structure would delight a connoisseur in mediæval

antiquities, for a more ancient-looking collection of tumble-
down houses I never saw collected together. Here stand the
first palace of the Grand Masters, and the cathedral of
Malta, celebrated for the pertinacity with which its bells are
rung. But the great sight we had all come to see was
the catacombs. Guides and lights were procured, and the
whole party descended to them. Incongruous, indeed,
seemed the light dresses of the ladies, the glittering uniforms of the officers, and the merry laughter of the party,
with the solemn, silent gloom of this vast receptacle for the
dead. These catacombs consist of long galleries or streets
cut in the rock, extending a great distance, and intersecting
each other at right angles about fifteen feet beneath the surface of the ground. The gloom, the chilly, confined atmosphere, the dark shadows, the mysterious passages and
recesses, the undefined shapes which flitted before us, were
ill calculated to dispel poor Miss Seton's melancholy. She
walked on, however, silently by my side, avoiding rather
than courting the attention of Sir Lloyd Snowdon, who at
length joined us, and who, seeing this, devoted himself with
much tact to her mother.

"If you have any intention, Sir Lloyd," thought I,
"you'll win the day, notwithstanding the present appearance of matters."

We could hear behind us the cheery voice of Captain Rullock, and every now and then a laugh from Hearty, who
seemed to be in high spirits.

"He feels that he does not stand ill in the good graces of
Miss Mizen, I suspect," thought I. "Most sincerely do I
rejoice at it; for though not to be compared in point of
beauty to the lovely girl by my side, she will make him a
very far better wife. Her straightforward honesty, her
modesty, her bright intelligence, her well-cultivated mind,

her unvarying good temper, her genuine wit, her loving disposition, are certain to secure her husband's affections and
respect."

Little did the lady by my side dream of the comparison I
was drawing, and yet I verily believe that she might have
been not much inferior to Miss Mizen in all those womanly
qualities, had they not been crushed or perverted by the
false system of education which her mother had adopted.
Such were the somewhat incongruous thoughts which passed
through my mind in the catacombs of Citta Vecchia. I
ought to have been duly oppressed with the gloom of the
place, and to have thought of nothing but ghost-like forms
flitting through the mysterious passages. I do not know
what my companion was thinking about, but she sighed
deeply and sadly. That sigh touched my heart with pity,
and reminded me how little I had attempted to do to restore
her mind to a state of composure.

We had, as I said, walked on somewhat ahead of the rest
of the party, and old Rullock and Hearty had just hailed us
to return, when directly before us appeared the figure of a
man who was evidently endeavoring to conceal himself in
one of the niches cut in the rock. It had, however, been
blocked up, and he was frustrated in his intention. He wore
a large cloak, such as the Italians call a *feriuoligio*, with
which he was attempting to hide his head, but the light of
the torch carried by our guide fell directly on him, and re-
vealed the features of Miles Sandgate.

He must have guessed that he was known, for he advanced a step or two rapidly towards us, but then, whatever
were his intentions, he must have changed them, for he retreated as hurriedly, and was lost to view amid the surrounding gloom. I knew that Miss Seton had discovered him

by the way in which her arm trembled in mine, and most certainly she would have fallen had I not supported her.

"I fear, Miss Seton, that the atmosphere of this place oppresses you; we will get out of it as soon as possible," said I.

"Thank you, thank you," she answered, leaning heavily on my arm. "I long for a breath of fresh air; I shall be better then."

Sir Lloyd Snowdon was much concerned at finding that Miss Seton was unwell, and the whole party hurried to the mouth of the catacombs.

It was very provoking to have Sandgate almost within one's very grasp, and yet not to have the power of punishing him.

On reaching the open air, Miss Seton at first nearly fainted. Restoratives of all sorts were recommended by her friends, but before any could be applied, she recovered, and endeavored to laugh off any disagreeable inquiries as to the cause of her attack. The exertion necessary to do this still further aroused her, and she speedily became one of the most lively and animated of the party. I saw that she could now do very well without me, so I retired from her side. Sir Lloyd Snowdon took my place. He was enchanted, and abandoned himself to the happiness of the moment. She saw her advantage, and not unmindful of her wise mother's instructions, seemed resolved to make the most of it. Still I thought that I detected at times the signs of unnatural spirits, and forced laughter, and I would not have answered for the consequences had the so-called Count Gerovolio appeared in the midst of us with a hundred well-armed followers, and summoned her to accompany him.

From the catacombs we drove to the Grotto of St. Paul, which is at no great distance. Whether the apostle to the

Gentiles ever took shelter within it matters but little; the monks of old decreed that he did, and therefore a fine statue of white marble has been placed within it, and the faithful have been encouraged to offer their gifts at his shrine. The statue stands in the farthest from the entrance of three grottoes, one within the other. We looked at them very much in the way that people in general look at sights with very little interest, but thinking it necessary to give utterance to certain set expressions of surprise or admiration. The most interesting sight was a portion of the cavern which resembles the nave of a church, overgrown with verdure. It is surprising that vegetation should flourish in such a position.

When we had all satisfied our curiosity, we proceeded to a small sheltered bay, where the most important part of the day's entertainment was to be performed. There was no great beauty of scenery, but the blue sea, and the pure sky, and the fresh salt breeze, and the rugged rocks, made it pleasant to the sight and feelings; and as most of the party had very good appetites, and tolerably clear consciences, we were altogether very merry. Captain Rullock, Hearty, Bubble, and Mite did their best to make it so. Miss Mizen was naturally very happy; so was her mamma, for Hearty had that day very palpably declared his intentions. Sir Lloyd Snowdon was happy because he thought he had won the beauty of the season; and Mrs. Seton, because she fancied that the great object of her life was on the point of being accomplished.

Several vessels had been for some time in sight, but we had been so much engaged in our own immediate occupation, that neither I nor any of the other naval men had paid them much attention.

The heavier portion of the feast had been concluded, and

sparkling wines filled our glasses, and luscious grapes our plates. Bubble had been called on for a song, and Sir Lloyd Snowdon for a speech, when we were somewhat startled from our propriety by a loud exclamation from Porpoise.

"Why, by the Lord Harry, there's that rascally polacca-brig again!" he cried, pointing to a vessel which was standing under full sail in shore.

Our pocket-telescopes were in instant requisition. The vessel in question was a polacca-brig, of the same size, and paint and build, and appearance aloft as the one which had attacked us; but still it was impossible to be certain as to whether the vessel in sight was the pirate or not. Porpoise was the only person who was positive as to her being so. Hearty was inclined to side with him. Still, what was to be done? Captains Rullock and Arden were ready enough to go in chase of her, but their ships were on the other side of the island, and by the time they could have got back to Valetta and obtained permission from the admiral, and been under way, the suspicious brig would have been far away again.

This discussion once more nearly upset poor Miss Seton, but she seemed relieved, and recovered somewhat of her vivacity when it was resolved not to take any notice of the stranger. I, of course, as she did, could not help connecting the brig in sight with the appearance of the pretended Count Gerovolio in the catacombs. He had, I suspected, been hiding there for some reason or other, till he could get on board his vessel.

After a little time the fun of the pic-nic went on as before. I, however, not being in love, nor having any lady to whom it was necessary to pay exclusive attention, kept my eyes about me, and every now and then swept the line

of the coast with my telescope, while I also did not neglect
to watch the movements of the brig.   As she came clearly
into the plane of my glass, I observed a dark cloth on her
foretopgallant-sail, which I suddenly recollected to have
remarked on the same sail of the brig from which Sandgate boarded us, as she lay becalmed before the squall
came on.   This to my mind was conclusive evidence ; but
my suspicions were further confirmed by seeing the polacca-
brig lower her topgallant-sails, and bring her head up to
the wind.   When hove-to, she lowered a boat, which, well-
manned, at once made for the shore.   I said nothing, but
narrowly watched the point for which she was steering.
As she drew near, I saw a figure climb a rocky point and
waive to her.   The dress and air of the person left no
doubt on my mind that he was no other than the Greek
count, or rather Miles Sandgate.   It was, indeed, provoking
to see the rascal escaping before our very sight.   Had we
taken upon ourselves to make chase after him, he would
have got on board the boat before we could have reached
him.   Still I felt that I ought to point out the state of
things to Rullock and Arden, and let them judge what
should be done.

"Go in chase after the fellow, by all. means," they exclaimed ; " we must not be too sanguine as to catching
our bird, or proving him a culprit if we do catch him, but
still we'll try."

It was arranged, therefore, that while the ladies and
military men, and non-combatants, should take their time
to return, we naval men should hurry back to Valetta, and
take the necessary steps to go in chase of the pirate.
Hearty looked at Miss Mizen and thought he should very
much like to stay with her, but his manhood would not let
him ; so he, with Bubble and Carstairs, settled to go away

in the yacht. Mrs. Skyscraper made an effort to detain the latter, but her admirer was not a man to shirk work where any was to be done, so he set off with the rest of us. This time we were more successful in finding the admiral. He was eager as we could be to catch the pirate, and instantly ordered the " Trident " and " Zebra " to go in chase of her. When last seen, after Sandgate, or the man we supposed to be him, had got on board, she was standing to the southward and east, with the wind from the northward; in which direction she would ultimately shape her course it was impossible to say. Calculating that she might probably be still hovering about the island, the " Trident " was ordered, after leaving the harbor, to beat round to the northward of Malta; while the " Zebra " was to keep to the southward, so as to intercept her, should she steer a course for the Straits. It was arranged that the " Frolic " should accompany the " Zebra," but to keep to the nor'ward of her, within telegraph distance.

" This is exciting," exclaimed Bubble, as we bowled along in company with the brig-of-war, away from Malta Harbor. " It seems like real work, going in chase of a pirate; only I hope that he may not give us the go-by in the dark."

The sun sank into the ocean before we had rounded Gozo, so that we were not able to see what vessels were to the eastward of us. We kept, however, a very bright lookout on either hand, so that we thought no vessel could pass between us and the land on one side, or us and the " Zebra " on the other. We were to stand on till we fell in with the " Trident " at day-light, and then the three vessels, spreading wide apart, were to continue the chase all day, and return or not at discretion.

It was at first a lovely night, starlight and bright, with

just such a breeze that we could carry our gaff-topsail, and yet the cutter scarcely heeled over to it.

None of us felt inclined to go below, notwithstanding the fatigues of the day and the previous night. Hearty, of course, had pleasant thoughts; Porpoise was eagerly watching for the pirate; I was running over the events of the day, and Bubble was whistling, while Carstairs was, I suspect, pondering on the advisability of proposing to Mrs. Skyscraper.

At first we had been very loquacious, but the silent solemnity of the night had an influence on all of us, and by degrees our remarks grew less and less frequent, till we were found standing, in meditative mood, in different parts of the vessel. The hours of the night passed by, and still we all kept the deck far later than was our usual custom. Towards midnight, either from a mist rising, or from some other cause, the darkness very much increased.

"If this continues we shall have to shorten sail," or we shall be running into some craft or other," observed Porpoise, who was no great admirer of romance, and would rather all the time have been listening to a jovial song.

"Yes, indeed," said I; "very little chance, though, of falling in with our roving friend, even should he be in the neighborhood."

"We'll get the gaff-topsail off her, Mr. Snow," said Porpoise; "the brig will be shortening sail, and if we do not, we shall be running ahead of her."

The order was given, and the hands had gone aloft to execute it, when an exclamation from the look-out forward made us open our eyes.

"A sail ahead, on the starboard-bow!" he shouted, with startling energy.

We looked in the direction indicated.

"Luff—luff all you can," cried Porpoise, with equal animation. "Luff! or she'll be into us."

The helm was put down; happily the gaff-topsail had not been taken in, and the cutter, having good way on her, shot up to windward. Close on our quarter appeared, towering up, it seemed, into the sky, a wide spread of canvas. The stranger rushed on past us, the white foam hissing and bubbling at her bows.

"What vessel is that?" shouted Porpoise.

I thought I heard a shout of derisive laughter in return. The next moment, as she came beam on, I distinctly made her out to be a Greek polacca-brig.

"The pirate — the pirate!" shouted all hands.

"We had a near chance of being run down by the rascal," cried Porpoise; "but we must be after him as soon as we can let the 'Zebra' know in what direction to make chase."

To do this we had to edge away to the southward, firing our guns to call the attention of the man-of-war brig. This was not so easy to do as might be supposed. We stood on and on, blazing away to no effect. We reached the track of the brig, but still we did not find her.

It was difficult to say what we should do next. Daylight came, and we had the satisfaction — a very poor one, thought I — of seeing her hull down to the eastward, while we had every reason to believe that the chase was merrily bowling away to the westward. There was no use going after the pirate brig by ourselves, so that all that we could do was to make sail in the hopes of catching up our friend.

Porpoise bit his nails with vexation. Hearty wanted to get the matter over to return to Malta.

It was noon before we came up with the "Zebra." This we should not have done had she not hove-to for us. We then had to wait for the "Trident," which appeared to the northward, standing towards us.

We were all so confident that the polacca-brig which passed us in the night was the pirate, that our naval friends were obliged to be convinced, so we all hove about, and stood back the way we had come in chase.

I think it better to make a long story short. We crowded every thing we could carry, and the little "Frolic" behaved beautifully alongside her big companions, shooting somewhat ahead of them in light winds, and keeping well up with them when there was a sea on.

We scarcely expected that the pirate would attempt to get through the Gut, and therefore we might hope to pick him up inside it. I could not help suspecting, however, that all the time Mr. Sandgate was laughing at us in his sleeve, and that we should see no more of him. So it proved. Ten days were fruitlessly expended in the search, and at the end of that time we were all once more at anchor in Malta Harbor.

Hearty very speedily reconciled himself to the disappointment in the society of Miss Mizen. Carstairs was soon at the feet of Mrs. Skyscraper, while I went to inquire for Miss Seton; but as I found Sir Lloyd Snowdon occupying her entire attention, I paid a short visit, and went to dine with Piper on board the "Trident."

CHAPTER XXIII.

WE had not been many days in harbor, when Rullock received orders to take a cruise to the westward to practise his crew, who, being mostly raw hands quickly raised at Plymouth, required no little practice to turn them into men-of-war's men.

As plenty of sea-air had been prescribed for Miss Mizen, and change of scene — not that I think she now required either — it was arranged that she and her mother should take a cruise in the "Zebra." Had Mrs. Mizen been his wife instead of his sister, Captain Rullock could not have taken her, as the rules of the service do not allow a captain to take his wife to sea with him, though he may any other man's wife, or any relative, or any lady whatever.

Under such circumstances, it was not to be supposed that the "Frolic" would remain at anchor. Accordingly she put to sea with the brig-of-war. Carstairs, however, had metal more attractive to his taste at Valetta, so decided on remaining on shore. We did not fail to miss him, and to wish for his quaint, dry, comic remarks, and apt quotations from Shakspeare. Never, certainly, was a party better constituted than ours for amusing each other, all of us. having that indispensable ingredient of harmony, perfect good humor ; and had not that arch mischief-maker Cupid found his way among us, we should have continued in united brotherhood till the yacht was laid up.

A light breeze brought off faintly the sound of the evening gun from the castle of St. Elmo, as, in company with the "Zebra," we stood away from Malta to the westward. Hearty walked his deck with a prouder air and firmer step than was his wont. Nothing so much gives dignity to a man as the consciousness of having won the affections of a true, good girl. His eye was seldom or never off the brig, even after the shades of night prevented the possibility of distinguishing much more than her mere outline, as her taut masts and square yards, and the tracery of her rigging appeared against the starlit sky. He had charged Porpoise to have a very sharp look-out kept that we might run no chance of parting from our consort; but, not content with that, he was on deck every half-hour during the night to ascertain that his directions were obeyed.

"I say, Bill, the gov'nor seems to fancy that no one has got any eyes in his head worth two farthing rushlights but hisself, this here cruise," I heard old Sleet remark to his chum, Frost. "What can a come over him?"

"What, don't you know, Bo?" answered Bill; "I thought any one with half an eye could have seen that. Why, he's been and courted the neice of the skipper of the brig there, and soon they'll be going and getting spliced, and then good-bye to the 'Frolic.' She'll be laid up to a certainty. It's always so. The young gentlemen as soon as they comes into their fortunes goes and buys a yacht. We'll always be living at sea, say they. It goes on at first very well while they've only friends comes aboard, but soon they takes to asking ladies, and soon its all up with them. Either they takes to boxing about in the Channel, between the Wight and the main; for ever up and down anchor, running into harbor to dine, and spending the day pulling on shore, waiting alongside the yacht-house slip for hours, and coming aboard with a cargo of boat-cloaks and shawls, or else, as I have said, they goes and gives up the yacht altogether."

Old Sleet gave a munch at his grub and then replied, —

"But if I don't judge altogether wrong by the cut of this here young lady's jib, I don't think she's one of those who'd be for wishing her husband to do any such thing. When she came aboard of us, t'other day, she stepped along the thwarts just as if she'd been born at sea. Says I to myself, when I saw her, she's a sailor's daughter, and a sailor's niece, and should be a sailor's wife; but if what you say is true, Bo, she's going to be next door to it, as a chap may say, and that's the wife of a true, honest yachtsman. No, no, there's no fear, she won't let him lay up the 'Frolic,' depend on't."

"Well, I hope so," observed Frost; "I should just like to have a fine young girl like she aboard, they keeps things alive somehow, when they are good, though when they are t'other they are worse than one of old Nick's imps for playing tricks and doing mischief."

"You are right there again, and no mistake, Bo," answered Sleet. "I once sailed with a skipper who had his wife aboard: I never seed such goings on before nor since. The poor man couldn't call his soul his own, or his sleep his own. She was a downright double-fisted woman, a regular white sergeant. She wouldn't allow a drop of grog to be served out without she did it, nor a candle end to be burned without logging it down; she almost starved the poor skipper — she used to tell him it was for his spirit's welfare. He never put the ship about without consulting her. One day, when it was blowing big guns and small arms, she was out of sorts, and says he,

"'Molly, love, I think we ought for to be shortening

sail, or we may chance to have the masts going over the sides.'

" 'Shorten sail?' she sings out, ' let the masts go, and you go with them, for what I care. Let the ship drive, she'll bring up somewhere as well without you as with you.'

" The poor skipper hadn't a word to say, but for his life he daren't take the canvas off the ship.

" 'My love, it blows very hard,' says he again, in a mild, gentle voice.

" ' Let it blow harder,' answers the lady; and you might have supposed it was a boatswain's mate who'd swallowed a marlinspike who spoke.

" Presently down came the gale heavier than ever on us. Crack, crack, went the masts, and in another second we hadn't a stick standing.

" 'Where's the ship going to drive to, now?' asks the skipper, turning to his wife. ' I've been a fool a long time, but I don't mean to be a fool any longer; just you get the ship put to rights, or overboard you go.'

" 'How am I to do that same?' asks Mrs. Molly, very considerably mollified; ' I don't know how.'

" 'Then overboard you goes,' says the skipper, quite coolly, but firmly. ' If the wind shifts three or four points only we shall have an ugly shore under our lee, which will knock every timber of the ship into ten thousand atoms in no time, and you may thank yourself for being the cause of the wreck.'

" ' Oh, spare my life, spare my life, and I'll never more interfere with the duty of the ship,' cries the lady, in an agony of fear.

" The captain pretended to be softened. ' Well,' says he, ' take the oaths and go below, and I'll think about it.'

"Mrs. Molly, as we always called her, sneaked to her cabin without saying another word. All hands set to work with a will, and obeyed the skipper much more willingly than we had ever done before. We got jury-masts up, and carried the ship safely into port, but from that time to this I've always fought shy of a ship with petticoats in the cabin, and so I always shall, except I happen to know the sort of woman who wears them."

I was much amused with old Sleet's remarks, and in most respects I agreed with him.

A day or two afterwards the crew had their suspicions confirmed by the appearance of Mrs. and Miss Mizen on the deck of the cutter. In the mean time Hearty had been constantly on board the brig-of-war. He dined on board every day, as indeed we all did, only we dined in the gun-room, and he with the captain and ladies. The accommodation, however, on board the brig was rather confined, and as the weather promised to continue fine, he became naturally anxious to get them on board the yacht. At last he broached the subject. Old Bullock did not object; the ladies finding that there was nothing incorrect in the proceeding were very willing; and to give them more accommodation, an exchange was effected between them and Bubble, who took up his quarters on board the brig. I should have gone also, but Porpoise begged I would remain and keep him company, so I doubled up in his cabin to give the ladies more accommodation. Hearty took Snow's berth, and the old man was very glad on such an occasion to swing in a hammock forward. The thought of those days are truly sunny memories of foreign seas.

Miss Mizen, by her kind and lively manners, her readiness to converse with the crew, her wish to pick up information about the sea and the places they had visited, and their own histories, and her unwillingness to give trouble, soon won the love of all on board; while her mother, whose character was very similar to her daughter's, was a general favorite, and I heard old Sleet declare to Frost that the old lady wasn't a bit like Mrs. Molly Magrath, and as for the young girl she was an angel, and old as he was he'd be ready to go round the world to serve her, that he would.

"Now don't you think Mr. Hearty, that you could find some one who can spin a regular sea matter-of-fact yarn about things which really have been?" said Miss Mizen, one fine afternoon, with one of those sweet smiles which would have been irresistible, even if a far more important request had been made.

The owner of the "Frolic" thought a little. "Yes, by the by, I have it," he exclaimed; "one of the men I have on board is a first-rate yarn-spinner. Once set his tongue a going, it is difficult to stop it, and yet there is very little romance about the old man. He has, I conclude, a first-rate memory, and just tells what he has seen and heard. I'll call him aft, and will try what we can get out of him."

Hearty on this went forward, and after a little confab with the crew, returned with old Sleet, who, instead of being bashful, was looking as pleased as Punch in his most frolicsome humor, at the honor about to be done him. Without hesitation he doffed his hat, threw his quid overboard, smoothed down his hair, and began his tale. I must confess that I have not given it in his language, which was somewhat a departure from the orthodox vernacular, and might weary my readers.

"Now, gentlemen and ladies all, I'm going to tell you

HOW JOE BUNTIN DID THE REVENUE.

The "Pretty Polly" was the fastest, the smartest, and the

sweetest craft that sailed out of Fairport; so said Joe Buntin, and nobody had better right to say it, or better reason
to know it, he being part owner of her, and having been
master of her from the day her keel first touched the water.
She was a cutter of no great size, for she measured only
something between thirty and forty tons; she had great
beam for her length, was sharp in the bows, rising slightly
forward, and with a clean run; she was, in fact, a capital
sea-boat, fit to go round the world if needs be — weatherly
in a heavy sea, and very fast in smooth water, though the
nautical critics pronounced her counter too short for beauty;
but Joe did not consider that point a defect, as it made her
all the better for running in foul weather, which was what
he very frequently wanted her to do. She carried a whacking big mainsail, with immense hoist in it, and the boom well
over the taffrail. Her big jib was a whopper with a vengeance, and her foresail hoisted chock up to the block. She
had a swinging gaff-topsail very broad in the head, and a
square-sail to set for running, with prodigious spread in it;
so that, give the " Pretty Polly" a good breeze, few were the
craft of anything like her own size she couldn't walk away
from. In fact, anybody might have taken her for some
dandified yacht, rather than for a humble pilot-boat, which
the number on her mainsail proclaimed her to be. Now
the " Pretty Polly," like other beauties, had her fair weather
and her foul weather looks, her winter as well as her summer
suit. She had her second, and third, and storm-jibs, a trysail of heavy canvas, and even a second mainsail, with a
shorter boom to ship at times, while her standing and running rigging was as good as the best hemp and the greatest
care could keep it, for every inch of it was turned in under
Joe's inspection, if not with his own hand. Joe Buntin
loved his craft, as does every good sailor; she was his care,

his pride, his delight, mistress, wife, and friend. He would talk to her and talk of her by the hour together; he was never tired of praising her, of expatiating on her qualities, of boasting of her achievements, how she walked away from such a cutter — how she weathered such a gale — how she clawed off a lee-shore on such an occasion; there was no end to what she had done and was to do. She was, in truth, all in all to Joe; he was worthy of her, and she was worthy of him, which reminds us that he himself claims a word or two of description. He had little beauty, nor did he boast of it, for in figure he was nearly as broad as high, with a short, thick neck, and a turn-up nose in the centre of his round, fresh-colored visage; but he had black, sparkling eyes, full of fun and humor, and a well-formed mouth, with strong white teeth, which rescued his countenance from being ugly, while an expression of firmness and boldness, with great good nature, made him respected by all, and gained him plenty of friends. Joe sported a love-lock on each side of his face, with a little tarpaulin hat stuck on the top of his head, a neat blue jacket, or a simple blue guernsey frock, and an enormously large pair of flushing trousers, with low shoes; indeed, he was very natty in his dress, and although many people called him a smuggler — nor is there any use in denying that he was one — he did not look a bit like those cut-throat characters represented on the stage or in print-shops, with high boots, and red caps, and cloaks, and pistols, and hangers. Indeed, so far from there being any thing of the ruffian about him, he looked and considered himself a very honest fellow. He cheated nobody, for though he broke the revenue laws systematically and regularly, he had, perhaps, persuaded himself, by a course of reasoning not at all peculiar to himself, that there was no harm in so doing; possibly he had an idea that those laws

were bad laws, and injurious to the country; so out of the
evil, as he could not remedy it, he determined to pluck that
rosebud — profit — to his own pocket.   Remember that we
are not at all certain that he actually did reason as we
have suggested; we are, we confess, rather inclined to suspect that he found the occupation profitable; that he had
been engaged in it from his earliest days, and therefore followed it without further troubling his head about its lawful-
ness or unlawfulness.   So much for Joe Buntin and his
cutter the " Pretty Polly."

His crew were a bold set of fellows, stanch to him, and
true to each other; indeed, most of them, as is usual, had
a share in the vessel, and all were interested in the success
of her undertakings; they were quiet, peaceable, and or-
derly men; their rule was never to fight, the times were too
tranquil for such work, and a running noose before their
eyes was not a pleasant prospect.   They trusted entirely to
their wit and their heels for success, and provided one cargo
in three could be safely landed, they calculated on making
a remunerating profit.

The days when armed smuggling craft, with a hundred
hands on board bid defiance to royal cruisers, had long
passed by, for we are referring to a period within the last
six or eight years only, during the last days of smuggling.   Now the contraband trade is chiefly carried on in
small open boats, or fishing craft, affording a very precarious
subsistence to those who still engage in it.   After what has
been said it may be confessed that the " Pretty Polly" was
chiefly employed in smuggling, though her ostensible, and,
indeed, very frequent occupation, was that of a pilot-vessel.

Now we must own that in those days we did not feel a
proper and correct hatred of smugglers and their doings;
the dangers they experienced, the daring and talent they dis-

played in their calling, used, in spite of our better reason, to attract our admiration, and to raise them to the dignity of petty heroes in our imagination. The dishonest merchant, the dealer in contraband goods, the encourager of crime, was the man who received the full measure of our contempt and dislike — he who, skulking quietly on shore, without fear or danger, reaped the profits of the bold seaman's toil.

Fairport, to which the "Pretty Polly" belonged, is a neat little town at the mouth of a small river on the southern coast of England. The entrance to the harbor is guarded by an old castle, with a few cannon on the top of it, and was garrisoned by a superannuated gunner, his old wife and his pretty grand-daughter, who performed most efficiently all the duties in the fortress, such as sweeping it clean, mopping out the guns, and shutting the gates at night. Sergeant Ramrod was a good specimen of a fine old soldier, and certainly when seeing his portly figure and upright carriage, and listening to his conversation, one might suppose that he held a higher rank than it had ever been his fate to reach. He had seen much service, been engaged in numerous expeditions in various parts of the world, and went through the whole Peninsular war; indeed, had merit its due reward, he should, he assured his friends, be a general instead of a sergeant, and so being rather an admirer of his, we are also apt to think — but then when has merit its due reward? What an extraordinary hoisting up and hauling down there would be to give every man his due! Sergeant Ramrod always went by the name of the Governor of Fairport Castle, and we suspect rather liked the title. He was, in truth, much better off than the governors of half the castles in the world, though he did not think so himself; he had no troops, certainly, to marshal or drill, but then he had no rounds to make or complaints to hear, and his little garrison, composed of his wife and grandchild, never gave him a moment's uneasiness, while he might consider himself almost an independent ruler, so few and far between were the visits of his superior officers.

The town of Fairport consists of a long street, with a few offshoots, containing some sixty houses or so, inhabited by pilots, fishermen, and other seafaring characters, two or three half-pay naval officers, a few casual visitors in the summer months, a medical man or two, and a proportionate number of shopkeepers. The castle stands at one end of the town, close to the mouth of the river, the tide of which sweeps round under its walls, where there is always water sufficient to float a boat even at low tide. In the walls of the castle are a few loopholes and a small postern-gate or port to hoist in stores, and close to it is a quay, the chief landing-place of the town. Here a revenue officer is stationed night and day to prevent smuggling, though there are certain angles of the castle wall which he cannot overlook from his post. This description we must beg our readers to remember.

One fine morning, soon after daybreak in the early part of the year, Joe Buntin and his crew appeared on Fairport quay with their pea-jackets and bundles under their arms, and jumping into their boat pulled on board the "Pretty Polly." Her sails were loosened and hoisted in a trice, the breeze took her foresail, the mainsail next filled, the jib-sheet was flattened aft, and slipping from her moorings she slowly glided towards the mouth of the river. The jib-sheet was, however, immediately after let go, the helm was put down, and about she came — in half a minute more, so narrow is the channel, that she was again about, and at least six tacks had she to make before she could weather the westernmost spit at the entrance of the harbor, and stand clear out to sea.

"I wonder which of the French ports she's bound to now," observed a coast-guard man to a companion who had just joined him on the little quay close to the castle. "After some of her old tricks, I warrant."

"We shall have to keep a sharp look-out after him, or he'll double on us, you may depend on it," replied the other; "Joe Buntin's a difficult chap to circumvent, and one needs to be up early in the morning to find him snoozing."

"More reason we shouldn't go to sleep ourselves, Ben," said the first speaker; "I must report the sailing of the 'Pretty Polly' to the inspecting commander, that he may send along the coast to give notice that she's out. Captain Sturney would give not a little to catch the 'Pretty Polly,' and he's told Joe that he'll nab her some day."

"What did Joe say to that?"

"Oh, he laughed and tried to look innocent, and answered that he was welcome to her if he ever found her with a tub of spirits, or a bale of tobacco in her."

"I'll tell you, though, who'd give his right hand and something more, to boot, to catch Master Joe himself, or I'm very much mistaken."

"Who's that?"

"Why, Lieutenant Hogson, to be sure. You see he has set his eyes on little Margaret Ramrod, the old gunner's grandchild, but she don't like him, though he is a naval officer, and won't have any thing to say to him, and he has found out that Joe is sweet in that quarter, and suspects that if it weren't for him, he himself would have more favor. Now, if he could get Joe out of the way, the game would be in his own hands."

"Oh, that's it, is it? Well, I think the little girl is right,

for Joe is a good fellow, though he does smuggle a bit; and
as for Lieutenant Hogson, though he is our officer, the less
we say about him the better."

While this conversation was going on, the "Pretty Polly"
had reached down abreast of the quay, when Buntin, who
was at the helm, waved his hand to the coast-guard men,
they in return wishing him a pleasant voyage and a safe return.

"Thank ye," answered Joe, laughing, for he and his opponents were on excellent terms. "Thank ye, and remember, keep a bright look-out for me."

The cutter then passed so close to the castle that her boom
almost grazed its time-worn walls. Joe looked up at the
battlements, and there he saw a bright young face, with a
pair of sparkling eyes, gazing down upon him. Joe took off
his tarpaulin hat and waved it.

"I'll not forget your commission, Miss Margaret. My
respects to your grandfather," he sang out.

There was not time to say more before the cutter shot out
of hearing. The flutter of a handkerchief was the answer,
and as long as a human figure was visible on the ramparts,
Joe saw that Mistress Margaret was watching him. Now,
it must be owned, that it was only of late Joe had yielded
to the tender passion, and it would have puzzled him to say
how it was. He had been accustomed to bring over trifling
presents to the little girl, and had ingratiated himself with
the old soldier, by the gift now and then of a few bottles of
real cognac; but he scarcely suspected that his "Pretty
Polly," his fast-sailing craft, had any rival in his affections.

The day after the "Pretty Polly," sailed, Margaret was
seated at her work, and the old dame sat spinning in their
little parlor in the castle, while Mr. Ramrod was taking his

usual walk on the quay, when a loud tap was heard at the door.

"Come in," said the dame, and Lieutenant Hogson made his appearance.

Now, although by no means a favorite guest, he was, from his rank and office, always welcomed politely, and Margaret jumped up and wiped a chair, while the dame begged him to be seated. His appearance was not prepossessing, for his face was pock-marked, his hair was coarse and scanty, and sundry potations, deep and strong, had added a ruddy hue to the tip of his nose, while his figure was broad and ungainly. He threw himself into a chair, as if he felt himself perfectly at home. "Ah, pretty Margaret! bright and smiling as ever, I see. How I envy your happy disposition!" he began.

"Yes, sir, I am fond of laughing," said Margaret, demurely.

"So I see. And how's grandfather?"

"Here he comes to answer for himself, sir," said Margaret, as old Ramrod appeared, and, welcoming his guest, placed a bottle and some glasses before him, while Margaret brought a jug of hot water and some sugar. The eyes of the lieutenant twinkled as he saw the preparations.

"Not much duty paid on this, I suspect, Mr. Ramrod," he observed, as he smacked his lips after the first mouthful.

"Can't say, sir. They say that the revenue does not benefit from any that's drunk in Fairport."

"A gift of our friend Buntin's, probably," hazarded the officer.

"Can't say, sir; several of my friends make me a little present now and then. I put no mark on them."

"Oh, all right, I don't ask questions," said the lieutenant.

"By the by, I find that the 'Pretty Polly' has started on another trip."

"So I hear, sir," said Ramrod.

"Can you guess where she's gone, Miss Margaret?" asked the officer.

"Piloting, I suppose, sir," answered the maiden, blushing.

"Oh, ay, yes, of course ; but didn't he talk of going anywhere on the French coast?"

"Yes, sir," answered Margaret, "he said he thought he might just look in at Cherbourg."

"And how soon did he say he would be back?" asked the officer.

"In four or five days, sir," said Margaret.

The lieutenant was delighted with the success of his interrogations, and at finding the maiden in so communicative a mood ; so mixing a stiffer tumbler of grog than before to heighten his own wits, he continued, "Now, my good girl, I don't ask you to tell me any thing to injure our friend Buntin, but did he chance to let drop before you where he proposed to make his land-fall on his return — you understand, where he intended to touch first before he brings the 'Pretty Polly' into Fairport?"

"Dear me, I did hear him talk of looking into —— Bay ; and he told Denman, and Jones, and Tigtop, and several others to be down there," answered Margaret, with the greatest simplicity.

"I don't think the girl knows what she's talking of, Mr. Hogson," interposed old Ramrod, endeavoring to silence his grand-daughter. "But of course any thing she has let drop, you won't make use of, sir."

"Oh, dear, no! of course not, my good friend," answered Mr. Hogson. "I merely asked for curiosity's sake. But I must wish you good afternoon. I have my duties to attend to — duty before pleasure, you know, Mr. Ramrod. Good-by, Miss Margaret, my ocean lily — a good afternoon to you, old hero of a hundred fights ; " and, gulping down the contents of his tumbler, with no very steady steps the officer took his leave.

As soon as he was gone, Ramrod scolded his grandchild for her imprudence in speaking of Buntin's affairs.

" You don't know the injury you may have done him," he added ; " but it never does to trust a female with what you don't want known."

" Perhaps not, grandfather," said Margaret, smiling archly. " But Joe told me that I might just let it fall, if I had an opportunity, that he was going to run a crop at —— Bay, and I could not resist the temptation when Mr. Hogson asked me, thinking I was so simple all the time. I'm sure, however, I wish that Joe would give over smuggling altogether. It's very wrong, I tell him, and very dangerous ; but he promises me that if he can but secure two more cargoes, he'll give it up altogether. I'm sure I wish he would."

" So do I, girl, with all my heart ; for it does not become me, an officer of the government, to associate with one who constantly breaks the laws ; but yet, I own it, I like the lad, and wish him well."

Margaret did not express her sentiments ; but the bright smile on her lips betrayed feelings which she happily had never been taught the necessity of controlling.

Mr. Hogson esteemed himself a very sharp officer ; and, as he quitted the castle, he congratulated himself on his acuteness in discovering Buntin's plans. He had spies in various directions, or rather, people whom he fancied were such, though every one of them was well known to the smugglers, and kept in pay by them. By them the informa-

tion he had gained from Margaret was fully corroborated,
and accordingly he gave the necessary orders to watch for
the cutter at the spot indicated, while he collected a strong
body of men to seize her cargo as soon as the smugglers attempted to run it.   His arrangements were made with considerable judgment, and could not, he felt certain, fail of
success, having stationed signal men on every height in the
neighborhood of —— Bay, to give the earliest notice of the
smugglers' approach.   As soon as it was dark, he himself,
with the main body of coast-guard men, all well armed, set
off by different routes, to remain in ambush near the spot.
While they lay there, they heard several people pass them
on their way to the shore, whom they rightly conjectured
were those whose business it was to carry the tubs and
bales up the cliffs to their hides, as soon as landed.   The
night was very dark, for there was no moon, and the sky
was cloudy ; and though there was a strong breeze, there was
not sufficient sea on to prevent a landing ; in fact, it was just
the night the smugglers would take advantage of.   Mr.
Hogson, having stationed his men, buttoned up his pea-
jacket, and drawing his south-wester over his ears, set off
along the shore to reconnoitre.   He rubbed his hands with
satisfaction when he perceived a number of people collected
on the beach, and others approaching from various directions.

"I'm pretty sure of forty or fifty pounds at least," he
muttered, " and if I can but nab Master Joe himself, I'll
soon bring his coy sweetheart to terms, I warrant.   Ah !
the cutter must be getting in with the land, or these people
would not be assembling yet."

Just then a gleam of bright light shot forth from the
cliffs, at no great distance from where he was standing ; it
was answered by the gleam of a lantern from the sea,
21

which was instantly again obscured. He watched with intense anxiety, without moving for some minutes, when he thought that he observed two dark objects glancing over the waters towards the shore. His difficulty was to select the proper moment for his attack. If he appeared too soon, the people on shore would give notice, and the boats would return to the cutter; if he did not reach them directly after they touched the shore, he knew from experience that he should certainly find them empty, a minute or two sufficing to carry off the whole cargo. At last he had no doubt that the smugglers were at hand; and, as fast as his legs could carry him, he hurried back to bring up his men.

We must now return to the "Pretty Polly." Besides Joe Buntin, the crew of the cutter consisted of Dick Davis, Tom Figgit, and Jack Calloway, as thorough seamen as were ever collected together, and all of them licensed pilots for the Channel, each having a share in the craft; then there were, besides them, twice this number of men shipped on certain occasions, who, though they received a share of the profits, had no property in her. Joe had determined to run great risks this voyage, in the hopes of making large profits, and had invested a large part of his property in the venture, which his agent had prepared ready for shipment at Cherbourg. The wind shifted round to the nor'ard, and the "Pretty Polly" had a quick run across the Channel. The evening of the day she left Fairport, she was riding at anchor in the magnificent harbor of Cherbourg. As soon as they arrived, he and his mates went on shore, and the agent, not expecting him that evening, being out of the way, they betook themselves to a *café* on the quay, overlooking the harbor. Joe always made himself at home wherever he went, and although he had no particular aptitude for learning languages, he managed, without any great difficulty, to carry on a conversation in French, and his thorough good-nature and ready fund of humor gained him plenty of friends among the members of the great nation.

The house of entertainment into which the Englishmen walked, is entitled "Le Café de la Grande Nation." The room was large, and had glass doors opening on the quay, through which a view of the harbor was obtained. It was full of little round tables, with marble slabs, surrounded with chairs, and the walls were ornamented with glowing pictures of naval engagements, in which the tri-color floated proudly at the mast-heads of most of the ships, while a few crippled barks, with their masts shot away, and their sails in tatters, had the British ensign trailing in the water. The prospect before them was highly picturesque. Directly in front was an old tower, the last remnant of the ancient Walls of Cherbourg. Beyond, spread out before them, was the broad expanse of its superb harbor, capable of containing all the fleet of France. In the centre, where laborers were busily at work, was the breakwater, the intended rival of Plymouth, one entrance guarded by the Fort of Querqueville, the other by that of Pelée; and on the western shore, guarded by numerous ranges of batteries, was the naval arsenal and dockyard, the pride of the people of Cherbourg, and which, when finished, is intended to surpass any thing of the kind possessed by the *perfide Anglais*.

Joe and his friends, having ordered some *eau de vie* and water, and lighted their cigars, took their seats near the door. They did not stand much on ceremony in passing their remarks on all they saw, particularly at the men-of-war's men who were strolling about the town.

" My eyes, Dick," exclaimed Tom Figgit, " look at them fellows with their red waistcoats and tight jackets, which · look as if they were made for lads half their size, and their trousers with their sterns in the fore part. Just fancy them going aloft."

"They are rum enough, but, to my mind, not such queer-looking chaps as the sodgers," answered Dick.

"Do you know, Dick, that I've often thought that a Frenchman must be cast out of quite a different mould to an Englishman? The clothes of one never would fit t'other. It has often puzzled me to account for it."

"Why, Tom, it would puzzle one if one had to account for all the strange things in the world," answered the other. "You might just as well ask why all the women about here wear caps as big as balloons; they couldn't tell themselves, I warrant."

Just then their conversation was broken off, that they might listen to Joe, who had entered into a warm discussion with the boatswain, or some such officer of one of the French ships-of-war, on the relative qualities of their respective navies. The *salle* was full at the time of naval and military officers of inferior grades, douaniers, gens-d'armes, and worthies of a similar stamp, all smoking, and spitting, and gesticulating, and talking together.

"Comment, Monsieur Buntin," said the Frenchman; "do you mean to say that you have got an arsenal as large as le notre de Cherbourg in the whole of England?"

"I don't know how that may be," answered Joe, quietly; "Portsmouth isn't small, and Plymouth isn't small, but perhaps we don't require them so big. We get our enemies to build ships for us."

"Bah," exclaimed the Frenchman, shrugging his shoulders; "les perfides!"

Just then a fine frigate was seen rounding Point Quer-queville. Like a stately swan slowly she glided through the water till, when she approached the town, her rigging was crowded with men, her courses were clewed up, her topsails and topgallant-sails were furled, and she swung round to her anchor. She was a model of symmetry and beauty, and the Frenchmen looked on with admiration.

"There," exclaimed Joe's friend, "n'est-ce pas que c'est belle? Have you got a ship in the whole English navy like her?"

"I don't know," answered Joe, innocently. "But if there came a war, we very soon should, I can tell you."

"Comment?" said the Frenchman.

"Why you see, monsieur, we should have she."

"Sare!" exclaimed half a dozen Frenchmen, starting up and drawing their swords. "Do you mean to insult La Grande Nation?"

Whereupon Tom Figgit and Dick Davis, though they did not exactly comprehend the cause of offence, jumped up also, and prepared for a skirmish, which might have ended somewhat seriously for the three Englishmen, had not Joe's agent at that moment appeared and acted as a pacificator between them, Joe assuring them that he had no intention of insulting them or any one of their nation, and that he had merely said what he thought would be the case.

Joe did not spend a longer time than was absolutely necessary at Cherbourg, and as soon as he got his cargo on board, the "Pretty Polly" was once more under way for England. Her hold was stowed with much valuable merchandise, chiefly silks, laces, and spirits. She had also on deck a number of empty tubs, and a few bales filled with straw. As soon as he had got clear of the land, the wind, which had at first been southerly, shifted to the south-west, and it soon came on to blow very fresh. This he calculated would bring him upon the English coast at too early an hour for his purpose, so when he had run about two-thirds of his

distance, he lay to, with his foresail to windward, waiting
for the approach of evening.

As he walked the deck of his little vessel, with Tom
Figgit by his side, he every now and then broke into a low
quiet laugh. At last he gave vent to his thoughts in
words.

"If we don't do the revenue this time, Tom, say I'm no
better than one of them big-sterned mounsieurs. What a
rage that dirty spy, Hogson, will be in! Ha, ha, ha! It's
a pleasure to think of it."

Tom fully participated in all his leader's sentiments, and
by their light-hearted gayety one might have supposed that
they had some amusing frolic in view, instead of an under-
taking full of peril to their personal liberty and property.
All this time a man was stationed at the masthead to keep
a look-out in every direction, that no revenue-cruiser should
approach them without due notice, to enable them to get out
of her way.

We must now return to Lieutenant Hogson. As soon as
he felt certain that the boats had landed, he hurried down
with his men to the beach. His approach was apparently
not perceived, and while the smugglers were actively engaged
in loading themselves with tubs and bales of goods, he was
among them.

"Stand and deliver, in the king's name," he shouted out,
collaring the first smuggler he could lay hands on, his men
following his example.

For a moment the smugglers appeared to be panic-struck
by the suddenness of the attack; but soon recovering themselves, as many as were at liberty threw down their loads
and made their escape.

"Seize the boats," he added. "Here, take charge of this
prisoner." And rushing into the water, he endeavored to

capture the boat nearest to him; but just as he had got his hand on her gunnel, the people in her, standing up with their oars in their hands, gave her so hearty a shove, that, lifting on the next wave, she glided out into deep water, while he fell with his face into the surf, from which he had some difficulty in recovering himself with a thorough drenching; the other boat getting off in the same manner. In the mean time, signals had been made by the revenue men stationed on the neighboring heights, that the expected run had been attempted, and the coast-guard officers and their people from the nearest stations hurried up to participate in the capture. Some came by land, while others launched their boats in the hopes of cutting off the " Pretty Polly " in case she should not have discharged the whole of her cargo.

With muffled oars and quick strokes they pulled across the bay; but if they expected to catch Joe Buntin, or the " Pretty Polly," they certainly were disappointed; for although they pulled about in every direction till daylight, not a sign or trace of her did they discover. Not so unfortunate, however, was Lieutenant Hogson, for although he did not capture his rival, he made a large seizure of tubs, and several bales of silk, as he supposed, and a considerable number of prisoners, which would altogether bring him in no small amount of prize-money. One prisoner he made afforded him considerable satisfaction. It was no other than Tom Figgit, who, having jumped out of the boat with a tub on his back, was seized before he had time to disengage himself from his load, and this, with many a grimace, he was now compelled to carry.

" I hope you've made up your mind for a year in Winchester jail, Master Tom," said Mr. Hogson, holding a lantern up to his face. " It isn't the first time you've seen its inside, I warrant."

"It would be, though; and what's more, I intend to spend my Christmas with my wife and family," answered Tom, doggedly.

The prisoners were now collected, and marched up to the nearest coast-guard station, but there were so many tubs and bales that the coast-guard men were obliged to load themselves heavily with them; for it was found that should only a small guard be left to take charge of them, the smugglers would carry them off. The wind whistled coldly, the rain came down in torrents, and the revenue people and their prisoners had a very disagreeable march through the mud up to the station, Tom Figgit being the only person who retained his spirits and his temper — though he grumbled in a comical way at being compelled to carry a tub for other people, and insisted that he should retain it for his trouble at the end of his journey. When he reached the guard-house, he slyly tumbled the tub off his shoulders, and down it came on the ground with so heavy a blow that it was stove in. The names of the prisoners were now taken down in due form, and they were told they must be locked up till they could be carried before a magistrate, and be committed to jail for trial. As soon as the officer had done speaking, —

"Please, sir," said Tom, "there's one of the tubs leaking dreadfully, and if it isn't looked to, it will all have run out before the morning; though for the matter of that, it doesn't smell much like spirits."

"Bring me a glass," said the lieutenant, who, wet and cold, was longing to have a drop of spirits. "I'll soon pass an opinion on your *eau de vie*, Master Tom."

. Tom smiled, but said nothing, while one of the men brought a glass and broached the leaky tub.

"Show a light here," said Tom. "Well, I can't say as

how it's got much of the smell of spirits — hang me, if I can make it out."

Tom filled the glass, and, with a profound bow, worthy of a Mandarin, presented it to the officer. Lieutenant Hogson was thirsty, and, without even smelling the potion, he gulped it down.

" Salt water, by George ! " he exclaimed, furiously, spitting and spluttering it out with all his might, and giving every expression to his disgust.

Tom, forgetful of the respect due to a king's officer, burst into a fit of uproarious laughter.

" Well, I warned you, sir. I told you there was something odd about it — ha, ha, ha — and now you find what I said was true — ha, ha, ha ! "

" What do you mean, you scoundrel? " cried the lieutenant, stamping furiously. " How dare you play such a trick ? "

" Nothing, sir, nothing," answered Tom, coolly ; " you see I should have been very much surprised if there had been any thing else but salt water ; for you see we was bringing those tubs on shore, full of sea-water, for a poor old lady who lives some way inland, and her doctors ordered her to try sea-bathing on the coast of France ; but as she couldn't go there herself, you see, she has the water carried all the way from there to here. It's a fancy she has, but it's very natural and regular, and we get well paid for it, sir."

" Do you, Master Tom, actually expect me to believe such a pack of gross lies? " stammered out the lieutenant, as well as his rage would let him.

" I don't know, sir," answered the smuggler ; " some people believe one thing, some another, and I hope you won't think of keeping us here any longer, seeing as how we've done nothing against the law in landing tubs of salt water for old Missis Grundy up at Snigses Farm, sir. You may just go and ax her if what I says isn't as true as gospel. It might be the death of her if she didn't get her salt water to bathe in, you know, sir."

"Old Missis Grundy! I never heard of her before," exclaimed the lieutenant, growing every moment more angry; "and Snigses Farm, where's that, I should like to know?"

"Why, sir, you see it's two or three miles off, and rather a difficult road to find," answered Tom, winking at his companions. "You first go up the valley, then you turn down by Waterford Mill, next you keep up by Dead Man's Lane, and across Carver's Field, and that will bring you about a quarter of the distance."

"Why, you scoundrel!" exclaimed the lieutenant, who recognized the names of these places, and knew them to be wide apart, "you impudent rogue, you — why, you are laughing at me!"

"Oh, no, sir," answered Tom, demurely, pulling a lock which hung from his bullet-shaped head, "couldn't think of laughing at you; besides, sir, you knows one can't always make one's face as long as a grave-digger's apprentice's."

"I'll make it long enough before I've done with you, Master Tom, let me tell you," exclaimed the officer. "Now let us see what are in those other casks and bales."

"What, all them that your people have had the trouble of carrying up here?" cried Tom. "Lord! sir, the tubs, of course, is all full of salt water, too, for Missis Grundy."

"We shall soon see that, my fine fellow," answered the officer, thinking Tom had only told the tale to annoy him;

but to make sure, seizing a gimlet, with his own hands he broached tub after tub, his face elongating as he proceeded, and the visions of his prize-money gradually vanished from his eyes. Tom and the other smugglers looking on all the time with a derisive smile curling their lips, though prudence prevented their saying any thing which might further exasperate the lieutenant.

At last, with an angry oath, he threw down the gimlet. They one and all contained nothing more potent than salt water. He then, with eager haste, anticipating disaster, tore open the bales. They were composed solely of straw and a little packing cloth.

"Them be life-buoys, sir," said Tom, quietly. "We carries them now always, by the recommendation of the Humane Society."

The smugglers now burst into fits of laughter at the rage and disappointment of the outwitted officer, and even his own men could scarcely restrain their tittering at his extravagances. There was, however, not a shadow of excuse for detaining the smugglers. They had a full right to land empty tubs and life-buoys at any hour of the night, and they had not offered the slightest resistance when captured by the coast-guard. In fact, as Tom expressed it while narrating his adventures with high glee to Joe Buntin, they "fairly did the revenue."

The next morning, the "Pretty Polly" appeared beating up towards Fairport, and before noon she was at her moorings, and Joe was exhibiting a variety of pretty presents to the delighted eyes of Miss Margaret Ramrod. Rumors were not long in reaching her ears that one of the largest runs which had been known for ages had been made on the coast at some little distance from Fairport, the very night Lieutenant Hogson seized the tubs of salt water; and Joe confessed that he had only one more trip to make before he settled for life.

We need not detail the events of the next few days in the quiet town of Fairport. Those we have narrated served for conversation to the good people for full nine days, and during that time poor Mr. Hogson never once ventured to show his face inside the castle walls, for he had a strong suspicion, though an unjust one, that pretty Mistress Margaret had something to do with his disappointment. For her credit, however, we are certain that she was innocent of any intentional falsehood. Joe suspected that Mr. Hogson would attempt to pump her; so, as we have seen the contents of a bucket of water thrown down a ship's pump to make it suck, Joe took care that the lieutenant should get something for his pains, by telling the young lady to answer, if she was asked, that she had heard him say that he intended landing at —— Bay.

For the three following weeks Joe Buntin contrived to spend several days on shore in the society of Sergeant Ramrod's family, though the "Pretty Polly" during that time made several trips down Channel, and was very successful in falling in with some large East Indiamen, the pilotage money of which was considerable; and besides that she landed several rich passengers who paid well, so that Joe was rapidly becoming a wealthy man. He would have been wise to stick to his lawful and regular calling; but there was so much excitement in smuggling, and the profits of one trip were so much more than he could gain in several winters' hard toil, that he could not resist the temptation. Had he taken the trouble of comparing himself with others, he would, we suspect, have considered himself a more honest man than the railroad speculators of the present day.

It was again the last quarter of the moon, and the nights were getting dark, when the "Pretty Polly" once more left her moorings in Fairport Harbor. Now it must not be supposed that she ran over at once to the coast of France, and taking in a cargo, returned as fast as she could to England. Joe was not so green as to do that. He, on the contrary, as before, cruised about the Channel till he had put two of his pilots on board different vessels, and, to disarm suspicion, they took very good care to present themselves at Fairport as soon after their return as possible ; and even Mr. Hogson began to fear that there was very little prospect of making prize-money by capturing the "Pretty Polly," or of wreaking his vengeance on Joe.

As soon as the last ship into which he had put a pilot was out of sight, Joe shaped his course for Cherbourg, where he found a cargo of tubs ready for him, but he this time did not take any silks in his venture. In a few hours he was again on his way across the Channel. The weather was very favorable. Now some people would suppose that we mean to say there was a clear sky, a smooth sea, and a gentle breeze. Far from it. It blew so fresh that it might almost be called half a gale of wind ; the clouds chased each other over the sky, and threatened to obscure even the stars, which might shed a tell-tale light on the world, and there was a heavy sea running ; in truth, it gave every promise of being a dirty night. Nothing, however, in this sublunary world can be depended upon except woman's love, and that is durable as adamant, true as the pole-star, and unequalled. The "Pretty Polly" was about fifteen miles from the land, and Joe and Tom Figgit were congratulating themselves on the favorable state of the weather, when the breeze began to fall and veer about, and at last shifted round to about east-south-east. Gradually the sea went down, the clouds cleared off, and the sun shone forth from the blue sky bright and warm.

"Now this is what I call a do," exclaimed Tom Figgit, in a tone of discontent. "Who'd have thought it? Here were we expecting the finest night Heaven ever made for a run at this time of the year, and now I shouldn't be surprised that there won't be a cloud in the sky just as we ought to be putting the things on shore."

"It can't be helped, Tom," answered Joe; "our good-luck has not done with us yet, depend on it."

"I wish I was sure of it," replied Tom, who was in a desponding mood:—he had taken too much cognac the night before. "Remember the story about the pitcher going too often to the well getting a cracked nose. Now, captain, if I was you I'd just 'bout ship and run back to Cherbourg till the weather thickens again. We should lay our course."

"Gammon, Tom. What's the matter with you?" exclaimed Joe. "One would suppose that you had been and borrowed one of your wife's petticoats, and was going to turn old woman."

"You know, captain, that I've very little of an old woman about me, and that it's for you I'm afeared more than for myself," replied Tom, in a reproachful tone. "A year in jail and the loss of a few pounds is the worst that could happen to me, while you would lose the vessel and cargo, and something else you lay more value on than either, I suspect."

"Well, well, old boy, we'll be guided by reason," said Joe. "We won't run any unnecessary risks, depend on it. I'll just take a squint round with the glass to make sure that no cruiser has crept up to us with this shift of wind."

Saying this, Joe carefully swept the horizon with his telescope, but for some time it rested on nothing but the dancing sea and the distant land.   At last, however, his eye caught a glimpse of what, to him, appeared a very suspicious-looking sail dead to windward.

" What do you make her out to be?" he asked, handing the glass to Tom Figgit, and pointing towards the sail, which appeared no bigger than a sea-gull's wing gleaming in the rays of the sun.   Tom took a long look at her.

" She's a big cutter, and no mistake," he answered, still keeping his eye to the tube.   "And what's more, she's standing this way, and coming up hand over hand with a fresh breeze.   I don't like the cut of her jib."

" Let's have another squint at her," said Joe, taking the glass from the mate's hand : then letting it come down suddenly, and giving a slap on his thigh, he exclaimed, "You are right, Tom, by George ; and what's more, if I don't mistake by the way her gaff-topsail stands, she's the ' Ranger ' cutter which we gave the go-by in the winter, and they've vowed vengeance against us ever since."

Davis and Calloway then gave their opinion, which coincided with the rest, nor did there appear to be any doubt that the approaching vessel was the " Ranger."

The wind, as we said, had fallen, but there was still a considerable swell, the effects of the past gale, which made the little vessel pitch and tumble about, and considerably retarded her progress.   Joe now scanned his own sails thoroughly to see that they drew well, and then glanced his eye over the side of the cutter to judge how fast she was going through the water.   He was far from satisfied with the result of his observations.

" It won't do," he remarked ; "we must be up stick, and run for it, or she'll be overhauling us before dark.   If we was blessed with the breeze she's got, we wouldn't mind her.

Rig out the square-sail boom, bend on the square-sail. Come, bear a hand my hearties, be quick about it. None of us have much fancy for a twelvemonth in Winchester jail, I suppose. That'll do ; now hoist away."

And himself setting an example of activity, the helm being put up, the main-sheet was eased off, a large square-sail set, and the cutter, dead before the wind, was running away from her supposed enemy. The square-topsail was next hoisted, and every stitch of canvas she could carry was clapped on, and under the influence of the returning breeze, the " Pretty Polly " danced merrily over the waters, though not at all approaching to the speed her impatient crew desired. Tom Figgit shook his head.

" I thought it would be so," he muttered. " I knowed it when I seed the wind dropping. Well, if it weren't for Joe, and to see that b——d coastguarder, Hogson, a-grinning at us, and rubbing his paws with delight, I shouldn't care. If we might fight for it it would be a different thing, but to be caught like mice by a cat, without a squeak for life, is very aggrawating, every one must allow."

Tom had some reason for his melancholy forebodings, for the " Pretty Polly " most certainly appeared to be out of luck. Do all she could, the " Ranger," bringing up a fresh breeze, gained rapidly on her. The people in the revenue cruiser had evidently seen her soon after she saw them, and, suspecting her character, had been using every exertion to come up with her. They had, in fact, long been on the watch for her, and quickly recognized her as their old friend. The smugglers walked the deck, vainly whistling for a wind, but, though they all whistled in concert, the partial breeze refused to swell their sails till it had filled those of their enemy. Nothing they could do, either wetting their sails, or altering her trim by shifting the cargo, would make the

" Pretty Polly" go along faster. One great object was to retain a considerable distance from her till darkness covered the face of the deep, when they might hope more easily to make their escape.

As the sun went down the heavens grew most provokingly clear, and the stars shone forth from the pure sky, so that the smugglers saw and were seen by the revenue cutter, and the character of the " Pretty Polly" was too well known by every cruiser on the station to allow her to hope to escape unquestioned. Still Joe boldly held on his course. He never withdrew his eye from his pursuer, in order to be ready to take advantage of the slightest change in her proceedings, but he soon saw that he must make the best use of his heels and his wits, or lose his cargo. Poor Joe, he thought of his charming Margaret, he thought of his good resolutions, he thought of Tom's evil prognostications, but he was not a fellow to be daunted at trifles, and he still trusted that something in the chapter of accidents would turn up to enable him to escape.

The breeze at last came up with the " Pretty Polly," but at the same time the " Ranger" drew still nearer. All their means of expediting her movements had been exhausted, every inch of canvas she could carry was spread aloft, and even below the main-boom and square-sail-boom water sails had been extended, so that the craft looked like a large sea-bird, with a small black body, skimming, with outspread wings, along the surface of the deep. The land, at no great distance, laid broad on their beam to the starboard. With anger and vexation they saw that all their efforts to save their cargo would probably be fruitless.

" It can't be helped, my lads," cried Joe ; " better luck next time. In with all that light canvas. Be smart about it, stand by the square-sail halliards — lower away ; hoist

22

the foresail again ; down with the helm, Bill, while we got
a pull at the main-sheet. We must run into shoal water
and sink the tubs. It will come to that, I see."

As Joe said, there was no time to lose, for the revenue
cruiser was now a little more than a mile distant, looming
large in the fast-increasing obscurity of night. There promised, however, to be too much light during the night for them
to hope to elude the sharp and practised eyes of her look-
outs. While the smuggler, with the wind nearly abeam,
was running in for the land, her crew were busily employed
in getting the tubs on deck, and slinging them in long lines
together, with heavy weights attached, over the side, so as to
be able, by cutting a single lanyard, to let them all sink at
once. No sooner did they alter their course than their pursuer
did the same. They had, at all events, gained the important
advantage of escaping being overhauled in daylight. They
now stood steadily on till they got within a quarter of a
mile of the land, the revenue cutter not having gained materially on them. By this time every tub was either on
deck or over the side.

"Starboard the helm a little, Tom — steady now ! " sung
out Joe ; " we'll have the marks on directly ; I can just
make out Pucknose Knoll and Farleigh church steeple. Now
mind, when I sing out cut, cut all of you."

It was not without some difficulty that the points he mentioned could be distinguished, and none but eyes long accustomed to peer through darkness could have seen objects on
the shore at all. His aim was to bring certain marks on the
shore in two lines to bisect each other, at which point the
tubs were to be sunk, thus enabling him to find them again
at a future day.

"Starboard again a little, Tom — steady now — that will
do — luff you may, luff — I have it. Cut now, my hearties,

cut!" he exclaimed, and the next moment a heavy splash told that all the tubs slung outside had been cut away, and sunk to the bottom. "Stand by to heave the rest over-board," he continued, and a minute afterwards, with fresh bearings, the remainder of the cargo was committed to the deep. "Now let's haul up for Fairport, and get home to comfort our wives and sweethearts. Better luck next time."

With this philosophical observation, Joe buttoned up his pea-jacket, and twisted his red comforter round his neck, determined to make himself comfortable, and to bear his loss like a man. By the "Pretty Polly's" change of course she soon drew near the "Ranger," when a shot from one of the guns of the latter came flying over her mast-head. On this significant notice that the cruiser wished to speak to her, Joe, not being anxious for a repetition of the message, let fly his jib-sheet, and his cutter coming round on the other tack, he kept his foresail to windward and his helm down, thus remaining almost stationary. A boat soon pulled alongside with the mate of the cruiser, who, with his crew, each carrying a lantern, overhauled every part of the vessel's hold, but not even a drop of brandy was to be found, nor a quid of tobacco.

"Sorry, sir, you've taken all this trouble," said Joe, touching his hat to the officer. "I thought, sir, you know'd we was a temp'rance vessel."

It was diamond cut diamond. The officer looked at Joe, and burst out laughing, though disappointed at not making a seizure.

"Tell that to the marines, Mister Buntin," he answered. "If you hadn't, half an hour ago, enough spirits on board to make the whole ship's company of a line-of-battle ship as drunk as fiddlers, I'm a Dutchman."

"I can't help, sir, what you thinks," replied Joe, humbly; "but I suppose you won't detain us? We wants to get to Fairport to-night, to drink tea with our wives and nurse our babies."

"You may go, my fine fellow, and we will bring in your tubs in the morning," answered the mate, as he stepped into his boat,

"Thank ye, sir," said Joe, making a polite bow, but looking very much inclined to expedite his departure with a kick, but discretion withheld him.

"Let draw!" he sang out in a voice which showed the true state of his feelings, beneath his assumed composure; "now about with her."

In a short time after, the "Pretty Polly" was safely moored in Fairport River.

The next morning at daybreak, the "Ranger" was seen hovering in rather dangerous proximity to the spot where the tubs had been sunk. She was then observed to get her dredges out, and to be groping evidently for the hidden treasures. In the course of the day, Joe and his crew had the mortification to see her come into the harbor with the greater part of their cargo on board. Of course they all looked as innocent as if none of them had ever before seen a tub, for there was nothing to betray them, though it was not pleasant to see their property in the hands of others. The revenue cutter then hauling alongside the quay, sent all the tubs she had on board up to the castle, where they were shut up securely while she went back to grope for more.

Joe watched all these proceedings with apparently calm indifference, walking up and down all the time on the quay, with a short pipe in his mouth, and his hands in his pockets. No sooner, however, had darkness set in, than he and his companions might have been seen consulting earnestly

together, and going round to the most trustworthy of their
acquaintance. What was the subject of their consultations
may hereafter be guessed at. Their plans, whatever they
were, were soon matured, and then Joe repaired to pay
his accustomed visit to Sergeant Ramrod and his grand-
daughter,

Joe Buntin was, as I have hinted, not the only lover
Margaret Ramrod possessed, which was, of course, no fault
of hers. One of them, for there might have been half-a-
dozen at least, was James Lawson, a coast-guard man, belonging to Fairport; and if he was aware that he was a
rival of his superior officer it did not afflict him. As it happened, he was stationed at the castle to guard the tubs which
had been captured in the morning. Having seen that every
thing was safe, he soon grew tired of watching on the top
of the castle, for it was a dark, cold night, with a thick,
driving rain, and a high wind, so he persuaded himself that
there could be no harm looking into Sergeant Ramrod's
snug room, lighted up by pretty Margaret's bright eyes, and
warmed by a blazing fire. The sergeant welcomed him
cordially, and Margaret mixed him a glass of hot brandy
and water, while discussing which, a knock was heard at
the castle-gate, on which Mistress Margaret, throwing her
apron over her head, ran out to admit the visitors. She
was absent a minute or more; probably she had some difficulty in again closing the gates on so windy a night: at last
she returned, followed by no less a person than Joe Buntin,
and his shadow, Tom Figgit.

A smile stole over Margaret's pretty mouth as she watched
Joe, who looked as fierce as he could at Lawson, and by
Ramrod's invitation, sat himself down directly opposite
the revenue-man. Lawson was not to be stared out of
countenance, so, notwithstanding Joe's angry glances, he

firmly kept his post. Tom Figgit quietly sipped his grog, eyeing Lawson all the time much in the way that a cat does a mouse she is going to devour, so that at last the revenue-man, feeling himself rather uncomfortable, he scarcely knew why, helped himself thoughtlessly to another stiff glass. Joe laughed and talked for all the party, and told several capital stories, contriving in the interval to whisper a word into Margaret's ear, at which she looked down and laughed slyly. She was soon afterwards seen filling up the coast-guard man's glass, only by mistake she poured in Hollands instead of water. The error was not discovered, and Lawson became not only very sagacious, but brave in the extreme. After some time he recollected that it was his duty to keep a look-out from the top of the castle, and accordingly rose to resume his post. Joe on this jumped up also, and wishing the old couple and their granddaughter good-night, took his departure, followed by Tom; Sergeant Ramrod and Lawson closing the gates securely behind them.

No sooner were Joe and his mate outside the walls than they darted down a small alley which led to the water, and at a little sheltered slip they found a boat, with a coil of rope and some blocks stowed away in the stern-sheets. Joe, giving a peculiarly low whistle, two other men appeared crawling from under a boat, which had been turned with the keel uppermost on the beach, and then all four jumping in, pulled round underneath the castle-wall to a nook, where they could not be observed from the quay even in the daytime.

It was, as we have mentioned, blowing and raining, and as dark as pitch, so that our friends had no reason to complain of the weather. After feeling about for some time, Joe discovered a small double line, to which he fastened one of the stouter ropes, and hauling away on one end of it, brought it back again into the boat. Who had rove the small line we cannot say, but we fear that there was a little traitor in the garrison ; perhaps Joe or Tom had contrived to do it before they entered the sergeant's sitting-room.

" Hold on fast," Joe whispered to his comrades ; " I'll be up in a moment." Saying this, he climbed up the rope, and soon had his face flush with the summit of the castle walls. Looking round cautiously, he observed no one, so he climbed over the parapet, and advanced across the platform to the top of a flight of steps which communicated with the lower part of the building. He looked over the railing, but his eyes could not pierce the gloom, so he descended the steps, and had the satisfaction to find Lawson fast asleep at the bottom of them, sheltered from the rain by one of the arches. " All's right : he won't give us much trouble, at all events," he muttered to himself ; and returning to the parapet he summoned his companions. Two other boats had now joined the first, and, one after the other, twelve smugglers scaled the walls. Others were, it must be understood, watching at various points in the neighborhood, to give the earliest notice of the approach of the coast-guard. Joe stationed two men by the side of Lawson to bind and gag him if he awoke, which he was not likely to do, while the rest proceeded with their work.

They soon contrived to break open the door of the store, opening from the platform, where the tubs had been deposited ; then each man, carrying one at a time, like ants at their work, they transported them to the parapet of the castle-wall. From thence, with great rapidity, they were lowered into the boats, and then conveyed round to the foot of a garden belonging to an uninhabited house, which, of course, had the character of being haunted by spirits. Joe and his friends worked with a will, as much delighted with the thought of doing the revenue as at recovering their property.

The greater nunber had been thus secured when the rain ceased, and the clouds driving away, the smugglers were afraid of being seen by their opponents. They therefore secured the door of the nearly empty store, and all descending, unrove the rope from the breech of the gun to which it had been fastened, so as to leave no trace of their proceedings.

The next morning Lawson, on recovering from his tipsy slumbers, seeing the door closed, reported that all was right. Mr. Hogson was the first person to make the discovery that all was wrong, and his astonishment and rage .may be more easily imagined than described. Nearly every tub of the rich prize had disappeared ; and the lieutenant swore he was certain that wicked little vixen, Margaret Ramrod, had something to do with it.

Neither Sergeant Ramrod nor Lawson could in any way account for it ; and as it would have been a subject of mirth to all their brother officers, who would not have shared in the prize, the authorities of Fairport thought it wiser not to say much on the subject. Several persons were suspected of having had a hand in the transaction ; but the smugglers were known to be too true to each other to afford the remotest chance of discovering the culprits.

Soon after this Joe Buntin married Margaret Ramrod ; and, wonderful to relate, forswore smuggling ever after. Whether her persuasions, or from finding it no longer profitable, had most influence, is not known ; at all events, he is now one of the most successful and active pilots belonging to Fairport, and though he does not mention names, he is very fond, among other stories, of telling how a certain friend of his did the revenue.

As soon as old Sleet had finished his story, which was much more effective when told by him than as it now stands written down by me, he scraped his right foot back, made a swing with his hat, and was rolling forward, when Hearty cried out, " Stop, stop, old friend, your lips want moistening after that long yarn, I'm sure. What will you have, champagne, or claret, or sherry, or brandy, or rum, or " ——

The honest seaman grinned from ear to ear.

" Grog," he answered, emphatically. " There's nothing like that to my mind, Mr. Hearty. It's better nor all your French washes put together."

Due praise was bestowed on Joe Buntin's history, but he evidently thought the extra glass of grog he had won of far more value.

" Health to you, gentlemen and ladies all, and may this sweet craft never want a master nor a mistress either," he rapped out; then fearing he had said something against propriety, he rolled away to join his messmates forward.

CHAPTER XXIV.

It was now time for the officers of the "Zebra" to return on board their ship. Another night and day passed away much in the same manner as its predecessors. All this time we were edging over to the African coast. Miss Mizen was rapidly recovering her strength, indeed she could no longer be declared an invalid, and it was very evident that a sea-life perfectly agreed with her.

Though I missed Bubble's fun and anecdotes, and his merry laugh and good-natured visage, I must confess that I much enjoyed the society of the two ladies. Mrs. Mizen was a kind-hearted, right-minded, good-natured, sensible, motherly woman, without a particle of affectation or nonsense of any sort. She had seen a good deal of the world, and of the people in it, and could talk well of what she had seen. Under present circumstances, indeed, I preferred her, as a companion, to her daughter. Barring the difference of age, they were very like each other. Miss Mizen also treated me with the utmost frankness and kindness as the friend of her intended husband, and I often enjoyed a pleasant conversation with her, though, of course, it more frequently fell to my share to entertain her mother.

While the fine weather lasted, the life we led was excessively pleasant; but as winter was now rapidly approaching, we knew that we must look out for squalls and heavy

346

seas. We had, as I before remarked, been making our way to the westward along the African coast, now making the land, and then standing off again at night-time.

One morning when daylight broke, we found ourselves rather in-shore of the brig. As I came on deck to relieve Porpoise, I saw her signalizing. We got the signal-book.

" What is Bullock talking about?" asked my brother-officer, as I was looking over the leaves of Marriot's well-known work.

" A suspicious sail to the north-west. Stay where you are. I shall chase, but be back by nightfall," said I ; on which Porpoise ordered the answering signal to be hoisted.

The brig now crowded all sail, but as she kept away I saw that the bunting was again at work.

" If we do not appear by noon to-morrow, return to Malta," said I, interpreting the flags. " And so our pleasant cruise will be up : but all things pleasant must come to an end. I wish it could have lasted longer."

" Well, Porpoise, what do you make of the stranger he is after? "

" By —— that she is no other than our friend the Greek polacca-brig," he exclaimed, almost letting his glass fall from aloft, where he had gone to get a look of the vessel the brig was chasing. " I have a great mind to rouse Hearty up, and get him to disobey orders, and go in chase of her also. I don't like the thoughts of the pirate being captured without our being present."

" Remember that we have ladies on board, and I don't think Hearty will be inclined to run the risk of carrying away our spars or mast for any such gratification," I remarked. " He'll be for obedience in this case, depend on it."

" That's the worst of having ladies on board," answered

Porpoise with a sigh. "But, I say, they have been rather more alive on board the brig than I should have given them credit for. How could they have suspected that the polacca out there was our friend?"

"You forget that Will Bubble is on board, and probably he was on deck, and aloft, indeed, at sunrise, and made out the Greek," I answered, not that I considered that there was any want of strict discipline or sufficient alertness kept on board the brig, though the crew were any thing but first-rate specimens of men-of-war's men.

By the by, that reminds me that I should like to say a few words about manning the navy. But I won't, though, simply because the subject is just here somewhat out of place. We are off the northern coast of Africa in a yacht with some ladies on board, and they might be bored, and we have to watch the proceedings of the brig-of-war and the vessel of which she is in chase. Only I would strongly urge any members of parliament, or other law-makers, or persons of influence, whose eyes may glance over these pages to think, and talk, and *do* very seriously about the matter. It will not bear letting alone or sleeping over. Something must be done, and at once. I've known ships-of-war go to sea with not a quarter of the men seamen — because seamen were not to be got. How would it fare with us had we to engage in a downright earnest naval war? Our men, it will be answered, will fight like Britons; so they will, I doubt not, but is it just to oppose landsmen to the well-trained seamen of other nations? Is it just to the able seamen to make them do the work which should be shared by others? But now we will again look after the brig-of-war and the chase.

The polacca, as soon as she saw that the British man-of-war was in pursuit of her, made all sail to the northward and westward. Old Rullock was evidently determined that she should not escape from any neglect on his part of carrying enough sail. Royals and studdingsails were quickly set, and under a wide spread of snow-white canvas away stood the " Zebra," leaving us jogging slowly on, with the purpose of returning to the spot whence we started. Hearty's surprise, as may be supposed, was very considerable, and so was that of his lady guests, when they found that the brig had run away from us.

" However, Mrs. Mizen, I suppose we must obey orders, must we not?" said he, with a shrug of his shoulders. " If you do not blame Captain Rullock for his treachery, I am sure that I do not, since he has left with me hostages of so much value for his safe return."

Mrs. Mizen and her daughter seemed to think the affair a very good joke, only they could not understand why the cutter should not go in chase of the polacca as well as the brig-of-war.

" Perhaps the captain wishes to have all the honor of capturing the pirate by himself without our assistance," observed Porpoise ; " I suppose the fellow will show fight should he come up with him."

" No fear of that," I remarked. " The truth is, I suspect, that Captain Rullock feared, that had he allowed the yacht to proceed in chase of the pirate, we might have come up with her before he could, and had to bear the brunt of the action. He probably would not have cared very much about that, had there been only four yachting gentlemen on board to be shot at, but the case was very different when his sister and niece might be placed in danger."

" He did very right. There can be no dispute about it," said Hearty. " We must bear our disappointment like

men, and during breakfast we will consider what amusement we can afford our guests, to recompense them for the
absence of the brig in the landscape — or rather seascape
we ought to call it — for little enough of the land have we
had this cruise."

We had a great deal of amusing conversation during
breakfast. It is a pleasant meal everywhere, if people are
well and in spirits, and nowhere is it more pleasant than at
sea under the same provisions.

"What do you say to a look at the African coast, Mrs.
Mizen?" exclaimed Hearty. "We could get there very
soon — could we not, Porpoise?"

"We should be well in with the land, so as to have a
good view of it before the evening, and if the wind holds,
we might be back here before the brig-of-war returns to
look for us," was the answer.

"Capital; then let us stand in there at once," said
Hearty. "It is a fine, mountainous, bold coast, very picturesque. You will have your sketching things ready, I
hope," he added, looking at Miss Mizen. He had not
learnt to call her Laura when any one else was present.

Miss Mizen said she would get her drawing-board and
color-box ready, and Porpoise went on deck to put the
cutter's head to the southward. A steady breeze from the
south-west enabled us to stand in for the land close
hauled. As we rapidly approached it, the mountains, with
their lofty peaks and wooded sides, seemed to rise out of
the water like the scene at a theatre, till the lower lands at
their base — rocky, undulating heights, and even the sea-
shore — became clearly visible.

"How very different is this scenery from the common
notion of Africa !" said Miss Mizen, as, with Hearty's help,

she was arranging her sketching-board, to make a view of the coast. "I have hitherto always pictured it to myself as a country of arid sands and dense jungle."

"You'd find jungle enough and sand enough in many parts, Miss Mizen, where I have been," observed Porpoise. "But both in the north and south there are districts which will vie in fertility with most in the world. Just think of Egypt; what an abundance of corn does that produce! All along this north coast are many fertile districts: so there are on the west coast, only it is rather too hot there to be pleasant; and then at the Cape and Natal are to be found spots rich in various productions."

"You draw a glowing picture of the country, Mr. Porpoise," observed Mrs. Mizen.

"I do, ma'am, because the country deserves it," he answered. "The world owes a great deal to Africa, and I should like to see every possible attempt made to repay it by continued and strenuous efforts for the civilization of her people. The work is a very great one, there is no doubt about that, and a few feeble and isolated efforts will not accomplish it. The merchant princes of England must take the matter up, and send out several expeditions at the same time. The officers should be experienced, energetic men, the vessels well supplied with merchandise, and well armed to protect it. But what can we hope for while the abominable slave-trade still flourishes? England is doing her best to put it down, but she is but ill supported by other nations. America, with all her boasting about freedom, protects and encourages those engaged in it; while France, professing to be the most civilized and liberal of countries, does the same. Spain and Portugal only occasionally pretend to interfere with a very bad grace, and secretly aid and abet the wretches carrying it on under their flag. I say, at any cost

and at every cost, England must put it down. No matter
if she goes to war with all the world to do so. It will be a
glorious war for the most holy cause, and honest men will
be able to pray with sincerity and faith, that heaven will
protect her in it."

"I am very glad to hear you speak so, Mr. Porpoise,"
said Mrs. Mizen ; "I will answer for it, that no war would
be so popular among the women of England as a war
against slavery and the slave-trade. No one worthy of the
name of an Englishwoman would refuse to sell her jewels
and every thing of value to support it."

"That's the spirit that will put it down, ma'am," exclaimed Porpoise, enthusiastically. "When we sailors know
that we have the prayers and good wishes of the ladies of
England with us, we should very soon sweep all our enemies
from the seas."

The rest of the party responded in most respects to these
sentiments. Hearty suggested that much might be hoped
for from a wise and firm diplomacy, and by calmly waiting
the course of events.

"No, no," answered Porpoise. "That's what the people
in parliament say, when they want to shelve a question.
Do nothing, and let affairs take their own course. It's a
very easy way of doing nothing, but that is not like you,
Mr. Hearty. You would manage the matter in a very different way, I'm sure, if it was left to you."

"I should be very much puzzled if the question were left
for me to decide it," said Hearty. "What do you think I
should do?"

"Oh, I will soon tell you what you would do," replied
Porpoise. "Why, you would look out for all the energetic,
dashing officers you could find, and send them to the coast in
command of as many fast steamers, and other small craft,

with orders to overhaul every suspicious sail they could find on the coast. Then you would have a whacking big fleet in the Channel, and several others in different parts of the world. You would not forget to keep your coast defences in good order, and to have a compact well-disciplined army on shore, and a numerous trained militia, ready to call out at a moment's notice. That's what you and every other sensible man would do, Mr. Hearty, and then I think we need have no fear that any one would causelessly attempt to molest us, or that we should be unable to make other nations keep their treaties with us."

" Bravo, Porpoise, bravo !" cried Hearty. " I wish that you were Prime Minister, or First Lord of the Admiralty, or Dictator, or something of that sort for a short time. I doubt not but that you would get things in prime order in a very short time."

While this conversation was going on, we were rapidly drawing in with the coast. Miss Mizen made two or three very masterly sketches, though the blue sea and water filled up the larger portion of the paper. The less there is in a subject the more does it exhibit a master's talent if the picture is interesting.

A fresh breeze had been blowing all day, but towards evening the wind fell, and the cutter lay floating idly on the water. We were assembled after dinner as usual on deck, laughing, talking, yarn-spinning, and occasionally reading aloud, enjoying the moments to the full, and little dreaming of what a few short hours were to bring forth.

.   .   .   .

Evening was about to throw its dusky veil over the African shore. The idle flap of the mainsail showed us that there was a stark calm. A fish would occasionally leap out of the water, or the fin of some monster of the deep might

23

be seen as it swam by in pursuit of prey, or a sea-bird
would come swooping past to ascertain what strange craft
had ventured into its haunts, ere it winged its way back to
its roosting-place for the night, amid the crags of the neighboring headland.

I was taking a turn on deck, when, as I looked over the
side and measured our distance from the land, it appeared
to me that, although the calm was so complete, we had considerably decreased our distance from it. Walking forward,
I asked Snow if he had remarked any thing particular.

"Why, yes, sir ; I was just going to speak to you or Mr.
Porpoise, about the matter," he answered.   "I've been
watching the land for an hour or more past, and it strikes
me that there is a strong current, which sets in-shore to the
westward hereabouts ; it's just the sort of thing, which, if
we hadn't found out in time, might have carried us much
too close in on a dark night to be pleasant ; as it is, if a
breeze doesn't spring up, and we continue to drift in, we
must just get the boats out and tow her head off shore, so
there'll be no great harm come of that."

"You are right," said I ; "there's little doubt about it ;
I'll mention the matter to Mr. Porpoise, and he'll approve
of what you propose.   But I do not think there's any use in
letting the ladies know, or they'll be fancying all sorts of
dreadful things — that they are going to be cast on shore, or
eaten up by lions, or murdered by savages.   I should not
like to give them any uneasiness which can be helped."

I watched the old man's countenance while I was speaking, to ascertain what he really thought about the matter.
The truth was that I was not quite satisfied myself with our
position.   I had been along that coast some years before,
looking into several of the ports ; and I remembered that
the Moors inhabiting the villages just above there, bore any

thing but a good character. I began to blame myself, when
too late, for not having thought of this before. When the
brig-of-war was with us, it mattered little ; for no pirates
would have ventured to come out to attack her : they would
have known that she would have proved a dear bargain,
even if they could ultimately have taken her, and very little
value to them if taken, but with a yacht the case was different. We could not fail to appear a tempting prize, and
easily won. Had we, however, been without ladies on
board, we should, I expect, all have enjoyed the fun of
showing the rascals that they had caught a Tartar, and am
fully certain that we should have been able to render a good
account of them.

I remember that these ideas crossed my mind as I walked
the deck, waiting for an opportunity of speaking to Porpoise, who was still engaged in conversation with Mrs.
Mizen ; then I burst into a fit of laughter at the thought of
the ideal enemy I had so busily conjured up to fight with.
Porpoise, who just then joined me, inquired the cause of my
merriment.

" It suddenly occurred to me that we were off a somewhat ill-famed part of the coast, and I could not help
fancying I saw half-a-dozen or more piratical row-boats
come stealing out from under the cliffs there, with the intention of cutting our throats and rifling the vessel," I answered ; " but of course it is a mere fancy. I never heard
of an English yacht being attacked by pirates hereabouts,
and it would be folly to make ourselves anxious about such
a bugbear."

Now even while I was saying this I was not altogether
satisfied in my own mind about the matter. If, as I before
said, we had had only men on board, we might have fought
to the last, and could only then have been killed ; but

should we be overpowered, the fate of the women committed to our charge would be too horrible to contemplate.

" I'm glad that you think there is no cause for apprehension," said I to Porpoise. " Still it might be as well to keep a sharp look-out during the night, and should a breeze spring up, to give the coast a more respectful offing."

" I'll do that same," he answered. " I feel no inclination to turn in myself, so that should any of the natives of whom you are suspicious be inclined to visit us, they may not find us altogether unprepared."

The ladies soon after this retired to their cabin ; we only then had an opportunity of mentioning the subject to Hearty. He rather laughed at the notion, but begged that he might be called when the fighting began. After taking a few turns on deck, he also turned in, and Porpoise was left in charge of the deck. I, after a little time, went to my cabin ; it seemed too ridiculous to lose my night's rest for the sake of an idea. I had slept about a couple of hours, when I awoke by hearing the sound of Porpoise's voice. He was standing directly over my skylight, which, on account of the heat of the weather, was kept off.

" Can you make any thing out, Snow?" he asked.

" I think I can now, sir. It seems to me that there are four or five dark spots on the water, just clear of the shadow of that headland in there," was the answer. " I can't just make out what they are for certain."

I was on deck in a few seconds, with my night-glass at my eye pointed in the direction indicated.

" What think you of their being row-boats?" said I. " They look wonderfully like them."

" I can't say that they are not," answered the old man. " They may be rocks just showing their heads above water.

But what, if they are boats, can they be doing out there at this time of night?"

"Coming to pay us a visit, perhaps," I remarked. "We really should be prepared in case of accidents, Porpoise. By timely preparations we averted danger once before, when otherwise, in all probability, we should have had our throats cut. Do not let us be less wise on this occasion."

"Certainly not," said Porpoise; "and as discretion is the better part of valor, we will try and tow the cutter off-shore. It will prolong the time till our visitors can over-take us, and will give us a better chance of having a breeze spring up. If we get that, we shall be able to laugh at any number of such fellows. They are only formidable when they can find a vessel becalmed. After all, I don't say that those are pirates, and if it were not for the ladies on board, we would very quickly learn the truth of the case."

The thorough John Bull spoke out in these remarks. Porpoise did not at all like the idea of flying from an enemy under any circumstances, and as he had to do it, he wished to find every possible reason for so doing.

"Turn the hands up and get the boats out, Snow; we'll see what towing will do," he continued. "You see that this current is setting us far too much in-shore, and, at all events, it is necessary to get a better offing before daybreak, lest no breeze should spring up in the morning to carry us back to the spot where Rullock was to find us."

Three boats were got into the water and manned forth-with; Porpoise, Hearty, Snow, and I, being the only people remaining on board. The crews gave way with a will, and the cutter soon began to slip through the water. She went along, probably, faster than the current was carry-ing her in an opposite direction. These arrangements being made, I took another scrutiny of the suspicious objects under the land. I had no longer any doubt in my mind that they were boats, and that they were pulling out to sea towards us. It was now time to call up Hearty. We had seen no necessity before this of making him unnecessarily anxious, and the noise of lowering the boats had not roused him; indeed, he would have slept through a hurricane, or while a dozen broadsides were being fired, I verily believe, if not called. He was brisk enough, however, when once roused up. As I expected, he was very anxious at the state of affairs.

"We were thoughtless and unwise to stand in so close to this shore," he remarked. "Brine, my friend, we must sink the cutter or blow her up rather than yield to those villains!"

He spoke with much emotion, and I could sincerely enter into his feelings. He did not utter a word of complaint against Porpoise or me, though I think he might have had some reason in blaming us for allowing the cutter to get into her present condition. He paced the deck with hurried steps, looking every now and then anxiously through the glass towards the objects we had observed, and then he would hail the boats.

"Give way, my lads — give way!" he shouted; "if any one knocks up, I'll take his place."

Again he looked through his glass.

"Can they be rocks?" he exclaimed. "I seen no alteration in their appearance."

"I do, though, I am sorry to say," I answered. "They have got considerably more out of the shade of the land since I first saw them."

This became very evident after some time; nor could Hearty any longer doubt the fact. I counted five of them, largish boats (I suspected), each pulling some twenty oars or more, probably double-banked. Very likely each boat carried not much fewer than sixty men — fearful odds for the "Frolic" to contend with. The "Zebra" would not have found them altogether contemptible antagonists, if, as I said, my suspicions were correct as to their size. Still, I hoped that I might be mistaken; we could not be certain as to their object. They might be mere fishing-boats magnified by the obscurity, or coasters which had pulled out in the expectation of getting a breeze in the morning to carry them alongshore, or to get into some current which might set in the direction in which they wished to go. All these ideas I suggested to Hearty; still my original notion outweighed all others in my mind. Indeed I have always found it wisest to take the point of view which requires the most caution; precautions can, at the worst, only give a little trouble; the neglect of them may bring ruin and misery. On this principle I was most anxious to get as far as possible from the shore. No one was idle. Happily the ladies slept on, so that we had not the additional pain at feeling that they were left in a state of anxiety. Porpoise took the helm; Snow went forward to direct the boats how to pull; while Hearty and I busied ourselves in getting out the arms, arranging the ammunition, loading the guns, and muskets, and pistols; indeed, in making every preparation for a desperate struggle. The boats came on very warily. I suspected that we had been seen in the afternoon from the shore, and that as we appeared a tempting prize, the expedition had been planned to capture us.

"A very short time longer will settle the question," said I to Hearty. "We must endeavor to keep them at a respectful distance as long as we can; should they once get alongside they would overpower us with their numbers. Happily these sort of gentry are as great cowards as they

are scoundrels, and a firm front is certain to make them consider whether the profit is likely to be worth the risk of a
battle."

I have gone through a good many anxious moments in the
course of my life, but never did I feel more apprehension
for the result of an adventure than I did for that in which
we were at present engaged. A waning moon had now
risen, and showed us very clearly the number and character
of the strangers — whether friends or foes was hereafter to
be decided. Another look at them through my night-glass
showed me that they were large boats, as I had suspected,
and full of men.

"There is little use in making any farther efforts to escape," said I to Hearty ; "I would hoist in the boats and
serve out some grog to the men. They want something after
their exertions, though they do not require Dutch courage
to defend the ship."

Porpoise agreed to my suggestions ; they were immediately put into execution. The men threw off their grog as
coolly as if they had been about to sail a match at a regatta,
instead being about to engage in deadly fight.

"Here's to your health, Mr. Hearty, and gentlemen all,
and may we just give those scoundrels out there a thorough
good drubbing if they attempt to attack us," quoth Snow,
in the name of his shipmates.

"Thank you — thank you, my men," answered Hearty ;
"you'll act like true-hearted Englishmen, and what men
can do you'll do, I know, to protect the helpless women we
have on board. I won't make you a long speech, you don't
want that to rouse your courage, but I do ask you not to
yield while one man of us remains alive on deck."

"That's just what we are resolved to do, Mr. Hearty ;
no fear, sir," answered all hands, and they would have

cheered lustily, had I not restrained them for two reasons :
I was unwilling to awaken the ladies sooner than was necessary, and also should the pirates have expected to surprise
us, it would be a great advantage if we, on the contrary,
should be able to surprise them. I mentioned this latter
idea to my companions, and they immediately entered into it.
The Moors had been too far off to allow them to perceive us
hoisting in the boats, so they could not tell but that we were
all fast asleep on board. Accordingly, the guns were loaded
up to the muzzle with langrage and musket-balls ; pistols and
cutlasses were served out to the men, and it was encouraging
to see their pleased manner as they stuck the one into their
belts, and buckled the other round their waists. Some had,
in addition, muskets, and a reserve of small-arms was placed
amidships to be resorted to in case of necessity. The men
then went and lay down so as to be effectually concealed
under the bulwarks : Porpoise and I only walked the deck,
as if we were the ordinary watch, and we agreed to pretend
to be looking seaward when the boats drew near, as if unconscious of their approach. Meantime Hearty went below
to perform the painful task of informing the ladies of our
dangerous position. He did it with his usual tact.

" Mrs. Mizen," I heard him say, " I must beg you and
Miss Mizen to dress, but not to come on deck. We have
got too close in-shore, and some Moorish boats appear to be
coming off to us ; they may not mean to do us any mischief, but it is as well to be prepared, and we do not intend
to allow them to come too near to us."

There was a short pause. I heard no exclamations of
surprise or terror—no cries, or lamentations, or forebodings
of evil, but Mrs. Mizen simply answered in a firm voice :—

" We trust, then, Mr. Hearty, to you and your companions

to defend us, and may a merciful God give you strength to
fight and beat off our assailants ! "

" That's a speech worthy of a true heroine," exclaimed
Porpoise, who had likewise overheard it. " Just the thing
to strengthen our nerves, and to put true courage into us. I
trust, Mrs. Mizen, we shall not be long in beating off the
pirates," he added, looking down the skylight ; " do you, in
the mean time, keep snug below, and don't mind the uproar."

" Now, my lads, be ready ; we mustn't let the blackguards
get on board to frighten the ladies, mind that. When I give
the word, be up and at them."

Porpoise having thus delivered himself, in accordance
with our plan, pretended to be intently looking over the taffrail. The row-boats were all the time drawing disagreeably
near, and I had no longer in my mind any doubt as to their
character and intention. We, also, were anxiously looking
out for a breeze which might enable us to meet them at
greater advantage. I took a glance at the compass ; as I did
so I felt a light breeze fan my cheek ; it came from the
westward. The cutter's head was at that time tending in
shore, for as soon as the boats had been hoisted in she had
again lost all steerage-way, and had gradually gone round.
Again the puff of air came stronger, and she gathered sufficient steerage-way to enable us to wear round just before
the boats reached us. The pirates must have thought that
we were very blind not to perceive them. Silently they
pulled towards us in two columns : we let them approach
within a quarter of a cable's length. Just as a tiger springs
on his prey, they pulled on rapidly towards us, evidently
expecting to catch us unprepared.

" Now, my lads, up and at them ! " sung out Porpoise,

in imitation of the speech of a somewhat better-known hero.

Our jolly yachtsmen did not require a second summons. Up they sprang to their allotted duties.

"Steady!" added Porpoise, "take aim before you fire. Those forward aim at the headmost boats; let the after guns give account of those coming up next astern. Now give it them."

The orders were comprehended, and executed promptly and well. Cries and groans and shouts from the row-boats followed the simultaneous discharge from our great-guns and small-arms. The pirates ceased rowing, and a second intervened before they fired in return, but their shot generally flew wide of us, our unexpected commencement of the action having evidently thrown them into not a little confusion. For an instant it occurred to me that we might have been too precipitate, and that perhaps after all they might not have been pirates, but for some reason or other had come off to us at that unseasonable hour. It was therefore, in one respect, a positive relief to me when they began to fire, and I discovered their real character. Still undaunted, on they came. Before, however, they could get alongside, our people had time to load again and fire; this time not a shot but took effect. The Moors did not relish the dose; some attempted to spring on board, but were driven back by pike and cutlass into the sea, Hearty setting the example of activity and courage by rushing here and there, cutting and thrusting and slashing away, so that he did the work of half a dozen men. Indeed I may say the same without vanity of all on board, or we could not have contended for a minute against the fearful odds opposed to us. The low deck of a yacht, it must be remembered, does not present the difficulties to assailants which even a brig-

of-war or an ordinary high-sided merchantman is capable of
doing.   Ours was literally a hand-to-hand fight without the
slightest protection, our slight bulwarks alone separating us
from our enemies when they once got alongside.   Happily
the breeze increased, and giving us way through the water,
the Moorish boats having failed to hook on to us, we once
more slipped through them.   Some of the men in the bows
continued firing at us, but a little delay occurred before the
rest could get out their oars to follow the cutter.   The chiefs
of each boat appeared to be holding a consultation, and I
only hoped that they would come to the decision that the
grapes were sour, or rather that the game was not worth
the candle to play it by, as the Frenchmen say, and give up
the pursuit.   But they were not so reasonable; they probably thought that if we fought so desperately we had something on board worth fighting for; not considering that our
lives and liberties were of very much consequence, and so they
showed a resolution once more to attempt to overhaul us.
This hesitation was much to our advantage, as it enabled us
once more to load our guns up to the muzzle, and to take a
steady aim as they came up.   In all my fighting experience
I have come to the conclusion that there is no system equal
to that of waiting for a good opportunity, mustering all re-
sources, and then, once having begun the attack, to continue
at the work without relaxing a moment till the day is won.
The Moorish pirates did not follow this course.   At last
came the tug of war.   Their fury and thirst for vengeance
was now added to their greed for plunder, and the boats
ranged up on either side of the little "Frolic" with seemingly a full determination on the part of their crews to overpower us at once.

"Steady, my good lads, steady!" shouted Porpoise.

"Remember, fire as before, and then load again as fast as you can."

Off went our guns with good effect; while Hearty and I, and three or four others, armed with muskets, blazed away with them, taking up one after the other as fast as the steward could load them. The report of the guns must have been heard on shore, and far out to sea over that calm water, while the bright flashes lighted up the midnight air. Musket-balls and round-shot don't often fly about without doing some damage; and while ours were telling pretty well among the thickly crowded boats of the Moors, we were not altogether free from harm. Two of our people had been wounded. One of them fell to the deck, and, from the way the poor fellow groaned, I was much afraid that he was mortally hurt. I drew him close to the companion-hatch, that he might, in a slight degree, be protected from further injury; but we were too hard pressed to spare any one for a moment from the deck to take him below. Hearty was passing close to me, when, by the flash of the guns, I saw him a give a sudden, convulsive movement with his left arm. I felt sure he was hit. I asked him.

"Oh, nothing, nothing," he answered. "Don't say a word about it. I can fight away just as well as ever, and that is all I care about just now."

One of our chief efforts was to prevent the Moorish boats from hooking on to us. This they frequently attempted to do, and each time the lashings they tried to secure were cut adrift. I was indeed surprised to find them so pertinacious in their attack, for a resolute resistance at the commencement will generally compel those sort of gentry to give up an enterprise, unless they are certain a great deal is to be gained by it.

The breeze was now increasing, and old Snow stood at

the helm, with his left hand on the tiller, and his right hand
wielding a cutlass, with which, aided by another man, he
kept at bay any of the Moors who attempted to climb on
board over the stern. Still, so overmatched were we by
numbers, that I felt even then, in spite of our determined
resistance, that the result was very doubtful. I almost
sickened at the thought; but I was very certain that, before
such a sad consummation should occur, not a man of us
would be left alive on the deck.

"And then, should the day be evidently going against us,
should no help remain — not a shadow of hope — would it
be right to blow up the vessel, and preserve those innocent
ones below from an ignominious slavery — from a worse
than death?"

"Impious man," responded a voice within me, "think
not to rule the providences of thy Creator. Do not evil
that good may come of it. Who can tell what means he
has in store, even at the very last moment, to preserve
those whom, in his infinite wisdom, he has resolved to
preserve?"

I felt the frailty of human thoughts and human intentions, and banished the terrible idea from my mind. Still
I could not feel but that our case, to outward appearance,
was very desperate. Porpoise himself was wounded, I
found, though the pain he suffered did not allow him for a
moment to relax in his defence of the vessel. His voice
was heard everywhere as loud and cheering as before,
encouraging our crew to persevere.

Once more the pirates drew off.

"Huzza, huzza!" shouted all hands; "they have had
enough of it."

But no.

"Load your guns, load your guns!" shouted Porpoise. "Don't trust to them."

It was fortunate this was done. With terrific cries and yells they for a third time gave way towards us, completely hemming us in, so that some boats going ahead almost stopped the vessel's way through the water. Keeping up their hideous yells, firing their pistols, and flourishing their cimiters, they flung themselves headlong on board. Many were driven back, but their places were speedily filled by others. The physical power of the cutter's crew, exerted so long to the utmost stretch, was almost failing, when, far in the offing, to the northward, the bright flash of a gun was seen, followed shortly afterwards by another and another. I pointed them out to Hearty.

"There's help coming, my lads!" he shouted. "Never fear; but let's have all the glory of the fight to ourselves, and drive these scoundrels off before it arrives. Huzza, huzza! Back with them! No quarter! Cut them down! Drive them into the sea!"

All this time he was most completely suiting the action to his words. At last some of the pirates saw the flashes. The morning light was just breaking in the east, for the action had endured far longer than it has taken to describe it. They must have suspected that they foreboded no good to them, and that the sooner they were off the better. Orders were shouted out by the chiefs. Those who could obeyed them, and, leaping back, the boats in a body shoved off from us; but some unfortunate wretches were still clinging to our bulwarks. They fought as they clung with all the fanaticism of Mohammedans; but our seamen made quick work of them, and in less than two minutes not one was left alive. The gray light of dawn showed us the dark boats pulling in-shore, and as the sun arose its early beams lighted up the canvas of a man-of-war brig, close hauled, laying up towards us. Our people shouted lustily when they saw her; and Hearty, forgetting his wound and his begrimed and war-stained appearance, hurried below to assure his charges of their safety. We quickly recognized the "Zebra," and were not long in getting within hail of her, when Rullock, accompanied by Bubble, came on board of us, to inquire into the particulars of our adventure.

Old Rullock at first was somewhat inclined to be angry with us for getting so close in-shore, and Will almost pulled his hair off in his vexation that he had not been with us to share in the honors of the fight and defence.

Our loss had been serious; the poor fellow who had been the first wounded had died just before sunrise, and the surgeon of the brig pronounced the other cases to be somewhat bad. Porpoise's was a flesh-wound—the advantage, as he observed, of being a fat man; but he forgot that if he had not been fat he might not have been wounded at all. Hearty, though he made light of his hurt, was very much injured; and the surgeon, with a somewhat significant look, advised him to get on shore as fast as he could, and to get carefully nursed for a time.

"You'll have no great difficulty to get some one to nurse you," he remarked.

I really believe that he did not think so badly of the case as he pretended. Be that as it may, we made the best of our way to Malta Harbor, where we all took up our abode on shore, while the cutter was undergoing some necessary repairs. The brig also requiring repairs, Rullock took lodgings, and in the most considerate way had Hearty conveyed to them, and invited his sister and neice to stay with him—a very indelicate proceeding, I dare say; but the jolly old sailor observed, "Who was so fit to look after a wounded man as the girl he was going to marry, and in whose defence he was wounded? A fig for all such rigma-role prudisms, say I." As the parties concerned did not disagree with him, so the matter was arranged to the satis-faction of everybody.

24

CHAPTER XXV.

THE BACHELORS AT SEA—THE IONIAN ISLANDS—RETURN
TO MALTA—SAD NEWS—HOMEWARD BOUND—HORRIBLE
SUSPICIONS—THE PIRATE'S HANDIWORK—A BURNING SHIP
—TRACES OF OUR FRIENDS—THE RESCUE—THE BACHE-
LORS BECOME BENEDICTS, AND THUS TERMINATES IN THE
MOST SATISFACTORY MANNER IMAGINABLE THE CRUISE OF
THE "FROLIC."

It took nearly two months before Hearty recovered even
partially from his wound; and at the end of that time, the
"Frolic" being ready for sea, the surgeons insisted that to
re-establish his health he must take a trip away for a few
weeks in her. This proceeding became somewhat more
necessary, as the "Zebra" had been ordered off to the
Levant, and he could not well remain the guest of Mrs.
Mizen during Captain Rullock's absence. Among the
lovely isles of Greece, then, it was resolved we would take
a cruise. Both Carstairs and Bubble joined us : the former,
in his usual way, had been carrying on with Mrs. Skyscraper; but the widow had been unable to hook him firmly;
indeed, as Bubble observed, he was somewhat a big fish to
haul on shore. He, on his part, also, could not tell whether
the lady cared for him or not. In my opinion she did, but
could not quite make up her mind to lose her liberty.

Once more we five jolly bachelors were afloat together,
on our passage to Greece. Hearty was in fair spirits. The
fresh air after the confinement of a sick-room, raised them,
in spite of himself; indeed, considering that he was certain

of Laura's affection, and hoped in a few months to be united
to her, though parted from her for a brief space, he had no
reason to be melancholy. We had a fine run to the eastward. What words can describe the picturesque beauties
of Corfu and the Albanian Coast — the classic associations
of Athens and the varied forms of the isles and islets scattered over the Ægean Sea! Bubble and I revelled in them ;
but it must be owned that Carstairs, and even Hearty,
thought more of the wild fowl and snipes and woodcocks to
be shot in the marshy valleys or thyme-covered heights, than
of their pictorial effects, or classic association.

Whenever we were at sea our people kept a very sharp
look-out for Sandgate's polacca-brig, in the hopes that she
might be cruising in those parts. After, however, the
various pranks he had played in the Mediterranean, I suspected that he would have shifted the scene of his exploits
to some other part of the globe.

Greece and her islands, lovely and interesting as they are,
have been so often described by more graphic pens than
mine, that I do not think my readers would thank me for
filling my pages with an account of what we saw.·

We had not much personal communication with the
Ionians. What we saw and what we heard of them did
not raise them especially in our estimation. However,
what could be expected of a race so long under the dominion
of Venice, during the worst times of her always nefarious
system of policy? By the Venetian system discord was
fermented among all the states subject to Turkish rule, and
miscreants of all classes who could help to·effect that object
were protected and supported. Crime was thus openly encouraged ; the assassin who had committed ten murders
was only sent to the galleys for the same number of years ;
and any one speaking disrespectfully of any person high in

office was actually punished with the infliction of a like sentence. The young men of the noble families were brought up in Italy, and while they learned all her vices, were taught to despise their native land, and to forget their mother-tongue. Falsehood, revenge, a foolish vanity, a love of political intrigue, were but some of their most glaring vices; justice was openly sold; public faith was unknown; their peasants were grossly ignorant; their nobles were without honor; and their merchants were destitute of integrity; while their priests were generally illiterate and immoral in the extreme. *Heu mihi!* a pretty picture of a people. Well, I fancy they have improved somewhat under British protection; and when I was among them I do not believe they were so bad as all that. Still they were in an unsatisfactory state, and a very difficult people to govern. They may have improved still more now; and I hope they have.

We sailed about from island to island, and visited them all in their turn. First we went to that of the ancient Teleboans; once conquered by King Cephalus, who gave it his name, and whose descendants for many generations reigned over them — so Bubble informed us; and we were not a little interested in visiting various cyclopic remains, and among them those of the ancient city of Cranii. The island is very rugged and mountainous; the highest mountain, that of Montagna Negra, being upwards of three thousand feet above the level of the sea. We spent a couple of days also at the handsome city of Zante, the capital of the island of that name, famous for the longevity of its inhabitants, and its currants, oil, wine, and fragrant honey. Santa Maura, once known as Leucadia, was our next resort. Little cared we for its classical recollections, but far more interested were we in visiting the tomb of the gallant Clarke, who fell under the walls of its fortress, which was attacked

by the English in 1810, under General Oswald. The island
is separated from the main land by a narrow channel.
There is a curious natural mole running out from the island,
which has exactly the appearance of being the work of art.
We all anticipated much pleasure in visiting Ithaca, the
birth-place and patrimony of Ulysses; but when we got
there none of us felt inclined to envy him his rugged, inhos-
pitable-looking territory, and were not surprised that he was
anxious to get a footing in a more fruitful portion of the
globe. Still it is a very romantic and picturesque spot;
and produces the vine, orange, lemon, and other fruits in
abundance.

Pasco also we saw, once noted as a retreat for pirates,
and Cerigo and Cerigotto; and thus, having made the tour
of the Septinsular republic, we sailed back to Malta, with
the anticipation of a hearty welcome from the friends we
had left behind there. How glittering white looked the
houses of the city! how blue the water! how gay the caps
and sashes and jackets of the boatmen as they pulled about
in their fancifully painted boats, and came vociferating
alongside as we beat up the harbor of Valetta, and dropped
our anchor not far from the landing-place. We all of us
hastened on shore; Hearty to see his betrothed, and I to
take care of him; Carstairs to throw himself at the feet of
Mrs. Skyscraper; Bubble, as he himself said, to see that no
one got into mischief; and Porpoise to order certain stores
for the cutter. Hearty and I walked up at once to Mrs.
Mizen's lodgings. He knocked hurriedly at the door. Perhaps some of my readers know how a man feels under similar circumstances — I don't.

An Italian servant appeared, a stranger. "Que vuole,
signori?" he asked.

"Are Mrs. or Miss Mizen at home?" inquired Hearty,

in an agitated voice, not heeding the man's question. " Do you understand me? An English lady and her daughter? "

" Oh, capisco, capisco! " answered the Italian, running away up stairs.

I thought he was going to announce our arrival; but he speedily returned holding a letter. I saw that the address was in a lady's handwriting as he delivered it to Hearty. Hearty opened it with a trembling hand. His countenance assumed a look of blank disappointment as he read its contents. As soon as he had glanced hurriedly through it, he began and read it over again; and then as he held it in his hand his eye still rested on it.

" What has occurred, my dear fellow? " I asked, anxiously.

I must confess — and oh! my fair readers! don't be angry with me, an old bachelor — I did truly suspect that it was the old story, and that the fair Laura had for some reason or other thought better of it; that she had heard something against her intended's character, and believed it; or that Sir Lloyd Snowdon, or somebody else, whose metal was more attractive, had stepped in and cut him out. I say these ideas glanced through my mind. They were very wrong and very disparaging to the sex, and most unjustifiable, and I was quite angry with myself for entertaining them, but I had seen so much that was bad in the world that they came in spite of me — I crave for pardon. I had also seen much that was good, and noble, and excellent; examples of the most devoted, self-sacrificing, all-enduring affection, and I ought at once to have remembered those examples and balanced them against all my evil suspicions. I did not, however, at that time; so I waited with no small amount of anxiety for Hearty's answer.

"They are gone," he replied; "gone away to England."

Then my suspicions are correct, I thought.

"It is a very sad case, I fear. Soon after we sailed, Mrs. Mizen received notice of Tom Mizen's illness, and the next post brought out such alarming accounts that she and her daughter resolved at once to return home. A fine fast-sailing merchant-brig, the 'Success,' was on the point of sailing, so, as a journey by land through Italy and France would be injurious to Laura, they determined to go by her. What was their surprise on going on board to find the other berths occupied by Mrs. Seton and her daughter, and Mrs. Skyscraper, who, for some business matters connected with property left them, had to go England. Miss Mizen wrote as they were on the point of sailing, and the people of the house took charge of the letter to deliver to me. She speaks in favorable terms of the brig and of the master, Captain Hutchins, so I trust that they may have a good passage home. But it is disappointing. You'll not mind, my dear fellow, sailing at once to follow them? I am afraid there is no chance of catching them at Gibraltar, but if the 'Frolic' behaves as well as usual, we may get to England almost as soon as they do. Not that I wish that either — I would far rather the 'Success' had a speedy passage. I am certain also Carstairs will be ready to start; and as for Bubble, he'll wish to do what is reasonable; so I suppose there is nothing to prevent our sailing as soon as we have got a fresh supply of water, and a few more provisions on board."

I assured my friend that I was perfectly ready to go to sea that very hour, if the necessary preparations for the voyage could be made; and volunteered at once to go in search of Porpoise, to hasten what was required to be done; while he himself went to his bankers, and settled a few bills he had left unpaid. On my way I encountered Carstairs, who had received no notice of the widow's departure, and was therefore still engaged in searching for her, as much puzzled as Hearty had at first been. I never saw a fellow more taken aback than he was when I communicated the truth to him, and he directly became all eagerness to put to sea. What his feelings were I cannot exactly tell. I suspect that his confidence in the durability of Mrs. Skyscraper's regard for him was not quite up to the mark of Hearty's for that of his intended.

"Why hasn't she written to me, to tell me what she was going to do, and why has she hurried away to England? Hang it, they are all alike, I suppose, and delight to make fools of us poor men. Now let us go and hunt up Porpoise. Bubble said he should tend to him while I was paying my visit to my — my — hang it, to the widow, I mean."

Poor fellow, he was sadly put out I saw. Porpoise was soon found; and when he heard the state of the case, he set to work as if life and death depended on it, in getting the cutter ready for a long voyage. He had plenty of lieutenants in us three gentlemen; and while one went off in one direction another started away in an opposite one to order what was required, and to see the orders executed, while the crew did their part with right good will. Water and coals, and stores and provisions, were soon alongside, and quickly hoisted on board and stowed away below. Hearty was surprised and highly gratified when he got on board and found what was done.

"Where there's a will there's a way," is a very true saying; and "If you want a thing done, go and do it yourself," is another. The Portuguese say, "If you want a thing *go*, if you don't want a thing *send*."

That very evening, with a fair wind, we were running

out of Malta Harbor. Away glided the " Frolic " over the moonlit Mediterranean, with every stitch of canvas she could carry set alow and aloft. We had a sharp look-out kept ahead so that we might avoid running down any boat, or running into any vessel ; while the three landsmen agreed to keep watch with Porpoise and me, to add to the number of hands on deck. Porpoise prognosticated a very rapid passage home, and certainly, from the way we commenced it, we had reason to hope that he would not prove a fallacious seer. We speedily lost sight of Malta, and its rocks and fortifications ; with its scanty soil and swarthy popula-tion, and noisy bells, and lazy monks, without any very great regret on our part. We had altogether passed a pleasant, and not unexciting time there ; and I, for my part, look back to those days with fewer regrets as to the way I spent them than I do to some passed in other places. I am somewhat inclined to moralize. I must own that often and often I wish that I could live my early days over again, that I might employ them very differently to what I did. Deeply do I regret the precious time squandered in perfect idleness, or the most puerile frivolities, if not in absolute wickedness ; time which might have been spent in acquiring knowledge which would have afforded the most intense and pure delight in benefiting my fellow-creatures ; which would have assuredly afforded me happiness and peace of mind in the consciousness that I was doing my duty. But ah ! time has gone by never to be recalled ; but happily it may be redeemed while health and strength and vigor of mind remain. Often have I thought to myself, " Why was I sent into the world? Why was I endued with an intellect — with a heart to feel — a soul to meditate on things great and glorious — with powers of mind which I am conscious are but in embryo, and which but await separation from this frail body to com-

prehend some, if not all, the great mysteries of nature!
Surely I was not placed here merely to kill time — to amuse
myself—to employ my faculties in trifles; still less, to in-
dulge myself in mere animal gratification. No, no; I am
certain of that. I was sent here as a place of trial — as a
school where I might learn my duties — as a preparation for
a higher sphere. When I understood this, the great problem
of existence was at once solved; difficulties vanished; the
whole government of the world at once seemed right and
just and reasonable; and my thoughts, feelings, tastes, and
aspirations became changed. I was led to look upward as
to the only source of happiness, and a pure and unfailing
source it has ever since proved to me.

Brother yachtsmen who may glance your eye over these
pages, meditate seriously on this matter. As you walk the
deck on your midnight watch, looking up ever and anon
into the dark sky where flit countless numbers of brilliant
stars to guide you on your path across the ocean, ask yourself the question, "Why was I sent into this world?" and
do not be satisfied till you have found an answer, and resolved to profit by it.

I do not pretend that I thought much about this matter
when I was on board the "Frolic," yet now and again some
thoughts of the sort did flash across my mind, but my companions rallied me on my seriousness and they vanished.

But to my history: away sailed the saucy little "Frolic"
over the blue waters of the Mediterranean. We laughed
and sang and chatted, much as usual, and Carstairs quoted
to as good effect as in days of yore; but we failed entirely in our long stories, for our pens had been idle, and
our imaginations were much at fault. What we might have
done I do not know, had not a reality occurred which effectually put all fiction to flight.

We were about half way between Malta and Gibraltar, a succession of light winds having made old Snow confess that he was afraid his prognostications of a rapid passage were not likely to be realized, when one forenoon when I came on deck, I found Porpoise scrutinizing through his glass an object which he had discovered on the water nearly right ahead of us.

" What is it, do you think?" I asked.

" I can't quite make out," he answered, handing me the telescope. "It looks to me like the hull of a dismasted ship — an ugly thing to run foul of on a dark night with a heavy gale blowing."

" You are right as to its being a ship's hull, I am pretty certain," I answered. " We shall be up to it soon, and that will settle the question."

Some of the people, however, declared that what we saw was a rock or an island, and others that a dead whale had floated in through the Straits. As we approached, however, our opinion was found to be the correct one, and then it became a subject of discussion as to what she could be.

" She is a good-sized craft, whatever she is," observed Hearty, who had joined us on deck. " Is she an English or foreign vessel do you think?"

" English by her build," replied Porpoise, observing her narrowly through the glass; " I cannot make it out. I see no one on board. How she came into that state puzzles me."

" My dear fellow, have you any idea what sort of a vessel the ' Success ' is? Does any one on board know her?" exclaimed Hearty, suddenly turning pale, and literally trembling from head to foot, as all sorts of horrible suspicions and fears flashed through his mind.

Inquiries were made, but no one recollected to have seen

the brig in which our friends had taken their passage. We did our best to calm Hearty's apprehensions, but under the circumstances they were very natural, and in spite of all we could say, they rather increased than diminished, as we approached the wreck. Carstairs shared them, but, being of a far less excitable temperament, in a much less degree; indeed, Hearty seemed to look on him as being very callous and insensible, for not making himself as miserable as he felt.

The breeze was very light, and our progress seemed terribly slow to the impatient feelings of our kind-hearted host. His glass was never for a moment off the wreck; indeed we were all of us constantly looking at her, in the hopes of seeing some one appear. The afternoon was drawing well on, before we got up to her. The instant we approached her, two boats were lowered, and Hearty and I jumped into the first, and away we pulled as fast as the men could bend to their oars — the men evidently entering fully into the feelings of their master. I went with him that I might really look after him, should his worst anticipations be realized. We were soon alongside, and in an instant scrambled on board.

The masts, and rigging, and sails, hung over the side; the former in their fall having carried away the bulwarks and smashed the boats. I saw before we got on board, that she had lost her masts with all sail set, in some unaccountably lubberly way it seemed. The sea had washed away some of her spare spars and the caboose, but she had apparently righted directly her masts went, and there seemed no reason why she should have been deserted by her crew. As we pulled up under the stern, we looked out for a name painted there, but a sail hung over it, and if there was a name it was not perceptible. Hearty, the moment he was on board, rushed with frantic haste along the deck, to ascertain the important fact, and very nearly fell overboard in his attempt to remove the sail, till others could aid him. The sail was soon dragged aside, and as we hung down over the taffrail, a large S appeared, there could be no doubt of it. There was the word "Success" of London. I had to help my friend on board again.

" What can have happened! What can have happened ! " he exclaimed, as soon as he could find words to speak.

" Why, I trust that they fancied the brig in a much worse condition than she appears to us to be, and that they quitted her in the boats, or some other craft which was fortunately passing soon after the catastrophe." But as I spoke, our eyes fell on the shattered boats, and I recollected that the former hypothesis could not be correct, "They must have fallen in with some vessel," I remarked to Hearty. " The ladies were happily conveyed on board her, but why the crew deserted the ship I cannot say."

" But where can they have gone to — what port can they have put into — what sort of vessel can they be on board?" exclaimed Hearty, almost frantic with agitation. " It's very dreadful."

By this time the other boat had got alongside, with Carstairs, Bubble, and Porpoise in her. Together we commenced a search over the deserted vessel. The appearance of the cabin again raised our doubts as to the reason of the desertion. The ladies had evidently been at work just before the catastrophe. Their work-baskets were on the floor, with their work, in which needles were sticking ; and needle-cases, thimbles, and reels of cotton, skeins of silk and worsted, and similar articles, were strewed about.

As I looked more minutely into the state of affairs, I observed that every thing of value had been carried off; not a silver spoon or fork, not a piece of plate of any description remained. The ladies' jewels were all gone. This was what was to be expected, but I was also certain that they would not leave their daily work behind. I did not increase Hearty's apprehensions by pointing this out to him. Carstairs all the time, though he took matters in a very different way, seemed to be much alarmed and anxious. I saw the chronometer, sextants, charts, compasses, and every thing in the captain's cabin had been carried off. The ship's log and manifest could nowhere be found, nor indeed could any of her papers.

From the cabin we went to the hold, and there also the cargo had evidently been disturbed, and I judged that a considerable quantity had been carried away; a few bales of silk and velvet only remaining. This was a very suspicious circumstance. Still, had there been time to remove any thing, the captain would of course have carried away what was likely to be of most value. The fore-peak was next searched. The seamen's chests had been broken open, and the contents of many of them were strewed about — why the men did not use their keys was surprising. Still, in their hurry they might not have had time to find them. Hearty went about looking into every hole, and making his observations on all he saw. He had collected every thing belonging to the ladies as treasured relics, and had them packed and conveyed on board the "Frolic," while Carstairs took charge of all Mrs. Skyscraper's property, and sighed over it with a look of despair, and we were about to quit the vessel, when one of the men declared that he heard a voice proceeding from the fore-hold. Forward we all went again. Certainly there was a groan. Guided by the sound, and by removing some of the cargo, we arrived at a space where lay a human being. We lifted him up, and carried him out

of the dark noisome hole, and the fresh air speedily revived
him. At first his startled look showed that he did not know
what to make of us, but by degrees he recovered his senses,
though his first words increased our apprehensions.

"What! are you come back again? Don't murder me!
— Don't murder me!" he exclaimed, with a look of terror.

"Murder you, mate! What should put that into your
head?" asked one of our men who was supporting him.

By pouring a little brandy and water down his throat, he
in a short time recovered altogether. He told us that he had
been the cook of the brig. He was an old man, and almost
worn out, and that this was to have been his last voyage.

"Well, gentlemen," he continued, "when I see a number
of young ladies come on board, and their mothers to look
after them, and no parson to make Davy Jones angered
like, which he always is when any on 'em gets afloat, says
I to myself, we shall have a fine run of it home, and the
chances are that the 'Success' will make a finer passage
than she ever did before. Well, we hadn't been two days
at sea before we falls in with a polacca-brig, which speaks
us quite civil like, and a man aboard, though he was rigged
like a Greek, asks us in decent real English, quite civil like,
what passengers we'd got aboard. So, thinking no harm,
we told him, and he answered 'that he'd keep us company,
and protect us, for that to his knowledge there was a notorious pirate cruising thereabouts, and that if he fell in with
us he might do us an injury.' The captain did not seem
much to like our new friend, and would rather have been
without his company, but as he sailed two knots to our one,
we couldn't help ourselves, do ye see. For two days or
more he kept close to us, and then it fell almost to a calm,
and what does he do, but quietly range up alongside with
the help of some sweeps he had, and before we knew where

we were, he had thrown some twoscore or more of cut-
throats aboard of us, who knocked some of our crew down,
drove others overboard, and very soon got possession of the
brig.   I was ill below, but I popped my head up to see what
was happening, and when I found how things were going,
thinks I to myself, the best thing I can do is to be quiet ; if
they cut my throat, they may as well do it while I'm comfortably in bed as struggling away on deck.   Instead, however, of turning into my berth again, I thought that I'd just
go and stow myself away in the hold under the cargo, where
they wouldn't be likely to look for me, so there I went, and
there I've been ever since.   I felt the ship some time afterwards thrown on her beam ends, and thought she'd be going
down, but she very soon righted.   I felt the masts shaken
out of her, but I could not tell what else had happened.   I
tried to get out to see, but the cargo had shifted and jammed
me in so tight that I couldn't break my way out.   I suppose
I should have died if you hadn't come to help me, gentlemen."

"But can you not tell what became of the passengers
and crew?" exclaimed Hearty, interrupting him.

"No more than the babe unborn, sir," answered the old
man ; "I suppose they were all carried aboard the pirate.
From what I know of some of our crew, I don't think they
would have much minded joining the villains, and several I
myself saw killed and hove overboard."

This fearful information gave us still more concern than
we had felt from what we had already discovered.
There was some cause for hope before, now there was none.
There was no doubt whatever that our friends had fallen
into the power of the villain Miles Sandgate.   Grown desperate, it was impossible to say to what extremes he might
not venture to go.   Still I had less apprehension for the

fate of Mrs. and Miss Mizen than for that of Jane Seton. It could scarcely be expected that he would again let her out of his power. I was offering what consolation I could to Hearty as well as to Carstairs on these grounds, in which I was joined by Bubble, whose heart was overflowing with commiseration for them and those they were so deeply interested in, when Hearty suddenly exclaimed, —

" But, my dear fellow, is it not possible that the same squall which struck this vessel and reduced her to a wreck may have struck the pirate, and sent her and all on board to the bottom? or can you answer me that this is not possible? Still it may have preserved them from a worse fate. Oh, horrible, horrible ! "

" I do not think it is probable that people so thoroughly acquainted with these seas should not have been forewarned in time to guard against even the most sudden squall. There are always some indications ; only those who do not regard them are the sufferers. Just as likely after he had rifled the brig, Sandgate (for I doubt not that he is the culprit) may have put the passengers on shore somewhere or other, and made some plausible excuse for having taken them on board his vessel. I think, in truth, that for the sake of making friends at court, he is much more likely to have treated them with perfect civility than to have ventured in any way to insult or injure them."

All the time I was trying to persuade myself that I was speaking what I thought ; but I must own that I had very serious apprehensions for their safety. There was no object in remaining longer on board the wreck. To prevent any vessels running into her, for that night at all events, we secured a large lantern with a burner full of oil to the stump of the mainmast. We were very unwilling to quit her, but we could not venture to leave anybody on board to

25

look after her till we could despatch a vessel to bring her
into Gibraltar, lest before this could be done a gale might
spring up, and she might founder. So, taking Tom Pancake, the old man we had found, on board with us, we
returned to the cutter. We forthwith held a council of war,
when it was resolved to steer a direct course for Gibraltar,
that we might then get vessels sent out in all directions to
look for the daring pirate. I never saw any one suffer so
much as did Hearty. A few nights of the anxiety he was
now doomed to suffer would, I feared much, not only turn
his head gray, but completely prostrate him. Carstairs
suffered a good deal, but his regard for Mrs. Skyscraper
was of a very different character to the deep affection
Hearty entertained for Miss Mizen ; and if he was to lose
her, I suspected that he would have no great difficulty in
supplying her place as the queen of his affections. No
sooner had we left the unfortunate ship, than a fresh breeze
had sprung up, and before sunset we had run her completely
out of sight. For all the first part of the night the breeze
lasted, and we made good way on our course for Gibraltar.
For a long time poor Hearty would not turn in ; but at last I
persuaded him to lie down and take some of that rest which
he so much required. I also went below, but I was restless, and just as the middle watch was set, I returned on
deck. Porpoise and Bubble were there. I found them
watching a bright glare which appeared in the sky. I considered a moment our whereabouts.

"That must be from a ship on fire," I exclaimed.

"There is no doubt about it," replied Porpoise. "She
has been blazing away for the last hour or more, I fear, for
all that time I have observed that ruddy glow in the sky.
I hope we may be in time to render some assistance to the
unfortunate crew."

The wind freshened even still more as we advanced towards the burning ship, but not enough for our impatience. Hearty and Carstairs were called, and when they came on deck they exhibited equal eagerness with the rest of us; indeed, Hearty seemed for a time almost to forget his own anxiety in his zeal in the cause of humanity. Surely we seldom know even our most intimate friends without seeing them tried under a variety of circumstances. Sometimes I must own that I have been sadly disappointed in them; at other times I have been as agreeably surprised by the exhibition of self-denial, courage, warmth of heart, and judgment, which I did not believe to exist in them. Such was the case with my friend Hearty.

We got the boats ready to lower the instant we should be close enough to the vessel. The interval which elapsed before we drew up to her was one of great anxiety. All sorts of ideas and fears crossed our minds, and at all events we felt that many of our fellow-creatures might be perishing for want of our assistance. Through our glasses, as we drew on, we discovered that the greater part of the vessel was enveloped in flames; the poop alone was not entirely consumed, though the devouring element had made such progress that the people were already seeking for a momentary safety by hanging on to the taffrail quarters.

"Stand by to shorten sail!" sang out Porpoise.

The squaresail and gaff and square topsail were taken in, and the foresail being hauled up to windward, and the jib-sheets let fly, the cutter was hove-to and a boat instantly lowered. As before, Hearty and I went in her, while the other gig immediately followed us.

Our appearance took the poor wretches by surprise, as from the darkness of night our approach had not been perceived. They raised a cry to implore us to hasten to their assistance. Our men shouted in return. They needed no cry to urge them to exertion. By the bright glare of the flames we saw that the men clinging to the wreck were by their costume Greeks, while the hull itself had a foreign appearance. The vessel was a brig, we observed. The foremast had already fallen, the flames were twisting and twining in serpentine forms along the yards and up to the very maintop-gallant mast-head. Some, as I said, were still clinging to the wreck, others had leaped overboard, and were hanging on to spars and oars and gratings, and a few were in a boat floating near the vessel; but she appeared to be stove in, and to have no oars or other means of progression.

With all these people, blinded with terror and eager to save their lives, it was necessary to use much precaution to prevent ourselves from being swamped by too many leaping on board at a time. The first thing was to rescue those who were in the most imminent danger of being burned. While we pulled under the stern, and as the people dropped into the water picked them up, the other boat hauled those on board who were already floating, and seemed most to require help. We had got most of the people off the burning wreck, but two still hung on to the burning taffrail, and seemed unwilling to trust themselves in the sea.

"Never fear, jump, jump, my lads!" sung out our men; then turning to the Greeks whom they had saved, added, "Tell them to jump in your own lingo; they don't understand us."

The Greeks said something about "Inglesi," but I did not understand what they meant. At last, however, the flames rushing out from the stern ports and along the deck, gave them no alternative, and they had to throw themselves into the water, whence we quickly picked them out, and with a boat loaded almost to sinking, returned on board the cutter. I was especially struck by the appearance of the two men last saved. Certainly they were much more like Englishmen than Greeks. No sooner, however, did the old man we had saved from the "Success" see them than he exclaimed, "What mates! is that you? How did you get aboard there? Why, as I live, that craft must be the Greek pirate which plundered us, and carried off the ladies."

The worst suspicions which had been floating through my mind were confirmed by these remarks. Poor Hearty seemed thunderstruck. Carstairs had not yet returned. The men could not deny their identity, and they instantly began to offer excuses for having been on board the Greek.

"Never mind that!" exclaimed Hearty. "Tell me, my men, where are the ladies? what has become of them? Help us to find them, and all will be overlooked. They could not have been left to perish on board the burning vessel."

"We can't say much about it, sir," answered one of the men, who seemed to be the most intelligent. "We were forward when the fire broke out, and it was with great difficulty that we managed to crawl aft. When we got there we found that a raft had been built and lowered into the water, and that the boats had been got out, and that several people were in them. Some got away, and we don't know where they went, but we towed two of them after us. One was swamped and went down, and the other, as you saw, was stove in. What became of the other two we don't know; we believe that the ladies were in them, but we can't say for certain; all we know is, that we did not see them on the deck, or in either of the other two boats, when we got aft; still we believe that nearly half the people on board, in one way or another, have been lost."

Then, supposing the seaman spoke the truth, there was still hope; but how dreadful at the best must be the condition of our friends, exposed in open boats with the most lawless of companions! While we were still examining the men, Carstairs and the rest returned on board. He had also with him one of the crew of the "Success," who, on being examined, corroborated the statement of the other two. The character of the men whose lives we had preserved was now clear; but, wretches as they were, and deserving of the heaviest punishment, we could not have avoided saving them from drowning, even had we known the worst at first. Scarcely were they all on board before every portion of the burning vessel was enveloped in flames. Porpoise all the time was fortunately not forgetful of the safety of the cutter, and, having let draw the foresail, we had been standing away from her. Suddenly there was a fiercer blaze than before — a loud, deafening report was heard, the remaining mast and deck lifted, the former shooting up into the air like a sky-rocket surrounded by burning brands, and then down again came the whole fiery mass, covering us, even at the distance we were, with burning fragments of wreck, and then all was darkness, and not a remnant of the polacca-brig remained together above water. After the character we had heard of the rescued crew, without giving them any warning, we suddenly seized them, and, lashing their arms behind them and their legs together, made them sit down in a row under the bulwarks. They seemed to be very much surprised at the treatment, but we did not understand their expostulations, and should not have listened to them if we had. We, however, served out provisions to them, and they very soon seemed reconciled to their fate. The three

English seamen vowed that they had been kept on board the brig by force, and, as we would fain have believed this to be the case, we did not treat them as prisoners, though we kept a very sharp eye on their movements; so, especially, did old Pancake, who appeared to have no little dread lest they should play him some scurvy trick in return for his having betrayed them.

These arrangements were very quickly made. The most important consideration, however, was the best method to pursue in order to discover what had become of the raft reported to have been made, and the missing boat. Unless by those who have been placed in a similar situation, the nervous anxiety and excitement which almost overcame every one of us would be difficult to be conceived. Hearty thought of sending the boats away to range in circles round the spot, in the chance of falling in with the raft or boat; but Porpoise overruled this proposal by assuring him that the raft could only have gone to leeward, and that the boat probably would be found in the same direction. Keeping, therefore, a bright lookout, with a light at our mast-head, we kept tacking backwards and forwards so as to sweep over every foot of the ground to leeward of the spot where the fire first burst out. We had hinted to the English seamen taken from the pirate that their future prospects depended very much on the success which might attend our search. They accordingly gave us all the information and assistance in their power, by showing us how the pirate had steered from the moment the fire was discovered, and how far she had gone after her captain had placed the ladies on the raft. Nothing could we discover during the night. Hearty was in despair; so was Carstairs; only he was rather inclined to be savage than pathetic in his misery. Daylight came; as the dawn drew on nothing could be seen but the clear gray water surrounding us. Then, just as we had gone about and were standing once more to the westward, the sun rose from his ocean bed, his beams glancing on a small object seen far away on our port bow.

"Huzza! huzza!" shouted Bubble, who was the first to bring his glass to bear on it. "Some people on a raft! There is no doubt on the subject. White dresses, too! It may be the ladies! It must be! Oh, it can't be otherwise! Keep up your spirits, Hearty, my dear fellow; all will go well! It will, Carstairs, I tell you! Don't be cast down any more! I think I see them waving!"

Thus the worthy Bubble ran on, giving way to the exuberance of his feelings and sympathy for his friends. Every yard of canvas the cutter could carry was pressed on her, and each moment rapidly decreased our distance from the raft; for that a raft it was, or a piece of a wreck, there could be no doubt. Our telescopes were kept unchangeably fixed on it. It was with no little apprehension, however, as we drew nearer, that I perceived that there were but three persons on it. One was standing up; the other two were seated on benches, or chests, or something of the same size, secured to the raft. The figure standing up was that of a man in the Greek costume; the other two were females. I had little doubt in my own mind who they were. As we got still nearer I fancied that, under the Greek cap, I could distinguish the features of Miles Sandgate. The features of the ladies were more difficult to make out, but I heard Hearty exclaim, "Yes, it is her — it is her!" meaning Miss Mizen; and I felt sure he was right. But who was the other person? The figure was not like that of either Mrs. Mizen or Mrs. Seton, but whether it was Jane Seton or Mrs. Skyscraper was the question. Poor Carstairs, he must have felt that, in all probability, it was Miss Seton.

What would Sandgate do when he found himself thus completely brought to bay? It was a serious question, for he
had the two ladies entirely in his power, and, had he chosen,
might, holding them as hostages, make any terms with us
he pleased. I saw him watching the approaching cutter.
He must have recognized her as soon as she hove in sight.
Yet he did not quail, but stood up boldly confronting us.
Then he seemed to be addressing one of the ladies. I looked
again; I was certain she was Jane Seton; and I clearly
recognized Miss Mizen. Jane had given her hand to Laura.
The pirate seemed to be urging her to fulfil some request;
he half knelt before her with uplifted hands; then he sprang
up, with a look of bitter reproach. By this time the cutter
was close up to the raft, and a boat was on the point of
being lowered. Again, with an imploring gesture, the pirate
urged his suit. Miss Seton shook her head. He seized her
hand. She struggled violently. It appeared that, in his
rage, he was about to drag her into the water. He would
have succeeded, had not Miss Mizen held her hand and
drawn her back.

Hearty and Bubble were in the boat pulling rapidly to
the raft. The pirate let go Miss Seton's hand, and drew
himself up to his full height; he seemed to be uttering some
strong reproaches. The bows of the boat were almost
touching the raft, the oars were thrown in. At that moment
the pirate, uttering a fearful cry (and if ever I heard the cry
of a madman that was one), turned round, and plunged
headlong into the water. Down, down, he sank! Scarcely
an eddy marked where he had sprung in, with such determination had he endeavored to reach the bottom. I watched
for him, but he never rose again. Such was the dreadful
end of Miles Sandgate. The next moment Hearty was on
the raft, and had clasped Laura Mizen in his arms, while

Miss Seton was borne fainting into the boat by Bubble. They were quickly conveyed on board, while the raft and its freight were allowed to go adrift. The two young ladies were immediately carried to the cabin, where Laura rapidly described to Hearty all that had occurred. Poor Miss Seton, however, required their whole attention, and for the moment drew them off from all thoughts about themselves. Not that Miss Mizen for a moment forgot her mother and her other companions, and it was a relief to us all to find that she had seen them placed in the first boat which had left the vessel just before they had been carried by Sandgate to the raft. He intended, it seemed, to have taken possession of one of the other boats, and when she was swamped he managed to get on the raft, and clear away from the burning vessel before any one else reached it, while he left the rest of his companions in crime to perish without an attempt to afford them aid. The general opinion was that the boat would be steered to the southward, for the purpose of making the Moorish coast, where the pirates fancied that they might find protection.

" The chances are that they will all get murdered if they reach it," observed Porpoise ; " but we must try and catch them up before they get there."

Fortunately we had the whole day before us. All sail was again made on the cutter ; the sun rose high in the heavens ; tolerably hot came down its beams on our heads. At noon a meridional observation was taken, and just as we were shutting up our sextants, Bubble, who was keeping a sharp lookout on every side, sang out that he saw a speck on the water almost ahead of us. I went immediately with my glass aloft. After waiting a little time I made out distinctly that the speck was a boat. As we drew on we made out that the boat was strongly manned, and that the people in her were doing their utmost to keep ahead of us. They could not have known what the "Frolic" was made of to suppose that they had a chance of escaping. The breeze freshened. Hard as they were pulling, hand over hand we came up with them. There were women in the boat, or we should have sent a shot after her to stop her way; we ran a gun out to frighten them. On we stood; the women in the boat now first observed us.

"Oh, help us! help,us! help us!" they shrieked out.

We required no summoning, however. There were three ladies, we saw, the number we expected to find. We soon ran up alongside the boat, though it required nice steering not to sink her. Our earnest hopes and wishes were realized. In the stern-sheets sat Mrs. Mizen and Mrs. Seton, and, to the very great relief of poor Carstairs, the fair Mrs. Skyscraper. The pirates saw that they had not a prospect of escape, so they threw in their oars, and quietly allowed us to get alongside them, and to hook on their boat to us. I need not describe the joy of the two mothers at finding their daughters safe, or that of the daughters at seeing their mothers; nor will I do more than touch on the effect which the risk she had endured, and the satisfaction Carstairs displayed at having her restored to him, worked on the heart of the widow.

We very soon got to Gibraltar, where we at once landed our very troublesome prisoners. Mrs. Mizen had written to England to desire that letters might be sent to meet her there. In a day or so they arrived, and they gave so favorable an account of her son's health that as there was no necessity for her hurrying home, she was able to wait till we were at liberty to accompany her, having given our evidence against the pirates. Several of them suffered, as the papers say, the extreme penalty of the law, and it was

certainly a pity, for the sake of justice, that Miles Sandgate
had not been alive to keep them company. At length we
all reached England, and not long afterwards I had. the
satisfaction of seeing my friend Edward Hearty united to
Miss Laura Mizen, and the next week was called away to
act as best-man to Captain Carstairs on his marriage with
the fair relict of the late Lieutenant Skyscraper, of the Rifle
Brigade.

Poor Miss Seton suffered much from the severe trial she
had gone through. It was, I rejoice to say, not without
good effects, and I had the opportunity of observing a great
improvement in her character. Some years passed by,
during which she remained single, but on the death of her
mother she became the wife of Sir Lloyd Snowdon ; and,
living constantly on his estate in Wales, proved a blessing
to her family, and to the poorer inhabitants of the surrounding district. May all the trials any of us have to endure
have a like good effect; for we may depend on it for that
purpose are they sent.

I am happy to say that, notwithstanding old Snow's prog-
nostication, Hearty's yacht was not sold, and that many a
pleasant summer cruise did I afterwards take with him on
board the " Frolic."

THE END.